UNITAS: TRIO

Unitas: Trio

Copyright © 2022 by J. Houser.

This book is a work of fiction. Names, characters, businesses, organizations, places, events and incidents either are the product of the author's imagination or are used fictitiously. Any resemblance to actual persons, living or dead, events, or locales is entirely coincidental.

For more information, visit: JHouserWrites.com

Cover design by Jervy Bonifacio

Edited by Nia Quinn

ISBN:

978-1-7370621-6-5 (ebook)

978-1-7370621-7-2 (paperback)

978-1-7370621-8-9 (hardback)

First Edition: March 2022

10 9 8 7 6 5 4 3 2
*Page numeration is slightly different than the first published version.

Note from the Author

Thank you for investing in the Seeder & Ivy story, following the central trilogy to completion!

I'm thoroughly blessed with supportive friends and family in this journey, as well as fantastic readers, and continue to enjoy working with my editor, Nia Quinn, and my cover designer, Jervy Bonifacio.

*

Make sure to sign up for my newsletter to get updates on upcoming publications, promotions, and bonus content!

Book-related merch can also be purchased on my author website!

Content Warning

Select scenes and topics in this novel may be more difficult for some readers, along the same lines as those found in book 2, Trouble in the Green Lands.

These topics include: mental health, self-harm, assault, discrimination, ableism, etc. There is a brief mention of suicide.

My intention is never to glorify or justify harmful behavior, even if a fictional character doesn't get it quite right. If you find yourself struggling with any of these issues in real life, please know you're not alone, not past hope, and not beyond help from professionals, friends, and family.

~J. Houser

"We read to know we are not alone." ~ William Nicholson

UNITAS: TRIO

J. HOUSER

Pronunciation Guide:

People

Beata: bay-AH-tuh

Boman/Bomen: BOW-man

Guillen: GUY-en

Kaylah: KAY-luh

Kyas: KAI-us

Lyza: LIZ-uh

Magda: MAWG-duh

Marigold: MARE-ih-gold

(**Mari:** mah-ree)

Murial: MYUR-ee-ul

Nuren: NYUR-en

Rian: ree-ann

Saffrona: suh-FRONE-uh

(**Saff:** saff)

Sanath: SAN-uth

Teagan: TEE-gun

Thod: thawed

Tobias: toe-BYE-us

Places & Things

Arcadia: are-KAY-dee-uh

Cassa: CASS-uh

Domiten: dome-IDE-en

Fortinda: for-TIN-da

Guenjalis: gwen-YAWL-iss

Siqendra: sick-EN-druh

Tonoru: TONE-oh-roo

Unitas: OO-knee-tas

The Outer Rim
Arcadia
Tonoru
Grand Sea
Siqendra
Seeder
Territory
South
Fortinda
Neutral
Woods
10
9
8
7
6
5
4
3
2
1
Ivy
Kingdom
Ivy Palace
The Green Lands

Prologue

KAYLAH STOOD IN FRONT OF the gilded mirror in her chambers, straightening her lace dress. It was striking; she missed getting dolled up, dressing like a princess. She tugged at her itchy sleeve and wiggled a bit. Maybe she didn't miss it as much as she used to. Her human-world, average-teenager clothes were much more comfortable.

But it was still nice to be home. Kind of. The warmth of the Green Lands was always refreshing, but the palace was so cold. At least the people in it were.

A knock at the door claimed her focus.

"It's unlocked."

A woman opened the door and curtsied. "Your Highness, your uncle called for you."

Kaylah bit the insides of her cheeks, forcing herself to not roll her eyes. "Yeah, I'm on my way." *No time to rest. Always about the project.*

After making her way down the quiet palace corridors, she arrived at the entry to the duke's study. She knocked.

"Enter."

Plastering a smile on her face, she opened the door and was greeted by her uncle, and to her surprise, her older brother, Soren.

Daylight bathed the room, backlighting one of dozens, perhaps hundreds, of stained glass inlays in the palace. The room was modest compared to most, but better than her uncle deserved.

"Come on in. We're just discussing our project," Duke Nuren said, running a hand over his bearded chin, sitting at a table with well over a dozen books.

She scowled at Soren. "Why is *he* here?"

Standing next to their uncle, Soren flashed pouty lips. "What kind of a greeting is that? We all missed you so terribly, Your Highness!"

"Not mutual," she drawled.

"That's enough of that." Duke Nuren scolded Kaylah with his eyes. "You two are going to have to learn to get along, because Soren's moving over with us before the next school year begins."

Her jaw dropped. "Why?!"

"To ensure our success," Nuren replied, placing a bookmark and closing one of the books he'd been studying.

She clenched her fists. "I'm doing exactly what I'm supposed to be doing. Why do we need *him*?"

Soren sneered, taunting her.

Duke Nuren set the book on a stack beside him. "We want all angles covered. He'll be dating her."

Kaylah busted out laughing. "Soren? Soren! Dating Rachel?"

Soren glared with cold eyes.

She stifled her laugh. "Sorry, but you're not exactly her type. That would never work."

Nuren raised his voice. "You'll make it work. You're in charge of making sure it does."

"But … they're nothing alike!" *Because he's horrible!*

Nuren lifted his eyebrows with finality. "Just because you've been away, doesn't mean he hasn't been excelling in his training. That's not your call to make."

She held her tongue while Soren wiggled his eyebrows in triumph. His stupid green eyes teemed with pride.

"I can be charming. I can be whatever she wants me to be."

Kaylah wanted to vomit. "Your precious Beata will be so disappointed."

Soren casually studied his nails. "She won't mind. I'll be back often enough."

"We'll talk later, Soren," Nuren said, dismissing him with a wave of the hand.

Kaylah hung back, giving her latest report. Nothing exciting or big had happened recently in the human world. "What are we even doing?" she asked. She wouldn't get an answer—she never had in the past.

Nuren wagged a finger at her as he stood. "Don't worry about it. You're right. You're doing a great job." He walked to the window, adjusting the curtains. "Just keep her trust. Guide her to Soren. Hopefully she'll bloom early and we can really get things started."

Clamping her mouth shut again, Kaylah forced herself to not reply. All of her protests to her uncle or parents over the years had only earned her their scorn and disappointment.

"That's all," he said. "Enjoy your visit."

She glanced at the table he was now standing over, stacked high with books. "Those look interesting. I'd love to help ... or just learn more?"

He didn't bother to look up. "As long as they don't go missing from this room, I don't mind you perusing. Lots of curious stuff here."

She nodded, planning on coming back soon. Not that she didn't have friends to hang out with, or family to catch up with, but ... she was becoming more distant the longer she was stationed in the human world. "Thank you. I'll see you later."

***

A week later, Kaylah found herself alone in her uncle's study; his visits were more frequent than hers, but never as long. Sitting sideways in a comfy armchair, she skimmed one of the old books, reading history.

"Your Highness?" a woman called through the partially open door.

"Yes?"

"You have a visitor."

Kaylah instantly beamed. "I'll be right there!"

Saving her place in the book and replacing it on the stack, Kaylah darted down the corridors to the main entrance. Seeing her visitor, she wore a toothy grin.

"Guillen!" she squeaked, giving her cousin a big hug.

"Hey, kiddo! Someone requested that I visit?" He released her and looked her over. "Want to go for a walk?"

She glanced down at her dress. "Yes, let me go get changed!"

***

Kaylah returned to meet Guillen, now dressed in clothes she didn't have to worry about ruining.

Soren strolled by. "Guillen, so nice of you to visit!" His tone was as arrogant as his grin. "They let you get away from your special people, just to grace us with your presence?"

Guillen glared, then turned to Kaylah. "Ready to go?"

She threw a stink eye at her brother. "Beyond ready."

They walked for quite some time, following their usual path through the dense forest, further into the mountains. They caught up with whispers, always cautious no one followed them to their secret place, a place of refuge.

The cave was chilly; she rubbed her arms as he offered to grab their sparring weapons. Returning from the depths of the cave, Guillen tossed a wooden staff, which she caught.

Without hesitation, Kaylah made the first strike. "I'm so tired of this crap."

He blocked and pushed her off. "Is it so bad?"

She huffed before grazing his arm with another attack. "They're having Soren join me. Like I can't do my job. They're going to make her date him."

"Then I feel sorry for her even more." He landed a blow in her ribs.

She clutched her side, clenching her jaw.

He halted, raising his eyebrows. "Do I need to go easy on you? You're out of practice."

She straightened out. "No."

"Alright. Fight now. Talk later."

They sparred for a good half hour. In the end, they sat on the cool cave floor, catching their breath and wiping their brows.

"Good workout," she said. "Way better than human gym classes."

"Yeah? You talk about it like you hate it there."

She frowned, tucking her knees under her chin. "I kind of hate it everywhere right now."

He matched her frown. "What's going on?"

She shook her head. "She's a nice girl. Sometimes I just want to come out and say everything. I'm delusional to think she'd understand. Who would understand that kind of thing?"

He turned the staff in his hand, inspecting it. "The end goal, right? No matter what the plan is, it won't be good for her. And you're attached."

She stared at the ground. "Yeah."

He took a deep breath. "Teenage drama. Can't say I miss it." He winked once she looked up.

She squinted. "You stopped being a teenager, what? A month ago? You're all older and wiser now?"

He chuckled. "Yep. That's me."

"Then please, wise sage," she bowed her head, "what would *you* do?"

He scratched his chin. "I'd find a way to make them listen. Or, you know, at least do my best to tick them all off."

She let out a breathy chuckle. "Great advice." She sighed. "I just don't get why my parents listen to him so much. Nuren thinks he's the next best thing. And Soren is so much like him."

"I'm always here for you. You know that, right?"

Kaylah smiled. "Definitely my favorite cousin." She stood, extending her hand for his staff.

Walking to the back of the cave, she placed the staves next to the rest of their training weapons they'd hidden away there. She furrowed her brow, studying something on the wall. Something that had always been there, but she'd never made much of. The symbols—they reminded her of something she'd just read. She took a mental photograph, planning to pick that book up after her visit with her cousin.

She couldn't help but wonder… *What if…*

Chapter 1

Four Years Later

THE IVY QUEEN AND KING were dead, assassinated. But the war was far from being won.

Rachel balanced in the breeze with the three others near her, flying home. At least, to the only place she could *call* home anymore. She hadn't chosen this realm, this life—the life of a Seeder in the Green Lands. And if she was going to have to live the rest of her life here, she wanted to make it worthwhile. But the war council wouldn't let her stay and help her best friend, Princess Kaylah. Instead, Rachel was being sent back to her village and had been warned to edit the truth.

Passing over hills and valleys lush with plant growth, wooden rooftops and dirt lanes, Rachel tried to smile. It was gorgeous. People were kind. But her heart wasn't here. Samantha, the human mom she'd grown up with, was in a Unitas safe house back in the human world. Her best friend was back in the village they'd just left, now in custody, where Rachel couldn't do anything to keep her safe. And the only guy she was interested in was an Ivy, one of the enemy.

Not technically an enemy—he was a Unitas spy, one of the good guys, but that only made it harder. He was out there, somewhere, possibly in danger.

Rachel shook the memory of Guillen out of her mind. Instead, she tried to commit to memory the lies she'd have to tell people once they landed. Her ex-boyfriend, Prince Soren, had killed his parents and blamed it on the Seeders, adding to the false accusations that they'd also kidnapped his sister Kaylah. That meant the truth of Kaylah being behind Seeder borders and working with their council needed to stay a secret while they sorted things out. The council was giving Kaylah a chance to prove herself, to make an alliance. But trust in an Ivy was hard to come by with Seeders, especially after Kaylah had spent years undercover, with her mission eventually leading to Rachel and others getting hurt. Leading to Seeders getting killed.

A gust of wind hit Rachel from the side, and she shifted the energy in her body to compensate. With the energy in her hands, she pushed back, righting herself. The air had a springiness to it. Compensating when catching a breeze felt a lot like pushing on a trampoline; there was a gentle give.

Flying straighter and glancing at the three others soaring nearby, Rachel took a deep breath, her brown hair flapping in the wind around her. So much in her life was out of her control, but she was going to try and make the most of it. To try to find the positive. She was alive. She could fly and heal. She had a huge Seeder family; she just hadn't given them enough of a chance. And she had hope for helping Kaylah with Unitas, with her movement to end the centuries-old war between their peoples.

~

Saff communed with the wind, her eyes and heart facing forward, toward her home village of South Fortinda. She yearned to be home, to see the people she loved most. To be reunited with her mother and all twenty-three of her siblings. *No. Twenty-two. Ben is dead, and I missed his burial.* She swallowed hard, trying not to cry.

She'd done it again—been impulsive. With her closest brother dead in the war, and at the end of her rope, she'd risked her life to experiment with her powers to take Rachel to the enemy princess. As much as she wanted to hate Kaylah for what her people had done to Seeders for centuries, for what had happened to Rachel, Saff had to admit that Kaylah had done a lot to prove herself already, in the few days she'd come to know her. But now, Kaylah and her fate were in the council's hands.

Saff pondered the meetings they were leaving behind. The intel Kaylah had provided about Ivy assassins was being acted upon immediately. With few formal laws binding Seeder society, most decisions were based on group consensus, tradition, and each family's preferences. But with the war so bleak, and this new information coming to light, the war council had immediately sent out an edict on how families were required to handle the care of blooming girls in the human world. The jade charms were a tool they'd always intended to keep hidden, as they hadn't been sure whether the enemy knew anything about their purpose. The Ivy assassins hadn't. But now they did, and they'd be laser-focused.

Conflicted about the terms of the edict, Saff still knew it was for the best. They couldn't leave it up to family preferences anymore. Before, if a family was careless about their own daughters' protection, they had paid the heartbreaking penalty for it. But now, if they dropped the ball, the price was even worse than assassination—those daughters would be kidnapped and subjected to the same torture as Rachel. The kind of torture that helped the War Vines tear down Seeder border walls.

One wrong move could jeopardize *everyone* in Seeder society now.

Thousands of Seeder girls were hidden in the human world, unable to survive in the poisoned Seeder lands until their powers came in. A lot of lives were about to change abruptly. Most girls bloomed between the ages of fifteen and eighteen, and the majority of the time, human host parents waited to tell them about their heritage until their blooming had been completed with the charm. But now, they would no longer be afforded the luxury of normal teenage lives free from worry of assassins on the hunt, able to spend carefree time with family they loved before moving away forever. *Every* Seeder girl thirteen and up was now to learn the truth. They could be their own advocates when looking for the enemy, spotting early signs of budding, and keeping the jade charms that controlled their changes well-hidden and used consistently.

Saff's heart was heavy. She would have hated losing out on that precious time with her human parents, blissfully unaware. But she also keenly recalled how poorly things had gone for her own family because of her ignorance. Despite that, she didn't blame her family—they'd done the best they could. And there were rarely ideal options in war.

Saff glanced to her right, at Thod, her Seeder dad. He was disappointed. Saff's stomach knotted. She had a lot of family, which meant a lot of people to love, but also meant a lot of people to hurt. She really should have at least waited another day to run away. It had been just a week ago that Ben died, and she'd slipped out before the burial to meet Kaylah in the human world.

Her guilt piled up when her mind turned to Devin, her husband. She wanted nothing more than to be with him, to hold him, to have him hold her. But she'd betrayed him, sneaking away in the dead of night without a word, leaving only a letter. She loved nothing more than her family, and she wanted to end the war, but her needs and wants were at odds, and she'd made a choice. A choice she hoped had been the right one.

She prayed Kaylah wouldn't betray them, and that Saff could make amends.

***

Approaching a central park good for landing, the four Seeders coasted lower and slower, floating to the ground. Saff had mastered a graceful landing long ago. Rachel's landing was a bit rough, as the least experienced of the group, but she caught herself and landed on her feet. Saff and Rachel had argued before taking off. Saff had wanted to go home; Rachel hadn't. But their hours in the air had allowed them each to do some thinking, and they hugged.

Saff forced a smile. "Maybe, if we're lucky, they'll let us keep working together for now. And hopefully we'll hear from Kaylah soon."

"Yeah. Maybe. Thanks for taking me."

Saff gave her another hug, and they parted ways to their own sections of the village. Saff and Thod walked in silence for a while down the semibusy dirt lane. One of her former students smiled and waved. Soldiers plodded along everywhere.

"Do you want me to drop you off at your cottage?" Thod asked. "Or do you want to stop by and see the family first?"

Both. Neither. She simultaneously wanted to hug everyone, and to shrink from the uncomfortable, but inevitable, meetings all at once. It was still early enough in the day that she figured Devin wouldn't be home yet, and she wasn't sure she could sit all alone in their empty cottage. "Let's go see Mom and the others."

"Okay." After a minute, Thod reached out an arm and slid it around Saff's shoulder, pulling her closer—an olive branch after he'd chastised her back in the village they'd just returned from.

They entered the family cottage, and Murial, Saff's Seeder mom, hugged her within an inch of her life. "You're home. In one piece," she breathed in relief. "Please don't worry us like that again."

Despite Saff's actions, Murial was just happy to have her home safe and sound. Saff's decision to go to the human world to parley with Kaylah had been a dangerous one. It shouldn't have even been possible, according to their understanding of their powers. And the fact that she might have been stranded in the human world in the attempt, had made it a potentially lethal decision. Seeder women's health and powers were tethered to the energy of the Green Lands. Unable to rift back on her own, she could have been dead by now.

A half dozen of Saff's brothers and sisters dropped by during the hour she was back home. Most of them still lived in the kids' housing in the back lot. Things were tense, but she had hope of their relationships bouncing back. None of them seemed to focus on her defiance of council orders. The pain they chiefly expressed was from her walking out before Ben's burial.

"So, how did you even do it?" Tabatha asked, sitting across from her in the cottage living room.

Saff shrugged. "I just … thought I'd test the limits of my extra capacity with energy."

Tabatha shook her head. "Wow, that's crazy. So, you can make *two* trips to the human world in a year?"

Saff's muscles tensed. She *hadn't* actually made two round trips—not on her own. She probably wouldn't have been able to, and would have died from root rot in the human world, if it hadn't been for Kaylah guiding her home through an Ivy rift.

But they had to edit their story. It might keep Seeders safer, not knowing Kaylah was in their custody, but it made Saff's justification for leaving her family sound a lot more hollow. "Yeah, two round trips. Crazy, right? But I don't plan to ever do it again. It hurt pretty bad. One trip is enough." She rubbed her chest at the echo of intense pain she had endured when she'd punched through the rift into the human world; it had been so bad that she'd almost died just from losing her focus during flight, plummeting in a free fall.

Tabatha frowned. "That would have been cool, to figure out a way to visit the human world more often."

"Yep."

Hesitantly, Tabatha dared to ask the same question the others had. "So, what came of your visit there?"

Saff poked her finger through the open pattern of an afghan. "Um, unfortunately we didn't actually get to meet the princess. But we found some intel that will be important regarding their assassin networks."

"Oh… Then … I guess something came out of it. We … missed you, at Ben's burial."

Saff closed her eyes, trying not to cry, *again*. "I know. I'm sorry."

"Well, I'm just happy you're home now."

After another round of hugs and some food, Saff walked next door to her in-laws' cottage. She was welcomed in by Heather, Ben's fiancée at the time of his death. She wasn't her usual cheery self, not that Saff would have expected her to bounce back so soon.

"I'm so sorry," Saff said as she held Heather tight.

Heather took a while to respond. "I'm glad you're back."

The members of Devin's family who were home acted more casually. One sister even asked questions about how the 'adventure' to meet the princess had gone.

Devin walked in the door, and his eyes focused on Saff. He didn't run to her, instead standing there as if deciding what to do. Seated on the couch, Saff also waited a moment, not sure if he would come to her, or just turn back out the door in anger at her betrayal.

She cautiously stood and walked to him; he grabbed her, closing the gap, and wrapped his arms around her.

"You're really home," he whispered.

She bit her lip. "I'm sorry. I love you. I missed you so much."

They stood there for a while, embracing, and not saying anything more. Not releasing each other. Saff didn't yet know where to go from there; perhaps Devin didn't either. Eventually, he was the first to pull away.

"Just checking in," he told his family.

She wanted to grab his hand, or feel his arm around her, something naturally affectionate. But instead, he was like a stranger, as awkward as when they were teenagers, before dating.

"I think I'm going to head home," she said, hoping he'd follow.

"I'll see you in a little while," he said, looking down. "I'm going to spend some time here."

Saff swallowed a lump in her throat. She could hardly just say she'd changed her mind and hang out there, if he was intentionally staying behind as a way to avoid being with her.

"Okay. I'll see you soon." She frowned and gave him a kiss on the cheek before saying goodbye to the others and heading out the door.

Chapter 2

SAFF ARRIVED BACK AT HER COTTAGE. It was quiet. Too quiet. She'd only spent a few days apart from Devin, but it felt like months. Perhaps it was the gap she'd forced into their relationship. She'd essentially left for a suicide mission and hadn't had the courage to even tell him to his face.

Passing their wedding portrait and wall of photos in the living room, she stepped into their bedroom. On their dresser sat the note she'd left him, now torn in half.

Her heart ached—she was solely to blame for the wedge in their marriage. She'd made an impulsive decision, had been pushed over the edge with Ben's death. Devin would have stopped her from going to meet Kaylah. She hoped he'd come to understand that she'd had to do it.

By the time Devin returned home, Saff was fast asleep. She woke in the morning to him getting dressed.

"Any chance you could stay and eat breakfast together?" she asked.

"I should get going." He put on his shoes without looking at her.

"You're sure?" She pleaded with her eyes.

"There's work to do." He leaned over and kissed her on the forehead. "I'll see you tonight."

"Yeah," she whispered as he walked out of the room.

After getting ready for the day, she rendezvoused with Rachel to meet with their village council. They were again deposed, individually. Saff couldn't help but wonder if she was taking on the brunt of their anger. She ought to, as Rachel's mentor.

Once they both rejoined the meeting, Saff waited for the hammer to drop, for them to take away her welcoming mentor position and reassign her elsewhere.

They didn't.

"For now, on a *trial* basis, we'll be reassigning you both to the healing clinic you were stationed at before you went AWOL. Standard temple deposits will also be expected," a councilwoman instructed. "Do you think you two can manage that?" There was obvious censure in her tone.

Both girls hung their heads. "Yes, ma'am."

"Good. You're dismissed."

The crunch of gravel under their shoes filled the awkward silence between them as they left the council meeting, headed toward the temple.

"That could have been worse," Rachel timidly encouraged.

"Yeah. I half expected them to order me to the front lines," Saff said wryly.

"You … do still want to work together, right?"

Saff's eyes shot to Rachel. "Yeah. I just… I guess we'll see what the council makes of our 'trial.'"

***

Saff was able to leave her work early that first day to visit the graveyard before dark.

She shuffled her tired feet to the edge of town, all alone. She'd only visited the village graveyard a couple of times before, but it hadn't meant as much to her then, as it did now.

Seeder graveyards were one of the most beautiful ways one could witness the Seeders' close ties to nature. In the center of the field rose a giant leafy tree. It stood vibrant, almost glowing. It was said that its roots took the energy from the fallen Seeders and recycled it back into the realm, and that those who came to visit the area could gain comfort and strength from the echoes of their loved ones giving back.

Regret filled her. She didn't even know which plot was her brother's—they didn't mark them. Seeders didn't waste time and money on expensive caskets or anything like that; Seeder funerals were simple, natural, practical.

Sitting on a knotted wooden bench, Saff surveyed the area. There were too many bright flowers. It made her hollow inside to behold such a floral display. Visitors knew that a plot was occupied, and how fresh the burial was, by the flowers that emerged from it. Ben would be under one of the patches of bright purple flowers. The field had several plots of purple flowers, and almost as many with yellow flowers. They would fade as the energy was released, as the bodies decomposed, and then the dirt would be barren, ready for the next.

There was a poetic parallel to human funerals, how people would bring cut flowers to put on the graves as a sign of respect. How over the years those flowers would often stop coming—a mirror of what nature did on its own over here.

Saff tried to talk to Ben, tried to apologize out loud; it felt right. But she choked on her words, instead sobbing.

The snap of a branch down the path announced someone's approach. She wiped at her eyes and turned to see who would be joining her. She wanted it to be Devin, but it wasn't. Heather gave her a sympathetic frown as she approached. Saff scooted over on the bench to make space, and Heather sat down without a word.

They both stared over the field. Only the chirp of crickets coming out for the night pierced the stillness.

Heather rested her head against Saff's shoulder. "He's that one, right over there." She pointed at a plot with fresher flowers.

Saff sniffled. "I'm sorry."

"Me too."

Saff leaned her head onto Heather's. They still had a strong bond. They'd still be sisters-in-law, with Heather being Devin's sister. But Heather had lost her fiancé, and Saff her brother. They were close before, and while they had naturally grown closer when Ben proposed to Heather, they were now brought together by something that ached deep in their souls.

Saff realized she hadn't really elaborated on her blanket apology. She was sorry that Heather hurt, that Ben was gone, but also that she'd deserted them before his burial.

"I'm sorry I wasn't here… That I left," she added.

"It's okay," Heather whispered. "He knew you loved him."

"I hope so," Saff squeaked. "I let him down."

"You didn't. No more than I did," Heather reassured her.

Saff sat up, looking over, confused.

Heather continued, "I gave everything I had when he came in. And you know I'm one of the best healers our age, at least in our village." She pursed her lips. "There's only so much we can do."

For work during this onslaught, Heather was often stationed out on the edge of the borders, healing those more severely wounded.

Saff nodded. While she was a talented teacher, training the young girls, she admired Heather. Heather's natural nurturing was something Saff loved about her; she'd always believed it had helped Ben with his temper and rigidity.

"Do you think it will make a difference, what you and your friend did?" Heather asked.

Saff wished more than anything that she could tell Heather about Kaylah and the council's plans. But she'd only been given permission to disclose that to Devin and her parents. "I really hope so. We need something to change. We can't keep going on like this."

Heather gave her a faint smile. "Then I'm glad you went. And if it's something that can end this, I want to help, too."

While surprised by Heather's declaration, Saff appreciated the support.

Heather fidgeted with her hands. "How are you and Devin?"

Saff opened her mouth, unsure of what to say at first. "I don't really know. Maybe someday I'll find out … if he'll stay in my presence long enough to talk to me."

"He'll come around, you know. You two are strong." Heather tapped her own knee. "But take my advice? Don't waste a day being apart from the one you love."

Saff nodded. She wasn't sure if she should ask what she wanted to. It could be seen as insensitive or impertinent, but she also hated taboos that restricted people from being able to talk about hard things. She hesitated, but took the plunge.

"Do you wish you had gotten married earlier? Knowing he'd be gone so soon?" Being a widow or divorcée in Seeder society was complicated. The mating bond didn't sever just because one of them left or died. Once a Seeder had been mated, a physical relationship wouldn't be the same with future suitors, and they wouldn't be able to have kids with them. In a way, Heather had dodged a dart; she could still find a mate down the road and have a 'normal' life.

Heather didn't answer Saff's question, instead shedding fresh tears. Saff leaned her head against hers again, and held her hand. The two looked out over the field of flowers as all light faded from the sky.

After a while, Saff dropped Heather off at her parents' place and then headed home for the night. Devin was asleep, or pretending to be, by the time Saff got back to their cottage. She slid into bed and cuddled up to him; he didn't react.

Devin's movements in bed woke her in the early morning. She opened her eyes to him studying her face, just inches away.

"Hey, you," she said with a small smile.

"Hey." Instead of returning a smile, he started to get out of bed.

She grabbed his hand. "Just stay for a little while?"

He shook his head, freeing his hand. "I have people counting on me. I need to get to work."

Her heart dropped. Had that been aimed to hurt her? Implying she'd deserted her people, left for a week, when they were counting on her?

She sat up in bed. "Please stay, just for a little while. Don't leave."

He met her gaze with narrowed eyes. "Like you left me?"

Devastated, she looked down. "I know you're mad. I deserve that."

He changed his clothes and continued to get ready, leaving the room.

She followed him to the kitchen. "Please, just talk to me."

He clenched his jaw and sat at the table. His hands were balled into fists. Slowly, he stretched them out onto the wood. "You weren't there when your family needed you the most. I don't know what you expect me to say."

Gripping the back of a kitchen chair, she uttered the only thing she could think to say. "I did what I felt I had to."

"Well, I hope it pans out." He stood as if to leave.

"I want to hear what you have to say. I'm ready."

"Are you really?" he snapped.

Saff swallowed, emboldened by Heather's advice to not waste a day. "Yes."

He scoffed. "I doubt that."

"Try me."

"I don't get to be mad at you. You don't *get* to be mad at someone that just had a family member die!" His glare was piercing. "It doesn't matter that you think you're smarter than the council. Or that he was one of *my* best friends. Or that a lot of people were depending on you for training and healing. Or that *every* family member on both sides felt your absence as they mourned. You get *your* way, and that's *all* you care about!"

His face was growing redder with each offense he spewed out. "And you didn't give a shit about my feelings, enough to even tell me to my face that you were endangering your life. It's like you're a human teenager all over again—inconsiderate and selfish."

Her eyes stung at his assessment of her. She and Devin were only twenty-one. She still had a lot to learn. "I'm not perfect. You knew what I was like when you married me."

"Yeah, well maybe I thought you'd grow out of it."

She pursed her lips, gripping the kitchen chair tighter. They rarely fought, and never like this.

He continued, "It's like you always have to take it too far. You couldn't just find a way to say goodbye to your human best friend— you had to reveal our entire society's secrets to him first. You couldn't just fly off to meet the leech princess, you had to do it before Ben's burial, and without even talking to me. Your husband. Your mate. The person you should be able to talk to and trust the most."

She'd asked for it, but she hadn't prepared herself for his tirade. She was at a loss on how to answer any of it.

When she didn't respond, he finished letting out his frustration. "I don't want to go to more burials, Saff. And as much as Ben's burial hurt, do you know what hurt more?" He paused. "Imagining my wife, signing her own death sentence in the human world. I wouldn't be there to keep you safe. I wouldn't be there for your burial. The person that matters the most to me."

She frowned. "I don't always need protection."

"Then maybe you don't need me." He studied her face. "You healed me once, when I told you not to, and you said that *you* deserved some say in the matter, that you take care of your family. Where did you extend that same courtesy to me?"

He was right. Absolutely right. They were supposed to be a team.

"I need you." She choked on her words as tears fell down her cheeks. "I love you. I won't do it again. I won't leave you again. I'm sorry. I really am." She couldn't yet bring herself to ask for his forgiveness.

Devin closed his eyes, clenching his fists again. "I love you too. I'm going to work." He left without further discussion.

Saff lay down on the couch, sniffling and wondering if she'd done the right thing by pushing Devin to talk. She felt like she'd done the right thing by going to meet with Kaylah. And she still felt guilty about the way she'd done it. But now she wasn't sure if she should have forced him to talk if he wasn't ready.

Either way, it was out in the open, and she'd made a vague promise she hadn't intended to. She'd said she wasn't going to leave again. If Kaylah asked for her to go help with the cause, she wouldn't be joining Unitas. Saff's marriage meant too much to her.

***

After forcing herself to get up and dress, Saff jogged halfway to work to clear her mind. Rachel was already there, tidying up bandage wraps.

"Hey, stranger. How's it going?" Rachel asked.

Saff set to work helping her. "I've been better."

"Sorry."

Saff managed a tight-lipped smile. "It's not all about us, right?"

~

As they worked with the younger girls, healing the wounded as they came in, they would occasionally chat.

"I thought it would be busier, to be honest," Rachel confessed.

"Calm before the storm," Saff replied. "I'm sure the Ivies are building something big to make up for the assassination and kidnapping."

Rachel nodded in agreement. She finished healing a minor head wound on a soldier, and he thanked her. She wasted no time starting on her given assignment from Kaylah. "Saff? Kay—um, *someone* asked me to look into something—the name of our village. Do you know where that came from?"

"No idea." Saff moved over to a newly returned girl who was healing a young soldier. "Not that much. Just enough to heal the immediate area. If you expend that much energy on every scrape, you'll be useless in a couple hours."

"Where do we find the history of our villages?" Rachel asked.

"They keep older relics safely locked away in the temples; there are some interior rooms people don't usually go into. You'd have to ask a temple leader, or a council member."

Rachel welcomed in another wounded soldier, mentally making plans for her time after work. It wasn't like she had friends to hang out with, or a desire to spend copious amounts of time with her Seeder family.

***

Rachel was at a dead end. After a week of asking around, she was finally allowed to spend some free time perusing old records of their village. But there wasn't much information that seemed pertinent. South Fortinda didn't have much written about its establishment. It was just another village, created as Seeders had spread out over time. From what she could gather, it was fairly identical to the others. And there wasn't really a meaning to the name; it wasn't named after a flower, or a river, or anything like that. She was curious about the fact that it was 'South,' and that other villages shared the same name—there was a North and West Fortinda.

Nothing jumped out as useful, until a certain passage piqued her interest. Rachel sat up straighter, sliding her clear-quartz-and-jade lightkeeper closer to the page. They'd all been named Fortinda because they shared the same rift space. *Hmm...* She sat back in her chair, lightly tapping the tabletop. Seeders were quite different from the Ivies in that regard. Seeders created their rifts to the human world in the air—they could fly. Ivies created their rifts through the sacrifice of trees.

The particularly interesting thing was the precision with which Ivies would travel. Seeders had to prepare for a long strenuous journey, flying for hours to find the right place to cross between realms. Ivies could practically pick any old random tree, and choose whatever destination they wanted in the Green Lands. She'd experienced it herself. She wasn't sure what this meant, but it might mean something to Kaylah. Rachel made a mental note of it so she could report back when, or if, she were to see her friend again.

After she flipped one last page, Rachel's eyes grew wide with curiosity. Intriguing symbols covered the parchment, similar to a type she'd once seen before, carved on a cave wall near the Ivy palace. She jotted them down, knowing that *these*, for certain, meant something.

Chapter 3

A COUPLE OF WEEKS PASSED without incident. Devin was still cold with Saff, the Ivy attacks were still eerily tame, and no word had come to their village—from or about Kaylah. Saff and Rachel would meet daily for work at the training and healing clinic, passing questioning glances, only to be met with frowns and heads shaking. They were both in the dark.

~

Rachel hated this. She was grateful they hadn't been punished, as the council had warned about possible 'consequences.' But they probably needed her and Saff healing too much to worry about anything punitive. Maybe, she hoped, they were also not being harder on Saff and Rachel because Kaylah was doing a good job. The part that killed Rachel was that there was no way to know. She'd promised Eric, Kaylah's human boyfriend, that she would watch out for her and keep her safe. She couldn't do that from here.

These weeks were lonely for Rachel. When she'd first met most of her Seeder family, it had been in shame. She'd been stupid enough to trust Prince Soren and had allowed herself to be kidnapped and used as a weapon against her own people. She'd found it hard to talk to her new family about the trauma she'd endured. Weeks later, she'd taken off, running away to go back to meet Princess Kaylah, one of the people at fault for Rachel's kidnapping. And returning to her village now, all she could say was that they'd 'found intel to mitigate the Ivy assassin network's efforts.' It all sounded like Rachel was weak and ungrateful.

She hadn't yet met her Seeder dad—he was still undercover taking care of her last sister in the human world, who was midbloom. Other than Saff, the only confidant Rachel had who knew the truth about Kaylah, was her Seeder mom, Lyza. But their relationship was the touchiest of them all. The tension between her Seeder and human moms—once best friends, now at odds thanks to Rachel's foolishness—made Rachel feel like she had to walk on eggshells around Lyza. And she wished, more than anything, that she could find some strength in talking with her siblings, even with the edited story. But things hadn't been going well with them, either.

***

Midafternoon at the clinic one day, Rachel and Saff were slogging through their daily tasks. Rachel collected bloodied rags and threw them in a bucket to be rinsed and boiled. Saff sighed heavily nearby, leaning back against a table, supervising a few trainees while they healed.

"What's up?" Rachel asked, approaching her and leaning against the table as well.

Saff shrugged.

They hadn't really talked about it, but Rachel knew things weren't exactly going well back home for Saff. She'd sometimes talk about spending free time with her family, or going on nature walks, but she never talked about her husband anymore. Rachel dared to ask, "How's Devin?"

Saff wouldn't make eye contact. "He's fine."

Rachel nodded.

"How about your family?" Saff asked.

Rachel grabbed a bar of soap and dipped her hands in a basin of clean water. "They're all safe."

What more could she say? Saff was already struggling with her marriage, and Rachel didn't want to add to that. But things had gone from awkward to silent back home for Rachel. She avoided Lyza more often than not, too ashamed to talk about her human mom and all the trauma Rachel had been through. Her brothers were nice in passing, though often busy fighting at the weakened Seeder border walls, or working other jobs, or dating. Her sisters were plenty occupied, but they all shared a space in their family dormitory; they were in closer proximity to her than anyone else. Rachel had to lie to them, had to keep secrets about Kaylah. The sisters that didn't judge her for her actions had originally tried to be there for her, but that support had died off. She wasn't sure how much of it was them being tired of trying to coax information out of her, or if, with eleven of them, they all assumed someone else had her covered.

But she felt adrift in a sea of pain and memories. She couldn't handle the looks she sometimes got in the mornings after she'd woken from haunting nightmares. It wasn't often, but it still happened—she'd wake up sweating and moaning or screaming.

The walls were too thin for her mental health. And what was she supposed to say? 'Sorry, just dreaming about my ex-boyfriend attacking me again. Yeah, and then I was strapped to a chair, and they drilled my arms with Ivy leaves to steal my energy?' Or the other nightmares. 'This was the one about my stepdad being the villain, and then being beheaded by my best friend. Did you have any dreams last night? Oh, unicorns—how fun.' She'd *tried* to open up, but it hadn't been easy, and it hadn't helped.

A pair of soldiers entered the clinic, one aiding the other as he limped.

"I've got this one." Rachel dried her hands on a clean rag. She approached the men as the injured one lay down on the stretcher and his helper left. Luckily, it was only a flesh injury. His leg had been sliced, no doubt by sharpened leaves on Ivy vines. One cut was down to the bone. She moved a hand over that one first. She still got a bit queasy at the larger injuries, but was starting to get used to it after so much exposure.

"Sorry," she said as he flinched, and she pinched the skin together, channeling Seeder energy from her heart to her hand. Her hand glowed as the bone, muscle, and skin healed. She preferred this kind of healing to anything internal. Internal was tricky.

Saff and Heather were as well-trained as any fully-rooted matriarch at those techniques. This was a training clinic, so they didn't get the most severely wounded, but when they did get bad ones, it was usually busy enough that the girls were needed for healing elsewhere, and couldn't be spared to train on the worst injuries. But recently, Saff had started to call Rachel over to watch and learn, to study the techniques of deeper healing.

As Rachel finished up on the man, a soldier entered the clinic, and Saff left with him. When Saff returned, she was practically beaming. She spoke to another mentor who had been working with them, and approached Rachel. "Find me outside when you're able to take a dinner break." She left the room again straight away.

Hope swelled in Rachel. It had to be word from Kaylah. Maybe they were being called to action? Though, it was odd they wouldn't have spoken to Rachel, too… What if she had to stay here, forced to work in the drudgery of it all, while Saff was put to work for Unitas? Rachel shook away her doubts. *Any* news that brought a smile to Saff's face was good news.

Finding a lull in healing work, Rachel quickly cleaned up her work area and stepped outside, searching around the wooden building for Saff. She spotted Saff's strawberry blond hair out in the garden. She was giving two girls a private lesson. Rachel hadn't seen these girls before, and something about Saff's instruction seemed … off. She walked closer to observe. Saff was gesturing, teaching these girls things Rachel had learned from her brother, Jeff. Basics. Like, *really* basic.

~

Having noticed her spectator, Saff perked up. "Alright, girls, drink lots of water, and you can go grab some dinner, if you're ready."

Rachel strolled up to her. "What's going on?"

"Kaylah." Saff smiled. "They're letting her do it."

"What do you mean? Give me all the details!"

They sat on the ground, watching the new girls from a distance as they collected food and water from a station at the clinic.

"Those girls are sisters from the neighboring village," Saff explained. "The one with long brown hair—she finished blooming just over a month ago. The one with shorter blond hair—they stopped using the jade four days ago."

"Four days!" Rachel blurted, clearly astounded. "So ... they have no training?"

"The one that bloomed earlier has some under her belt, but nowhere near enough to catch a breeze. They were guided home through an Ivy rift." Saff grinned from ear to ear. She was overwhelmed with excitement at seeing some good come from her tumultuous decision.

"Wow," Rachel whispered. "Then it's really happening? We're working with Kaylah?" She stared at the girls for a moment. "Any more information about how things are going? About how Kaylah's doing? When we'll be needed?"

Saff pulled a weed growing near her foot. "No, they only gave me the bare minimum, letting me know these girls would need training in the basics." She thought of Devin. Would he be allowed to train new girls like this with Saff? If he was, would he even accept the responsibility? He'd done a great job of speeding her through learning the basics when she was at that stage.

The girls returned to where Saff and Rachel were sitting, and Saff made the introductions.

~

"Welcome!" Rachel said. She would have said 'welcome home,' but the Green Lands didn't always feel like home to newly returned girls; it hadn't for her, at least. "You girls are … really brave to come here. You know everything that's going on?"

Brielle, the one with long hair, seemed jittery, poking at a hole in the knees of her human-world jeans. "They said I would be safe, that I wouldn't have to fight."

Rachel smiled reassuringly. These sisters had bloomed, but not rooted. Technically, either could still choose to go back to the human world and live the rest of their lives there if they wanted to forfeit their powers and home realm. "There's lots you can do within the safety of our borders. Like us—" She gestured to herself and Saff. "We know how to fight, but we help more with healing and training, and energy deposits at the temple wells. We really appreciate you being here."

The short-haired girl, Coral, finished chewing a mouthful of salad, her long dangly earrings swaying. "I hated high school. And that tiny town. This sounded a lot more fun."

Rachel smirked at such a casual description of a life-altering decision. "Adventure of a lifetime."

Saff got up and grabbed dinner for herself and Rachel before rejoining the conversation—the cooks had prepared a thick vegetable stew with rice and salad.

The new girls were itching to talk about their experiences, learning about their identities, and how they'd made their choices to come home. Rachel assumed they'd probably been told to keep quiet about Unitas, like she and Saff had been ordered to, but she couldn't help herself.

"What was it like? Coming through with Ivy help? Do you know the names of the people involved? How many were there?" She poked at a parsnip in her stew, trying to act casual, despite the far-from-casual string of questions she'd just rattled off.

Brielle seemed more nervous to talk about that part. Coral happily obliged.

"I don't know why they think it should be some great secret— there were tons of people there."

"Tons?" Saff raised her eyebrows.

"Well, I mean, you know." She flourished her hand in the air. "There were, I think, like five or six of us girls, so at least that many Ivies to take us through. And then lots of humans and our kind at the forest to make sure things were safe, and to say goodbye."

Saff and Rachel shared a heartfelt glance.

"It was freaky coming to this side. The energy's awesome, but there were like, a thousand guards to escort us through the walls."

"And you don't remember any names? Any of the Ivies or humans?" Rachel asked.

Both girls shook their heads. "No. Sorry," Coral said. "There was a lot going on."

Rachel's heart was light with relief—Kaylah was alive, and the Seeders had decided to work with her! And hopefully, Rachel would soon be requested to help in the Unitas cause.

****

Saff worked well past sundown training the new girls. She was beyond grateful to know things were progressing, that Kaylah was serving as a beacon of hope in the war.

She caught a breeze straight home, figuring Devin would already be in bed. To her surprise, a lightkeeper still lit up the cottage. She moseyed a bit on her approach to the front door, pondering their relationship. Worse than their fighting was the silence.

Had Devin overreacted? Probably. But as Saff's mate, her husband, her best friend—he knew her better than anyone else. He also had more invested in her than anyone else. Others might think that Saff's impromptu unsanctioned mission with Rachel had been more altruistically motivated than it really was. Devin could see right through that, even if he wasn't empathizing.

Stopping by the front door, Saff checked the pea planters to see if any pods were ready to pick.

Her actions might have brought about some good in the war, but her motivations for leaving in the first place had been primarily about avoiding grieving at Ben's funeral, and seeking revenge for his death.

Then there was the letter she'd left Devin when she snuck out in the middle of the night. Without imagining how hard it would be to stand alone at his best friend's funeral, Saff had scratched out the sorriest of apologies. It hadn't been much more eloquent than 'Sorry. Going to experiment with my life. Please forgive me. Love you.'

Had it been the other way around, she would have been just as devastated to face the funeral alone, having to inform both of their families of Devin's disappearance, defiance of council orders, and general recklessness, all the while worried for his safety, unable to protect him.

None of the pea pods in these planters were quite ready. She sniffed the blossoms, bolstering her courage to head inside. She should stop avoiding the subject, and try apologizing again.

A bundle of daisies greeted her from the kitchen table when she walked inside. Devin was cleaning dishes. He turned around and gave her a hesitant smile.

He glanced over at the kitchen table. "I, uh, I know it's more of a human thing, cutting flowers to bring them inside… I just wanted you to know I was thinking of you."

"Thanks. They're beautiful." She looked into his handsome brown eyes, appreciating the gesture, the shift in tension between them. When she had been sick in high school, going through her bloom before being given her charm, he had shown up with a vase full of daisies. That had been the day they'd first kissed.

"Why don't you sit down?" he said. "Let's talk."

Her chest tightened. "Why?" The flowers were proof she hadn't completely ruined things, right? It wasn't like he was going to move out, right? Seeder divorces were rare, given the strength of the mating bond, but they did happen.

Or maybe someone else close had died? Half of the time, she got bad news—news of the fallen, deaths like Ben's—from Devin.

He read her face. "Nothing's wrong, Saff. I just want to talk."

She swallowed and sat on the soft living room sofa, glancing at him over her shoulder.

"Are you hungry?" he asked. "I made some fruit salad."

"Sure." She pulled off her shoes, tucking them under their wicker coffee table.

He returned with a bowl of mixed fruit—cantaloupe, pomegranate, young coconut, and blueberries.

She smiled. "Thanks." She awkwardly dug in, unsure what was prompting his actions. His sweet treat hit the spot after an exhausting day. He'd always been the better cook between them— he even made a simple bowl of fruit taste amazing.

He sat next to her in silence for a minute. "It was a rough day. We're starting to see more of their soldiers in the woods again." He frowned.

She matched his frown.

"I just…" He rubbed his face with his hands. "I wanted to say I'm sorry for getting so mad at you. And I'm tired of living like this. You and me, just passing each other." He scratched at a spot of dirt on his pants. "Pretending like we're not both hurting. Missing Ben. Coming home drained every day."

She'd lived every day, for *weeks*, riddled with guilt, without her usual confidant to hold, to talk to. Saff grimaced as she fought tears. "I don't want your apology. I just want your forgiveness."

He twisted his wedding ring around his finger. "I don't know if I can say I completely forgive you, yet. I'm not sure if I know what that fully means." He looked up, reaching over to wipe away her tears. "But I know I will. I love you. It might just take more time."

"Okay," she whispered. "I love you too."

He paused, pensive. "I understand you were struggling. I do. And we both could have handled this better." They shared a look of shame. "I just wish you would have been here, that you would have given me the chance to come with you, to be there for you."

"I know."

"And you didn't even *try* talking to the council first, before you ran away like that." His voice was soft as he presented his argument this time.

She opened her mouth to protest. Rachel had never gotten anywhere with her appeals to the council.

He anticipated her response. "Yeah, the council didn't trust Rachel. I don't blame them, considering she's spent years under Ivy influence. But you, Saff—they trusted you to be her mentor. You didn't even *once* suggest this plan to them, or ask to go. They *might* have listened to you. You didn't even give them a chance. Or me."

She sniffled, nodding. Had she been thinking logically, that would have been the right approach. Even if the council had turned her down, like they had Rachel numerous times, Saff still could have absconded during the middle of the night and done as she pleased.

"Come here." He managed a small smile.

Saff put down her bowl and crawled into his arms. "I do love you." After a few minutes wrapped in his embrace, she decided it was her turn to talk about her day.

"I worked with some new girls today." She shifted in his arms to see his face. "They were brought home with Ivy help."

He squeezed her hand. "That's great, love. That's really great. I'm glad to hear things are working out."

"I thought about you. How you trained me in the basics of energy. I wondered if we could work together to train these girls. You were a great trainer for me." She searched his eyes.

Leaning closer, he gave her a kiss on the lips. Since her return, he'd kissed her on the forehead, or on the cheek, but not on the lips. She'd been longing for his touch; the sweet familiarity of it took her breath away.

"Just because I made a decent trainer for you, doesn't mean I'm the best for everyone," he said. "But … we'll see. You never know."

Saff lightly poked him in the chest. "You're not decent."

He smirked. "I'd like to think I'm a decent person."

She chuckled. "You know what I mean."

He gave her the biggest smile she'd seen in a long time. "I do. Let's get some rest, okay?"

***

A week down the road, the Ivies made it clear they were taking the war seriously, flooding the Neutral Woods with troops. The Seeders were grateful for the lull they'd been given—time to repair their borders, allowing reinforcement of weak places in the thicket—but they had known it would only last so long.

Rachel was surprised when she and Saff were pulled from training and healing one day to meet with a local council member.

"You're both being asked to report for a special assignment, leaving tomorrow. Our ally has requested assistance in Siqendra."

Rachel was beyond ready to start a new adventure, to help in a different capacity. Siqendra was one of the oldest known Seeder villages, and also one of the more central ones.

"I won't be going." Saff twisted her lips. "I'm needed here."

Rachel furrowed her brow. "Really?"

"You were requested by name," the councilwoman said.

~

Technically, this was only a request, not an official order. Saff hesitantly answered the question in Rachel's eyes. "I need to be here. For my family. I'm sure someone else can help just as much as I can."

She'd given her word that she would help with Unitas, but she'd also given her word that she wouldn't leave Devin again. If she left her village, she'd be breaking one of those promises.

Rachel bit her lip and nodded slowly. "Don't say no without even asking him."

Saff turned to the councilwoman with a heavy sigh. "I'll discuss it with my family. Can I give you an answer in the morning?"

The woman said that she could. Saff mulled it over during the day and tried to head out from work early that night.

Making it home just before Devin, she paced around their cottage. The moment he came home, she ran up to greet him with a hug.

"Well, I'm happy to see you too!" He let out a soft moan. "Everything okay?"

"Yeah, of course. I just couldn't wait to see you." She smiled. They'd grown closer in the last week, but still had some work to do in their marriage.

He leaned in and placed a lingering kiss on her lips. "I missed you too. I wish we could go back to our old jobs, teaching at the school together."

She searched his eyes; her smile faded as her breathing picked up. If she reported to her assignment, they wouldn't just be a quick flight or a couple of hours of walking apart; they would be several days' walk apart.

"What's wrong?" he asked.

She grabbed his hand and led him to the couch. "I've said no. But … they wanted me to double-check. I made you a promise."

He cocked his head in confusion.

"The council wants me to go to Siqendra. Kaylah requested help on something. I'd be leaving with Rachel in the morning." She frowned. "I told you I wouldn't leave you." She reached for his other hand. "And I meant that."

He freed his hands and rubbed the back of his neck. "Siqendra? Staying inside the walls? No human-world trips?"

"They didn't give me a lot of details."

He scrunched his face. "You're not sure how long?"

She shook her head.

He nodded. "You should go."

"But … we've been doing so good. And I need you to know I care about you, that I'm not being impulsive, not ignoring you. Kaylah can find someone else. I don't even know what she wants me for."

He held her hands again. "If the council wants it, it's safe to say you have my blessing. It's not my place to disregard their orders."

She felt a pinch of guilt at that. Though, he'd said it in a kind way, not as though he were rubbing it in that she had done that exact thing—defied council orders while deserting him to meet with the princess.

"Love, it's pretty clear there's something different about you. Your extra energy and second trip make that apparent. And we both know I was first attracted to you because you were the smartest Seeder girl in that stupid human-world trigonometry class of ours."

"None of our siblings were in that class." Saff grinned. "I think it's safe to say I was the *only* Seeder girl in that math class."

He winked. "Either way, you're smart, and you're powerful. And I would never want to stop you from fulfilling your potential, especially when you're capable of doing some amazing things."

Her heart melted at his sweet words.

He smirked. "We've already seen some good things come out of your … *passionate* … decision-making, haven't we?"

He was always a giving person, down to calling her defiance 'passionate' instead of 'impulsive.' She couldn't resist smiling.

"You're sure? I mean it—I'll stay. I don't want to ever jeopardize our relationship again."

He looked her straight in the eyes. "I forgive you, Saff. Right now, asking you to stay would only show *my* selfishness." He frowned. "Go. But be safe. Send word when you can?"

"Thank you. You know I will. And I won't be gone a second longer than I need to be." She launched herself onto his lap, giving him a huge hug. "I love you. You're more than I deserve. And definitely more than just a decent man."

He chuckled. "What if I don't want to be decent right now?"

She leaned back, eyebrows raised quizzically.

His handsome dimples made an appearance as he thumbed the collar of his shirt. "We're both pretty decent right now. You're not leaving until the morning?"

Her heart rate doubled as she blushed. "That's right. And I'm not leaving this house a second earlier than I need to tomorrow."

***

Rachel arrived at their designated meetup point fifteen minutes early, pacing around and imagining what they would be asked to do. The councilwoman greeted her on the hour, and they stood, waiting for Saff.

"She would come to let us know if she turned down the position, right?" the woman asked.

"I'm sure she would. She'll be here." Her words were more confident than she was. As excited as she was to see Kaylah, she didn't want to go it alone. Saff had hesitated to accept the assignment, and her ties to her home were stronger, and touchier still.

Ten minutes later, Saff ran up, a light bag thrown over her shoulder. They couldn't carry things with them when they caught a breeze through rifts, but if experienced, they could carry a bit when flying within the Green Lands. And flying would take days off of their journey.

Rachel was all smiles, taking the bag as a good sign.

"I am *so* sorry!" Saff apologized. "Had to pack everything and talk to my family this morning."

Saff and Rachel didn't talk about such things, but Rachel spotted good news and hid a grin. She scratched at a spot on her lower neck, flashing her eyes neon green at Saff.

Saff slapped her hand to her own neck, blushing and healing a hickey. "So … what now?"

They were given instructions, and then with a good running leap, took off—soaring to meet Kaylah. Catching a breeze required considerable focus, and it could be hard to hear, so Seeders rarely chatted while traveling. But Saff guided Rachel, letting her know the names of the villages she recognized as they passed. She and Devin had toured a lot of Seeder territory together before their wedding.

After a long day of exhausting travel, they touched down, Rachel still significantly wobblier due to her lack of proper training.

They drank water and caught their breath. "Thanks, Saff. For coming." Rachel smiled. "And I'm glad things are good back home."

Saff blushed again. "Yeah. I got a good one. But that's enough of that for now. Let's get to work."

They'd been instructed on where to meet in the old village, knocking on a door as it got dark. They were greeted by a stranger, a kind elderly gentleman, who showed them to their accommodations.

"Is the princess not here?" Saff asked.

"She'll be here first thing in the morning," the man replied.

Saff and Rachel settled in for the night. Rachel struggled to sleep, wondering what the next day would bring, somewhat comforted by the tossing and turning in Saff's bed as well—at least she wasn't the only one with racing thoughts.

Chapter 4

KAYLAH EMERGED FROM THE RIFT, straight away sensing the dimmed energy of the human world. She was almost immediately greeted with a warm smile and a strong hug from Nathan, one of her Ivy deployment guardians.

"It's so good to see you," he whispered in her ear.

"You too."

"We all set here?" a voice asked.

Kaylah pulled back from the hug and paid more attention to the large group surrounding her. Nearly a dozen Seeders, Ivies, and humans had gathered for this exchange. At least that was what it felt like—a highly inconvenient prisoner exchange rather than a dignitary on a visit.

"We've got it covered," another answered.

An older Seeder male gave a single nod, then turned and stalked deeper into the woods. He had to be the one assigned to catch a breeze back to the Green Lands to inform their council that she'd arrived at the correct location, that she hadn't deserted them and gone on the run.

Kaylah fought the building bitterness. As if she would have done that. She'd walked willingly into their territory, offering to help. And they were holding her deployment 'mom,' Ginger, hostage, unable to do any work while Kaylah was afforded the rare privilege of visiting the human world. Kaylah wasn't going to just skip out on them all. She'd worked too hard for this.

"Then are we ready to go?" another Seeder asked, all business, no compassion. This time, the question had been aimed at Kaylah.

"Am I allowed *two seconds* to talk to Nathan?" She barely even attempted to hide her frustration.

The Seeder raised her hands. "It's your time. Be our guest."

Kaylah turned her focus back to Nathan, keeping her voice low, keenly aware of all the eyes still on them. "They're treating you okay?"

Nathan wore a soft smile. "I'm perfectly fine. And they've let me chat with Eric a few times."

That gave her at least a little relief. "I'm sorry you haven't been able to see Ginger." She looked down.

"How is she?"

"She's good. Real good."

"I'll be alright, Your Majesty..."

She shook her head. "Don't call me that. No coronation: no title."

He held her hand, squeezing it reassuringly. "By all rights, it should be your title. Formalities or not, you're already our queen."

That only made her feel worse, the weight of her failed strategy digging deeper. "Yeah, well... Maybe if I can manage to turn things around..."

"How are you holding up?"

She forced a half-smile. "Things really are looking up."

Sparing a glance at the group still watching on, Nathan squeezed her hand again. "Well, I know you're not here to visit me, but I'm glad I'm stationed here to see you. And..." He cleared his throat. "Well, I'm sure Ginger's sentiments are the same... Not that we'd presume to fill their places, and now that the undercover gig is up… Just … if you still ever want to call us 'Mom' and 'Dad,' we'd be more than happy to hear it."

She lunged forward, throwing her arms around him for another hug. "Thanks, Dad." Her words caught in her throat. "I…" She whispered in his ear. "I'm so sorry I told them about you."

He released her, holding her at arm's length. "You did what you had to. If sharing my secret saves lives, especially yours, then don't you dare hold any regrets, okay?"

"Yeah. Okay. Love you."

She pulled out a letter from Ginger and handed it to him. She'd see him the next day and would get another short chance to chat. After a quick goodbye, she was escorted from the woods to a car.

***

Kaylah sat quietly in the car. Her jaw hurt from clenching it as she mulled over her conversation with Nathan. She shouldn't have needed to share so much with the Seeders, but Soren had disrupted the power dynamics of the entire realm. She'd been at the Seeders' mercy, forced to give more intel than she would have liked. She'd sworn to keep Nathan's secret gift just that—a secret. Now the Seeder council held that information, and his skills, over their heads.

Cracking her neck and sitting up straighter with a sense of satisfaction and a hint of defiance, Kaylah allowed herself to calm. She hadn't given away *all* of her knowledge, her secrets. Some things, she kept only between herself and her closest Unitas followers. Others were only known by herself and Eric.

And some secrets were hers alone.

With each speed bump and pothole on the way to their destination, Kaylah's anger subsided, her anticipation grew. She glanced down at the burner phone in her hands and smiled. She read the message again. He'd given the right code word to assure her things were safe, but her favorite part was the 'XO' he'd included at the end, just like in the good old days.

"You said we're leaving at two tomorrow afternoon?" she asked the pair of Seeder guards in the front seat. With the time zone change and extra transit time, they expected to leave the human world, travel through the Neutral Woods, and make it to Siqendra early the following morning.

"Yes, ma'am."

"No chance that could be pushed back?"

"Not likely," the male drawled.

"Okay." She forced a smile, not quite thrilled with the idea of having less than twenty-four hours with Eric on this visit. But after weeks of proving herself, having not seen him since Rachel and Saff had come to meet at this safe house, she was just grateful to have this much.

Her heart nearly beat out of her chest as they turned down his street, but she waited as patiently as she could while they made a first pass, then came around again to the simple house with the nicely manicured lawn.

The garage door opened on their approach, and the white SUV pulled in. Kaylah followed orders, waiting with one of the guards as the other went in to inspect. She sighed. Seeders were so paranoid. She'd earned their trust, but she was pretty sure their dictionary defined that word differently.

Finally, the all clear was given, and she made every effort to walk into the house calmly, like the dignified almost-queen she was, and not like the giddy teenager that she also was.

Spotting each other, she and Eric instantly beamed, but she kept herself back.

"Thank you for getting her here safely," Eric said.

"Yes," the female Seeder said. "Where will we be staying?"

"Let me show you to your rooms. Have you eaten dinner?"

"We're fine, thanks."

"Okay, great. The fridge is stocked, if you change your mind. Follow me."

Eric led them down the hall to the guest bedrooms. Kaylah's smile grew after the doors clicked and he turned back to her. In no time flat, he was in front of her, pulling her into the tightest possible hug.

"You came back," he breathed.

She squeezed a little more. "I'll always come back."

He was the first to pull away, before quickly leaning in for a kiss. "How are you doing?"

She reached up, feeling his freshly shaven face and the strong jawline she'd missed so much. "A thousand times better now that I'm with you."

His eyes twinkled. "Are you hungry?"

Kaylah bit her lip. "Mmm, maybe later." She took his hand and led him down the hallway, quietly opening his bedroom door and leading him inside.

Once the door closed, she stood tall and held him closer, laying a kiss on him she'd been counting down the days for. She reached for his belt and undid it.

He broke from their kiss. "Alright, you. That can wait two seconds. I want you to see what I did for you."

She glanced around the room.

"Flowers for my favorite girl, and all her favorite snacks."

Kaylah smiled wide. "*You're* my favorite snack." She reached for the top button of his shirt. "Too many of these." She undid the top two.

"Come on, babe. Look, I got a love seat too. Over in the corner."

"Mmm." She undid another button. "I prefer the bed." She kissed him again.

He held her by the arms, frowning. "Kaylah, why don't we talk first? There's plenty of time for that later."

"That also means there's plenty of time for talking later, too."

He raised an eyebrow, giving a disapproving glance.

She knew what he was uptight about, but she didn't want to think about it. She didn't want to think about *anything*, other than him, and her, and them. "Seriously?" She nuzzled his neck. "You don't see me for weeks, and you want to *talk*?" She cocked her head to the side. "I must be wearing too much clothing." She pulled her shirt over her head and dropped it on the ground.

Eric didn't budge. "How are you doing?"

She slid another button out of place, then kissed his exposed chest. "I told you, I'm great."

"Kaylah … we should get caught up."

"That's what I'm trying to do." She reached for another button, and he grabbed her hand.

"No. Not like this."

She frowned, meeting his gaze. "I told you—I'm fine. I just want to be here with you. Happy."

He read her face. "Don't do this. Don't shut me out."

She swallowed hard, looking down. "The Seeders haven't hurt me. I'm really fine."

"You know that's not what I'm talking about. Sweetheart … your brother killed your parents."

She met his gaze again. "I don't want to talk about that right now."

"But maybe you should," he said softly. "Come on." He took her hands and led her to the love seat, pulling her onto his lap.

She leaned against him with a sigh. "What do you want me to say, Eric? We knew they probably had to die." No matter how much she knew it, how much she'd repeated the facts to herself—it hadn't actually made it any easier.

"I know. And your relationship was complicated. But you can't pretend you don't feel anything."

"Maybe I don't even *know* how I feel about it," she whispered, staring at his hand on her knee.

"Have you cried?"

Kaylah shook her head. Silence hung in the air.

"It's not like you *have* to cry. Everyone handles things differently. And they didn't exactly win any awards as parents or leaders. But … how do you feel about Soren being the one to do it?"

She shrugged weakly. "I should thank him. This way I didn't have to do it myself."

"I don't believe that."

She wilted. "Like I said, I don't know. I just wish it meant things were over. But now … I don't know. It just makes things that much more complicated."

A hesitant smile crept onto his face. "Okay. But you have a solid plan. And you got the Seeders working with you. And a human or two." He poked her knee. "One, I might add, that is madly, hopelessly in love with you."

A genuine smile grew on her face. "Yeah?"

He nodded. "And he worries about you—every day."

"You don't need to worry about me. Now that my entire kingdom is aware of my absence, I get guards wherever I go. I'm safe."

He wrapped his arms around her. "Your physical safety is not all I worry about."

She drew a deep breath. "I know."

"Give me an update. They haven't told me much."

Kaylah reluctantly recounted what she'd had to do to earn Seeder trust. She'd endured endless days introducing her most loyal and available Unitas followers, discussing plans and proposals, divulging information. She had hesitated to share information about Nathan's special gift, even with Eric. It wasn't that particularly helpful or harmful to the human part of the equation, or even the Seeder part of it all. She'd only told the Seeders because they knew how to drive a hard bargain. And her life and hopes to rule her own kingdom had been the trump card she couldn't beat.

She'd originally hoped they could make some headway negotiating with her parents. But then Soren had murdered them and pinned it on the Seeders. And lied about her being kidnapped, so she could no longer meet with her own spies in her own lands, or claim the throne that should be hers. She'd had to pivot. Her knowledge and research were no longer tools to negotiate with; now she had to dig deep and actually use it all to prove herself for this alliance, and to get her throne and end the war.

"It might be slower than you want, but it's going in the right direction," Eric said. "You haven't said anything about Rachel. How's she doing?"

Kaylah pouted. "They haven't allowed me to see her, or really know anything." A faint smile formed. "But that's what I'm excited about for tomorrow. She'll be joining me. And Saff, that other one."

Eric's eyes widened. "Saff? She was a bit of a spitfire. How's that going to work out?"

Kaylah shifted off of his lap, sitting next to him on the love seat. "You know? She really came through at the last moment. I think we'll be okay."

"Good." He rubbed her leg. "What else is bugging you?"

"Why would you think something else is bugging me?" She put on a brave face.

"Because I know you."

She blew out a long breath. "It's up to seven." Her comment required no extra explanation—Eric knew exactly what that meant. That meant her personal body count. Her uncle had been the fifth. The soldier she'd killed in front of Rachel had added to the tally, making it seven.

"I see," he said. "Why did you do it?"

"He… I don't know." She shrugged. "I was mad. And … he probably would have slowed us down too much. And he refused to join, even though he *knew* my mother was dead."

Eric squeezed her hand. "What did you feel, right before and after?"

They'd done this exercise before. It helped sometimes. Not always. "I don't know. Like I said—mad."

"That doesn't sound like you, just killing someone out of anger. What was happening?"

Her heart beat faster, just like it had that day. "We were close to the border, about to be surrounded by fighting troops. I…" She swallowed hard, her ears pounding with the echo of soldiers closing in on them. "You should have seen Rachel's face."

"So, there was you, and Rachel, and Ginger, and Saff. Imminent danger. One of your own?"

She nodded. "It was frantic. I was panicking. I…"

"Did what you needed to do. And not out of anger. That number could be a thousand and it wouldn't be wrong, if you're doing it for the right reasons."

"I didn't even bother to learn his name." She picked at her fingernails. "What does that say about me?"

"It means you're strong. And having to make decisions no one else in the world is making. And shouldn't judge yourself that way."

She finally found her tears. "I feel like I'm losing myself, Eric. I just… I feel like it's getting easier. And it shouldn't be that way. And I'm just a damned transport half the time, bringing back these Seeder girls instead of helping my people from the palace I have a birthright to be in charge of right now. I'm useless, and I'm sinking, and… I don't know."

"I'm sorry." He pulled her in for another embrace, and she silently shed more tears in his arms.

After several minutes, he sweetly rubbed her back. "It's not possible to lose yourself. Not completely."

She sniffled, sitting back and wiping at her cheeks. "How do you figure that?"

"Well…" He smiled. "You told me a part of your heart was always here with me. And I'm keeping that part safe. So, if you get a little fuzzy on the rest of it, I'm always happy to give you a refresher."

She matched his smile.

"Plus, I think we're each a new version of ourselves, each and every day."

Kaylah took a cleansing breath. "I love you."

He raised her hand, kissing it. "Ditto."

Her stomach growled loud enough for them to both hear.

He chuckled. "Does that mean I should figure out dinner?"

"Nah. Not yet." She stood, taking a peek at the goodies he'd bought for her. A few chocolate bars, jerky, breakfast bars, and her favorite cheese crackers covered the top of the dresser. Opening the box of crackers, she leaned in, sniffing the perfume of the dozen red roses he'd bought for her. He'd been a gentleman from day one.

She took the box back to the love seat, sitting on his lap and crunching into a couple of crackers. "So, all this talk about me. What about you? What have I missed in the last thousand days?"

Eric grabbed a handful of crackers from the box. "Thousand days? I feel like that count might be off."

"*Feels* like a thousand."

He grinned. "Well, I'll have you know it's been as wild and crazy for me as it has been for you."

She arched an eyebrow in disbelief.

"I mean … if you consider online Economics 101 exams to be as stressful as open war and revolution in a realm of supernatural beings."

Kaylah laughed. "It's probably about the same."

"But, in all seriousness … mostly quiet here. Nothing big. I keep thinking about enrolling in more classes, but then I get nervous that Unitas will pick up. So…" He shrugged.

She winced. "Sorry."

"We've talked about this. This is my choice. No apologies." He cleared his throat. "And … I'm a little insulted you didn't notice while you were trying to strip me down—but I've been using my free time to work out more."

Smirking, she set the box of crackers on the floor and dusted her fingers off. "You don't say." She placed a hand on his exposed chest, and he flexed. "Oooh, nice." She threw a glance at the bed.

"What do you say we pick up with my original idea and get a little workout together?"

"I might be okay with that." His face softened with hesitance. "Sure there's nothing else you want to talk about first?"

She paused. "I'll be okay. Thank you for making me talk. I needed that." She pressed her lips together. "You know, there *is* one more thing I'd like to get off my chest."

"What's that?"

She couldn't keep a straight face. "This bra. Think you could help with that?"

Looking relieved, he slid his hands to her mostly exposed back. "I think I could manage."

***

An hour and a half later, Kaylah sat on Eric's bed in a pair of his boxers and an oversized t-shirt, drinking a tall glass of water. Eric reentered in similar attire, holding a large box of pizza.

"Oooh, I am *starving*." She got up, setting down her glass and approaching him.

Eric held the box high above his head.

Kaylah placed her hands on her hips. "Excuse me? You know I could take that from you with my vines in two seconds flat, right?"

"You wouldn't dare! I'm the one that ordered this. If you want me to share, it's going to come at a cost."

She narrowed her eyes. "Fine. How much per slice?"

"Two kisses."

Her jaw dropped. "That's highway robbery. That's price gouging, and I won't stand for it. One kiss."

He stood firm, shaking his head. "You don't know what kind of pizza this is. It's worth every pucker."

She struggled once again to keep her face straight. "You drive a hard bargain. I will acquiesce this once." Standing on her tiptoes, she gave him two pecks. "We'll start with one slice." She grinned. "Now gimme!"

Eric didn't budge. "Do you want dipping sauce? That'll cost you extra."

She wrinkled her nose. "Now you're just getting greedy."

He chuckled, lowering the box.

Her eyes widened as she read the logo on the top of the box before he opened it. "Davino's?" She grabbed a slice of meat-lover's pizza and sat on the love seat, tucking her legs under her. "How the heck did you get Davino's all the way out here?!" She bit into it— the cheese pull was nothing short of a masterpiece, and the symphony of sauce and toppings was akin to poetry. She moaned, splaying a hand over her heart as she chewed. "My people don't know what they're missing."

Eric laughed, joining her with a slice of his own. "Careful now, I might get jealous of that pizza if you keep moaning that way."

She finished her bite, giving him a toothy grin. "If you had told me it was Davino's, I would have paid *three* kisses per slice. Lucky for you, the night is young and I am a *very* generous tipper."

He wiggled his eyebrows, taking another bite. "They opened a new branch nearby, and they deliver pretty late."

She peeled open a garlic butter sauce packet, dipping her crust into it. "That's it, I'm petitioning to visit *every* weekend now."

"So, you want me for my body *and* my pizza?"

Kaylah giggled, covering her crust-filled mouth. She finished her slice, grabbing a second. "Add this to my tab."

He winked.

She looked over at the flowers and then back at him. "Thanks for everything, babe. This is perfect. I really do wish it could be every weekend. Every day … really."

He gave her a half-smile.

"I haven't … found anything yet. You know…" She hadn't found a way to get a human into the Green Lands. And she didn't know that she ever would. That was the hardest part of being with him. She wanted to be a queen, to be there for her people. But she also wanted to be with Eric.

He picked up a second slice of pizza, meeting her gaze in understanding. "I'm here for the long haul—you know that."

She nodded. "And frankly, I'm too selfish to tell you how foolish it is for you to go along with all of this."

Eric pointed at her with his slice of pizza. "Say what you want. I know I'm the lucky one."

She rolled her eyes, taking another huge bite. "Did you ever suspect Rach was anything other than human?"

He looked taken aback. "What? No… I had no idea she wasn't human until you told me. But I might just be dense. Then again, I didn't know back then that green folk even existed…"

Kaylah bent forward, grabbing a napkin from a little side table. "Yeah, I guess. Just thinking about work stuff, now that they're finally letting me have more say." She pondered the past, and the hopeful future. "Last time I saw her, I told her she'd see Guillen soon."

"Yeah? How's your cousin doing?"

She smiled, picking up her glass of water. "He's good." She mused on the pair. "I think they'd be good for each other."

"Really? Is she over David, er, Soren?"

Kaylah eyed Eric with adoration. "Sometimes, you just know."

He swooped in and stole a kiss.

She ran her thumb over the bumps in the water glass design. "Plus, they both like each other."

"Good for them. I hope it works out. He sounds like a great guy."

She wore a sad smile. "He really is. You'd like him. I wish you two could meet." Eric couldn't enter the Green Lands realm. Guillen couldn't leave it. "Maybe someday, if I can…"

Eric gently squeezed her knee. "I think we need to talk in terms of 'when' and not 'if.'" He searched her face. "Please."

She swallowed, nodding. "There's no 'if' in how I feel about you."

"Same."

Chapter 5

THE HOUSING WAS COMFORTABLE ENOUGH, and Rachel slept solidly after finally drifting off. A loud knock on the door woke the two of them in the morning.

Rachel stumbled out of bed and answered it with one eye open. She was practically knocked off her feet as Kaylah lunged forward and hugged her.

"Finally!" Kaylah squealed. "I am so excited for this phase! And that you both came!"

Rachel blinked a few times, still groggy, then returned to her bed and sat down.

Saff pulled herself up in bed. "Hi, Kaylah. How's it going? Why didn't we see you last night?"

"Good. Slow, but good. Last night… I brought another Seeder home this morning. I figured you guys could use a rest after traveling yesterday, so I held off until now."

Unexpected jealousy flared up in Rachel. Had Kaylah put off her departure to spend more time with Eric, back in his safe house in the human world? All of this love around her, and Rachel had no one. A tiny infatuation, perhaps, with a guy she hadn't seen in a while, who she probably meant nothing to, who she was trying to put out of her mind.

"So, what's the plan?" Saff asked.

"We can spare a few minutes to get caught up!" Kaylah insisted. "How are things back in your village?"

Rachel smirked. "Do you remember Jeff, my brother?"

Kaylah nodded.

"He's dating someone."

Kaylah busted out laughing. "Is she as awkward as he is?"

Rachel made a funny face. "Yep. That one's … unique." She felt kind of bad, but none of them had really taken to Jeff that much in the human world. He was painfully socially awkward, especially around humans. Rachel sometimes wondered if her Seeder parents had been scraping the bottom of the barrel by sending him, out of all of her brothers, to train and protect her. Seeder brothers sent to the human world were *supposed* to blend in seamlessly. But he was a nice guy, and it was wartime … so…

"How's everyone else?" Rachel asked.

"Good. Jon and Guillen are recruiting. Ginger is helping with bloomed Seeder girl runs. Nathan is helping Unitas in the human world right now."

Rachel smiled at hearing that Ginger and Nathan, Kaylah's Ivy deployment parents, were safe. And that Jon was helping. And at hearing Guillen's name at all.

"And Eric?" Rachel arched an eyebrow.

Kaylah grinned. "Safe, and handsome as ever."

Rachel tried to hide her envy. "When did you get to see him last?"

Kaylah bit her lip. "I had a few hours with him in the human world." She reached into a pack she'd carried in with her. "I haven't seen your mom since we all left together, but Eric gave me these." She handed Rachel a few folded papers.

Guilt for judging Kaylah mingled with pure gratitude for word from her mom in the human world. "Thanks!" She unfolded the pages.

"No prob. Eric helped set up a secure messaging system and wanted to make sure we could keep you two in touch when possible." She sat down next to Rachel on the bed, shoulder to shoulder with her.

~

As usual, the chitchat was mostly Rachel and Kaylah getting caught up. Saff waited for a good moment to bring them back on task.

"I was happy to start training a couple new girls your people brought back. Thank you."

Kaylah pointed at Saff. "And you doubted me."

"So, what's the plan?" Saff asked again with raised eyebrows.

"Alright," Kaylah drawled. "Getting to business, as usual. Hopefully it won't take us too long before we can move to the next steps of my strategy, but for this part in particular, I wanted *your* help, Saff."

"Okay?"

"A little bird told me you were a good student in high school. I need help with research. And with that research, we're going to change the game. No more needing an Ivy for each Seeder girl we bring home. No more pain in the process. We need to make better use of our resources."

Saff scrunched her face skeptically. "I feel like my high school report cards are *not* that significant here."

Kaylah adjusted her messy bun. "You didn't let me finish." Her tone was friendly. "They granted me access to your archives. And I was able to confirm something. Something that makes you different than other Seeders. And helpful to me."

Saff narrowed her eyes. "Okay. I'm curious."

"Everyone says you're really powerful compared to others your age." She crossed her arms. "You never told me your visit to meet me was a second visit in one year—something that shouldn't have been possible."

Saff grinned. "You'll have to forgive me for not divulging something so sensitive to the enemy princess."

Kaylah smiled in return. "I asked about your story. You didn't go through your whole bloom with the charm on, right?"

"No." Saff rolled her eyes. "I screwed that up and almost got myself and my family killed in the process."

"But … that's what makes you so powerful."

Saff furrowed her brow. "What? Our theory was that I was born immune to Ivy poison…"

Kaylah chuckled. "I've never heard that one." She extended a short vine tendril from one wrist. "Want to test out that theory?"

Saff eyed the tendril. She definitely wanted to know, but wasn't eager to be stabbed and poisoned. "I'm good. Tell me more about your theory."

Kaylah crossed her legs, sitting further back on Rachel's bed. "Your people use the jade charms to suppress the change so it's hidden and manageable. But it dulls your ultimate potential. Back in the day, before the poisoned lands forced your women into the human world, blooming happened here without them, and you were all stronger."

"Yeah. It was the first generation after the poisoning that showed diminished energy. We assumed it was a lingering effect passed on to the next generations."

Kaylah shook her head. "No. I can understand why you'd draw that conclusion. But if you look *really* hard, and find the exact right scroll, paired with some of the books from my uncle's private collection—it paints a pretty clear picture."

Saff sat speechless. No one had ever been able to explain to her why she was different. She and Devin had just guessed at the poison immunity theory. But this made sense. "But … Devin told me if we don't wear the charm, the change can be so bad we slip into a coma.

What I went through was a nightmare—I wouldn't wish it on anyone."

Kaylah held up a pointer finger with knowing emphasis. "That's because it was done in the *human* world. Once we can heal the land and figure out how to get the unbloomed back, they can change *here,* and it's not like that at all. The saturation of energy here makes it practically seamless, from what the books imply."

"Really?" Saff was still confused. "I can't be the only one that slipped long enough without their charm."

Kaylah shrugged. "I'm sure you're not. Your change must have happened over there at just the right time. They said you were about three-fourths of the way through your change?"

Saff nodded.

"I don't know. Maybe that's far enough along to not fall into the coma that usually lasts until you root, but not so far along that this benefit is lost. There must be a narrow sweet spot. I doubt you're the only one like this, but we don't exactly have social media, and your people kinda keep to themselves."

Saff blinked a few times. 'Sweet spot' didn't feel like an accurate description; nothing about her botched bloom had been sweet. It had been over four years ago, and she could still vividly remember the agony of that day. This, however, was a refreshing discovery. "That's awesome. But … that's also a ways away, right? Blooming here so they have their full powers? Have you been able to heal the land? Find a way to bring an unbloomed girl through a rift?"

Kaylah frowned. "No, not yet. One thing at a time. Speaking of … Rachel."

~

Rachel gave Kaylah her full attention, setting down the letters from her mom that she'd been scanning while listening. She was glad to finally be acknowledged in the plan.

"You researched your village's name and history?"

"Yes! Those symbols you drew back at Eric's, like the ones in the cave near your palace—they were in a book about our history."

She pulled out a piece of paper from her pack sitting against the bed. "Here."

"This is brilliant." Kaylah beamed. "We've got homework to do."

~

The Seeder girls dressed and followed Kaylah out the door. She was still accompanied at all times by at least two Seeder guards. Kaylah led them to the nearest temple and into the old library.

Saff sat down to a pile of books. "I still don't understand why this is a priority when the fighting is picking up, and we still have girls being tortured in your palace, every single day."

"I think about them too," Kaylah said, her voice soft and regretful. "And we'll get them out as soon as we can. But we really need to crack this. We're wasting too much time, with the limited people I have, to keep going back and forth to bring your girls home. Once we can solve this, we can bring back girls faster, easier. *Your* travel time will be significantly faster, too, between realms. And my people can focus on other things—learning to heal the land, protection, finding more to join our cause. Your dads and brothers can help here, too."

"Alright. Then explain what it is we're looking for."

Kaylah rubbed her forehead. "How do you know where to fly, back in your village, to go through a rift? Is it always in the same place?"

Saff searched her memories. "I don't really have to think about it. I mean, I was directed to the general area the first couple times, but I just know when it's time to open it."

"And when you're leaving the human world, is it the same?"

"Yeah…"

"It's intuitive. You feel the pull; there are set locations there for you Seeders, up there, in the sky. I think my people hone in on how it works more naturally, and that's why we can travel so quickly, through a wider variety of rifts."

Rachel looked as lost as Saff was.

Kaylah sighed. "I don't know what to call it. I hesitate to call it magic, or a spell, or anything like that. But the names of your villages—their names match these old symbols, and by knowing the words, you know where the rift is. It's like coordinates. When you know the coordinates and how it works, then you can create more possibilities."

Saff opened one of the books they'd pulled to study. "So, you mean to say, that if I knew a word that connects with my GPS location, I could step outside of this building and form a rift in the sky above, coming out wherever I wanted to on the other side?"

Kaylah rocked her head side to side. "Not that simple … but along those lines. Your temples and border walls make it so you can't just rift right here, and *we've* never been able to rift into your lands. But further out, we've scouted locations." A giant smile spread across her face. "We're going to open a cave."

"A cave?" Saff and Rachel asked in unison.

"Yeah." Kaylah shifted some papers, revealing a map. She pointed to a location near the mountains in the far north, technically in neutral territory. "It'll be a permanent location. It can be guarded, and a way for Ivy and Seeder alike to travel to that area of the Green Lands. If they know the word, if they know how to do it right."

Rachel cocked her head. "It's been done before. Like the cave by the palace?"

"Yeah," Kaylah said. "I hadn't been able to sort that out. But I'm sure that's what it used to be used for."

The girls pored over old books for hours, jotting down helpful tidbits. The guards had changed shifts once, and a home-cooked meal of lettuce wraps and coconut-carrot juice had been brought to the girls in the temple.

"Alright, I think we have what we need." Kaylah rolled up one last scroll, replacing it on a shelf. "But we can only do so much here. Once we find the right cave, I hope I'll be able to pinpoint the location. And we can make history." She smiled triumphantly. "I know you girls could fly so much faster, but since I'm not able to do that … let's get on the road and start making our way to our next destination."

"What do you mean, next destination?" Saff asked hesitantly. Her excitement over the research had caused her to gloss over the mention of moving their operation to the far north.

"Like I said, we need to be away from the border walls to open a rift like this. We're going to Arcadia, the village where your people without powers live. We've found a prime area over there."

~

Rachel perked up. She'd been waiting for this. This was where her interests really lay.

"But I…" Saff tucked her hands into her pockets. "I thought we'd be inside the borders. That's what I told Devin."

"Why don't you go check in?" Rachel suggested. "You can take a day to head back, then rest up for a day or two, turn around and join us? By the time you do the back-and-forth, we'll have been able to walk there."

Saff gnawed on her lip. "How many girls have you brought back so far, with Ivy assistance?"

Kaylah shouldered her pack. "A drop in the bucket considering the entire Seeder nation, but I figure forty-seven isn't horrible."

Saff's eyes grew large. "That's a lot of extra womanpower!"

"It's just the beginning." Kaylah's calm and confident voice matched her expression.

"Alright. I'll meet you both there."

Chapter 6

WALKING THROUGH THE VAST STRETCH of Seeder lands was as much a tour for Rachel as it was for Kaylah. Seeders had only one steam engine that crossed their territory, for the purposes of carrying heavier materials and goods across the nation. Its path was less direct than just walking the route to where Rachel and Kaylah were heading, and the train stopped so often for loading and unloading that catching a ride would have been a waste of time.

Instead, they enjoyed rekindling their friendship and discussing the differences between Ivy and Seeder lands. Seeder territory was much greener; homes and property were shared in the communities, usually built out of wood, whereas the Ivy Kingdom mostly built with stone.

Their conversations were perhaps a little surface level, but Rachel wasn't ready to talk about how much she hated it back in South Fortinda, how much she still struggled with her mental health. She was just happy to see her friend and explore along the way.

Each of the girls carried their personal necessities in a pack, weighed down more now with an extra book or two. Rachel glanced at the soldiers walking with them. Each of them had huge backpacks, carrying even more books and scrolls.

"Why aren't there horses in the Green Lands?" Rachel asked. "That would certainly be helpful."

Kaylah picked up a fresh green pine cone in her path. "Wish I had all the answers. Why don't we have electricity the same way humans do?"

As Rachel pondered that, an echo of pain surged in her body. "When I was held captive at your palace, the nurses ... they would..." Her breathing intensified as she remembered their heartless actions.

Kaylah frowned. "Olivia told me about having to tase you, to keep her cover."

Rachel's eyes moistened as she nodded.

"That's not really electricity, at least not in the way you grew up with. Deep in the mountains by the palace, there are some plants, kinda like cacti. We call them static nettles. Their needles have a bit of a staticky spark, when you get enough of them together. Our scientists have been working with them for decades to see how to propagate them better, how to maybe harness their charge. But the plants are tricky to deal with, and we've never made much progress." She hurled the pine cone into the trunk of a nearby banana tree. "I was *so proud* that they'd decided to put them to use *that* way, out of anything." Kaylah frowned again. "I'm sorry they did that to you."

"You don't have to keep apologizing. I forgave you."

Kaylah linked arms with her. "Doesn't mean I'm not still sorry."

***

With their soldier escort and no significant hang-ups, Rachel and Kaylah reached the far end of the map. Rachel was apprehensive about stepping outside of the safety of their borders.

Kaylah gave her a reassuring pep talk. "The people who live in the village we're going to are the most vulnerable, but they're safe in there, and we will be too."

After leaving behind the border wall thickets, and making their way through a short stretch of the Neutral Woods, Rachel soon realized why this area was better protected.

"A cliff!" Rachel stared at the rocky landscape before her. It was a *massive* drop from where they stood at the top.

"A canyon, actually. A good natural border, hiding an area that wasn't poisoned."

Swallowing hard, Rachel thought of the Grand Canyon. She'd never been there, but she wondered if this was comparable. This probably wasn't quite as 'grand,' but it was still plenty deep. Stubborn bushes clung to the occasional crack in the almost-sheer grey rock, the canyon snaking its way toward the nearby goliath Outer Rim mountains, taking a sharp turn to the right a few miles from Rachel's current position. "How are we supposed to get there?"

Kaylah chuckled. "Well, you can fly, right? At least you're not the one who has to use hands and vines to make your way down the walls."

Rachel laughed. Catching a breeze was still a novelty for her, not a default she considered naturally. All of her takeoffs thus far had been into the sky, not plunging from a great height. She side-eyed one of the guards. "Do either of you want to go first?"

One smirked. "Sure." He tugged his backpack straps, securing his cargo, and without a speck of hesitation, he jumped into the canyon.

Letting out a little gasp, Rachel watched closely. Other than the eyes on a mated male, nothing on Seeder men glowed, so for the unknowing bystander, he would have looked like he was plummeting to his death with his arms and legs outstretched, his arm blades extended, his hair tips purple. She was actually a bit concerned with how quickly he descended, but after a little while he slowed, and then did a smooth, wide loop in the air. Rachel smiled. "Show-off."

"I expect you to do one of those things on the way down, too," Kaylah kidded.

"Right…" Rachel was pulled back to reality. It was her turn now.

"Wait," Kaylah said. "Um … have you flown carrying this much weight before?"

Suddenly, Rachel was acutely aware of the straps digging into her shoulders. "You have a point…"

"I can take your extra books," the other guard offered.

She didn't need to be talked into it. Taking off her pack, she opened it and handed her extras to the guard. "You're just worried about the precious books, Kaylah. You've seen how well-trained I am at catching a breeze now, and you want to make sure I don't dirty them if I splat."

Grinning, Kaylah cleared her throat. "I don't know what you're talking about. Smoothest flier I've ever seen."

Rachel matched her grin; they both knew that was a bald-faced lie. Securing her pack again, she prepared for her own leap. Taking a few paces back to ensure she'd safely clear the wall she'd be jumping from, Rachel drew a deep breath, then sprinted and jumped off. At first, it was terrifying. A small scream escaped her mouth before she calmed and almost even enjoyed the fall. Not wanting to build up too much speed, and not being a show-off, she stretched her energy throughout her body, balancing in the wind and coasting.

Approaching the base of the canyon, Rachel now had a clear view of the small river cutting through a millennium of stubborn stone. There was plenty of bank on either side to land on. Squinting to find the first guard, she was thrown off by a bug flying *right* up her nose. Distracted and freaking out, she tried to dislodge it with short forceful bursts of air out of both nostrils. Already struggling to focus as needed on balancing her energy, she quickly moved a finger to her itching nose. And then she plummeted. Screaming again, she straightened her posture, but it was too late—she smacked into the river in a far-less-than-graceful belly flop.

Startled by how cold the water was, Rachel swiftly found her way to the surface, gasping. Every inch of her exposed skin stung from the impact.

"Are you okay?" The guard on her level came running to her aid.

Moving energy to her arm muscles, Rachel fought the lazy current and swam to the bank, dripping like a drowned rat as she crawled out. "I'm good." She let out one last solid burst of air from her nose, making sure the offending creature had been expelled.

"But the books…" The guard looked at her pack with concern.

Rachel instantly burst into hysterical laughter, still on all fours. Kaylah would love the irony. The guard, however, didn't see the humor in Rachel's casual treatment of precious ancient research literature. She waved a hand dismissively, forcing herself to stop laughing. "They're fine. Totally fine. Your partner has them up there."

He relaxed. "Okay. Well, now we wait."

Rachel picked herself up, still dripping. It would take quite some time for Kaylah to make her way down, so Rachel slung off her bag and found a sunny spot to unpack her belongings for them to air-dry. She also needed a good rest from all the travel, and she certainly wanted to dry off herself, so she lay down with her hands under her head, watching clouds roll by and keeping an eye on where Kaylah would be descending.

Kaylah was astonishingly quick. Then again, she had vines to not only help her securely descend the wall, but also multitask. Two feet, two hands, two vines. At times, as she was nearing the floor of the canyon, she almost even reminded Rachel of a monkey, swinging with an acrobatic flair. Once she was almost to the bottom, probably a couple of hours later, the second guard finally flew down and met her.

Rachel started to repack her things, as Kaylah and the guard had a few dozen yards to walk to meet her. Most of her things had dried, though she was personally still rather soggy.

"Are you okay?" Kaylah's voice came between panting breaths as she ran to Rachel.

"I'm great. Just thought I'd do some laundry," Rachel said, standing up and closing the latch on her pack.

Kaylah dropped her own pack, which was heavy with her books. She opened her arms and hugged Rachel. "Gosh, you had me worried! Samwise here refused to leave my side to go check on you."

Rachel pulled back from the hug, confused. "Samwise?"

Still breathing hard, Kaylah raised a hand. "Never mind."

"She's fine," the guard drawled. "And you know the escort requirements of your agreement with our council."

Rachel realized Kaylah had meant the guard was 'Samwise.' Scrunching her eyebrows, she pointed to the guard. "His name is Cecil, Kaylah."

Kaylah chuckled, wiping sweat from her brow. She was absolutely drenched from descending the wall. Her face was red. Hair wisps were plastered to the back and sides of her neck. "It's from a super long movie Eric made me watch with him once. He thought green folk sounded like flipping hobbits."

Rachel still didn't get the reference. She shrugged. "Either way, now I feel like I should have joined you. Looks like a good workout." She winked. "And here I was napping the day away."

"Sure. Feel free next time. I'm sure it's even more fun on the way up!" Kaylah stuck out her tongue. "But seriously, what happened? I'm glad we didn't send the books with you."

Rachel whistled. "Bug flew up my nose."

Kaylah grinned. "Yeah, I'd say that too, if I'd biffed it."

"It's the truth!"

Kaylah continued grinning. "If you say so."

"Lovely reunion. Shall we continue?" Cecil asked.

Kaylah glanced at him with subtle annoyance. She had often referred to him as 'the buzzkill' when it was just her and Rachel talking. "Being the one who just exerted the most effort, how about we give me half a second to catch my breath and cool down?" She approached the river, bending down and splashing her face with water.

"You're pretty sweaty. Maybe you should just take a quick swim. Rather refreshing," Rachel kidded.

Kaylah hummed. "Maybe I will." She slipped off her shoes. "Or at least I'll soak my feet for a minute." She waded up to her calves, just below her long shorts.

"I don't think that's going to cut it," Rachel said. "Did you smell yourself? I just hugged you. You do *not* smell like a princess right now."

Kaylah glared playfully. "And for that, you're joining me."

Before Rachel could react, she had vines around her wrists, yanking her back into the river. Emerging from the water, she cleared her nose again. "You are so dead." She grabbed Kaylah's legs, pulling her in the rest of the way.

They screamed and giggled and splashed for a couple of minutes, then pulled themselves back onto dry land. They wrung out their hair as the guards approached where the girls had gotten out after drifting down the river, also carrying the girls' packs. "Just the dignity one would expect from the would-be queen of the Ivy Kingdom," Cecil chastised. "Can we go now?"

Kaylah's smile dropped at his censure. "Yes, we can go."

Rachel glared, snatching her pack from him. "That's uncalled for. Maybe we *should* call you Samwise."

Kaylah did a poor job of stifling a laugh. "Rach, don't use insults you don't understand. You kind of just complimented him." She accepted her own pack from the other guard, slinging it over her shoulder. "Lead the way."

The guards both turned and started walking.

Rachel linked arms with Kaylah, following after them. "But you said it like it was a bad thing," she whispered.

"I'll explain it later."

***

The guards led the way to a cave—a tunnel—where they were greeted by more Seeders. This was the entrance to Arcadia, the village that gave Seeder boys born without powers a chance at life. Against impassable mountains, tucked away on the floor of a canyon that separated them from the Neutral Woods, the village barely even had any security measures set up.

Once they passed through the tunnel, lit with lightkeepers, they entered a wide clearing. Rachel was in awe at the lush surroundings. Drawing her attention in particular were some beautiful orange flowers she'd spotted before in the Neutral Woods and Ivy Kingdom.

"It's always nice to have guests," an elderly woman greeted them, shaking hands. "I'll show you to your accommodations."

Making Rachel feel a bit like an exhibit in a zoo, eyes of the locals followed them along the way until Kaylah and Rachel were shown to the building with their beds.

The old woman scanned them with a smile. "Would you young ladies like to change before getting a tour?"

"Yes, thank you," Rachel said.

"Alright. I'll be waiting out here."

Kaylah and Rachel went inside the stone building, quickly tossing their packs on a set of beds and stripping out of soggy clothes. Rachel rummaged through her pack to find the driest of her clothes while Kaylah explained the Samwise thing. Apparently, it was from '*Lord of the Rings.*' Kaylah also had to clarify that it had nothing to do with a shell and little boys murdering each other. That had been '*Lord of the Flies.*'

Rachel sighed, brushing out her wet hair. "Too many lords to keep track of, if you ask me." She'd hated half of the books they deemed mandatory reading in English classes back home... Back in the human world.

Kaylah started braiding her own hair. "By the way, Guillen's on his way here. Not sure how long it will take him to make the trek, but I figured it might give you something to look forward to."

Rachel hid a smile at his name; she didn't want to get her hopes up. And luckily, this time Kaylah wasn't hassling her about him too much. "Good to know."

Kaylah nudged Rachel's arm. "So, be honest, was it really a bug up your nose?"

"Yes!"

"Hmm. Was it a … glow-butt bug?" She smirked.

Rachel set her jaw, recalling the joke Kaylah had made weeks ago at their parting, comparing Seeders to lightning bugs. She grabbed the damp towel off of her bed, twisting it. "I spent two years on the high school volleyball team. I know how to wield one of these from my time in the locker room."

Matching her game face, Kaylah held out her wrists, inching out vines. "You think you could snap me with that before I could rip it from your hands?"

Changing her strategy, Rachel instead chucked it at Kaylah's face. Kaylah erupted into laughter.

Rachel shrugged. "Strategy, not strength. Come on, let's not keep our tour guide waiting."

They quickly tidied up the room and left the wet clothes draped over drying racks. Rachel loved taking in the sights and interviewing residents. From Kaylah's knowledge of the Ivy population born without powers, the Seeder nation could theoretically hold upwards of one to two thousand male Seeders born without powers, assuming the frequency of the birth defect was equal amongst both races. Just as many female Seeders without powers would likely be in existence, trapped over in the human world.

There were less than three hundred Seeders without powers who resided in this village. Saff's words from their time back in the human-world safe house haunted Rachel. The 'helpless babies' born without powers were susceptible to the poison in their lands, and only stood a chance if their mothers caught it soon enough, and if they were strong enough for a journey across their lands, and through a small stretch of Neutral Woods to get to the canyon.

Rachel's heart ached for these boys and men, and their families. Essentially human, they'd always be susceptible to this poison.

At least half of the people that lived in the village had powers, family members of those born with the rare disability. They considered the sacrifice worth it, to be removed from their kind, to be able to live together. Rachel asked why they couldn't just have girls come to live there, instead of needing to be raised in the human world, but she was reminded that the area was too small, and unable to be expanded, tucked away in stone. Other attempts made by Seeder families to escape their borders and raise their families together in the Neutral Woods had always been met with deadly opposition by Ivy troops occupying what had been penned into the treaty as 'neutral.'

Few children lived in Arcadia. Sometimes only the affected boy and an aunt or uncle lived there, or his mother, with other family raising his brothers in regular Seeder lands. Once the boy's sisters and father returned from the human world, the mother would often leave, since the young boy was a man by that point. They'd visit him often, but he was stuck in a limbo, not able to leave, unless he wanted to find a way to scale the canyon and brave the dangerous Neutral Woods for some reason.

The gender ratio was definitely off as well. Finding a Seeder woman to settle down with wasn't easy for these guys. They had no powers. Unique Seeder physiology meant they could have no kids. And it was out of the way for any woman to come out there. But they weren't completely hopeless; there were always some women sentimental about the simpler 'human' ways of life there.

For Rachel's part, she'd known she would be sad to see the way they had to live as a result of the war, but she was happy to observe the contrast of her people's treatment versus that of the Ivies. Seeders didn't brand them as stunted. They didn't look down on them, or *force* them to live separately. And they didn't require them to do menial work, having little say in their own jobs and industries.

The community was its own little capsule oasis, functioning fairly independently, apart from regular society.

After a few hours of talking to some attractive and particularly attentive young men, the women were happy to have Saff finally join them.

~

"My goodness, this place really is tucked away, isn't it!"

Rachel gave her a hug. "Glad you made it."

"Thanks." Saff scrunched her eyebrows, glancing at a flower garden past Rachel. "Is that Guenjalis over there? Like … everywhere?"

Rachel looked around. "Um…"

Saff clarified. "Those gorgeous fire-orange flowers? I've only ever seen paintings of them back home. They're kind of like a myth."

"Those?" Rachel asked, doing a double take. "I've seen them past our borders, on my return from the palace."

Kaylah clicked her tongue. "I'd hoped we'd find a few things here. And I think those pretty flowers might be just what we need for one of my theories." She spelled out her meaning. "To heal the land of the poison, we really have to understand better what we're working with. Like you've said before—you can't see the poison. And you guys still have plenty of plant growth in your lands.

"So, I could try to heal the land, but we'd have no way of testing it without putting one of your vulnerable people there and just seeing … if they got sick." She cringed. "But I'm pretty sure these flowers grow everywhere in the Green Lands, *except* for Seeder territory. Transplanting these, with trial and error—this could save your people." She raised her eyebrows. "You're a floral race, you must share something … biologically."

Saff and Rachel looked at each other, hope smiling in their eyes. It might take a while before they could figure out the right treatment. And it would take a *ton* of female Ivy power, but in over a hundred years, this was the first time there was a light at the end of the tunnel.

Saff thought of Devin, and how they'd talked about having kids, though it was still years away. But the possibility of raising kids together in the same realm was feasible.

***

That evening, they ate out over a campfire in the center of the village, sharing time and food with the hospitable residents. Rachel explained to those around her how the Ivy Kingdom treated their citizens without powers. She'd expected more of a reaction, but they weren't as invested as she was. Most Seeders still didn't feel a need to sympathize with Ivies, though they did casually comment on how it sounded like the short end of the stick, having the lack of powers in common.

And none of the men there understood her World War II references, when she compared the Ivy Kingdom to Nazis, requiring those without powers to live in separate communities, not allowed to have kids, and forced to be tattooed with numbers. Whereas Ivies without abilities were *prevented* from taking classes about the human world, the Seeders in this community just didn't feel as much need for that curriculum. Their families generally focused as much education as possible on Seeder-focused history and culture, to help the boys stay connected to their people living in proper Seeder territory.

After a particularly attractive male Seeder asked Rachel if she'd like a refill of her pineapple juice, Saff leaned over and whispered, "A lot of eyes on you."

Rachel's cheeks warmed. "Yeah, on Kaylah, too."

"Yeah, but that's because they don't know what she is."

That rubbed Rachel the wrong way. She and Saff had come a long way, but she still had her annoying moments. "*What* she is, or *who* she is?"

~

"I'm just saying … if you don't fancy anyone back home, maybe you should give one of these guys a chance." Saff had to admit to herself that Kaylah could be trusted. Even the council thought so. But it was hard to not still worry sometimes, just the smallest amount, that there was deception lurking behind a helpful hand and smiling face. And Rachel was still… Saff had promised herself she wouldn't use the word 'naïve' in regards to Rachel again. But the truth was, dating an Ivy couldn't possibly be good for her. That would dredge up all sorts of pain from her past, even if Rachel didn't realize it. And unless it was for the purpose of kidnap or assassination, there hadn't been a Seeder-Ivy couple in centuries. She admired Rachel's desire for change, but Rachel didn't understand how complicated things were.

~

Rachel rolled her eyes. Saff was obviously bringing up her dislike of Guillen again. "Are you saying that because you think I have a fetish for human men? Or because you'd rather I be with a Seeder without powers, than an Ivy without them?"

Saff stared into the crackling fire. "I'm just saying … any relationship with a Seeder is less complicated than trying to work it out with an Ivy. Even if he *is* as good as you think he is."

"Again. Guillen and I are not dating. And I appreciate…" Rachel gripped her hands a little more tightly around her empty cup. "No. I don't think I *do* appreciate the advice. I don't consider who I date based on convenience. I don't need you to be a matchmaker." She huffed and stood up, marching over to refill her cup with water.

Leaning against a fence, Rachel surveyed this group of people, this village. It was like a little hideaway—safe, not as much constant talk about the war. It was idyllic in some ways. There wasn't a single overcrowded lane or temple or soldier in sight.

"How does it feel to be the center of attention?" The deep voice startled her.

She snapped her head to the right, taking in a tall muscular figure next to her. "To be honest, it feels like a meat market."

He looked confused.

"Right, sorry. It's … interesting." The phrase 'meat market' didn't mean much to a Seeder who hadn't had any dealings with the human world—they were all vegetarians here.

He wore a charming smile. "Well, hopefully we don't scare you off too quickly." He stretched out his hand. "I'm Zeus."

Rachel bit her lip, meeting his brown eyes. "Zeus?"

He flashed a look of embarrassment mingled with frustration. "I know. My mom thought it was a great idea; she told me about the human mythology behind it, some super powerful god?"

Rachel shook his hand. She could understand a mother wanting to boost her son's morale, with him being different, having no powers, but it honestly just came off as compensation, and his reaction made it apparent they were on the same page about that. "It's cute. I'm Rachel."

He cleared his throat, running a hand through his light brown hair. "I don't know about that. Most guys aren't hoping for 'cute' names. But I can pretend you meant that about me, and not my name."

She successfully suppressed a laugh; not as successfully, a grin.

"So … I just wanted to come say hi. I didn't want to seem like a desperate creeper or anything like that. I'm told we'll be working together."

Rachel took a sip of her water. "Well, I didn't think you seemed desperate, or that you were a creeper… We'll be working together?"

"Yeah, I'm one of the master gardeners here." He moved closer, whispering, "They told me about your mission, who that girl is over there." He pointed to Kaylah with a pinky. "And that you're going to do research with some of the flowers?"

He was close enough for the warmth of his skin to radiate onto Rachel's. And it was nice to be able to chat with someone in the know. Most of the time thus far, they'd pretended Kaylah was just another Seeder, for her protection, and plausible deniability.

"Yeah. It's pretty awesome, isn't it?"

"Yeah." He smiled. "Well, it was nice to meet you. I look forward to getting to know more about the girl hand-picked by our leaders for this special project. Do you know how long you'll be here?"

Rachel shook her head. "I'm not too sure."

He looked away, focusing on the dying campfire. "Hopefully long enough that we can get a real breakthrough. But not so long that you miss your boyfriend."

She pursed her lips at his fishing for information. "There's not one to miss."

He flashed flirtatious eyes. "I'll see you in the morning?"

"Sounds like a plan."

After he left her side, Rachel mused on poor Zeus and his name. Yes, that voice and body were certainly heavenly, but his mother hadn't known he'd grow into that when she'd named him. Eventually, Rachel's eyes landed on Saff, who was looking over at her, grinning. Rachel rolled her eyes again. She wasn't there to date or fall in love. She was there to work. And she *especially* didn't want to prove Saff right by falling for one of these men.

***

A cot was added to their shared room by the end of the day; Kaylah offered to take it so the Seeders could have the beds.

Saff and Kaylah took off together at first light the next morning to scout out a good cave rift location, while Rachel sat outside on a log at the extinguished campfire, drinking a cup of coffee as the sun rose. Zeus gave her a warm smile when he found her, sitting down next to her.

"It's peaceful here," she said wistfully. Compared to the constant noise of her war-torn village of South Fortinda, the silence and wonder of this hideaway made it so serene, like a balm to her soul. Well, it was mostly silent. The blue-breasted, yellow-winged chatterbirds were chirping away rather noisily in a nearby tree.

"It has some redeeming qualities, that's for sure," Zeus said. "Some think it's a nice place to settle down, away from the chaos." He took a sip from his own cup. "How do you like it back in the main villages?"

"I, uh… I don't know." She pictured her mom back in the human world, all alone, moving between safe houses. And her own serious lack of bonding with people back in her home village. "Sometimes I wish I could have just stayed back in the human world, stayed human."

"Why did you decide to come back?" He frowned. "Did you feel pressured into it?"

She grinned and shook her head. "I forget most people don't know much about me. Pressured into it… You could say that."

"Did you leave someone important behind?"

"You mean other than my mom?" She made sure she had eye contact. "Or like a boyfriend?"

He blushed and looked down. "It's not my place to ask. I didn't mean anything by it."

"It's okay." She chuckled. "Zeus, you have no idea. My last boyfriend is the reason I came here."

He pursed his lips.

"It's not like that, trust me. I'm here because he kidnapped me." His eyes shot back up to meet hers.

"I dated the Ivy prince for almost three years. And he brought me here to use my powers against our people."

Zeus's mouth was agape for a moment as he took in the revelation. "Oh… Uh…"

She set down her coffee cup. "It's okay. You don't have to say anything." She gave a half-hearted smile. "Ready to get to work?"

Chapter 7

ZEUS AND RACHEL LEFT THE campfire area to start their research. Seeders rarely wore long sleeves, owing to the impracticality of them when needing their arm blades for fighting or catching a breeze, and the climate was almost always pleasant enough not to need bulky layers. As Zeus strolled alongside Rachel toward his garden, she couldn't help but notice his sleeveless shirt, which put his biceps on full display. Where he lacked Seeder energy to make him strong, it looked as though he compensated with plenty of exercise.

"I just wanted to say, I wasn't judging you back there. I just wasn't quite sure what to say."

She tucked her hands into her pockets. "It's really okay. I don't know what I would expect you to say, to be honest. It's not really something I tell everyone."

He gave her a warm smile. "Then I'm glad you felt you could confide in me."

She returned his smile, but she really wasn't sure *why* she had blurted out her kidnapping and dating history to him. She barely knew the guy. Was it because she felt comfortable with him, like he assumed? Or was it because she was trying to put up an emotional barrier? She reminded herself it mattered little; she wasn't there to date. It was just kind of nice to have someone new to talk to.

They turned a corner, arriving at a community garden bursting at the seams with every possible flower, in every color of the rainbow.

"That's gorgeous!" She stood in awe with her mouth open. She caught his gaze from the corner of her eye; he was beaming with pride.

"Thanks. I'd like to think I have an eye for beautiful things."

She looked back at the flowers, assuming that was just another flirtatious remark. "Honestly, I'm not any better of a gardener than any other Seeder. I feel kind of useless here, being assigned to this project." She didn't want to say as much, but she felt like this was a 'filler' project, just something she could do until Guillen arrived. Kaylah still wouldn't explain what her plans for Rachel and Guillen were, nor did she have a better estimate on his arrival time. It could be days or weeks. Ultimately, working on the poison problem was something Rachel could do to contribute while Kaylah and Saff worked on the trickier, smarter job of locating a rifting cave.

Zeus gave Rachel a gentle nudge. "I'm sure you're better than you're letting on, otherwise they wouldn't have picked you, out of everyone."

Guilt stabbed at her as she suppressed the truth. She'd been picked to go there so she could learn about his way of life, the Seeder equivalent of Guillen. She was trying not to count the days, knowing Guillen was making his way across dangerous territory at that very moment, to meet up with her. And frankly, the only reason she'd been invited on this mission was because she was the princess's best friend.

She tried to change the topic, rubbing the petal of a Guenjalis flower. "So, what's so special about these? Why can't we just have the Ivies try to heal some soil, pluck a few of these up, and transplant them to see if they'll live?"

He shook his head. "They're really delicate, they wouldn't do well being transplanted."

"I guess that makes sense, that they're frail, if they don't survive in our regular villages." She instantly regretted the way she'd phrased that, as if she'd called *him* frail for his human nature, unable to withstand the poison. Luckily, he didn't appear to take offense.

She quickly moved on. "If we can't transplant them, how do we do this? Planting from seed has got to take forever."

"Not if you know what you're doing. You have it in you to accelerate plant growth."

She cocked her head to the side. "Really? No one's told me about that."

"Yeah, it's not something most people train for. The energy of the Green Lands already makes this place, well, green. But it's something you're capable of. It's kind of a hobby, in a way, for some of the women here. It's not like they have a temple well they deposit their energy at on a regular basis."

Her interest was piqued. But why wasn't she working with another Seeder woman who could train her, hands-on? She didn't ask, not wanting to insult him again.

"Alright, what do we do?"

"Let me show you."

They strolled down a dirt path until they reached an area thick with the special flower.

"The seeds are actually best when planted fresh, for what we're doing," he explained. He showed her how to pluck them from the center of the flower. The pollen stained their hands, but he assured her it would easily wash off. The flowers exuded a strong honey and lemon aroma. Once they had gathered a few seeds, he led Rachel to a clearing. "Ironically, these are the easiest for Seeder women to grow with their energy, but the hardest to keep alive. That's kind of where I come in as a master gardener."

They sat down in the clearing.

"We bury them about this deep." He dug up a little soil with a small spade, then replaced it after dropping a seed in. "Add some water." He poured from a watering can. "And this is where you come in." He held his hands up, pointer fingers touching and thumbs meeting, leaving a triangle empty in the middle. "Like this."

She followed along.

"Not too tricky thus far, right?" He moved his hands to demonstrate where hers should go, hovering the triangular opening over where the seed had been planted.

He removed his hands, and she scooched closer, placing hers on the wet soil. She figured it was pretty intuitive, like most Seeder abilities. Imagining energy stretching from her heart down to her hands, Rachel closed her eyes and took a deep breath. Once confident she'd done enough, she opened her eyes and saw … nothing. She frowned.

"It's okay. It doesn't come naturally to everyone," he coached. "Maybe you just need to focus harder."

She nodded and closed her eyes, taking a moment to clear her mind. She tried again, without success. "Yeah, like I said … maybe not the best pick for this."

"Give it another try."

She tried a third time, focusing all she could on that little triangle, trying to coax life into the seed. Large warm hands glided onto hers, weighing them down. She took a sharp breath and opened her eyes. He'd moved closer, looking at her with deep brown eyes.

"I think part of the problem is that you need more pressure on the soil."

"Yeah, okay." She swallowed, her breath irregular. He could have just told her that. He didn't need to get handsy, but he was obviously trying to start something. She allowed his hands to linger while she closed her eyes again, trying not to get distracted. It didn't feel horrible, though, to have someone holding her hands, touching her. She missed that.

"Open your eyes," he prompted moments later.

She did as instructed, and happily admired a sprout popping out of the dirt. Not a fully formed flower by any means, but she had done it—she'd grown something with her energy. Pulling her hands back, Rachel smiled. "Thanks." She scratched an itch on her cheek.

A grin spread across Zeus's face. He reached over and wiped at the spot she'd itched. A quick glance at her hands explained why; they were muddy.

"I don't mean to be forward, Rachel, but I'd like to get to know you better. Do you think you'll have any free time tonight?"

Her cheeks warmed. "I … don't know. We have a lot going on."

He did a poor job of hiding his disappointment. "Okay."

She tilted her head. "I'll let you know?"

His smile came back. "I'd like that."

They went back to her growing attempts until they were interrupted by a familiar voice, that of a redhead Rachel hadn't seen in weeks.

"Rachel!"

She opened her eyes and hopped up from the ground, running over to Ginger to give her a hug, being careful to not smear her with mud. "I'm so glad to see you! I hear you've been crazy busy!"

"Wouldn't have it any other way," Ginger said. Like Kaylah, she was escorted by a pair of Seeder guards. Ginger rubbed her hands together. "They tell me I'm here to practice killing a sad little flower until I can figure out how to fix it."

Rachel chuckled. "That's a horrible job description. And I'd recommend not letting anyone else hear you say that."

Zeus seemed a little bothered by their new companion, perhaps because she was Ivy, or because she'd intruded on his attempts at flirting. Either way, he formally greeted Ginger and led them to the far edge of the village, where they'd dedicated some space for their experiments.

Ginger knelt and practiced poisoning the ground, trying to only kill off the little flowers, not everything else in the area. Just like when Kaylah had first demonstrated this skill, greenery browned and went limp with Ginger's poison, then recovered with the chemical compound she followed it up with. It was tricky trying to narrow the toxins. She tired quickly, killing off and healing several times. After a few breaks, they decided to call it a night.

***

Rachel was conflicted when she agreed to spend the rest of the evening with Zeus. He was sweet, giving her options for what she wanted to see and eat. Conversation flowed fairly easily between them. Though, she couldn't help but wonder if she was holding back because of Guillen, or the prince. Or if she was just overthinking it all.

"So, you're keeping your human name?" Zeus asked. They stopped and sat on a wooden bench overlooking a small pond where minnows danced around.

She polished off the last of the pimple berries she'd pulled from a bush while on their stroll. "Yeah. Not all girls make the change." She'd mulled it over a lot since her return. Changing her name, despite it being a common Seeder tradition, felt like it would be severing another tie to her mom back home. Saff—short for Saffrona—was one of those girls who had embraced her new life wholeheartedly. But that wasn't Rachel. That wasn't her story. She hadn't genuinely chosen any of this. "Guess I'm just not really a fan."

"I understand different villages have different traditions about the names. What does your village favor?"

Rachel grinned, fingering a blade of tall ornamental grass swaying next to her in the evening breeze. "The most original— flowers." She looked Zeus dead in the eyes. "But can you believe my dad didn't give it a second thought before he named me *Pansy*? Out of all the flowers available…"

Zeus's eyes grew large as he bit his lip. "I thought my mom had bad taste. But…"

She busted out laughing, putting a hand on his arm. "I am *so* kidding. It's not that bad. It's Mari, for Marigold. Just not my thing."

He relaxed, nodding with a hint of a smile. "That's not so bad. Much better than Pansy."

***

At the end of the night, Zeus stopped short of returning Rachel to her door, where guards were positioned outside. He asked for a hug goodnight, and she obliged. It was nice to be in warm arms, just standing there, not letting go.

She'd forgotten how much she truly missed romantic companionship. How lonely she felt at times, even when surrounded by family and friends.

She wanted to blot out memories of Prince Soren, the last man she'd kissed. She wanted to blot out a lot of things. Stress. Anxiety. Frustration. Guilt.

Releasing Zeus from their hug, she gazed into his eyes. There may not have been instant chemistry, but there could be something there, if she allowed it to grow, if she would stop getting in her own way. Or perhaps a onetime thing with no strings attached could be enough.

She wrapped her hands behind his neck. "You're a nice guy, Zeus." She stood tall, caressing his lips with her own. Her stomach did a somersault. She leaned back to get his reaction.

He looked surprised, but was smiling. "Thanks."

One kiss wasn't enough. She needed more. Rachel leaned closer again, and he took the hint. She kissed him several times, more firmly, more involved with each pass. She wanted to feel something—something new, simple, uncomplicated. She pressed herself against him, and he pulled her in tight. Her heart and lungs kept pace with her lips, but fell short of giving her the spark she was looking for.

She pulled away. There was no warmth in her eyes—they hadn't even changed color.

"I should go to bed," she whispered, studying his face.

He continued to smile. "Yeah, me too." He tucked a strand of hair behind her ear. "I'll see you in the morning." He gave her one more peck and left her to return to her room.

When she entered, Ginger was snoring on a cot, and Kaylah and Saff were sitting in their pajamas, talking about their day.

Saff smirked. "You were out late."

Kaylah dodged eye contact. She had to be making the same assumptions, and disapproving, thinking of Guillen. But Rachel and Guillen were far from being an item. They hadn't made any sort of agreement. She didn't owe him anything.

"I just want to go to bed," Rachel said, heading to the bathroom to get ready for the night. Minutes later, she lay in bed, unable to sleep, beating herself up. *Why didn't that kiss feel better? He didn't seem very experienced.* Then it dawned on her that he may have never had a chance to kiss a girl before. And she'd used him.

She tried to lie to herself, saying it was just a mental block. But the fact was: she didn't feel the same way about him, as he apparently did about her. She stewed in self-hatred. She'd kissed him as a way to forget her previous mistakes, and all she'd done was dig deeper.

***

Zeus greeted Rachel at her door with a large smile and a coffee in the morning, once her party left the room. She sipped in silence as he sat next to her back at the fire pit. He rested a hand on her back, rubbing as she sat slumped over.

She sat straight up. "Zeus, I'm sorry. I shouldn't have kissed you last night." She stared at the cold black coals.

"It's okay. You took me by surprise." His voice carried a vulnerability that only made her feel worse. "But … I liked it…"

Knives twisting in her gut, she remained unsure of what else to say. "I just … don't know if I'm ready for that."

He rubbed her back again. "That's fine, really. I'm still open to spending some time together after work, if you're interested. But no pressure. I just want to get to know you."

She gave him a weak smile. She could do friendship, even if she knew that particular f-word was one no one wanted to hear right after they'd been kissed. "Yeah. If I'm not too busy, I'd like that."

Chapter 8

THE NEXT EVENING, RACHEL TOLD ZEUS she could only go on a short stroll after dinner. She ended up leaving him with an awkward hug, and going back to her room after their time together. She said she needed more time to coordinate with the others in her party, and then felt guilty, finding she was actually back quite a while before they were.

Saff and Kaylah returned late, clearly exhausted and frustrated.

"Going that well, eh?" Rachel asked, already tucked in for the night.

Saff tossed her pack on her bed. "It feels like we're wasting our time."

"I never said it would be easy," Kaylah snapped back.

Saff rolled her eyes and went to the bathroom.

Rachel lay in uncomfortable silence. *Would it really be Saff and Kaylah in the same room if they weren't bickering about how to get things done?* At least they'd moved past death threats—that had been a real treat in the safe house when they'd first met.

Kaylah explained their predicament to Rachel. "We go out there to find a place with good cover, nicely defensible, but there are a ton of variables. I can sense the location's name, but I'm not sure how close I am. Like, we could be twenty yards to the right, and we don't know it. Or we're not powerful enough between the two of us. I don't know. It could be a million things."

A knock on the door claimed their attention; Kaylah got up to open it.

"Hi, um … is Saff here?" a male voice asked from the door.

Saff came out of the bathroom. "Devin! What are you doing here?" She ran up and squeezed him tight, planting a kiss on him.

"I figured it was worth carving out some time to come all the way out here and see you." He rested his forehead against hers. "I missed you."

She stole another kiss, then looked back at the room of women. "Well…"

"Oh, for the love," Kaylah drawled. "Go ask someone about getting your own room."

Saff blushed. "I'll be ready first thing in the morning." She snatched up her pack.

Kaylah launched herself onto Saff's bed. "Yeah, yeah, yeah. Whatever. I could stand sleeping in."

As soon as Saff and Devin left, Kaylah turned to Rachel. "She had the more comfortable bed, anyway. It's a win-win. Now I get this one."

Rachel let out a half-hearted chuckle. "Then everyone wins." She pulled up her covers. "Almost everyone."

Kaylah gave her no pity. "What's with you and that tall thing? Are you rebounding with him?"

"I feel like such a jerk." Rachel frowned.

"Then don't do it!"

Rachel scowled. "I'm not going to, Mom." She huffed. "I just… I don't know."

"Were you rebounding with Guillen?"

"No! We never even kissed."

Kaylah lifted her eyebrows. "Why was he any different?"

Rachel looked away, aching, longing to see him again. "He just was. I don't want to talk about it." She turned off her lightkeeper. They were both nice guys. But she'd shared an instant chemistry with Guillen. And he was sweet and vulnerable in a different way. But she worried—that she had put him on a pedestal after all this time, that it wasn't the way she remembered. That he could have found some other girl who made him happy. That he wouldn't want a girl like her now, one who took advantage of sweet, innocent men like Zeus.

***

For the next few days, Rachel occupied herself, avoiding any actions with Zeus that might be misinterpreted. Ginger made progress in her attempts to poison and heal Guenjalis. Saff and Kaylah grew confident they were narrowing in on the right cave location.

Devin returned home to South Fortinda, and with Saff's recommendation and Kaylah's permission, he was going to ask Heather if she would want to join them.

***

Saff was ecstatic to see her sister-in-law at her arrival. "Thanks so much for coming!"

Heather seemed to be doing somewhat better. She still wasn't her bubbly old self, but she carried herself well. And Saff figured a change of scenery, working far away from where her fiancé had been slain, could only do her good.

"Thanks for inviting me." Heather tucked her hands into her pockets.

The group of Unitas women suspected they needed more energy to create the kind of cave rift they wanted, and while they had plenty of Seeder matriarchs available nearby, Heather had mentioned wanting to help. Heather possessed the average energy-wielding abilities of her peers, but her dedication and focus on learning the ins and outs of healing boosted her knowledge of how to harness it with more finesse.

Ginger and Rachel took a day to join Kaylah, Saff, and Heather—the day they announced they might finally have it. It required three hours of hiking to get to the new location from this village. They'd had to cross the river to find the cave, with a decent path to the top of the canyon. The Seeders easily caught a breeze to avoid getting wet, but Kaylah and Ginger had no choice other than to wade through it.

"I know it, it's got to be right here," Kaylah said. "The location, I can feel it. This is Tonoru. Run that through your minds as we try this."

Kaylah pulled a big book from Saff's pack; the front of it bore the Unitas symbol, a blossom in front of an ivy leaf. "One of my books I smuggled here." She turned a few pages. "This is one of the books where most of the research came from that helped us realize how we could access your powers." She dodged eye contact with Rachel.

"By accessing our blood?" Saff asked.

Kaylah nodded. "Yeah, umm … that. Anyway…" She found what she'd been searching for and showed everyone the pages pertaining to cave rifts. The instructions were written in the old language Kaylah had educated Rachel and Saff on, but they were hardly fluent. She pointed to a diagram and translated, explaining the gist of what needed to be done.

"But how does this work?" Saff asked. "You guys pull the energy from a tree to do your rifts. We always have to do it in the air. This doesn't make sense."

Kaylah looked exasperated. "Why does everyone expect me to have *all* the answers? I don't know. But this book hasn't been wrong, yet." She set it down on the ground.

"Then I guess we'll find out," Saff said, stretching her arms.

They stood near the opening, afraid of a potential cave-in, not certain how it all worked. Saff and Heather touched hands in the air, sweeping them apart, tracing the outline of the cave opening.

Simultaneously, Kaylah and Ginger extended vines, running them on the stone floor, climbing to meet the Seeders' hands.

A ripple formed, a surge of energy. They shared congratulatory smiles. It had *actually* worked. And the realm hadn't come crashing down on them…

"Should we go through?" Rachel asked. "Will it always take this much effort?"

"I really don't know," Kaylah confessed as the shining ripple dimmed. "Maybe we just needed to prime it… Let's step back and see. We need to focus on a specific destination to make this work. I'm going to think of Domiten. That's the closest forest rift I can sense to Eric's safe house."

One of the guards cleared their throat.

Kaylah's face showed frustration—she'd gotten ahead of herself. "Right, sorry. No leaving alone." She added with some sarcasm, "I might up and betray your people after *everything* I've done."

"It's okay, I'll try," Saff said, stepping up to the cave entrance. She ran her hand through the air, opening up a new rift like she had a few times in the past, though this was her first time doing it from the ground. Right before entering, she jerked back, her expression dropping in horror. "Wait! This goes to a forest? Is there someone there to get me back?" She kicked herself for being so reckless. *How could I already forget?* She couldn't catch another breeze back home from the human world this year, and she'd already risked her life once experimenting with their powers.

Kaylah recoiled. "Crap! Wait. You're right, I'm sorry. Got too excited. We need to find a cave or rock formation of some sort on that side to match it, for back-and-forth travel."

Saff took an uneasy breath. They were doing a lot of speculation on brand-new theories, and needed to proceed with more caution. "I, uh… I'm not going to be the guinea pig on this one. I couldn't do that to Devin again."

"I could go with whoever wants to try it," Ginger offered. "We can come back by tree, just experimenting. Then we know we can focus on a match." She looked to the guard, who gave a hesitant nod.

~

Rachel shrugged. "I could go. I don't have anyone that loves me."

"What?" Kaylah and Saff blurted in unison, both sporting a perturbed look.

Rachel grinned, feeling all the warm fuzzies. "I meant romantically, like Devin."

Kaylah and Saff both mumbled unintelligibly. Rachel was pretty sure Kaylah said something about Guillen, while somewhere in Saff's muttering 'Zeus' could be heard.

Rachel held a hand over her heart. "Wow. So much love *and* annoyance for you both right now."

Heather quietly chuckled. "I should go. I haven't taken a trip yet this year. And Rachel's been a few times. It's probably safest for me."

"Not a bad idea," Kaylah said. "Although, my impression is that it should be safe for *any* of us here to use it. And on a regular basis."

~

Saff loved the idea of it. All of them did. Regular visits to the human world? Not just once a year? Kaylah had already made it clear in negotiations that this permanent rift still wouldn't support Seeder matriarch travel. And while Saff's powers were near-matriarchal, though technically not fully-rooted, she still couldn't imagine taking the risk.

Saff's rift had timed out. Heather stepped forward, creating one of her own, and with minimal hesitation, walked through it. It closed, then Ginger ran a vine along the floor of the cave, opening her own rift, and stepped through. The others watched on in awe. This was the first time in modern history that a Seeder had created a rift from the ground, and an Ivy through something other than a tree.

Not two minutes later, Heather and Ginger reappeared, a vine around Heather's arm with a minor injury to get her back. They were both beaming.

"Mark this one off the checklist," Heather remarked in a cheery nasal voice Saff recognized. "What's next?"

They took some time to congratulate themselves. With permission and a warning from the guard, Kaylah and Rachel took a trip through the cave; knots in Saff's stomach kept her from even considering it.

They experimented with Ginger and Heather going through again, but the constraint seemed to remain that both races still didn't have enough energy to do more than one roundtrip rift in a day. If an Ivy tried more than once, a rift just wouldn't form. If a Seeder tried more than once, they could form a rift, but not travel through it—they would just continue walking deeper into the cave. Saff rubbed her chest, recalling the price she'd paid to get to the human world just weeks ago. She again declined a trip of her own, even after Kaylah and Ginger offered to have the guards fetch another Unitas Ivy to escort her.

Kaylah then went over the next phase of her plans. "Rachel, I'm going to pull you from flower duty to work on extra training. Saff and Heather, if you two can manage to stay, we could really use your help. Training new girls here, defending the rifting location, and helping me find the cave on the other side.

"Ginger, I'm going to want to get you set up to train here. Bringing some of our women, you can teach them how to better dose, as well as heal the land." She looked at the Seeders. "I've got to talk to your council, though, but everything is looking great!"

Everyone was on a high after their success; they took the rest of the day off after securing the cave with several guards, just in case. After they returned to the village for dinner, they chatted excitedly with the residents about their accomplishment. The Seeders without powers likely still couldn't use it, unable to enter a rift without Green

Lands powers, but Kaylah hinted she hoped for something like that down the road.

~

Knowing her time was short in the village, and with Zeus throwing Rachel sad puppy-dog eyes, she excused herself to go on a walk with him after dinner. They likely wouldn't visit Arcadia often after Kaylah established a training camp on the other side of the canyon.

"It sounds like a big win for you and your posse," he complimented, holding his hands behind his back.

"I was just there for the show, to be honest. But it's pretty cool."

They continued in awkward silence; he slipped his hand into hers. She gave his hand a squeeze and then released, shoving her hands into her pockets. He was definitely more clingy than she'd anticipated, which made it that much worse.

"It really wasn't fair of me to kiss you, Zeus. You're a really nice guy. But I'm confused about a lot of things, and I won't be here for much longer. I'm sorry."

He frowned. "Just do me a favor. Don't completely write me off? I know you're going to go out there, on all these adventures, and I'm … stuck here…"

She didn't respond right away. Part of her wanted to urge him to learn to fight, to tell him he could be like Guillen and leave the confines designed for his disability. But that wasn't fair. Guillen could freely walk around all of his own kingdom without harm. Zeus was *literally* stuck in his village, with the only alternative being dangerous territory. And he and Guillen were very different people. Guillen was a self-starting fighter. Zeus was comfortable as a gardener.

"I won't forget you, Zeus. And who knows, once we get this healing-the-land-thing done, I'd love to see you make the long trek all the way to my village." She smiled.

"Deal." He smiled back, holding out his arms for a hug. She obliged. She still felt crummy about the way she'd treated him, but she was grateful she might leave with a friend.

Upon her return to their room at night, Rachel was happily able to report to Kaylah. "All taken care of."

"Good. You both deserve better."

Rachel threw a pillow at her.

Kaylah caught it, giving her a playful we-both-know-I'm-right look. "Fancy going into the neighboring village with me tomorrow? I need to talk to the local council about approving the training camp and getting support. You and Ginger could do a test on the soil in an originally tainted area."

"Yeah, sure thing."

***

In the morning, all five women decided to make the trek to regular Seeder territory. Ginger tried healing the soil while Rachel showed Saff and Heather what she'd learned about sprouting the delicate flower using energy. It came with mixed results. She expended a lot of energy trying to sprout the seeds she'd brought, but when they would start to grow, most died quickly in the tainted soil. Ginger kept attempting to fine-tune the chemical composition she would inject into the ground. Worn out, she tried one last time before taking a break. They all watched as the flower bloomed. They stared at it, waiting for it to wilt any second.

Their anticipation rose with each moment that passed, signifying Ginger had properly healed the soil, giving hope for something on a much grander scale.

"Kaylah! Look!" Rachel yelled as Kaylah approached with her guards.

Kaylah rubbed her arm anxiously. "That's brilliant! I'm really proud of you guys." The flower stood tall, but Kaylah's smile didn't.

"What's wrong?" Rachel asked. "Did the council reject your plans?"

"No. That's all great. They're rushing to put it into action. There was just some other news."

Rachel's muscles tensed, and the others also looked at Kaylah with fear in their eyes—they all had someone to lose.

"Saff, you told me once that you could provide Unitas with names to help the network on the other side. I need those."

~

Saff had been so focused on their work in the Green Lands that she'd hardly given any thought to the humans working hard on their behalf. "Yeah, you've earned it. What happened?"

Kaylah frowned. "There's been an attack. I don't want to freak anyone out. Everyone's fine. It's just the first time they've turned on a human host family."

The Seeder girls stood with mouths wide open.

"Really? They've always left them alone before. It's just..." Heather said.

"Yeah, well, I think Soren's getting impatient. The fact that he hasn't found any new girls to kidnap proves my intel was helpful. But they might have noticed some movement. And opening that cave, there's going to be a lot more movement, and soon. And we need to be prepared to keep our people safe."

"Sure thing, right away," Saff said. "I can give you my mom's number. She was going to look up everyone and see who lived where by now. And I can give you the code word I gave her." Saff grinned. "I told her not to trust anyone without it..."

"That was smart," Kaylah said. "But how about calling her yourself?"

Saff wrung her hands, suddenly feeling warm. Of course she wanted to talk to her human mom again. More than anything. But just thinking about going back to the human world again this year made her anxiety peak. "Maybe Heather should go. I'll give you the password. My parents would love to hear your voice. And I'm sure yours would, too."

Heather gave her a grateful smile. Her parents still didn't know the wedding was off, that her fiancé was dead. "I'd love to."

"Sounds good." Kaylah added with a smile aimed directly at Saff, "And I'll have you know that Unitas has started to pay, to one of those tree-hugger foundations, for each tree we have to sacrifice for our rifts in the human world."

Saff laughed and grabbed Kaylah, pulling her into a hug. She'd always hated the destruction left in the wake of Ivies rifting.

Likely startled, Kaylah awkwardly patted Saff on the back during their first hug.

Chapter 9

THE NEXT FEW DAYS WERE a whirlwind of action in their tiny corner of neutral territory. Heather and Kaylah briefly popped over to the human world through a cave rift. Saff's human mom gave them their family contacts to grow the safety net for Unitas, and they took a quick look at a cave near Eric's safe house.

Not feeling confident enough to attempt an opening right away, they decided to return for it another day. They still weren't sure how it would affect the Seeder physiology, specifically, making multiple trips in a year like this, so they were going to be cautious.

A decently functioning training camp grew, practically overnight, near the new cave. Trees were cleared to build a defensible barricade, only leaving a few in camp for the purpose of emergency exit rifts for Ivies in the cause.

Rope ladders and a rope bridge were constructed to allow quicker travel across the canyon for Ivies, and Seeders without powers. With dozens of volunteers from Arcadia, and extras assigned by the local Seeder council, they gathered supplies and assembled tents.

Carefully, friendly Ivies made their way to the location—some through the cave, others arriving from the Neutral Woods on foot. With strict screening procedures, one by one, old enemies gathered as allies.

Like Rachel had learned to expand her skill set with growing, the Ivy women also experimented with using their abilities to fertilize. In war, troops needed to be fed. Together, Seeders and Ivies were able to start a garden in camp and make it flourish beautifully. Last, but not least, brave female Seeder teens kept a steady pace in their returns. Saff and others were busier than ever, training at the point of their arrival.

***

As the commotion of establishing the Unitas camp settled down, Rachel and the others were assigned tents. For now, Saff and Heather shared a tent. Rachel was assigned one all to herself, per her request. She hadn't woken from a screaming nightmare since leaving South Fortinda, likely thanks to less anxiety brought on by so many eyes on her, but she still had nightmares and would sometimes wake up sweating. She didn't want to disturb anyone.

Entering her tent for the first time, she placed her pack in a wooden chest that had been made for her, then sat down on the cot. She ran her hand over the thin blanket that had been donated by their previous hosts in Arcadia. The dirt floor was reddish, speckled with a few pebbles.

She enjoyed being here with Kaylah and Saff, Ginger and Heather, away from the chaotic, noisy border villages. But she also felt useless. She'd handed off her work with the Guenjalis flower to others, so what was she supposed to do now?

Before she had much time to dwell on the question, footsteps thumped outside her tent.

"Rachel?" a woman asked.

"Yes?" Rachel stood, sticking her head out of the tent.

"Please follow me."

The woman turned, and Rachel did as ordered. Just yards away, the woman led her to Kaylah's larger tent, gesturing for Rachel to go inside. Two guards watched on as she entered.

Expecting to just see Kaylah, Rachel was surprised to be met by an additional leader. Sitting in a chair next to Kaylah was Lionel, a grey-haired Seeder councilman who'd been permanently assigned to the Unitas camp to co-lead with Kaylah.

"Hi…" Rachel said nervously.

He smiled. She barely knew the man, so she wasn't sure how genuine the smile was. "Thank you for meeting with us, Rachel. Please take a seat." He gestured to a third chair in the tent.

She sat down.

"You don't need to look so worried, Rach," Kaylah said. "This isn't the principal's office." She winked.

Rachel settled in with more ease.

"But what we're about to discuss should not be taken lightly," Lionel added.

Kaylah sat up straighter in her chair. "Also true."

Lionel scrutinized Rachel. "Her Highness assures me you know how to be discreet? How to keep a secret?"

Rachel looked between them and nodded.

"Good," he said. "Even if you choose not to participate, you will not be allowed to discuss what's shared in this meeting with anyone."

"Okay…" She threw a questioning glance at Kaylah. "Even Saff?"

"No one," Lionel said.

That didn't sit quite right with Rachel, given how much Saff had struggled to trust her and Unitas. But Kaylah nodded.

"Okay. I won't say a word."

Kaylah crossed her legs. "Great. We're here to discuss a mission. It's … not a small favor." She scanned Rachel's face. "I—I mean *we*—need a, uh, spy." She glanced at Lionel. "Ambassador?"

He nodded. "Ambassador."

Spy? Ambassador? Rachel hadn't exactly been trained as either. "To do what?"

"You don't have to say yes, but I'd like you to go behind enemy lines, helping in my kingdom," Kaylah said.

Rachel blinked in shock.

Kaylah's lips twisted into a smirk. "With Guillen."

Rachel's stomach knotted as she looked between the two leaders. She wanted to see Guillen, but this wasn't exactly the way she'd imagined it. "Come again? I thought he was coming *here*, to help with research or something…"

Kaylah rested her hands on her knees. "That was the plan before Soren took over. I need your help in a different capacity right now."

"This Guillen, a quote, unquote, Ivy stunt—you've worked with him before?" Lionel asked. "Her Highness seemed to think you would feel comfortable working with him?"

A hint of annoyance flashed across Kaylah's face. "Please stop calling me that. Just call me Kaylah."

"Right, sorry."

Both leaders focused back on Rachel.

"Well, yeah." She wouldn't have phrased it that way. She hadn't so much 'worked' with him, as she'd been *saved* by him, and had developed a tiny, miniscule, kinda huge crush on him. "I trust him. I wouldn't have problems working with him. I just didn't envision myself going behind enemy lines…"

Surely Kaylah wouldn't be so frivolous as to assign a dangerous mission to Rachel just to be a matchmaker, right? "Could I speak to Kaylah alone for a minute?"

Lionel wrinkled his nose. "I think it would be prudent to keep this discussion open between the three of us. If you have any concerns, it's important that I know."

What was Rachel going to say? No? Her best friend—the leader of Unitas, the future queen of the Ivy Kingdom—was asking this of her. And this time, she had the support of the Seeder council. "What do you need me to do?"

"Historically, the disadvantaged population of Ivies without powers has been met with severe punishment for uprisings," Lionel said. "You'll be touring their communities, posing as one of them, to provide a little encouragement."

Kaylah held up her hands. "Nowhere near the palace, I promise. And if Guillen can sneak you out of my kingdom, he can sneak you there and back. Just an ambassador."

"We need more influence from within to weaken Soren's hold," Lionel said. "And to pave the way for Her High— For Kaylah, when we're able to take back the palace to right things."

Rachel didn't immediately respond, pondering the task being asked of her. Part of her yearned to go there—to see what it was like in the Ivy Kingdom, to be there for and with Guillen. But who was she, really? She still wasn't a spy or ambassador.

Kaylah must have read the doubt on her face. "You know, Rach, in the human world, you never once slipped to your best friend that you were a Seeder. And if I hadn't already known your identity, I wouldn't have guessed that you were one—I never spotted any hints of Seeder transformation. No green eyes, yellow hair, any of it. Even when… Well, never."

Rachel picked at her fingernails. That was all true. She'd been so paranoid about discovery that she'd done everything she could to suppress that part of herself. But had that last part Kaylah hinted at really been true? Even when she'd walked in on Rachel hurting herself, not even her eyes had turned green? Seeders often specialized in different powers based on natural skill, or sometimes based on their desire and dedication, like Heather with healing. Perhaps that was one of Rachel's unique gifts, that she was better at concealing Seeder transformations during emotional times.

"And you've been trained to fight and heal, not that we're obviously hoping for any of that," Kaylah added.

That was also true, though so much focus had been placed on healing with Saff at the clinic, Rachel wasn't exactly battle-ready, should she and Guillen meet opposition. "You're sure I'm the best person for this? There's not a soldier or someone else better qualified?"

Lionel didn't have to speak for Rachel to understand his feelings on that topic. He pursed his lips, looking as if he agreed with her. "There *are* definitely other candidates with more impressive résumés."

"We'll train you as much as we can before he gets to camp," Kaylah said. She locked eyes with Rachel. While there was a steady composure to her voice, her eyes reached out in pleading. "We could send someone else, but I want someone I know I can *trust*. With my kingdom. And with Guillen's life."

Rachel read the message loud and clear. Guillen and Kaylah were unfailingly loyal to each other. He was her favorite cousin, one of her best spies. And it made sense that she wanted Rachel with him, out of anyone. The council's cooperation with Kaylah had become increasingly encouraging, but she still wanted to make sure he'd be safe. Some random Seeder going undercover with Guillen wouldn't do. Guillen had once told Rachel that Kaylah herself didn't know who to trust half the time.

"I'll do it."

Relief washed over Kaylah's face. "Thank you," she mouthed.

Lionel drew a deep breath. "Then it's settled. Extra training. We'll brief you more later. And not a word of this to anyone."

"Okay."

After a few more words on the topic, they dismissed Rachel, and she departed Kaylah's tent. Half-dazed, she returned to her own tent and lay down, trying to grasp the reality of what she'd just signed up for. Her heart warmed at the idea of spending time with Guillen, but her stomach knotted at the same time. What if she'd gotten it all wrong when they'd first met? Her brain and nerves protested the mission altogether.

Needing to walk off her jumble of emotions, Rachel got up and strode through camp.

***

Early afternoon, Saff helped in the camp garden, harvesting moon melons. She'd just sent off her latest pupil to return to her family in proper Seeder lands, and was waiting for a new one to arrive.

Lionel, the camp's councilman, approached her. It was a little surprising to have him single her out to chat, but she'd been friendly with plenty of village elders and council leaders back in South Fortinda.

Her suspicion grew when the topic changed to Rachel.

A request to train a Seeder teenager wasn't new to Saff. However, a request to train *Rachel*, focusing primarily on more advanced fighting techniques, was definitely out of the ordinary.

"Can I ask why fighting?" she asked warily.

"You two come from a border village, right? She may return home soon, and we know she's missed valuable training, so we just want to ensure she's prepared for any eventuality." He wore a politician's smile.

"She's going home? Is this Kaylah's doing?"

He tilted his head to the side. "No. You can ask the girl yourself."

"Yes, of course. I'd be happy to train her."

"Thank you for your services." He gave her a nod.

Saff eyed him with suspicion as he walked away. She asked another Seeder she'd been working with to take care of the melons, and set out to do just that—ask Rachel.

Once she found Rachel, their conversation went nowhere. Rachel shrugged a lot, claiming she was homesick. That couldn't have been further from the truth; she'd seemed so relieved to leave South Fortinda behind. Her anxiety had even seemed to calm a bit with the slower pace of the remote village.

Saff abandoned her line of questioning. She knew who she needed to talk to. This whole thing reeked of Kaylah.

After Saff marched to Kaylah's tent, the guards announced her, and Kaylah let her in. Kaylah sat behind a table covered in research books and scrolls. "Nice of you to visit. How can I help you?" She didn't look up from the table.

"Why am I training Rachel on fighting techniques?"

"Is that what the councilman ordered?" Kaylah drew a line across a page with her finger, still not meeting eyes with Saff. "He said he talked to her and wanted to change her assignment."

"Really?" Saff tucked her hands into her pockets. "And she's going to need those fighting skills back in South Fortinda?"

Kaylah frowned, grasping a pen and jotting something down in a notebook. "It's a pity, really. But she *has* been homesick. I'll miss her."

"*Bull.*" Saff crossed her arms. "What's *really* going on?"

Kaylah finally looked up, leaning back in her chair. She splayed a hand across her chest and opened her mouth as if shocked or offended. "What's this? Are we back to not trusting me again?"

Saff glared.

Kaylah smiled triumphantly. "Funny, because your council finally does. But you know everything, right?"

"No. But I deserve to know what's going on with Rachel."

Kaylah pointed at Saff. "Ya got me. I convinced your council to ship her off to the front lines. We're going to pop some popcorn and see how long she lasts. So you better train her well."

"You're not funny. You know that, right?"

Kaylah shrugged. "I don't know. It seems to me like *you're* the one who can't take a joke."

Saff shook her head, examining Kaylah. She'd spent enough time with her now to recognize when she was deflecting, when she was putting on a facade. "You know, you once told me that I had the talent of being a pain in the ass."

Kaylah grinned.

"You know *your* talents? Being flippant and callous."

Kaylah's grin melted away. Saff had hit a nerve.

"Please, just tell me what's going on," she asked, simply and to the point.

Kaylah kept quiet, closing the book she'd been studying. "You know, Saff. You're a mentor. Not a council member. Not a soldier. Not a politician or strategist of any sort." Kaylah set the book on a large stack next to her desk. "You don't *need* to know."

"Then maybe someone else should train her."

Kaylah sat back down, a small smile crossing her face. "Fine. But *she* wanted you to be the one to train her."

"That's unfortunate. She wants me to train her. I want to know the truth. We don't always get what we want." Saff turned to exit the tent.

"Wait," Kaylah called.

Saff sighed, facing her once more. "Yes?"

Kaylah gestured to an empty seat, and Saff sat. "Do you know why you and Rachel were reassigned to work together after you brought me to your council?"

Saff had assumed it was because the council was too busy with the war, and that they'd needed Saff and Rachel working where they'd already been trained. "I guess maybe not…"

"Rachel vouched for you."

Saff swallowed, guilt washing over her.

"To me, and to your council. And I vouched for the both of you. And I worked my ass off to do my best to ensure you weren't punished to satisfy your council's pride."

"Just tell me," Saff whispered, pleading.

Kaylah buried her face in her hands, mumbling from behind them. "I know you care about her. But why was she assigned the most stubborn Seeder in existence to be her mentor?"

With a measure of satisfaction, Saff let out a breathy chuckle. "I was basically raised a shut-in, only child. Blame it on my human parents." She pictured them in the human world, hoping they were okay. "You earned the council's trust—that's great. But don't I deserve something after trusting you with the names and locations of my family and other human host families in the human world? Plus, after we brought you to our council, I vouched for you too. I may have been hesitant, but I signed up for this."

Kaylah dropped her hands, staring at Saff, seemingly worn down.

Saff pointed to the tent door flap. "No one else out there knows Rachel like I do. They'll buy this 'she was homesick' crap. I know how to keep a secret, if that's what you're all worried about."

After a calculating moment of silence, Kaylah sat up straight again. "If I tell you, you can't speak of it to anyone. I can't even have your council knowing that I told you."

"Done."

"Remember those two guards outside of the tent are not only here to babysit me, but also to protect me, okay?"

Kaylah needing to be protected after disclosing something to Saff? That wasn't at all foreboding. "That sounds like a promising start."

"She'll be working a low-profile mission on the other side of the realm."

"Other side of the realm?" Saff narrowed her eyes. "Why do I have a feeling you don't mean southern Seeder lands?"

"She'll be safe."

Saff's heart dropped. "Like hell she will! What kind of thanks is that for your friend's loyalty? You really are marching her up to death's door."

Kaylah shushed her, pointing to where the guards stood on the other side of the tent door. "She'll be fine. She won't be alone."

"Who will be with her? I can go." Saff's mind flashed to Devin, not sure why she'd volunteered.

"No. She'll be working with one of my best spies."

Saff read Kaylah's face. "Who?"

"Guillen."

"Your cousin? The one she has a thing for?"

Kaylah rolled her eyes. "Yes. Guillen is my cousin. They'll keep each other safe."

"No."

"It's not your choice."

Saff was flabbergasted, unable to believe the council had agreed to this plan. "Even *if* she comes back alive… Do you… Remember how I said you were callous? Hasn't she been through enough? She was lucky to escape your kingdom with her life last time. Don't pretend she came out the same girl you once knew."

Kaylah looked away with a pained expression. "She's doing better. And… Well… She's the best person for the job. It's not up for debate. I've known her since we were little girls. I think she can handle it."

Rachel needed community, and support from people around her, not to be isolated and marching into a den of wolves.

Saff stood, preparing to exit the tent.

"What are you going to do?"

More than she was angry, Saff was disappointed, hurting for Rachel, that she was being used for Kaylah's agenda again. "I'm going to go talk some sense into her."

***

Rachel ambled to the edge of camp, pensive. She fought her fears of the task ahead of her, choked down the dislike of lying to Saff, and battled her usual onslaught of guilt. Nodding at a couple of Ivies as she passed, she allowed herself to savor the satisfaction of having helped move Unitas forward.

Finding a soft patch of white clover, she sat down. The normal drama played through her head—the hurt her actions had caused others, her own pain from betrayal, attack, and torture. Recently, though, she'd mostly dwelt on the realization that she honestly didn't know whether she was all that likeable.

Tyler, her first kiss, had only kissed her because of spin the bottle. Jeremy, her first date, had probably only asked her out because she'd grown a bra size over the summer break between ninth and tenth grade. David—Prince Soren—had only dated her to use her. And Zeus was only interested because he had limited options, tucked away in that tiny village.

Rachel was no Kaylah. She wasn't a supermodel with full lips and jet-black hair. She wasn't even Saff, with good grades and quick thinking. Rachel was average, at best.

And why did it even matter if Rachel was likeable? Was she not capable of being alone? Of not having a relationship for two seconds? Hadn't that been the reason she didn't dump Soren after he'd attacked her the first time, in a hot tub?

She wasn't even nice. She'd judged her own brother, Jeff, for not having more trendy clothes. *Who does that?* She'd grown up with a princess for a best friend, a prince for a boyfriend, and a duke for a stepdad, all easily affording what they'd wanted thanks to the queen's coffers in the Ivy palace. The palace that still held three Seeder girls hostage, suffering a daily horror Rachel knew too well.

As she fixated on drugged, hazy memories of the palace, her breathing picked up. She couldn't let herself go down that path. She needed to focus on the good. Or better yet, the *possible* good that she could do. She would be far from the palace. She could make a difference.

Plucking one of the clover blooms, Rachel sniffed it and smiled, the vanilla scent reminding her of baking Christmas cookies with her mom, Samantha, back in the human world. Rachel calmed a bit. Her mom was safe. Rachel could help keep Guillen safe on her upcoming mission. She could make a difference.

***

Saff scoured the Unitas camp to find Rachel again. Luckily, she *wasn't* easy to find. Saff's prolonged search gave her time to calm down, to think through her approach. She wanted to point out how crazy Rachel was to accept this mission, but remembered all too well how that had worked to dissuade her from wanting to defy council orders to meet up with Kaylah in the first place.

Passing a wild red gooseberry bush, Saff finally spotted Rachel, sitting in a patch of white clover.

"Did you know those are edible?"

Rachel looked up, twirling the little blossom in her fingers. "Oh, yeah. I think one of my sisters taught me that."

"Mind if I join you?"

Gesturing to the ground next to her, Rachel popped the clover blossom in her mouth. "Are we starting training tonight?"

Saff sat cross-legged. "I wanted to talk first." She studied Rachel's face. "You're sure you want to leave camp?"

"Yeah, like I said: I want to go home."

"Hmm. You could continue your training back there. I'd love to visit my family. How about we pack up tonight, and I'll take you home?"

Rachel's mouth hung open for a moment. "I… Well, I want to go alone. After I've had more training."

Saff nodded. "Yeah? You don't want Guillen to take you there either? After your mission?"

Rachel's eyes grew wide. "How'd you find—"

"Kaylah."

"Oh…"

"I wish you'd reconsider," Saff said in a soft voice.

Picking another blossom, Rachel shook her head.

"I worry about you."

"I know what I'm doing this time, Saff." Her tone was confident, but not argumentative.

A fluffy bumblebee buzzed around and landed on a nearby blossom.

"After what you went through at the palace, you're the *last* person that should ever have to go back there."

Rachel tucked her knees up under her chin. "Which is why I'll be the last person they'll expect to be there. I don't plan on wearing a t-shirt stamped 'Prince Soren's Ex-Girlfriend.'"

Saff glanced at the garden and tents in the distance. She had about a thousand arguments she could make, but nothing she'd ever tried seemed to get through to Rachel. "Would you be doing this if it weren't with Guillen? If it were with someone else?"

Rachel's nostrils flared. "I'm going to pretend you didn't just ask that."

"It's a valid question."

"No. I don't think I would. Because I know I can trust him, and I wouldn't go over there with someone I didn't know."

Saff rubbed the back of her neck. "What's it going to take to convince you to stay?"

Leaning in, Rachel glanced around, then whispered loudly, "The war to end."

Saff sighed. "What would you do if I didn't train you?"

"I guess I'd ask Heather."

"No, you wouldn't. She's a better healer, but she's *not* a soldier."

Rachel raised her eyebrows. "Then teach me."

"I'm not a soldier, either. I've never actually taken a life." Saff ran a hand over the tops of the clover around her.

"You've taken *every* class offered in our village, and you wouldn't have the position you do if you weren't good. I have faith in you. I wish you'd have a little in me."

Saff frowned. "I believe in you."

Giving her a half-smile, Rachel stood, dusting off her shorts. "Great, then let's train."

"Well, I…" Saff certainly hadn't planned to leave it at that, to just give up so quickly.

"When we first started training, you told me I was a quick learner, didn't you?"

"Yeah, but…" It was true that she'd complimented Rachel about being talented. What with having her powers suppressed in the human world by Kaylah's poison, Rachel had been given no choice but to work twice as hard as others, so now that she was in her home realm and not poisoned, and adding the energy boost that came with rooting in the Green Lands, she wasn't half bad.

"I'm eighteen now," Rachel firmly asserted. "I'm an adult in *both* Green Lands nations, *and* the human world. The moment I next step foot outside of this camp, you'll cease to be my mentor. But I hope we can still be friends."

Hesitantly, Saff stood to join her. "You know what this feels like? Like I'm handing you a bottle of vodka as you sit in the driver's seat."

Rachel slipped her hands into her back pockets. "If you're so worried about my safety, maybe you should look at it as tossing me a life preserver when I'm in the deep end of the pool."

She was right. Saff still wanted to convince her to let someone else go, but perhaps she could do that *while* training her. "Alright, let's get started."

Chapter 10

RACHEL WOKE WELL-RESTED ONE MORNING, just over a week after starting intensive training with Saff. She sat on a boulder that gave a good vantage point, a place she'd found for a quiet break to think. Saff had used every argument in the book to dissuade her from going. None of it had made a difference in the slightest.

Surveying the area, Rachel could finally smile with real pride and genuine contentment at what they were doing. Unitas—unity between green folk. Growing gardens, eating, and training together. There wasn't a day that went by without at least one new Ivy Unitas member arriving at camp. Her old friend, Jon, had arrived a few days prior, and they'd enjoyed getting caught up.

The sun was barely rising for the day. The air was crisp and quiet. A sea of beige tents stood firm against a slight breeze.

Rachel pondered her mistakes of the past. She saw the evidence of her attempts to make amends. She found purpose. She looked into her future. What Kaylah was asking of her was terrifying in many ways, but she didn't let that feeling win. The challenge made her feel alive; thinking of the success it might bring was exhilarating.

And while she'd never admit it to anyone, she couldn't stop smiling, because it would be a mission with Guillen.

Mulling over one of her previous conversations with Kaylah about Guillen, Rachel asked herself why he was different from Zeus, other than the obvious racial difference. She worked herself into a frenzy analyzing the situation and her feelings. Had she just been hypersensitive when she'd met Guillen? Did she like him because she needed fixing, and he was kind? Or because she needed saving, and he was a project? Or was it that he had been key in literally saving her life? Was it just a friendship, and she'd been manipulated for so long in a fake relationship with Prince Soren that she'd assumed too much?

She made herself sick and gave up on it all. None of the answers could be figured out on her own right then, anyway. Guillen would arrive. They'd work together on the mission. She'd see from there if anything developed.

A scraping from her side broke Rachel's concentration. Jon was scaling the rock to join her. This time he was clean-shaven, unlike when he and Guillen had helped save her and escort her to Seeder borders. She stood and gave him a hug, ecstatic to see his familiar face. He stayed rigid, definitely still not comfortable with hugs.

"Well, look at this." He smiled once she let him go, overlooking the area with her.

"This is my special spot." She gestured at the boulder. "You'll have to keep it safe for me." Jon was one of the few people Rachel could talk about her mission with.

"You've got it. For as long as I'm here."

"I knew I could count on you." She nudged him, then they sat down together. "I'm curious—when was the last time you saw Guillen?" She'd tried to slip it in coolly, though she'd done a poor job of it.

"It's been a while. We've been on vastly different missions."

"Okay." She failed to hide the concern in her voice.

"You're worried about him?"

Rachel picked at her fingernails. "No. I'm sure he's fine. I just thought he'd be here by now. Kaylah said she sent for him a while ago."

"Last I heard, he was on the far side of things. He has a cover to worry about, and lots he can accomplish on the way. Plus, he's got to use those two legs of his. He's fine."

She nodded. "You're right." Movement in the camp caught her attention. A couple dozen occupants made their way from the tents and gardens over to a training area at the far end of camp, near the laundry station. "What's going on?"

He watched them as well. "Training exercises."

Rachel furrowed her brow, zeroing in on the movement. "Just the Ivies?"

A grin grew across Jon's face. "Well, now that I think of it, I do remember seeing Guillen more recently."

Her energy pulsated in her chest. "When?"

"Mmm." He scratched his chin. "About fifteen minutes ago at the camp security tent?"

Her eyes grew wide with excitement. Jon chuckled.

Rachel hopped up, about to jump down from the rock to go meet Guillen. Realizing she may not get to see Jon again before leaving camp, she quickly gave him another hug. "Thank you. Again. For everything you've done. Saving my life. And being here, still, for my people." She beamed. "Our people."

He shared a warm smile with her. "The more people talk like that, the better it sounds. Stay safe, kiddo."

Without further delay, she jumped off of the boulder and sprinted across the camp.

A handful of Seeder guards had been stationed at the entrance to the camp security tent, definitely more than normal. They nodded her in without a single word.

Familiar voices and laughter broke through the silence as she pulled back the tent flap. Guillen stood with his arms crossed, sharing a laugh with Olivia, the nurse who had also helped in Rachel's escape from the Ivy palace.

Kaylah entered right behind Rachel. "Look at that, some of my all-time favorite people."

Rachel gave Olivia a tight squeeze. "I never got to say thank you for how you helped me. Thank you. *So much!* I'm really happy to see you doing well." Only the two of them knew how much Olivia had really done to keep Rachel safe. Not only had Olivia helped with her escape from the palace, she'd disrupted Soren's advances, his assault on Rachel. She could never thank Olivia enough for risking her neck.

"Of course." Olivia gave her a bright smile in return.

Guillen wore a handsome smile as well. This was the moment Rachel had been waiting so many weeks for. His pale blue eyes, soft face, and the large scar on his temple were exactly how she'd remembered. His brown hair was neatly trimmed. A little more awkwardly, Rachel extended her arms, and he accepted, bringing her in for a hug. His embrace was like that of a close friend. The kind she *really* wanted to kiss… Apparently, the attraction was genuine still—she could check that fact off of her mental list.

"I…" She wanted to say 'I missed you,' but was worried it might sound too forward. "I'm glad you're safe. And thanks again, for your part in getting me home."

"Any day." He gave her another smile, before breaking eye contact.

"I'm guessing by your arrival at this hour, that you're rested?" Kaylah asked Guillen. "Or did you walk through the night?"

"I'm set to go when everyone else is." Guillen cracked his knuckles.

"Me too," Olivia said. "We had hoped to arrive last night, but we got so tired that we took a nap."

A pang of jealousy coursed through Rachel. Was Olivia coming now, too? Or … were they an item, and she'd just never known?

"Sounds great," Kaylah said. "We could always use some impromptu training for anyone who might recognize Guillen in daylight." She winked, obviously referencing the diversion Rachel had already witnessed with Jon on the boulder. Kaylah poked her head outside of the tent, speaking to one of the guards. "Please have Craig report to my tent."

"Yes, ma'am."

Kaylah looked between Rachel and the new arrivals. "I'm just going to do a debriefing with these two. Join me at my tent in a few?"

Rachel glanced down at her clothes; it was time to get changed, anyway. "Sounds like a plan."

"Fantastic. Then we can get the show on the road."

***

Rachel made her way to Kaylah's tent, and the guards allowed her entrance.

Kaylah welcomed her and introduced the newcomer, someone Rachel had seen in camp, but hadn't formally met yet. "Craig is one of the official tattoo artists—also an amazing Ivy stunt."

Rachel and Craig exchanged a handshake. Olivia was present, presumably for numbing. Guillen was also there, sitting in a chair.

Rachel eased herself down on the open chair next to Guillen.

Guillen looked at Rachel with a concerned frown. "You're sure you're up for this?"

She smiled reassuringly. "I'm ready. Plus, I hear Olivia's the best Ivy nurse when it comes to refined medicine."

"I heard that rumor too," Guillen acknowledged, nodding at Olivia. Olivia blushed.

Guillen's demeanor again showed worry. "I just remember … how much you're opposed to this."

His sweet concern warmed her heart. "Thanks. It's worth it."

Kaylah stood in the back of the group and winked at Rachel. "Plus, once the mission is done, I'm sure we can saw that chunk of flesh off and Rach can heal it, in like, two seconds flat, right?"

Rachel laughed. "It's great to hear your concern for me. I know my best friend will *always* have my back."

Kaylah chuckled. "Any last words?"

"Let's get this over with."

Olivia approached, wrapping a vine around Rachel's upper arm. "Just a tiny pinch is all."

Rachel winced more than she needed to for the tiny prick. The numbing poison was fast-acting, and, from what she understood, amazing compared to what humans used for numbing when getting tattoos.

Craig got to work, pulling out a bottle of clear liquid, a clean rag, a small vial of black ink, and a stick with a needle embedded at the end. Rachel would be the first Seeder taking this mark.

As an official Ivy Kingdom tattoo artist, Craig was familiar with the work at hand. He poured a little of the clear liquid onto the rag and wiped down Rachel's upper arm and his tools. It was alcohol, by the smell of it. "You'll need to hold still."

Sitting up straight, Rachel rested her hand on her thigh, holding it in place with her other hand. Craig dipped the needle into the ink, and traced a rough outline. Without speaking, or hesitation, Craig held Rachel's arm, dipped for more ink, and plunged the needle in. With quick and precise movements, the needle dug in. Dozens, hundreds, perhaps even thousands of times.

Rachel observed those around her in the completely silent tent. Kaylah stood still, frowning, with arms folded. Olivia stood straight, her gaze traveling between Craig's hands with a look of curiosity, and Rachel's face, checking on her patient. Guillen sat with a pensive frown, his gaze shifting to the ground anytime his eyes would meet Rachel's. She couldn't tell if it was nerves or guilt.

Craig looked to be in his forties, with shoulder-length curly hair. He was laser-focused on the work. She glanced at his arm, wondering what number hid under his sleeve. What his story was. What it felt like to have to do this to teenagers of his own kind. Ivy 'stunts' were taken from their homes at the age of fourteen to be branded and relocated to stunt communities, denied many freedoms

Ivies with powers had. This ink meant the rest of their lives would be spent in hard labor.

Just minutes in, the silence was tense; Craig's work, quick. It felt like overkill to have everyone standing around them to watch. Or at least to not talk. But Rachel didn't know what to say herself. The experience thus far hadn't gone exactly how she'd expected it to go. When she'd agreed to get a tattoo, she'd imagined the buzz of modern equipment. But that wasn't what this was.

Rachel finally dared to turn her head to watch. Craig dipped the needle and poked Rachel's arm. In and out. Over and over again.

She observed how her skin gave way. How her arm moved slightly under the pressure, with each intentional injury.

Poke. Poke. Poke.

It was steady, rhythmic, mesmerizing. The needle deposited the ink in her skin without drawing any blood. Especially odd for Rachel because she knew what it was like to shove a needle into her own skin, drawing blood. In and out. Over and over again.

"Craig, let's take a break," Kaylah said.

"Yes, Your Highness," he replied. A moment later, his voice carried concern. "Are you alright?"

Rachel continued to stare at the ink on her skin. Registering his question, she looked up. Craig shyly pursed his lips. She swallowed.

"Do you need more numbing?" Olivia asked with an equally concerned tone and expression.

There was a warmth behind Rachel's eyes; they'd changed. Then it registered that her breathing was a bit quick. Kaylah wore a deeper frown. Rachel didn't dare look at Guillen.

"Let's go get some fresh air," Kaylah said.

Rachel stared at the beige fabric of the tent, wishing she could shrink from all the eyes on her. "Yeah." She stood and exited as quickly as she could, Kaylah following after her.

They walked several paces from the tent. Kaylah faced her. "Are you okay?"

Rachel returned her energy to her core and focused on her breathing. "Of course." She'd been trying so hard, in preparation, to make sure she could control her energy. And she was normally so good at it. She couldn't slip like this.

"I'm so sorry," Kaylah whispered, taking one of Rachel's hands. "I really didn't think this part through."

Unable to make eye contact, Rachel looked down. "I'm fine. My mind just drifted."

"I never should have asked this of you."

Rachel finally met her gaze, frowning. Kaylah's eyes expressed profound guilt.

"I'm fine. It's just different than I thought it would be."

Kaylah shook her head. "No one would think less of you, if you didn't go through with it."

Rachel bit her lip. She'd been trying to be strong. She wanted to prove herself. She wanted to make a difference. "I'll be fine once it's over. I promise. I just won't look at it."

Reading Rachel's eyes, Kaylah slowly nodded. "I can have Olivia leave the tent. The numbing she gave you should be fine for the whole process. And I can dismiss Guillen, too. Would it help to have less of an audience?"

Rachel's heart raced. She fought tears, fought to keep her energy from traveling again. "No. I don't want people to look at me that way." She glanced at the tent. "None of them know, right? You haven't told anyone?" Rachel had never confided in anyone else about hurting herself. Kaylah had walked in on her doing it. And had helped her through that tough time. Kaylah had also been the *cause* of Rachel having turned down that dark path, by poisoning Rachel, causing her to spiral. Their relationship was complex.

"No!" Kaylah said. "I've never told anyone. Not even Eric, and I tell him everything."

Rachel closed her eyes. "Alright. Then let's just walk back in there and get it done. I'll be fine, I promise. This is too important." Before Kaylah could object or question anything else, Rachel took off back to the tent, putting on a smile as she entered. "Sorry, just tired and kind of out of it, I guess."

"Ready to continue?" Craig cautiously asked.

"Of course."

Kaylah reentered the tent.

Avoiding eye contact with her audience, and forcing herself not to look at the needle again, Rachel fixed her eyes on the table of books tucked in the corner of the tent.

Over an hour later, Craig had repeatedly wiped, dipped, and stabbed. He ran over the lines with a second round before packing up his equipment. Rachel's tattoo matched Guillen's, except hers had the number five in the center, where his had a crown. They'd strategized on which community she should be 'assigned' to, had created a backstory for her, forged paperwork, the whole nine yards.

Once everyone agreed that Craig's work was done, Rachel carefully healed the area, making it appear as though she'd had the tattoo for years.

"Well. That's that…" Rachel said. Beyond grateful for this live-time flashback to be over, she now found herself getting nervous about going. "I think I'm going to double-check that I've packed everything I need, and go find Saff."

"Olivia and I have work to do, so we're going to say our goodbyes right now." Kaylah gave Rachel a long, tight hug. "I'm proud of you. Stay safe. Look out for each other." Kaylah had tears in her eyes. "You're amazing, and brave, and one helluva woman." Kaylah gave her one more quick hug, whispering, "And I'm not the only one who knows that." She pulled back with a wink.

Rachel threw her a dirty look. Couldn't let their special moment go without hinting at romance. She internally mused that perhaps that was what it took to pull off this kind of crazy movement—a hopeless romantic.

"You stay safe too. Could you have imagined a year ago that we'd be where we are now?" Rachel let out a breathy chuckle. "Well,

I guess you had a better idea of where we'd be. I was thinking about college."

Kaylah laughed. "Right? Ten times better than college." She smiled softly. "I love you. Guillen knows how to send word through the network. I'll keep in touch as much as I can."

Kaylah turned to Guillen, giving him a tight squeeze. "I'm sorry we don't have more time to catch up. I love you."

"You too," he said, not shying away from the hug.

Olivia offered Rachel another hug as well, and she accepted. "So, you're not coming with Guillen and me?" Rachel asked.

Olivia looked confused. "No…"

Rachel was just as confused. She'd obviously misunderstood something earlier. "Well, I'm glad you'll be able to help your women here learn more about your powers."

"Thanks. Stay safe." Olivia and Kaylah left the tent. Craig offered a handshake and followed the others out. Guillen and Rachel were left alone.

Rachel swung her arms with nervous energy.

"I, uh, thought they'd told you it would just be the two of us."

"What? Yeah." She clasped her hands together to stop her fidgeting.

"Okay." He seemed unsure. "But you thought Olivia was coming?"

"Oh. Yeah, I just… No. I know it's just you and me."

It was silent for a moment. Painfully silent.

"You're going to be okay with it just being the two of us?"

Would she be okay with that? Was that question aimed at the butterflies in her stomach?

Or did he genuinely worry about the fact that they didn't have another companion like Jon on this journey, like they had last time? Rachel was much better trained now. Either way, her answer was the same.

"I'm fine with it being just you and me."

"Alright."

And then they just stood there again, like two people who hadn't shared hours and days of easy conversation before.

Rachel lifted a hand to her new tattoo. "I'm sorry if that was hard for you to watch. If it brought back any bad memories or anything."

He waved a dismissive hand. "No. Not at all. I'm just really impressed, is all. Can I take a closer look?"

She twisted to show her tattoo. His hand moved up to it, softly rubbing over the fresh ink. His touch took her breath away. She focused on keeping her energy in check, which was pretty silly for something so innocent. She quickly admitted to herself that she *really* hadn't just imagined her attraction to him this whole time. And it would be a long journey with him … for better or worse.

"It looks just like it should," Guillen said.

She nodded. "Good. Gotta make it look like the real deal, right?" She smiled, noting his hand still on her arm after rubbing at the ink. "Won't just wash or rub off. Like any good waterproof mascara, my mom would say."

He removed his hand, sliding it down her arm as he went. He looked down, pursing his lips.

"What's up?"

He met her gaze with narrowed eyes. "What's mascara?"

She arched an eyebrow. "Makeup? I'm assuming Ivies use it like Seeder girls do." Kaylah certainly did… "More natural stuff, definitely not as good as the commercially sold human kind, but it does the job better than nothing."

"Aha. Yeah. I know what makeup is. I think my sister uses some."

"Sister? I don't remember you talking much about your family when we met before."

Guillen shoved his hands in his pockets. "Yeah. Um … parents. I'm the oldest. Brother in the middle, then my sister."

Rachel sat back down, and Guillen followed suit. "Are you close?"

Guillen crossed his arms, leaning back. "Mmm … complicated. I'd say I'm closest to my sister and father."

"I get the good big-brother vibes."

He grinned. "What about your mother? The human one. It sounded like you were pretty close. Did you get to see her?"

Rachel's heart hurt at the mention of Samantha. This mission would take Rachel further from the cave, from the letters she would sporadically get. "I did get to see her. I think she'll be okay."

His smile widened a bit as he stood back up. "Guess I didn't just come here to get caught up. Have you had breakfast? Do you need help packing, or anything like that?"

"I ate, thanks. Did you guys?" Rachel stood to join him.

"Yeah, Olivia and I had plenty of food."

"Okay, great." She pointed to the tent door flap. "Well, if you want, you can wait here while I finish up, or you can keep me company."

"If I won't get in your way, I'd love to join you," he said shyly.

"Sounds great." She smiled. "Follow me."

It was only a few yards to Rachel's small tent. They both ducked inside.

"So, the makeup thing. What was that called again?" he asked.

She brushed her bangs to the side. "Mascara."

"And what does mascara do?"

"Longer, darker, thicker eyelashes."

He squinted, studying her face. "Are you wearing any?"

"No. No makeup since I left my village. Not really worth the hassle."

"I don't think you need any."

Her cheeks warmed as she folded up the blanket on her cot. "Thanks. Every girl could stand to hear that now and again."

"I guess you're right about Ivy girls maybe wearing that stuff, too. At first, I thought it was a human-world reference. But maybe it's just a girl thing."

Rachel chuckled, setting the blanket on the end of the cot. "Pretty sure the vast majority of guys, in either realm, are clueless about cosmetics."

Guillen pulled a folded piece of paper from his pocket. "Kaylah gave me this. A list of observations she's made from being around your people. And in the human world. We'll have time to go over it to help you blend in, so you don't accidentally say the wrong thing in public."

He handed Rachel the paper to look over. "It's not like the residents in stunt communities have never heard things about the human world, but we're just not taught as much, you know. We're more … isolated … ignorant…" He pressed his lips together.

Rachel tried to hide a frown. The way they were treated was rotten. Guillen had at least been afforded a more rounded education, having been provided tutors until he was eighteen. But that was considered an extra privilege for someone born without powers in the Ivy Kingdom, a privilege only given to him because he was so close to the Crown in the royal bloodline.

Rachel tucked the note in her pocket. "Take a load off. I shouldn't be too long." She gestured for Guillen to sit on her cot.

He lay down on it. "Nice. You're going to miss something like this as we cross the woods."

She blinked. He was casually stretched out on her bed, his biceps naturally flexed as he crossed his arms under his head for support. She swallowed and turned.

Focus on the mission.

"I'm sure I will. But I'll survive." She rummaged through her packed bag, double-checking she had the most important things with her. She glanced at the folded clothes she'd worn that morning, and then down at the ensemble she'd recently changed into. "How do I look?" She raised her hands and turned full circle.

Guillen wore a soft smile. "I think you look great."

"Good." She turned back to her bag, checking the pockets.

"Does my opinion matter that much?"

She faced him. "Of course it does. Don't get me wrong, I trust whoever smuggled these clothes over here, and Kaylah. But Kaylah's spent most of her life at the palace or in the human world, you know? You'd know better the right fashion for a girl in that region and type of community, right?"

"Right. That." He cleared his throat. "Yeah, you'll blend in great."

She nodded, that much more confident in the success of their mission.

She finished checking her bag. "Then again, I'm asking a guy for fashion advice. Makeup and fashion, all in one day."

He chuckled. "I may not know what all the things are called, but I'm not blind."

"Oh, dang it," she said, pulling her lightkeeper out of the last pocket. "This would be bad if my bag was searched by the wrong people. Definitely not something your kingdom would use."

"What is it?"

Rachel held it in her palm, kneeling next to where he lay on the cot. "Clear quartz on the top, jade stone on the bottom."

"Yeah, I saw some bigger ones out there. What's it do?"

She demonstrated with a touch of a finger at the top of the dome. It lit up, the jade releasing the energy she'd previously deposited into it. "Good as a lamp or flashlight. Would be handy at night, but I guess you guys more commonly use beeswax candles?"

"Yeah," he said, still looking at the lightkeeper. "It's amazing, what your people are capable of."

Rachel ran her hand across the jade to call the energy back. The powers were nice, though they sometimes felt more like a consolation prize since she hadn't been able to actually choose what world she'd live in. She stood, approaching the trunk in the tent. "Yeah. Our guys can turn them on and off, since they can channel energy. But we girls have to initially deposit the energy because they can't share theirs in that way."

After placing the lightkeeper in the wooden chest with the other belongings she was leaving behind, Rachel flung her bag over her shoulder. "Well, I think that's it."

"Rachel?" a deep voice called from outside her tent. She stiffened… *Oh crap.* Zeus had been making the trek to camp from his village on a regular basis. He helped in the garden and often dropped by for a visit.

"I'll be right back," she said to Guillen as she left the tent.

"Hey! They said you're actually taking off today." Zeus held a Guenjalis flower.

"Yeah, just heading out now." She was starting to sweat, wishing he'd talk quieter. "It was nice of you to drop by."

He handed her the flower. "I know it's delicate, so it won't last long like this, but I thought it was fitting."

She gave him a polite smile. "Thanks. That's sweet."

He reached for her hand and raised it, kissing it. "Don't be a stranger."

Her heart sped up as she desperately hoped Guillen wasn't seeing or hearing any of this. She gave Zeus a quick hug. "You keep up the good work. I'm excited to hear how the healing of the land goes! And thanks for everything you taught me."

"Of course. Be safe." He flashed his warm, friendly smile, giving her hand a quick squeeze before taking off.

She turned around, red-faced, nervously tugging on her ear. She then noticed she'd left a gap in the tent door that Guillen could have possibly seen out of, though she wasn't sure he had.

"Well … um … a couple more people to see on our way out," she announced after entering the tent.

Guillen hopped up. "Lead the way."

***

Saff was the goodbye Rachel definitely needed to have, but also dreaded the most. They'd argued recently. Saff had said that Rachel 'owed it to her family' to not take this kind of risk. Rachel had reminded Saff that their family dynamics weren't the same, and that she was planning on going no matter what anyone else said or thought.

But they'd forged a good friendship, and since they'd been the two to open this path, Saff deserved a proper goodbye. Saff had already been up at dawn, training new girls on energy exercises. Rachel stood nearby, hands folded in front of her, waiting for a moment where she wouldn't be interrupting too much. Guillen stood next to her.

Saff spotted her and frowned. "Alright, five minutes, everyone." She strode over to Rachel, offering her arms. "You're sure you know what you're doing?"

Rachel nodded, accepting the hug. "I've never been more sure of anything. In either world."

Saff sighed, surveying her face. "You're crazy, you know. Going back there."

"Yeah, well, I'd say the pair of us have made a lot happen by being a little crazy, haven't we?" Rachel smirked.

Saff cracked a smile. "Yeah, yeah, yeah."

"Do you want to see it?" Rachel twisted, raising her shoulder.

Saff wrinkled her nose. "I guess so…"

Rachel rolled up her sleeve to show the tattoo.

After a momentary glance at it, Saff shifted her focus to Guillen. "You're going to keep her safe?"

He gave her a single nod. "Absolutely."

Saff kept her gaze on him, straight-faced. "If not, I'll hunt you down myself."

Rachel furrowed her brow and unrolled her sleeve. "Okay, Mom."

Guillen chuckled.

"By the way, Saff—this is Guillen. Guillen—this is Saff."

They shared a handshake, and to Rachel's relief, Saff didn't say anything or give any looks that indicated they'd talked about him before.

Saff's attention flickered to the flower Rachel was holding, and she bit her lip.

Don't you dare.

"Is that from Zeus?" Saff smiled. "He's going to miss you."

Rachel's nostrils flared as she considered how to discreetly flash a look of rage, but it was hard with Guillen right there. "He's really *friendly,* isn't he?"

Looking down, Saff ground her shoe into the dirt. "Well, we'll *all* miss you, to be fair." She wrapped her arms around Rachel again, who stood stiff this time.

Saff pulled back, frowning, and added in a more apologetic and sincere tone, "Be safe. Come home soon."

Rachel sighed. "You be safe too. Remember what you promised?" They'd had a good heartfelt conversation recently, and Saff knew exactly what that meant.

Saff adopted a far-off look, rubbing her chin. "Eat my vegetables and wash behind my ears?"

"Right…"

Saff held her by the arms. "I'll do my best to play nice with the other kids."

"Good. Then I'll keep up my end of the deal and stay alive."

Rachel and Guillen headed out of camp, stopping for a hug with Heather as they went. Rachel promised Heather she'd deliver a letter to her family back in South Fortinda, which Kaylah and Lionel had already arranged for someone else to do. Guillen picked up his bag at the entrance, where he'd left it with the guards to search and watch.

As soon as they left camp, the silence was painful. It would be days until they'd reach Ivy territory. Just the two of them, and all the time in the world.

Chapter 11

NOT LONG AFTER WATCHING Rachel and Guillen leave, Saff gave her trainees a longer break. Camp would be terribly lonely without Rachel.

Saff approached Kaylah's tent. Once the guards announced her presence, she was permitted entrance. Kaylah sat at her table, next to a tall stack of books and a jumble of scrolls. She wrote on a piece of paper without looking up. "How can I help you?"

"Um…" Saff hesitated, nervous about how this conversation would go. "How's it going?"

"Everything is dandy." Kaylah set down her pen and blew on the fresh ink. "Just coming to say hi?"

"Well…" Saff shifted her weight from one foot to the other. "No. I mean, I hope things are going alright…"

Not responding, Kaylah grabbed a short candle of golden wax and a striker, lighting the wick and setting the candle upright in a holder as she folded up the paper she'd written on. She removed a ring from her finger, dripped some of the wax onto the folded paper, then pressed her ring into it.

It was cool to watch. Some things still felt foreign in the Green Lands, like the lack of technology. After spending her childhood in the human world, Saff sometimes still patted her pockets for her cell phone when she wanted to know the time.

"If you're too busy, I can come back later."

Kaylah finally looked at Saff, standing and grasping the sealed letter. "You're fine. Just a sec." She crossed the tent and leaned out of the door flap, handing the letter to one of the guards, rattling off some instructions.

"Sorry about that." She returned to her table, giving Saff her full attention.

"Who was that letter to?" Saff asked.

Kaylah studied Saff, looking as if she was deciding how to respond. This time, it wasn't sarcasm or defensiveness about how Saff ought to mind her own business. "Your council."

"Gotcha." She moved her hands awkwardly from her front pants pockets to her back pockets. "But how *are* you doing?"

Kaylah arched an eyebrow. "Me, personally? I'm fine."

This conversation was twice as awkward with Saff still standing. "Mind if I sit?"

"Yeah, sorry." Kaylah gestured to a chair. "Where are my manners?"

Saff sat. "I guess I just wanted to see how you're doing, and if you think they got out of camp without anyone suspecting anything, and, you know, stuff…"

Kaylah nodded. "Hmm. I'll miss her while she's gone. I'm confident they got out cleanly. And … stuff?"

Saff shyly averted her eyes. "Well, I guess I'm here because of a favor."

"Did she ask you for the same favor she asked me?"

Wait, what? Saff had wanted to ask Kaylah for a personal favor… *Oh…* Rachel had likely tried to prod Kaylah to make peace with Saff as well. "Maybe. Rachel said something about making sure you learned to understand that I'm always right. About everything." She tried to suppress a smile.

Kaylah smirked knowingly. "Funny. I swear she gave me the same talk. But she said that *I'm* the one who's always right."

Saff gave her a genuine smile. "For what it's worth, I'm sorry. You know, you sometimes remind me of one of my sisters that I knew in high school. We didn't always get along. I can ... sometimes be a bit judgmental. Especially in high-stress situations."

"I just wish you'd give me a little credit now and then."

Biting her lip, Saff crossed her legs. "Yeah. Did I mention I grew up as an only child? Well, kind of. And that my parents were overprotective, and kept me in the dark? I just ... don't like being out of the loop."

Kaylah glanced at her table full of books and scrolls. "I can appreciate where you're coming from. But you need to realize you can't control everything, and you don't always know what's best for everyone."

"I know. Though ... that's what you're aiming for, right? As a queen, to have control and decide what's best for everyone?"

Narrowing her eyes, Kaylah changed her tone. "Wow. That's the shortest olive branch I've ever seen. If this is how you put aside our differences," she pointed to the door flap, "then you can—"

"Wait." Saff furrowed her brow, confused. "I genuinely didn't mean that as an insult."

Kaylah crossed her arms, obviously unbelieving.

"I just meant... You still want to be queen, right?"

"Yes."

"That's a lot of power for one person. Have you considered finding a way to reorganize things? Have elections or something?"

Kaylah softened, but only a little. "Show me the perfect form of government, Saff, and I'll consider it. This is my birthright, and the way our Mother Vines work. And once I rightfully sit on my throne, I plan to address the balance of power within my kingdom." She grabbed a water bottle from the floor, unscrewing the cap.

"Don't you think your leaders and I have discussed our long-term goals? Concessions?"

Saff blushed as Kaylah took a swig. Of course they had. "For the record, I think you'll make a good queen." The fact that the council had been working side by side with her had genuinely surprised Saff. So far, she was doing a good job.

"Thanks," Kaylah said graciously.

While concerned about how things might work out in the long run, Saff wouldn't dare bring that up. Even if Kaylah could win and keep her kingdom, and fulfill her promises, what would happen if the next ruler just reversed all of their hard work? And who would that next ruler even be? The power of the Mother Vines passed down through the female bloodline. Kaylah loved a human. A man who couldn't enter the Green Lands, and couldn't give her kids.

"How's Eric?" Saff asked.

A twinge of longing flashed across Kaylah's face before she settled on a barely there smile. "He's good. Haven't seen him since you and I paired up, but I sometimes get letters through the cave."

Saff nodded, sorry for her. Kaylah had to be terribly lonely. Politics and leadership galore, but now her best—and locally, only—friend had left. At least Ginger was still here to keep her company. "Why doesn't your dad—well, you know, Nathan—come to camp?"

Kaylah looked down, lining up a few scrolls. "Your council feels he would be more useful on the human-world side of things right now."

Stopping herself from asking more questions like she wanted to, Saff decided it was best to bring up the reason she'd originally come to visit. "So the favor I came here for doesn't have anything to do with Rachel, really."

Kaylah straightened in her chair, taking a deep breath. "Shoot."

"Well, I…" Saff glanced at all the books and scrolls. The stack had grown since her last visit. "I guess, without Rachel, I'm trying to figure out my part. You talked about wanting my help with research, but I haven't done any since we set up camp. And I like training these new girls, but I guess I just…"

The truth was, Saff was a little lost at sea without Rachel. Rachel had been a special assignment for her. And Saff was starting to question a lot about herself and her own path amidst everything happening around them.

"Sorry," Kaylah said. "The research—I haven't had much time, myself. And I'd like to be here to go over it, so I don't want to just hand it off to anyone."

"Right." Saff fidgeted with her hands. She was also homesick. She and Heather got the occasional letter all the way from South Fortinda, but it was so far away. It wasn't fair for Saff to ask for what she wanted, not when Kaylah couldn't be happy in the same way. But she needed to. "I, uh, I understand new people allowed into camp have to be approved by both yourself and Lionel?"

"Yes…"

Saff rubbed at an invisible speck of dirt on her pants. "My husband was a fantastic teacher for me when I first got my powers. I think he'd be great here with me in camp as more girls return through the cave."

Kaylah gave her an understanding smile. "I wouldn't want you to be too exhausted, doing so much on your own. I might be able to do something about that."

Saff's heart somersaulted. "Thank you."

"Sure thing." Kaylah stood. "Is there anything else? I've got a meeting I need to head to."

Saff also stood. "No. That's it."

"You know," Kaylah picked up a pack, swinging it over her shoulder, "I think that me sending for your husband should earn me some forgiveness points for shipping Rachel off to Mordor."

Saff chuckled. "I don't know." She pointed at the ring on Kaylah's finger. "You didn't even send her with anything 'precious.'"

Kaylah busted out laughing. "Are you a Lord of the Rings nerd? Rach totally didn't get a reference I made before."

"My best friend growing up was a guy, so I've seen my fair share of fantasy and sci-fi." She surveyed Kaylah, the picture of traditional femininity. "I'm kinda surprised you're into it."

Kaylah held a hand to her chest. "Judging a book by the cover?" She winked. "Not a superfan, really. Eric made me watch with him once. The *extended* version."

That surprised Saff a little as well. Eric looked more like he ought to be commanding a yacht club or a gym rather than munching popcorn while geeking out on a couch. But then again, Saff barely knew him, and he'd spouted off all sorts of impressive information when she'd met with him and Kaylah back at the human-world safe house. About encryptions, codes, security walls, all of that.

Grabbing her water bottle, Kaylah approached Saff. She had to have read her mind. "He's just the way I like him—sexy and smart."

Saff smiled. She threw one last glance at the books and scrolls. "I need to get back to my girls, too. But let me know when you need help with research?"

"Will do." Kaylah reached for the tent door flap, then paused. "I do," her voice lowered, "have one favor to ask, something you can help me with."

"Okay?"

Kaylah sighed. "Well, there's one pain-in-the-ass Seeder I know who seems to need to control everything." They shared a knowing grin. "But I do understand her predicament, because I struggle with that as well."

"Okay…"

"I used to do the majority of recruiting for Unitas. Ever since Soren cut me off, I've had to rely solely on other Unitas members to take care of that. It just makes me a little uneasy to not know everyone here in camp. Maybe help me keep an eye out for suspicious activity?"

That apprehensive, nerve-filled feeling crept into Saff's mind. Everyone showing up at the cave and Neutral Woods entrance was thoroughly interviewed, but still… "You trust your people, though, right?"

"Of course."

"Yeah, I can help keep an eye out."

Kaylah wrapped an arm around Saff's shoulders, opening up the tent flap. "Fantastic. If we keep up more conversations like this, I might even be able to tolerate you by the time we end this war." She winked again.

Saff chuckled. "I might be able to tolerate you, too."

Chapter 12

A FEW MINUTES INTO THE open Neutral Woods, the mumble and rustle of the busy training camp faded, the only sound the crunch of fallen twigs and branches under Rachel and Guillen's feet.

Rachel thought about the time Kaylah had described Guillen as 'not very talkative,' but she really wished he'd be the one to get the conversation started. Glancing in his direction, and with no response, she decided to jump right in. "I guess we'll have lots of time to go over strategy and everything, right? And catch up." She smiled.

He turned and smiled back. "I look forward to it."

They kept walking … awkwardly…

"So, is that a human tradition?" He pointed to the flower Rachel wished she wasn't holding, but hadn't known how to ditch without being disrespectful.

"Yeah, kind of weird, right? Cutting flowers and giving them to someone? I'm assuming you guys don't do it?"

"No. Not an Ivy thing, either." He glanced around, doing a regular check to ensure they were in the clear. "What's it supposed to mean?"

She twirled the flower in her fingers. "Just something nice, and fresh, and pretty. They can mean different things based on what kind of flower it is, or the color."

"What does that one mean?"

She was happy to explain human customs to Guillen, given he'd been denied that education. But this ... was uncomfortable. "I actually don't think we have this flower back in the human world. Zeus, the guy that gave it to me—we worked together on the project to help heal the land."

"Sounds like you've kept busy. That's really great." Guillen adjusted his pack. "What about the kissing thing?"

Her eyes grew wide as she stared straight forward, tight-lipped. Had he seen something from the tent? Kaylah wouldn't have dared to mention anything else, right?

"He kissed your hand before you hugged him," he clarified.

She swallowed a couple of times before answering. He had seen the exchange... And ... she couldn't tell if Guillen was genuinely confused, or if he was trying to razz her, or if he was fishing...

"That? You've never seen anyone do that?"

"Or maybe that's a Seeder thing?" He shrugged. "I guess I sometimes don't know where traditions come from, right?"

"A kiss on the hand can mean different things. Just a hello or goodbye. It's kind of old-fashioned." She cleared her throat, glancing out of the corner of her eye to try and read his face.

"Okay."

Rachel stopped, turning to face him. She squinted. "You really haven't seen anyone do that before?" He'd expertly deflected a question about himself before, when they first met in a cave by the palace. "You didn't answer my question. And if I remember right, you're good at that."

His straight face changed into a smirk.

"I knew it!"

He chuckled. She loved the sound of it, and the way his eyes squinted when he laughed. "Sorry. I'm sure your boyfriend will miss you a lot. I'll try to get you back in one piece."

She shook her head. "This flower, as lovely as it is, was a kind gesture. From a *friend*. And not very practical. So, no offense to him, but I think I'll be leaving it here." She bent over and gently placed it on the ground before continuing to walk.

Guillen strolled alongside her again, grinning for another minute.

It was only fair for Rachel to throw something back at him and suss out where he was in relation to the singles arena. "So, you and Olivia arrived together. She's really great. I didn't realize you guys knew each other that well."

"Oh, Olivia? Yeah, she's nice, isn't she? Maybe I should ask her on a date when we get back, do you think?"

Rachel bit her tongue. That was *not* the direction she'd been intending to go at all. But she had no claim on Guillen. They were technically just friends. "Well … I … uh… I don't know your type."

"She's not my type," he calmly replied.

Perhaps it was best to leave it at that. They were both single, and she wasn't even the slightest bit mad about it; but she figured she'd give the butterflies in her stomach a rest. "So, what have you been up to lately? What damsels in distress have you been rescuing, and all that?"

"Hmm… No damsels. I did some location scouting. Went through the different stunt communities, getting a feel for who might be on our side, making connections to help us along the way. But I also went back to work for a while."

She raised her eyebrows. "Working construction? Why would you still be doing that?"

"Connections to the palace or not, I only have so much vacation time, especially during an active war."

"They really don't know you're in Unitas yet?" Her mouth hung open. "I figured, when you came to save me, that they'd know…"

"You were kind of out of it at the palace, so you might not have noticed the hood I was wearing at the time. That wasn't just a fashion statement. We'd hoped we could get you out cleanly, and that I wouldn't be identified. And, well, no one ever came for me." Guillen grinned. "Plus, Soren's cocky. He underestimates me." He shrugged. "I'm nothing to him. We have that on our side."

Rachel grinned from ear to ear. "He would, wouldn't he? I, for one, am glad to have you on our side."

They continued to chat, getting caught up and preparing for their mission. Guillen was fascinated to hear how Seeders without powers lived. He was still missing a lot of time from his day job with this campaign, but luckily his supervisor was a sympathizer, so he was able to help with forged paperwork, movement orders, and the like.

Rachel gave Guillen the highlight reel of how things had gone for her since they'd parted ways. Conversation flowed easily between them. She was grateful that if she had to traverse the Green Lands on foot, and go into enemy territory with anyone, that it was with him.

In the early afternoon, Rachel decided to listen to her stomach's complaints. She opened her knapsack and searched through the options she'd packed.

"How about we take a break for lunch?" he suggested.

"That's okay, I can keep walking while we eat."

"Mmm. Yeah, but I want a break."

"Oh. Yeah, sure."

They found a log in a shaded area, and Rachel sat down. Guillen chose to lie on the ground instead, propping his feet up on the log. "You may be all energetic, but I've been walking and sleeping on the ground for days." He closed his eyes and grimaced as he twisted his neck, as if trying to make it pop.

"Sorry, I didn't think about that. Let me know whenever you need a break." She glanced down at his shoes, his elevated feet. "I could help with that, maybe heal a little, so you're not so tired or hurting. Like I healed my feet after our escape, before Jon got me shoes."

"No thanks," he said.

"You're sure? I discovered with Saff that I'm a pretty good masseuse, learning how to incorporate my energy and everything."

"I'm fine."

She raised her eyebrows, unwrapping a granola bar from a dried corn husk. "Do you have gross feet? Are you afraid I'll judge you? I'm not weird about feet."

He shook his head.

She squinted. "Are your feet ticklish?"

He flashed a silly face like he'd been caught in a secret.

"Ooh, now *that* is good to know." She looked him over from head to toe. "Where else are you ticklish?"

"Psh! Like I'd tell you or anyone else." He wiggled his eyebrows. "Unless … you tell me where *you're* ticklish."

She frowned. "But what if I'm not ticklish at all?"

He crossed his ankles, wearing a knowing grin. "With the sincerity in that face, I'm sure that just *has* to be the case."

She laughed before taking a bite of the granola bar. "How about a shoulder massage? You look like you're in pain." Just in case that was too forward, she added, "I'm not coming on to you. I just figure … it's a long trip."

He drew a deep breath. "Sure. I'd hate to deprive you of an opportunity to practice your skills."

"Your sacrifice will be remembered."

He moved to sit in front of her, breaking out some food of his own to eat. He leaned back against her legs as she sat on the log. She couldn't help but smile, hoping he was feeling the same way she was. But she wanted to take things slow. Guillen was special. He wasn't a rebound. She'd worried that, even if she'd been right about them sharing an attraction, she'd have to get to know him all over again. But she was surprised by how quickly they were picking up where they'd left off.

After pulling back his shoulders for better posture, she focused energy into her fingertips, and set to work on his knots. "I'm guessing some of these are from your job, too, aren't they?"

He quietly moaned. "Maybe."

"I remember you not liking your construction job. What would you do if you had a choice?"

"You know, I thought about what you said, and I asked myself that question. But it's hard to imagine a lot of other opportunities here. What kinds of jobs do they have in the human world that they don't here?"

The human world seemed so far away sometimes—something she still longed for, despite the energy of the Green Lands realm. But talking about it with Guillen was a fun walk down memory lane. "Gosh, a lot. I could probably entertain you all day with them." She puckered her lips in thought, staring into the distance. "I'm sure you could do anything you put your mind to, you're obviously a determined person. But right off the top of my head, I'm not sure…" She dug a glowing thumb into a particularly big knot. "You and your knives and machetes, though, that makes me think of something funny. People pay for axe-throwing in the human world. Like, they show up at a building, and pay money to chuck sharp objects at a wall."

He laughed and leaned to the side, twisting to look back at her. "Really? You're not making that up?"

"I kid you not."

He straightened back up. "Hmm. Sounds kind of boring for a job every day, to just watch. What about you? What do you want, when all this is said and done?"

She sat pensively, continuing to work on his shoulders. "I… I honestly don't know. I think my life is kind of the reverse of yours. I started out with all the opportunities at my fingertips, and now I'm here, and the only thing I see in my future is this war."

He reached up and rested a hand on hers before turning to look at her again. "It won't be forever."

She smiled at the gesture. "I hope not. It's exhausting." She glided glowing fingertips up his neck, applying pressure. "I do know one thing for sure—one way or another, I'm getting my GED. Soren stole my graduation from me, but I'm not letting him win on that." Guillen probably had no idea what a GED was. "That's just the formal mark that you've completed your basic education in the human world. My grades were good enough that I still should have been able to apply for graduation, and get a diploma in my absence. If my high school hadn't thought I ran away and dropped out… Anyway, I just figured, since we have the cave for rifting now…"

Guillen tilted his neck to each side; a slight pop followed. "Thanks." He stood, offering his hands to help her up. "That's one of the things I like about you. You're smart. And you're not going to let his crap or anyone else's get in your way."

Chapter 13

RACHEL AND GUILLEN WALKED AND talked for hours about jobs in both worlds before stopping for a dinner break. They filled up their canteens and sat on some large boulders by a stream, facing each other.

"You're less scared than I thought you would be," he said.

She sloshed around the water in her canteen, staring at it. "Kaylah assured me there haven't been any Ivy soldier sightings this far north. With that camp and community being secret, and past our borders…"

"She's right. I didn't come across a single soldier on my way here. I guess I was just thinking about the mission as a whole."

"Do you think I should be more scared? I don't know." She met his gaze. She'd been so numb. His comment made her wonder if she was being foolish, or perhaps he really didn't think as highly of her as she'd hoped. "I think a lot of it has to do with being with you. I feel safe with you."

He tossed a peanut down to a happy squirrel. "I don't know that you *should* feel more scared. You're just not as combat trained as others, having been back home for such a short amount of time."

She frowned. Despite all of Saff's training, which had even been supplemented by time with some Seeder soldiers, Rachel still wasn't a soldier. "Do you think this is a mistake? I'm sure we could find someone else to help on the mission."

His expression showed a hint of confusion. "No. I didn't mean that at all. I wouldn't want to do this mission with anyone else." He raised his eyebrows. "I mean it. I don't think I would have gone along with it if Kaylah had made me pick a different Seeder."

She bit her lip. "You picked me? It wasn't just Kaylah's decision?"

His eyes gave off as much warmth as his smile. "I could rally by myself, but we need you to be the face of the Seeder part of this movement. We need to show someone who's passionate, brave, and caring. Kaylah always told me I'd like you, that you were kind. And after meeting you, I couldn't agree more. You're the perfect example of what we're trying to represent."

She blushed, fixating on a scratch on her canteen. She may have been a screwup, but she tried to be a decent person; it had never felt like any sort of extraordinary character trait. "Thanks."

"Hey," he said in a gentle voice, causing her to raise her head. "How are you doing? With everything you've been through?"

She shook her head. "I don't even know how to answer that, to be honest. Did Kaylah warn you I still have nightmares about it? Nothing as bad as before, but we'll need to be careful at night."

"You'll get through this." His voice was as soothing as ever. "And I'll stay close."

"Thank you." She packed up her things before sliding down the boulder.

The rest of the evening, they focused on the work at hand. They talked more about the route they were taking to avoid catching any suspicious eyes, and he filled her in on all things Ivy. They would primarily be going to the stunt communities, but would pass by regular towns. She would need to blend in seamlessly.

"Oh yeah, and you'll be going by Elizabeth."

"Really?" She stepped over a log as the sun began to set in the background. "Is that a normal Ivy name? That sounds very … human."

"Well, yes and no, and that's kind of the point. It's not what you'd consider a traditional Ivy name, but assassins and generals are notoriously proud of their 'calling' and often try to show it off."

Her stomach churned.

"So they'll use lingo or even name their children more human names to show that off. Not dissimilar from the upper class wearing nicer things." He bent over, picking up a pine cone and crunching it in his hands. "That way, your backstory will make a little more sense if you say too much that would give away your childhood in the human world."

"Oh. Then Elizabeth it is. I suppose we don't need people whispering about a Rachel going around."

"Nope." He glanced at the sun setting in the sky. "You know, we should probably get in a little training before it gets dark. I'd feel better that way."

"Yeah, sure."

While Rachel had trained with her Seeder abilities, they were only to be used as a last resort. Guillen would be rounding off her training with knives.

He picked up a couple of short thick sticks. "Alright, no need to risk it with the real thing." He handed one to her.

"If we had to, you know, kill someone to keep our cover … wouldn't they suspect a," she still hated saying the word, "stunt? The injuries would obviously be different from Ivy leaf cuts."

"Possibly. More than one murder has been pinned on a stunt because a knife was used." He tossed his stick in the air, then caught it. "Pretty flimsy reasoning, given every regular Ivy has a knife on their person somewhere."

"What? Really? I thought Kaylah did just because of you…"

"Nah." He pointed to the machete on his belt. "She knows how to use one of these, and other weapons, because of me. But it's pretty standard to tuck one in your boot or pocket, but only really as tools, not weapons."

"Oh."

"Think about it this way: Regular Ivies can disconnect their vines internally at the wrist, but once they've used that vine on something, say… to mend a broken fence or as a strap to pull a wagon or something, then they need a way to cut it for some reason, and cutting with a knife is just faster in a lot of cases than using vine leaves. Not to mention most women and children aren't efficiently trained in using their vines as weapons, so they might not have down the rigidity or sharpness required for that kind of cutting."

His explanation painted such a curious picture for Rachel, to imagine Ivy vines being used domestically like a piece of twine, rather than as weapons against her people.

"You look surprised."

"I guess. I dunno, Kaylah just hasn't talked about it that way."

He shrugged, tucking the stick he'd been carrying into his pocket. He then pulled out a smaller pocketknife and approached her. "My favorite servant gifted me this years ago. I've fashioned the others I have in a similar way." He handed Rachel the knife.

She ran her thumbs over the handle. It was made of a pearlescent shell of some type. "It's beautiful." She handed it back, and he slipped it back in place in a pocket. "Did you have many servants growing up?"

He looked embarrassed, rubbing the back of his neck. "Well, my family has money and position, so… Most people don't have any, right? But it's not like I have one now."

"Yeah, of course." She now wished she'd taken more time to ask Kaylah questions about Guillen to avoid making him uncomfortable, but she'd done everything possible to avoid Kaylah's pushing, prodding, and teasing about Rachel's crush on him. "So, um, knife practice before we lose all light?"

"Right, yes."

They only had about a half hour or so before it got dark, but they made good use of that time. He showed her a variety of restraint holds and targets to aim for with a dagger. He was all business, and she tried to be, but it was exceptionally hard at times when he'd have her in a hold for a while, explaining his technique. It was nearly impossible for her mind not to wander with her being so close, being held in his arms, even if it was for such a serious purpose. She could swear he smelled of mint leaves and juniper berries.

After agreeing to resume their training the next day, they walked long past nightfall, hoping to find a well-hidden place to stop for the night. If they could be confident they were tucked away well enough, they could both try to sleep, instead of taking shifts. They were still in the Neutral Woods, where the trees were fairly dense, and they found a spot Guillen was satisfied with.

They tried to get as comfortable as possible, sleeping on the ground under the stars. Lying down, they faced each other.

"So…" He yawned. "Is that your first tattoo?"

"Yep. What about you? Any others?"

"I've got a couple others."

She wished she could see him better, be able to view his face and not just an outline of his body in the dark.

"What are they?" She added playfully, "And *where* are they?" He'd seen her in a lot less clothing than she'd seen him in during their time together before.

"Hmm. Maybe I'll keep that a mystery," he returned in fun.

"Come on." She jabbed a finger in his direction. Meeting his shoulder, she poked a few more times. "I wanna know."

He grabbed her hand, giving it a squeeze. His palm was calloused, but she smiled at his tender touch, then her heart skipped a beat as a pair of lips met the back of her hand.

"Have you ever thought of getting one before? I'm sad this is your first experience with them." He rested his hand on the ground, leaving his palm open, as if letting her choose whether she wanted to keep hers there with his. Not seeing his face, his piercing blue eyes right now, that killed her. She tickled his palm with her fingers.

"I thought about it. My parents, um…" She still had a hard time not calling Duke Nuren one of her parents or her stepdad, but he didn't deserve that title in her life anymore. "My mom definitely wouldn't let me when I was younger. But just something simple, like a cute butterfly, would be fun."

"That suits you," he said in a soft and tired voice. "Just like you. You can both fly. And you're both beautiful."

She stopped drawing on his hand and settled her palm onto his. "Thanks," she whispered.

"Where do you think you would get it?" he asked.

Not that he could see it, but her cheeks had to be red with warmth. She'd just mentally undressed him, searching for his mysterious tattoos. Was he now doing the same? "I don't know. There are a lot of options." She was tempted to ask him where he thought she should get it, but that was pretty intimate, even if he was returning her interest. She gave his hand a gentle rub and then retracted her own. She didn't want to screw this one up. "Good night, Guillen."

His silhouette shifted positions, and he drew a deep breath. "Good night, Rachel."

***

Rachel woke in the morning to Guillen's face just a couple of feet away; he was peacefully sleeping. She studied him with a contented smile—his eyebrows framing his stunning eyes, the large scar on his temple, his perfectly kissable lips. She looked him over, now that she could see him, and wondered again where he'd placed his tattoos. Her eyes landed on his chest, which moved slowly with each breath he took. His breathing pattern changed, and she looked back at his face. His eyes were now open, his lips upturned in a smile. "How long have you been awake?" he asked.

"Not long. Just wanted to let you get some more sleep."

"Thanks." He shifted into a sitting position, then ran his fingers through his hair.

She followed suit, grabbing a comb from her pack.

"I'd imagine sometime past midday, we'll run into a river and be able to walk near that most of the way back to our borders," he said. They were entering Ivy lands on the opposite end from the palace; this was all new territory for Rachel. Luckily, it wouldn't take them as long to cross the distance as it had months prior, but it was still a couple more days at least. And they were going through areas less patrolled—their odds were good to approach without conflict.

"That sounds great. I'd love to wash up," she said.

"Yeah, I'm sure we can find a good spot for that."

She cleared her throat. "So, I don't have to be worried about what happened last time?" She smirked, referring to the time he'd tackled her when she was half-naked to avoid discovery by enemy troops.

"Hey! That was to keep both of us safe." His unamused face showed he'd taken offense. "I would never just grab you like that if I didn't have to."

"I'm just giving you a hard time. You're obviously a gentleman; that's one of the things I like about you."

He nodded. She then fought a grin. The bra she wore now was the same one he'd seen her in at the lake.

He furrowed his brow. "What?"

She pulled up the collar of her shirt to hide her face below the eyes. "I don't know what you're talking about."

He shook his head. "I hope you can be more convincing than this when we meet some of my people."

She dropped the shirt from her face, giving him a determined look. "I accept that challenge." She flashed her green Seeder eyes.

"I like a girl who's not afraid to take on a challenge." He winked.

***

Despite his flirtation and attention, Guillen really was a gentleman, and perhaps a bit shyer than Rachel had remembered. He'd probably only dared to hold her hand the night before because it had been dark. He didn't try to make any moves on her the next couple of days, and they had to split the nights to watch out for unexpected visitors. The Seeders described Ivy lands as 'a wasteland,' which was accurate, depending on your definition. Compared to the lush lands near the Ivy palace or Seeder territory, or even neutral lands, there was little plant growth in most of the Ivy Kingdom. They were more vulnerable in this part of the wilderness, closer to the wastelands.

On the last evening of their journey, they stopped early for the night. Taking a late dinner, they sat close to each other as they reviewed what the next day had in store for them.

Rachel rubbed her sore shoulder. "I'll just be glad to sleep indoors again."

"I think that means it's your turn." He invited her over with a nod.

"I don't know. I'm the one with healing hands." She stuck out her tongue.

"Hey now, I'm good with my hands."

She chuckled. "Now *that's* a good pickup line."

He cleared his throat. "I meant, you know, construction and knife work and all that…"

"If you insist." She sat down in front of him, cross-legged.

Guillen gently moved her hair to the side, and the butterflies took flight in her stomach. He started in with his fingers on her neck, then slid them down to her shoulders. She closed her eyes and soaked it all in.

He avoided her bra straps. "Here," she said as she slipped a hand under her collar and pushed the straps down, revealing each shoulder for a moment. Her breathing shuddered as his hands made more contact with her skin. He carefully straightened out her collar and started to massage again.

"Is that better?" he asked.

"It's great, thanks." She took a calming breath. "Speaking of you and your knife work." Reaching into her pocket, she pulled out the knife he'd given her. They had only ever used sticks for their training, for safety.

"You still have it." His smile was audible.

"I always have it with me."

He stopped massaging and glided his hands down her arms, meeting her hands. "Are you keeping it sharp like I taught you?"

She handed him the knife as he leaned forward, setting his chin on her shoulder.

It was intoxicating, being in his arms, having his face so close. "Yeah, I, uh, I've tried to take good care of it."

He checked the blade with his thumb. "Not bad." He slid it back into its sheath, handing it to her and lingering with his arms around her.

Her heart pounded so hard that she feared he might hear or feel it. "I don't think I can ever thank you enough. For this, for saving me that day in the palace, for everything."

"You're welcome," he whispered in her ear.

If she turned her head just a few inches, his lips would be right there. He wanted to kiss too, right? Instead, she panicked. "I owe you my life," she blurted.

He drew a deep breath, moving his hands back up her arms, to her shoulders. He planted a kiss on the top of her head as he shifted back. "You owe me nothing." He continued the shoulder massage.

They sat in silence for another few minutes. She tried to enjoy the vibrant orange-and-purple sunset, as she kicked herself for ruining their moment.

"We should turn in early," he announced.

He would take the first watch and wake her when it was her turn. They'd gotten lucky so far—Rachel hadn't woken up noisily from traumatic nightmares. His calming presence helped. But the stress of entering enemy territory the next day got to her that night, and she woke up, panting in a cold sweat.

"It's okay," Guillen whispered in the dark. He reached out and held her hand. "It's okay."

She focused herself, slowing her breathing and heartbeat.

"Can I do anything to help?" he asked, squeezing her hand.

She swallowed hard. "No. Thanks." She let go of his hand and rolled onto her side, crying. She remembered the look he gave her when she'd found out how poorly he was treated for not having powers. He'd told her he didn't want her pity. That same sentiment ached deeply in her soul right now. She wanted Guillen, but she didn't want him in that way. Not as someone who saw a broken girl to take care of, just because he was nice.

She woke in the wee hours of the morning to birds chirping in the trees above them. She startled and looked around; Guillen stood leaning against a tree. She rose, and he flashed a tired smile. Joining him, she leaned against the other side of the tree.

"You didn't wake me for my turn," she scolded.

"You needed it more." The exhaustion in his eyes begged to disagree.

She sighed. "I don't know about that. How about you try to get some sleep before we pack up?"

"No. I think we should get going. We're so close."

"Okay." She took a breath and decided to ask what was on her mind. "Can I hug you?"

He held his arms open. "Of course."

She wrapped her arms around him, and he pulled her in tighter and tighter. She closed her eyes and melted there. This was the safest place she knew in both worlds. In Guillen's arms.

His breathing matched hers. After what felt like hours, she decided she would finally have to let go, since he wasn't the first to move. She stepped back, glancing at his lips before meeting his heavenly eyes. "Thanks."

He gave his signature roguish grin. "Any time. Are you ready for this?"

Today would be the day she really put on her game face, infiltrating enemy territory. "I'm all in."

Chapter 14

SINCE A STUNT LIKE GUILLEN had no reason to be in the Neutral Woods, he and Rachel had to take a roundabout path to get into the Ivy Kingdom. Though, even with the war actively raging, the borders were barely patrolled, especially this far from the palace. Eventually, they hit the main path toward the stunt community furthest north.

Guillen had told her how small, and often remote, the communities were, but even still, the symphony of chatter, clangs, and thuds on the approach was deafening after days in the quiet woods. Rachel put extra effort into focusing her energy, tucking it away and calming her nerves. She was an Ivy. One born without powers. She was from Community Five. She worked in a textile workshop. She was visiting her friend Magda here in Community Ten. She was traveling alongside Guillen coincidentally, having met along the way to visit mutual friends.

As they approached the community entrance, a bulky guard stood ready to screen visitors. Guillen went first. He lifted his sleeve, showing his mark. The guard gave him a courteous nod. "Sir."

Rachel was already annoyed. He'd called Guillen 'sir,' and waved him in without travel documents, just because he was royalty, but he was still treated worse than a commoner with powers.

Guillen stopped shortly after entering, watching for Rachel to get through. She handed her forged documents to the guard, smiling as he looked them over. She raised her sleeve, showing her mark. As he read her papers, Rachel studied his face. *Please let this one be the right kind of guard…*

Guards had been front and center in Rachel and Guillen's discussion of culture and potential threats on their mission. The way Guillen had explained it, there were really only two types of guards at the stunt communities. The majority were nothing more than washed-up soldiers looking for an easy paycheck that still boosted their ego. They were also the type that saw the girls without powers in these communities as easy conquests.

The minority of guards were generally there for a good reason, wanting to stand in a place where they recognized an injustice being done. Some of them even had stunt family members they loved, though they'd never be stationed at a community where a family member resided.

The guard squinted, glancing between Rachel and the paperwork. It was taking him a long time to review the papers, and there was something in his eye that forced her to choke down her energy.

Something was wrong.

She looked past the guard, trying to keep her cool. Guillen had his hand subtly ready, concealing a knife, observing.

The guard grasped Rachel's upper arm, extending vines around it. "You're from Five?" He gazed into her eyes in a way that made her uncomfortable. She trained her expression to hide her panic.

"That's what the paperwork and skin say." She shrugged.

He rubbed his thumb over her tattoo. "I think I'd remember a beautiful face like yours—I just transferred from Five last month."

"Oh, really? That's neat." She feigned interest.

In their many hours together, she and Guillen had been able to discuss strategy for this kind of scenario. She likely knew that community better than half of its occupants, without having ever set foot in it.

"Did you work the north or south entrance?" she asked.

"North. Near your job," he replied.

Rachel nodded. "That makes sense. I approach from the other direction. Did you work days?"

"Nights. The schedule is why I transferred."

He was still holding on to her arm. Giving her a line about being beautiful had to mean he was the wrong type of guard… She slid her free hand up, then stroked the back of his hand and looked at him with seductive eyes, licking her lips. "That would be why. I guess I don't get out much. Trust me. I'd recognize you, too, if I had seen you." She winked.

He gave her a lusty grin, glancing at her chest. "I guess it's a shame I left."

"I'll be here a couple of days for my visit." She smiled. "When do you get off work?"

He looked at Guillen out of the corner of his eye. "You're not here with palace boy?"

By this point, she wanted nothing more than to vomit.

She bit her lip. "Acquaintance, at best. The guys in these kinds of places don't exactly do it for me, if you know what I mean."

He released his vines from her arm. "I know *exactly* what you mean. I get off at five. Will I see you at the pub?" He handed back her paperwork.

She tucked it into her back pocket. "I don't know my exact schedule. But if I can sneak away, I know where you'll be."

He nodded her in. As she started to pass, the guard's hand landed on her backside. "Don't lose that paperwork."

Get your hand off me or you'll be losing something much more dear!

"Thanks. I'll see you soon." She forced one last grin while looking back, then moved on.

The moment she turned away, her facade dropped. Her breathing was forced as she focused on controlling her emotions and energy. Guillen walked silently next to her. At the end of the dirt street, they turned the corner and stopped at the community café. They sat down and placed an order—both grateful for fresh, warm food. Once the waitress left, Guillen reached his hand across the table.

"I'm sorry." He frowned.

She shook her head, moving her hand up to his. "We talked about this." Guillen couldn't be seen questioning authority; he couldn't stand up for her. She moved her hand back down; they shouldn't be seen looking too familiar, either.

After an amazing breakfast of warm buckwheat, peppers, and zucchini, Guillen gave Rachel a brief tour. With his unique position, he'd enjoyed significantly more travel opportunities than most stunts. He not only had more freedom of movement, but also in how many vacation days a year he was granted. He'd spent time in every stunt community, and lived in more than one of the communities long-term.

The Ivy Kingdom had four steam engines that traversed their landscape. They had helped him travel between the communities in the past, but for the purposes of this mission, they'd be avoiding them, since they were packed with upper-class citizens, guards, and all the wrong people to avoid suspicion.

Community Ten was a notch or two above bleak. Other than a rare shade tree, there was no plant life to be seen. No yards. No flower gardens. Nothing. People plodded along, fulfilling their daily tasks, with the occasional neighbors stopping to chat with each other. All of the buildings blended together, built of dull grey stone, merging into the background of mountains from whence they were hewn. The air was more stale than in the Neutral Woods or Seeder nation, which wasn't all that shocking considering the lack of plant growth in the vicinity.

One of Guillen and Rachel's last stops was at the blacksmith's.

"This is my old friend, Jacob. He and his wife Magda are going to be hosting us."

Jacob, a man in his late twenties with dark brown hair, wiped his dirty hands on a shop rag, and shook Rachel's hand. "It's a pleasure."

"Thank you. Nice to meet you." Sitting on Jacob's workbench behind him was a basket, plumb-full of arrowheads. Rachel could almost hear Jon's voice from months earlier, when he'd explained how her stepfather had petitioned to issue soldiers in the woods with bows, not just guards at the palace. "How long does it take you to make one of those?"

He glanced behind him, instantly looking perturbed. "Too long, if you ask the folks in charge." Passing another dark, knowing look at Guillen, he added, "And if you ask me, still too long, given the public toilets can't be used until I fix the hardware." He reached into his pocket. "But that's obviously not a priority." He handed Guillen a key. "The place is all yours. Magda should be home in a little while, but she set out some towels and everything so you two can get cleaned up."

Guillen pocketed the key. "Any birthday celebrations tonight?"

Jacob looked at a pendulum clock on the wall, shaking his head. "Not enough time. Tomorrow."

"Alright. Well, it's good to see you." Guillen pointed to the basket of arrowheads. "And good to know about that."

A sinister smile spread across Jacob's face. "It sure would be sad if they went missing after I turned them in." He picked up his hammer to get back to work. "Happy to be the eyes and ears on the eyes and ears."

***

"You can go first," Guillen said, sitting down on the couch. Rachel willingly took the offer, hopping in the shower. While the materials the shower was built from were different than those she'd grown accustomed to back in South Fortinda, the simple plumbing was similar. She moaned at the refreshing sensation of warm water rushing over her, cleaning her better than the river along the way had.

The hot water didn't last long, which wasn't a huge surprise. Everything in these communities was built economically. Every apartment was a one-bedroom, since they weren't allowed to have kids. Uniform, tiny, boring. She toweled off and got dressed. Planning to warn Guillen he'd have to wait a while for hot water, she headed down the short hallway, then stopped to lean against the wall, grinning. He was fast asleep.

She quietly sat on the living room floor and perused some books on a shelf, flipping through them and looking longingly at Guillen. He was really out.

Not much later, the front doorknob twisted, and a woman with light brown hair entered, presumably Magda, returning from work. Rachel waved and put a finger to her lips, then pointed at Guillen. Magda tiptoed inside and eased the door closed, but the click of the door closing woke him.

He rubbed his eyes. "Gosh. Sorry. Hey, Magda, it's great to see you." He stood and gave her a hug. His voice still groggy, he motioned to Rachel. "This is my friend, Elizabeth."

Magda gave her a cordial smile and handshake. They chatted a while, and Rachel offered to help with dinner as Guillen excused himself to shower. He came out looking fresh and sharp.

After Jacob returned home, the four of them ate a dinner of bean soup and herbed salad, and talked for hours. Jacob and Magda were a cute couple, and Rachel could easily see why Guillen was friends with them. She allowed her mind to wander. How might things be if she and Guillen nurtured their relationship? Would they have friends like this? But ... where would they live? Her mood shifted when she remembered he probably couldn't even come to visit her at her family home in Seeder lands, assuming even Ivies without powers were susceptible to the lingering poison there. Would she be willing to join him in the Ivy Kingdom? That would be a huge commitment. She shook away the thoughts. She was getting ahead of herself.

At the end of the night, Magda pulled out thin pads and blankets for Guillen and Rachel to sleep on in the living room. "Sorry, you know how it is," Magda said.

"Don't we all," Rachel lied, as though she'd experienced the daily discomfort of stunt life. The couch was too short for either of them, but a padded floor was still better than a forest floor.

They wished each other a good night and settled in after all lights were out. Rachel lay on her side, facing away from Guillen.

"Are you warm enough?" he asked.

"Mmm. I'm perfect," she replied, already half-asleep. "Plus, I can warm myself if I get cold."

A moment passed, and she opened her eyes. *Wait a second. After a week of camping in the elements in the Neutral Woods, he asks me if I'm warm now? In a sheltered building? Is he offering … to cuddle?*

"You know what, it is a bit chilly," she lied.

She smiled as he shuffled behind her. Then he draped another blanket over her.

Stupid chivalry. "Thanks. Good night."

***

By the time Rachel woke in the morning, Guillen had folded up his pad and blanket. He sat on the couch, reading a book.

"Good morning, sunshine," he said once she stirred.

After stretching and pulling her shirt back down, she rose from the floor and folded her own bedding, before joining him on the small couch. "Is the book any good?"

He shrugged, setting it down on the floor. "Just passing the time. How did you sleep?"

She had woken up a time or two, and remembered some nightmares, though nothing too intense. "I've had worse."

He gazed into her eyes. "You know you can talk to me about them, right? And anything, if you want, if you're ready."

She scratched her arm. "Thanks. You're sweet." She wasn't ready to talk about it. Especially not with him, no matter how great he was at talking about hard stuff. It was complicated—having a romantic interest in the cousin of your ex-boyfriend who kidnapped, tortured, and assaulted you was *definitely* complicated. "You know what I'd love to hear about?" She reached up, cupping the side of his face and rubbing the scar on his temple. "Of course, only if you want to tell me."

He bit his lip. "That ... is a reminder of the day I learned I needed to stand up for myself, that I couldn't always depend on others. That's when I picked up a blade and decided I was tired of being treated like I was nothing." He leaned into her cradling hand, not breaking eye contact. "My mother had a temper when I was a boy."

She'd expected a story about injuring himself as a little boy, or getting in a fistfight, or something like that. She frowned as a coldness struck her heart. "Your mom did this to you?"

"It's okay. She's calmed down a lot over the years."

Rachel shook her head. "No wonder you're so nice to me. You understand crazy families and how things can get so messed up."

He let out a short breathy chuckle.

She looked down, pulling her hand from his face. "I do worry, sometimes..."

"What?" He moved a hand to caress her cheek, a look of concern on his face.

"I worry that you're nice to me just because you're a nice guy." Her heart raced. "And not because you like me ... the way I like you."

They locked eyes.

In no time flat, Guillen closed the gap, brushing his lips against hers. Smooth, sweet, perfect. He quickly pulled away. "Sorry, I should have aske—"

"Yes."

"Yes?" He lifted his eyebrows.

"Yes." Her smile grew as she leaned in, kissing him back. And he did not disappoint. His hands may have been rough from hard work, but his lips were perfectly soft. He moved his hand to the nape of her neck, drawing her closer.

The click of a door behind Rachel pulled them away from each other.

Guillen hid a sheepish grin behind his fist, looking past Rachel. "Hey, Magda. Good morning."

Rachel wiped her lips off, blushing. Guillen subtly tapped a finger next to his eye.

Crap! She closed her eyes, unable to stop smiling, and focused on bottling up her energy. She reopened them and looked at him. He winked that all was well. They hadn't even told his friends yet that she was a Seeder. They were going to feel out the meeting that night to see when it would be best to divulge that information.

"When Guillen said he was bringing a friend with him, he didn't mention *that* kind of friend," Magda teased as she passed them on the way to the kitchen.

Guillen cleared his throat. "Can I offer a hand in there?"

"No, I'm good. You two … don't mind me."

Rachel suppressed a laugh. It wasn't like they'd go back to kissing. It was a tiny place, and they were in full view of the kitchen. But they did sit there, holding hands, and chatting with Magda as she made everyone breakfast. Jacob came out of their bedroom and helped set the table as Magda finished up.

"Jacob, our Guillen has been keeping a secret from us," she kidded, and Guillen's face grew pink. Magda whispered loudly, "Elizabeth isn't just a friend." Then it was Rachel's turn to blush.

Jacob raised his eyebrows, smirking. "Really? This is the first time we've met one of Guillen's girlfriends. Why didn't you just say so?"

"It's…" Guillen looked at Rachel. "New."

Trying to stifle a laugh, Rachel instead snorted, which only made her laugh harder. *Right. New. Less-than-an-hour new.*

That garnered her some mixed looks.

"We expect to know all the details," Magda insisted as the group dug into breakfast.

They could hardly share the truth while keeping Rachel's identity a secret.

"We met through family, actually," Guillen offered up.

Rachel pushed around her parsnip hash with a fork, reveling in the ironic truth. They wouldn't have ever met if his cousin hadn't kidnapped her, so … it wasn't a lie.

Magda demanded more information, but Guillen told her they couldn't share too much, that some of their backstory had to do with secret Unitas business. She relented. "Alright, well, you make a cute couple. I hope you know what a great guy you've got here," she told Rachel, pointing at Guillen with a fork.

Rachel smirked. "I know. He is." He rested a hand on her knee under the table, and shivers raced up her spine. She blinked and double-checked that she was controlling her energy.

Chapter 15

GUILLEN AND RACHEL OFFERED TO clean up the kitchen while Magda and Jacob headed out for work. The meeting they were there for would happen at 7 p.m. They'd have all day in Community Ten.

"Make yourselves at home," Magda said on her way out. "And make sure to show her the garden."

Rachel stood at the sink washing dishes while Guillen wiped down the small dining table. His arms wrapped around her waist from behind, and she took a sudden, deep breath.

"Hey." She beamed.

"Hey back." He planted a kiss on her neck and reached up, removing her hand from the water pump.

Setting down her washcloth, she turned around; he rested his hands on her hips. His bright eyes were mesmerizing.

"I figured we might be able to try that again. Without interruption." His handsome smile lured her in.

"I mean…" She sighed and rolled her eyes. "If you want." She giggled at his stink eye.

He leaned in, taking his time to sweetly graze her lips with his. A fire was burning, radiating from her heart and reaching across her entire body. Her hands grasped the fabric of his shirt, pulling him closer. He matched her enthusiasm by pressing against her; she was snug against the counter now. As she offered more, his breathing picked up; he didn't hold back in the slightest. After a couple of minutes, he pulled back, catching his breath.

She, too, was catching her breath. If he hadn't still been holding her against the counter, she might not be standing at all at that point. *That* was the kind of kiss girls dreamed of.

He gazed into her eyes. "I've waited my whole life for you." He raised a hand, tenderly brushing aside some of her bangs. "How can you be so beautiful both ways?"

His whole life? He was moving … *fast*. But it also felt completely natural. She looked up; her hair was glowing Seeder-blond, a change that only happened with extreme emotion, much more intense than a simple glow of the eyes.

She swallowed, still catching her breath. "You don't mind the changes?"

"Are you kidding me?" He maintained eye contact. "Not even a little."

She blushed. "I wouldn't change a thing about you."

He responded with a contented grin and gave her a single peck before stepping back. "Let's finish up here."

She nodded and steadied herself, getting back to cleaning the dishes with a perma-smile. He grabbed a hand towel and dried.

When they finished, Rachel leaned against the counter, facing Guillen. "So … we have all day?"

"Yeah, I can show you around some more. We can grab lunch and dinner before the meeting. Do you have any requests?"

"Would you hate it if we bummed around here for a little while?" she asked.

He raised his eyebrows. "Because…?"

She didn't want him getting the wrong idea, that she was looking to make out all day. "Just to talk, and spend some time where we don't have to pretend to hardly know each other."

He set down his drying rag. "Of course."

They sat down on the couch and held hands, facing each other.

"Jacob said you've never brought a girlfriend around here?"

"That's because none of my previous girlfriends were worth the investment and introduction."

She chuckled. "Yeah. And they weren't here with you as a spy."

He scolded her with his eyes. "I mentioned the reason that mattered."

She rubbed the backs of his hands with her thumbs. "Is that what this is? Am I your girlfriend?"

"If that's what you want." He pursed his lips. "If you think you can get over the guy who gave you the flower. You seemed pretty attached."

She narrowed her eyes at his razzing. "I'll remind you that I know at least one place where you're ticklish."

He shot her a seductive look. "And I'll remind you I'm willing to find out where yours are."

She chuckled again and shook her head. "I like you."

"Come here." He opened his arms, and she snuggled against his chest. He held her close, whispering, "I've liked you for a while now." He gave her a gentle squeeze. "Kaylah would always show me pictures and tell me stories about her best friend. I knew you were beautiful, and that there was something special about you. And I saw that right away when we met."

"In that stupid prom dress."

"Right. That dress." Her body moved with his as he drew a deep breath. "I knew you had just been through a lot, and things were complicated. I didn't want to scare you off. But I thought about you every day after I had to leave you."

"I thought about you a lot, too," she whispered. "I feel safe with you." After a lifetime of lies and manipulation, she needed extra assurances if she was going to put her heart on the line again. "But … I need to be with someone that will be absolutely honest with me, about everything. Can you promise me that?"

"I can."

Every last muscle she hadn't even realized was tense, relaxed as she molded to his body. "I was so worried about you while you were gone. I'm really glad you're okay."

They sat cuddling for several minutes. He broke the peaceful calm with a whisper. "I know I've already asked, but are you alright? After everything that happened?"

She frowned. "I don't know."

"Have you been able to talk about it with anyone?"

She buried her head deeper into his chest. She had shared details with others, but not in depth, and with liberal censorship. "Not really."

"It helps to talk. I'd be willing to listen."

Her eyes filled with tears. "I'm not ready for that yet."

"That's okay." He hugged her tighter as her tears wetted his shirt.

She stayed in his arms for over an hour. Once she'd finished crying, she rested her eyes and let his body warmth heal her. She shifted in his arms, and he reciprocated with a kiss on her head.

"We should probably go do something, shouldn't we?" she asked.

"If you want to."

Sitting up, she faced him. "Thank you."

He acknowledged her words with a sympathetic smile.

Rachel went to the bathroom to finish getting ready for the day. Guillen took his turn while she perched on the back of the couch, glancing around the kitchen area. Everything was compact and purposeful in these tiny apartments. It wasn't likely she'd see the kitchen of a regular Ivy community home while on this mission, though her curiosity was piqued.

Guillen emerged from the bathroom and rested his hands on her waist. "Are you ready for this?"

She scrunched her face. "I guess."

"What's that about?"

"It's going to be twice as hard pretending I don't care about you, as pretending I'm not a spy."

He grinned and stole a kiss. "I know. But even Jacob and Magda agree it's for the best that we appear unattached. And they don't even understand it all…"

She sighed.

"We'll have tonight, after the meeting." He tucked a strand of hair behind her ear. "How do you feel about … um … cuddling tonight?"

She smirked. "To keep me warm? Because there are plenty of blankets here."

He threw his head back and laughed at her calling him out. "Come here, you." He started to kiss her again.

A key turning in the front door brought them back to reality.

"Your eyes," he whispered.

Rachel turned away from the door, toward the hallway, and closed her eyes to get things back in check. This was so hard with Guillen. She wished they would get it over with and tell Magda and Jacob she was a Seeder; they'd find out that night anyway. But he insisted they wait. He knew these people better than Rachel did, and had been a successful spy for quite some time now. He leaned in, covering Rachel more from the front door's immediate field of view.

"Well, hello again," Guillen greeted the intruder.

"Have you two seriously been here the whole time?" Magda's voice conveyed playful surprise.

Rachel gently pushed Guillen back. "Sorry, that's me. I was really tired; I just wanted some more rest. We were literally on our way out."

"She's not lying," he backed her up. "What are you home for at this time of day?"

"I forgot the lunch I packed."

"Well, that won't do. Grab it, and we'll take off with you."

He gave Rachel's hand a last reassuring squeeze before dropping it as they followed Magda out and headed down the street.

***

For the next few hours, Guillen took Rachel around the community, showing her the pantry, a ruddy little pub, and workshops. Along the way, he introduced her to a few people in the area, most of whom he anticipated being at the meeting that night, though they discussed no such topic in public. He smoothly called her Elizabeth and only a couple of times got a tidbit too close physically for an 'acquaintance.'

As Magda had recommended, they spent a good deal of time in the community garden. Almost all of the food needed for the entire community was grown here. It was as massive and lush as any Seeder family garden, though much larger, as it had to feed hundreds. Honey bees hovered from one squash blossom to another. Small vibrant-red birds landed occasionally to enjoy a buffet of beetles.

As much as Rachel enjoyed, or wanted to enjoy, the brilliant array of colors represented in the wide assortment of produce, her eyes kept landing on something unsettling—Mother Vines.

Propped up on a towering wooden structure in the center of the garden, the Mother Vine threw twisted tendrils into the soil. The tendrils were as thick as her thumb, the main Vine as wide as her arm.

Rachel's stomach physically hurt at the sight of it. Her arms, where leaves of the War Vines had once dug in to drain her of her energy, also ached.

"It's okay," Guillen reassured her, standing close. "They're not trained to do the same thing."

Rachel hugged herself. Kaylah had already explained that to her. The Mother Vines connected the communities in the Ivy Kingdom, distributing nutrients as they were 'trained'—essentially programmed—to do. They also kept a strong protective barrier around the palace. They weren't a weapon; they were central to the Ivy people's powers, their culture. The Mother Vines were a revered piece of every Ivy's identity, and what made a woman in the right bloodline a queen.

She'd have to get used to the sight of them, too. They stretched across the entire kingdom, on structures visible from the main highways, propped up like human power lines, just as this one was propped up.

"I know," Rachel said. Knowing the facts only barely took the edge off of seeing them. They literally couldn't hurt her. The way Kaylah had described them, Mother Vines didn't have sentience, but they did have a strict allegiance. A previous queen had trained them for their task, and without a change in orders, they continued to do their job, even without Kaylah's presence. Her mother's death had passed that allegiance down to Kaylah. She could do as she wished with the Mother Vines, but only by retraining them at the roots, which were dispersed throughout the kingdom, as opposed to the War Vines which were rooted at the palace, and continued to shred through Seeder borders.

"It's illegal to harm them, not that damaging them is even an easy feat," Guillen said. "But you can touch them."

Rachel stood still, considering. They looked *exactly* like the War Vines. Completely indistinguishable. If anything, she wanted to take a few steps back. But perhaps this could be helpful, like one of those therapies where people terrified of snakes force themselves to hold a harmless little garter snake.

She hesitantly stepped forward, bolstered by Guillen's hand on her back. Touching a tendril and a leaf brought flashbacks to when she was with Prince Soren back in the human world. Her trepidation was traded for pain. Crossing her arms, she decided it was enough to be in close proximity to them instead.

"Do you know what they say about the Mother Vines?" Guillen asked.

Rachel shook her head.

"They have eyes and ears."

Rachel side-eyed the Vine, then looked back at Guillen. "What?"

"Well…" He tucked his hands into his pants pockets. "It's just a silly personification, you know? They're plants. Powers or not, they don't actually have eyes and ears. They can't see or hear. But it's a saying." He reached out, running a finger along one of the tendrils. "It's a saying that aims to keep people in line. Across the kingdom, there are royal enforcers, law enforcement. They don't take too kindly to talk that doesn't agree with the royal family and their policies. Some people are superstitious enough to think the Vines have something to do with it. I think they just don't want to imagine their neighbors capable of turning them in."

Recalling something Jacob had said when they'd first met, Rachel furrowed her brow. "Jacob said something about that. Eyes and ears."

Guillen chuckled. "Yeah. 'Happy to be the eyes and ears on the eyes and ears.' Just his way of saying that we can be as secretive as those in power, that we're keeping our eyes on them, and plan to hold them accountable."

***

They sat down for dinner at the café, chatting about their day. The café was a breath of fresh air, really the only public place in the community with some décor. A little mural of the gardens was painted on one of the walls. In such a small community, with its residents paid so poorly, the café didn't need to be large. There were only eight little square tables.

"There are a lot of nice people here," she said, making sure to speak quietly under the chatter of a dozen other patrons.

Guillen stabbed a chunk of roasted potato with his fork. "You're surprised?"

"Of course not. I just wish people could see each other this way. Without labels and blame."

He smiled and shook his head. "*That* is precisely why you're here."

She sat back and sipped her water. "You know, now that I think about it, *you* are the reason I'm here."

He lifted his eyebrows in question as he brought his fork to his mouth.

She chuckled. "Not just for the," she cleared her throat, "exciting, new reason. But if I hadn't met you and the others," her eyes darted around the dining room, "the way I did … I would have held just as much prejudice as most others. You're better than me. You came to that conclusion on your own." She bit her lip. "You're the best man I know."

He blushed. "I don't deserve that much credit. Kaylah's an astonishing advocate. And you were her best friend growing up. You play a larger role in this than you allow yourself to believe, so the credit goes back to you." He winked.

She sighed. "How about let's toast to her, then. Without her, none of this would be possible."

They each raised their glass. "To Kaylah."

As they clinked, the elderly waitress returned to refill their glasses. "That's right! To Princess Kaylah, may we get her back from the weeds, sooner than later!" She filled their glasses and moved on.

Rachel had averted her eyes at the woman's pronouncement, stabbing at the last few morsels on her plate. When she looked up, Guillen searched her eyes as though unsure how she'd react to her people being called the filthy nickname. Rachel grinned. "She's right. We all want the princess safe, don't we?"

He stifled a laugh.

They moved on to dessert, a tropical pudding of some sort, as they had time to kill before the meeting.

"You said each of these communities is different based on the industry they provide, but are they all basically like this?" she asked.

"More or less. The closer you get to the palace, the richer people are, so that's why I'm in construction over there. People can afford bigger houses. All the way out here, the woods are still decent; that's why the main industry here is lumber."

She furrowed her brow. "From what you showed me, there's a ton of industry that takes place here. And not that many apartments. How does that balance out?"

"The factories and mills have a private entry for prisoner escorts. Prisons are situated outside of these communities, but they're used for labor as much as my kind."

She shook her head. "Prisoners? And lumber seems like a stretch for this community. The woods are still pretty thin compared to what I've seen. And the community gardens… That garden seemed barely adequate for the people here."

He leaned close so as to not be overheard. "That's one of the things people don't understand. Your temple roots, they transfer energy to your security walls. Our Mother Vines are kind of like that. But since your people aren't the aggressors, we don't focus our resources so much on one place like you do. Instead, the individual communities feed the nutrients from their soil to the palace, and the palace then distributes them as they like. It wasn't always that way. People relinquished their freedoms."

He leaned back, frustration growing on his face. "People blame irresponsible rifting habits for our lack of vegetation, but that's only one factor. Some of it is the Mother Vines. One person calls it progress. Another calls it prison. I think even regular Ivies should have more say over their own communities."

Rachel suppressed a smirk—Kaylah had talked like that once before. Which of the two had first phrased it that way? "So, it's like socialism? Or communism? I guess when I imagine royalty, it's something that's gone back for several centuries. I don't know how it is that people vote on having rulership like that."

He shrugged. "I don't know what those words mean. And honestly, you won't find the truth in what they teach in schools. At least not without a significant spin on it."

Setting her dessert spoon down, she grimaced. "Politics. No thank you… I was kinda surprised, though, that there weren't any jewelry shops, art galleries, museums, libraries—any of it. I mean, these are small communities, but *nothing* beyond the basic necessities? Well, and the pub, I suppose that's not a necessity. But I got the impression Ivies were more … well … different and more focused on that kind of stuff, compared to Seeders." She winced at the description. "More materialistic."

Guillen blew out a puff of air, pushing his bowl to the edge of the table. "Well, the pub replaces a good deal of interests. Alcohol can be easily brewed nearby, and booze takes minds off of hard work and hard times. It also makes for loose lips and loose wome—" His mouth hung open for a second. He looked positively mortified.

Rachel's eyes grew wide in shock. She hadn't expected something like that to come from Guillen. "Please, do continue."

"I… You know I'm not like that, right? I don't even drink. It's just … what people say."

He didn't seem the type, and she considered razzing him a bit for saying it, but decided to let it go. "So, free time consists of cooking and cleaning, drinking and," she raised an eyebrow, "related activities. And time in the garden." He'd already explained how strict stunt rules and restrictions were about possessions and travel; it was all rather ridiculous.

"That's basically it. There's plenty of the rest of it—art, jewelry, libraries—throughout the kingdom. Just not in a stunt community." His voice rarely carried resentment, and now was no exception.

She huffed, then bit down on the insides of her cheeks. These people weren't worth 'wasting' the 'finer things in life' on.

He smiled in appreciation of her silent protest. "We should head out. Let's go change things."

Chapter 16

THE SECRET MEETING WAS HELD in a community classroom. It wasn't fair to compare these communities to cruel concentration camps, but the stunts who lived there were treated like second-class citizens. Once they were taken from their family homes at the age of fourteen, they were no longer offered formal education; they didn't need school. But each community had a small building. It was multipurpose, helpful if training was needed for a shift in industry, if the guards needed to meet, for celebrations, that sort of thing. It reminded Rachel a lot of Seeder log huts used for education.

Having set everything up, Jacob was the first there. He welcomed Guillen and Rachel in.

Jacob stood at the door, greeting people and introducing them to Guillen and 'Elizabeth' as they trickled in. Magda gave Rachel a huge smile before sitting down. In total, there were just over a dozen new faces for Rachel. They had only invited those they were certain could be trusted, the most outspoken in the community against the treatment of their kind.

Rachel's anxiety bubbled as Guillen invited her to stand next to him at the head of the room. She looked over the crowd, her heart calming at seeing Jacob and Magda holding hands. Jacob was now sitting right next to the door, acting as guard. Magda sat beside him. Guillen had told Rachel how much they wished they could have a child. Just one. But they weren't allowed. This was personal for them.

Being born without powers was a random fluke of nature. But there *had* to be some sort of genetic component to it—if even *one* of the parents was a stunt, the child was also born without powers. The lack of powers was *always* passed down. Many people in society considered stunts inferior simply because they lacked powers, but others plainly saw them as a threat, as a curse. Like Kaylah had once explained about Ivy fears of Seeders overpopulating the Green Lands, Ivies feared losing themselves and their unique abilities if they allowed stunts to mingle with their peers with powers, or to even have kids at all.

Guillen spoke first in the meeting. He had prepared the whole presentation. They'd touched on points Rachel felt comfortable addressing, but he'd give her the green light after feeling out the room.

"Thank you, everyone, for making the sacrifice to be here. I'm honored to stand in this room with like-minded people. People who care about each other, and real equality." He gained some nods from around the room.

"My friend and I are here with a proposal. Something we know for certain will *finally* make a real change for our kind." He paused. "I think we first need to discuss the truth about our former queen and king, and Princess Kaylah."

"Screw them all!" a woman spat. "I hope she rots in enemy hands. Their family has had *decades* to do better!"

Rachel was taken aback by the woman's passion. Did this woman realize Guillen was Kaylah's cousin?

He tilted his head to the side thoughtfully. "You're right. They could have done better. And they will. The first thing you should know is that the queen and king were *not* assassinated by Seeder hands. Prince Soren was behind it."

Looks of confusion and whispers were exchanged around the room.

"I understand most of you don't know me all that well." He lifted his sleeve to show the royal insignia in the middle of his mark. "I'm close enough to know the truth. You can take my word on it." His voice filled the room with strength and authority. Rachel smiled at seeing this new side of him.

"The stories about Princess Kaylah are also false. She's the reason we're here."

Rachel watched the room, checking their expressions for buy-in. It was too early to tell.

"She's perfectly safe. The palace doesn't want our people to know she's turned from their ways. The kind of ways that weaken our lands, that fight senseless wars, that treat people like you and me as though we're only good for labor others don't want to do."

"Do you mean … the rebellion?" a man near the back cautiously asked.

"Yes. Princess Kaylah is in charge of the rebellion. I don't know what rumors you've heard, but we're here on her behalf. To forge an alliance. She cares deeply about the injustices of our people."

There were a lot of wide eyes and open mouths.

One man scowled. "The rebellion is about the war; I don't see how that has to do with us. If that's true, she's just a weed-lover."

"Please don't use that term," Guillen reproached him, crossing his arms. "And the rebellion has a larger scope to it. Yes, she wants to end this war. She wants to stop wasting our resources and tossing aside the lives of our people. She wants to grant people like us equal opportunities." He paused. "And yes, part of her plan involves the Seeders. I'm sure I've met more Seeders than any of you. They're decent people."

Several heads shook, many of them mumbling. None of them would have ever met a Seeder. Not on the battleground, not in the course of their daily lives.

"You may not want to believe it, but the Seeders care about the treatment in these communities. They want to fight for us, and are asking that we join in the efforts."

"That's the biggest lie I've heard all night!" a bitter-sounding woman yelled. "All they care about is watching out for themselves. This is just empty promises for us to stick our necks out."

Guillen looked at Rachel and nodded.

Rachel cleared her throat and tried to stand tall. "It's not a lie. They do care. I would know." She lit up her eyes to full glow.

The room *erupted*.

"Are you kidding me?!"

"You brought one here?!"

"I didn't sign up for this!"

Rachel choked down a lump in her throat as her heart raced. A lot of angry and skeptical glances swept over her. Jacob stood at attention in front of the door, ensuring no one could exit. His face held a look of contempt, or perhaps betrayal. He clearly didn't appreciate the surprise.

Guillen moved closer to Rachel, placing his hand on her back, brandishing one of his knives in the other hand and pointing it at a couple of aggressive attendees. "Sit down and listen! Don't be fools."

Rachel's eyes rested on Magda, and her heart shattered. Magda looked murderous with rage, her eyes burning a hole right through Rachel.

"You're here to listen, so shut up and listen!" Guillen boomed. "Give her a chance."

The room begrudgingly calmed as everyone sat back down.

"Go ahead," Guillen whispered. Rachel took a step away from him, so his hand was no longer on her back. Magda had been glancing between the two, and by the look she was giving her, she clearly didn't think Rachel was good enough for her friend, not anymore.

Rachel found her voice. "It's true. Everything he says. We didn't kill your queen and king. And Princess Kaylah is fighting for all of our rights, Ivy and Seeder alike. With or without powers. I know. Because I know her. I've worked alongside her in this movement. And I know Prince Soren and Duke Nuren. I was taken from my people and tortured at the palace, personally, at their hands."

Her eyes glowed green, not as part of a show, but as a result of her struggling to deliver the personally gutting speech she'd prepared. Her story softened a few expressions.

"I don't expect you to pity me. Ivies and Seeders, we fight, right? It's war. There are casualties. People get hurt. I don't matter to you. But your people matter to the movement. It's called Unitas. It means Unity. My people, we didn't know your people treated you this way. I was personally enraged when I found out." She and Guillen shared a knowing glance. "And now that we know, we *are* willing to fight for you, too. Seeders have people just like you, and we don't restrict them this way. We just want to live our lives in peace. And we believe you deserve the same rights as anyone else in the Green Lands. We can help each other." She stepped back, silent.

"She volunteered to take a mark; she wasn't forced to," Guillen added. "She walked across the Neutral Woods to come here, endangering her own life. That should hold some weight."

They spent the next hour discussing what Unitas was offering and asking for. Soren overlooked these communities, vastly underestimating the power held there. These people could slow production. Lose supplies. They could reach out to family members in other communities.

The night hadn't gone as smoothly as Rachel and Guillen had hoped, but the participants were more or less pacified and rallied by the end, and interested in their proposals. They reminded the group of their oath of secrecy, and invited them back for another meeting the next night to discuss more.

Only one Ivy approached Rachel at the end and shook her hand, thanking her. The rest filed out. Magda had been one of the first to leave, and Jacob lingered by the door. Guillen and Rachel walked up to him hesitantly.

"I guess that could have gone better," Guillen said.

Jacob's gaze flickered from Guillen to Rachel, then back. He pressed his lips into a thin line. "You could say that. We'll talk."

"Thanks, Jacob. For all you're doing," Rachel offered.

"You guys head back. I'll lock up here. Magda and I are going to take a walk, so we might be a while."

Guillen and Rachel quietly ambled through the dark streets. "We knew our first meeting might be bumpy." He failed to comfort her.

"Yeah," she whispered in defeat.

They got back to the empty apartment, and Guillen locked the door behind them, turning and offering Rachel a hug.

"She hates me," she squeaked into his shoulder.

He rubbed her back. "They just need time. We threw a lot at them."

She knew that. She hadn't expected fanfare in the meeting. But Magda's disapproval in particular pierced her. They had only known each other for a day, but they'd shared an instant connection. One that had corroded in the flash of a Seeder's eye.

Rachel and Guillen sat on the living room floor, opposite the doorway, holding hands. They didn't want to be on the couch with their backs to the entry when Jacob and Magda returned. When a key twisted in the door, Rachel took her hand back and shifted away from Guillen. Magda walked in alone. She glared with contempt at Rachel as she stalked past without a word, slamming her bedroom door behind her.

"It'll be okay," Guillen soothed.

A minute later, Jacob showed up. He poked his head in. "Can we talk?"

Guillen nodded and got up, giving Rachel a reassuring look before shutting the door behind him. Mumbles traveled through the wall, and she was grateful they hadn't walked away. Not that Magda was trained in fighting, and Rachel had her knife and Seeder blades. And she didn't expect Magda to leave her room to try anything, but still…

Guillen came back in after several minutes, his face marred with disappointment. He rejoined Rachel as Jacob entered the apartment and locked the door. Jacob turned to the both of them. "I'm sorry. Good night."

Rachel fidgeted with her hands as Jacob disappeared into his bedroom. "What did he mean by that?"

"They'll still help. We haven't lost them. They just…" He frowned and grabbed her hand. "They're letting us stay the night, but you and I are going to find somewhere else to stay in the morning." He forced a smile. "We'll grab some breakfast and spend the *whole* day together again."

"They're kicking us out?" Tears came to her eyes. "I thought she liked me. I thought she'd understand."

He wiped away some errant tears from her cheek as his own eyes moistened. "I really didn't think she would react that way. But … that's part of why we were supposed to just be friends, right? Or at least appear that way. Not add more complexities to the issues?"

She nodded. "Did he tell you why she reacted that way?"

"Honestly, this is more about me than you, okay? I have a precarious place in these communities." He held her gaze. "None of their misguided opinions about you, or us, mean anything to me, okay? Just … asking people who are focused on equality for their own people to start caring about ending a war with the enemy is a huge leap. Then asking them to be okay with a relationship like ours … it's a lot."

"I know." Her voice betrayed her as she struggled to choke back a fresh batch of tears. "That doesn't mean it doesn't hurt."

They set out their bedding and lay down to sleep. She would have been happy not staying there at all, but with curfew so close and guards patrolling the community, they couldn't risk raising suspicion. Guillen insisted on still sleeping close to her, for safety, but not nearly as close as either would have wanted earlier that same day.

Chapter 17

BACK IN THE TRAINING CAMP on the edge of Seeder lands, the diverse Unitas group was steadily growing in numbers. They'd successfully found a good cave in the human world to link to the one they'd created in the Green Lands. Saff was excited to greet newcomers as more and more Seeder girls could come home safely, now without Ivy escort. The Ivies who had been spending time on transport duty could focus their efforts elsewhere. Brothers and fathers of Seeder girls were able to come home early to help with defense on the home front. Where the Ivy War Vines lacked extra umph in piercing through the border walls, their troops made up for it with increasingly brazen attacks, the soldiers' zeal fueled by Soren's propaganda, as he hid away in the comfort of the Ivy palace.

In the human realm, Saff's contacts and those of other Seeders caused the Unitas network to grow exponentially. Some Seeders decided to pull all family members at once, placing the unbloomed in Unitas safe houses. Tensions rose as Soren ordered extra searches to try to bring back more girls to power the primed War Vines.

***

Saff and Kaylah sat together one morning, sipping coffee and preparing for the perpetual grind of war.

"Thanks again for requesting Devin's help," Saff said. "It means a lot to me, to have him here."

"No problem." Kaylah's shaky smile was soon replaced by a frown. "I know how hard it is being separated from the one you love."

"I'm sorry you haven't been able to go see Eric. He's really mature for his age. You got a good one."

"Thanks. He knew it might be tough. But he loves me. And sometimes that's enough, right?" Kaylah rubbed her hands together and stood up. "And about your husband… I did have it on good authority that he's great at training your girls on their energy." She gave a more genuine smile.

"He *did* come with some amazing references, didn't he?" Saff chuckled, then became more serious. "Still no word on Rachel?"

Kaylah shook her head. "I don't expect any for a while. They had a lot of travel to get there, but I'm sure they're fine. They're both capable. And he'll take good care of her."

Having Devin there with her had been a balm to Saff's soul, but she still worried about Rachel daily.

She took another sip of her coffee, cringing, wishing she'd made tea instead.

Kaylah sifted through some paperwork, sighing. "I really hope today's briefing is less brutal than yesterday's."

Saff set her mug on the floor, the canvas of the tent whipping behind her in the wind. "Brutal, huh?"

"You didn't hear?" Kaylah's lips puckered in obvious annoyance. "Yeah, well, a few of your people thought they were being *so* clever, expanding on their usual tactics."

Saff had no idea what that was supposed to mean. "Come again?"

"You know, the jade charms."

"Gonna need more than that."

"You know, the lies they tell their children." Kaylah sat back down. "Well, I guess you don't all use the same playbook. How did your parents convince you to wear your jade charm without telling you the truth about your identity?"

"Actually…" Saff smiled fondly. "They didn't. Devin gave it to me as a gift, and it was our little secret. We were kind of … sneaking around behind our parents' backs."

Kaylah splayed a hand across her chest, feigning shock. "Our dear Saff, the most upright Seeder, with an impeccable moral compass, a rebellious teenager?" She tutted.

Saff fought a grin. "Anyway, what about the jade charms?"

Kaylah frowned again. "Yeah, that's not a joking matter. Anyway, it sounds like most human host parents play the charm off as a naturopathic healing stone. Once their daughter's bloom starts, they get sick. So the parents say it's a 'healing' stone, and that's how they convince their girls to wear it all the time without worrying them about assassins for a few more months."

"Okay." Saff had never fixated on how other families took care of that particular part of the process. It sounded like a decent plan.

"Right, well, some families weren't too keen on the idea of trusting Unitas safe houses, so they got the bright idea to take to social media about the jade charms instead."

"What?!"

Kaylah held up a finger. "Popularizing *fake* jade charms. Well, it might have been real jade, but not from here. But they went to the lengths of sourcing manufacturers to make the charms, and then paying social media influencers to make them the next fad."

Saff laughed. If Soren's assassins came across a school full of girls wearing jade, they'd completely lose their advantage in the hunt. "That actually sounds brilliant. Now they can't tell who the Seeder girls are anymore."

Kaylah wasn't laughing. She silently nodded. "You're right. It really was a brilliant idea. But I have a feeling the half dozen murdered human girls would beg to disagree."

That sobered Saff up real quick. "What do you mean?"

Kaylah sat straighter in her chair. "I'm sure by now, the assassin networks know they can't just spot a jade charm around a girl's neck and kidnap her. But those first few they tried … when they didn't bloom, when they couldn't be forced through a rift and taken to the palace to hook up to the War Vines… Yeah, they couldn't have witnesses."

Saff's heart ached for them and their families. Seeders made it a point to try to keep humans safe and out of their affairs as much as possible. These girls wouldn't have even been part of host families, knowingly taking on the risk. They were just teenage girls following a trend.

A male Seeder announced himself and entered the tent. "Princess, we have your morning updates."

Saff stood to leave, still shaken.

"You're fine, stay." Kaylah motioned for her to sit back down.

He looked at a piece of paper with notes. "From the human world, we've been informed there's been more suspicious public news reports."

Saff and Kaylah looked at each other, eyebrows raised.

"What kind of reports?" Kaylah asked.

"Disappearances. Attacks. Nothing giving away specifics of our realm … but the actions are catching attention."

"Related to yesterday's news?"

He shook his head. "No, ma'am. It all sounded like regular assassin hunting activity. And the disappearances all matched up to families that have fled to Unitas safe houses."

Saff's muscles relaxed a bit. "I'm surprised the assassins aren't being more careful."

Kaylah gave a disingenuous smile. "If Soren wins, and your people are all dead, they have no reason to even go to the human world. The humans aren't exactly able to come here and prosecute my people, are they? It just means he's taking it seriously." She turned to the guard. "As for our part, we'll talk about how we can work on being more discreet while ensuring safety."

"Alright." He looked back down at his paper. "There was another fight last night."

Kaylah rubbed her temples, and Saff could only feel sorry for her. There had been a handful of altercations already in camp. From a brief argument, to a decent fight with injuries that had required healing. "What about?"

"The usual. It was a couple of Seeders and an Ivy, ma'am."

The usual. That was code for: Kaylah couldn't please everyone. Seeders were starting to resent her plans because she wasn't actively taking on the palace, to end the war, to get back their tortured girls. But it wasn't that simple. Security at the palace had been at least doubled or tripled. She insisted they allow more time for Guillen and Rachel, and others, to grow support from inside the kingdom, for a successful takeover.

Some Ivies also found themselves less than dazzled at the camp. The conditions were significantly humbler than they were used to, and some hadn't fully thought out their commitment. Fearing one might change their mind, Kaylah and the Seeder council had decreed that any Ivy who came to the camp (with the exclusion of her most trusted spies and transport help) was required to stay in camp. Bitterness was growing about not being able to leave.

"I don't know what they expect me to do!" Kaylah balled her fists.

Saff grimaced. She and Kaylah had already discussed all of this, but surely there had to be something they could do differently… "You're sure there's no way to speed up your timeline? I know you're working on a way to rift within the Green Lands, and on how to get the unbloomed back, but those really don't seem like the priority."

Kaylah closed her eyes, breathing deeply. "We need to give you-know-who and the others more time. As we get more progress reports, maybe we can reassess. But we need them. And I'm not giving up on my other goals while we wait."

It wasn't like Kaylah didn't have other spies, in addition to Rachel and Guillen.

Kaylah leaned forward. "The cave—that's crucial. Our Mother Vines ensure we have a border that can't be rifted into, even by our own kind. The War Vines have strengthened that twofold. And just like your people discovered during your last attack on the palace, the Vines make it harder to fly above, too. That border's a much smaller defense than your border walls, but it's right around the palace. And that cave is directly on that border."

The messenger stood there, awkwardly waiting for them to stop talking amongst themselves.

"Was there anything else?" Kaylah asked.

He pursed his lips. "Yes, just the one thing. The Ivy from the fight last night—he's missing."

"What do you mean, missing?" Kaylah shot up from her chair.

Knots twisted in Saff's gut.

"Well, from witness accounts, I don't think the argument was so bad that others would have harmed him … but he can't be found anywhere. We think he found a way out of camp overnight."

Kaylah pulled on her hair. "We need to find out what happened. Search again. Look for marks of a rift. A gap in the patrol perimeter. And request extra guards. If he's gone back to the Ivy army, and gives up our location … without the protection of your border walls…"

"Yes, ma'am. I'll talk to our council." He promptly exited the tent.

Kaylah turned back to Saff, who was giving her a sympathetic frown.

"Want to change places?" Kaylah asked.

Saff shook her head. "Not on your life."

***

It was well past dark when Saff and Devin retired to bed. They shared a wide cot, the soft glow of large lightkeepers in the camp shining through the tent fabric.

Saff snuggled up to Devin, thinking over their time together since joining Unitas, and the still-missing Ivy recruit. "How is it so easy for you to accept this change? They've tried to kill us both."

The rest, she left unspoken. The Ivies had also killed Ben—Devin's best friend and Saff's brother—and left Devin's sister, Heather, hurting. Every time a fight broke out in camp, Saff struggled with hope for their cause.

Devin drew a deep breath. "I figure the council wouldn't be working with Kaylah and letting her have this much freedom if she wasn't really trustworthy."

Perhaps that was true. Lionel wasn't Kaylah's constant companion anymore. A different council member had replaced him, and only visited daily, but didn't stay in camp overnight. "Yeah. I don't know. Definitely took me a while."

Devin gently rubbed Saff's upper arm. "Sometimes, I think you forget I'm a soldier. And not a human soldier. A soldier who didn't always know the difference between play and sparring growing up. I follow the council. I follow orders. It works for me."

She snuggled closer. "Sometimes I wish it was that easy for me."

"I don't know about 'easy.' I'd like to think I'm a *smidge* more complicated. That I have a *few* brain cells to think for myself, and that it's not *all* following orders."

She scoffed. "I'd never describe or imply that. I just wish I knew where to draw the line. And was better at following orders, sometimes. You know me."

"Mmm." He kissed her neck. "I *do* know you."

She smiled.

"That's part of why I love you so much," he said. "You keep me on my toes. You might drive me crazy sometimes, but most of the time, I'm just crazy *about* you."

She chuckled. "Either way, you're crazy. Sounds like I might not be good for you."

He pulled her in tighter, leaving another kiss on her neck. "Oh, you're good for me."

She grinned.

"I'd like to think we're good for each other." His voice softened more. "Why haven't you tried out the cave yet?"

She swallowed, frowning. "Just busy, you know?"

"Hmm. You're sure it's not because of our fight? Because I think you should give it a go. When things calm down, imagine the possibility of being able to visit your human parents more often."

She'd thought about it frequently. "I'm scared," she whispered.

Devin shifted in bed, reaching over and tapping a small lightkeeper by him; it lit up. "Why are you scared?"

She gazed into his eyes. "I could have died. I could have left you and everyone else without a goodbye. And this is still experimental."

He held her hand. "Kaylah's certain it would be safe. You understand your extra power capacity now. Others have taken the risk to prove it works without harm."

She looked away, contemplating it. Her fear wasn't rational; she knew that, too.

Devin tucked her hair behind her ear. "I'd hate to see you paralyzed by fear."

She sighed. She hated the idea of fear holding her back as well.

"What if we went together? There and back? I've always said we're better together."

As she gazed into his warm brown eyes, her hesitancy melted. "I'd like that. With you by my side, I think I could tackle it."

He beamed, scooting closer and nuzzling her neck. "Tackling. I'm a fan. Like football. A full-contact sport. I *like* full contact." He nibbled on her ear, and she slapped a hand to her mouth, quickly stifling a laugh that might wake others in nearby tents.

"Don't you feel guilty?" she asked.

He moved back, propping himself up on his side with an elbow. "For what?"

She rested a hand on his exposed chest. "Being together. Being happy. With all the ugly stuff going on in both worlds?"

Devin took a pensive moment before speaking. "No. I don't. We're not twiddling our thumbs out here. We're working hard, every day. But we still deserve to sleep, and eat, and have *a little* bit of time to recharge. Tomorrow's never promised."

She gave him a soft smile. "You're right. I love you."

He returned the smile. "I love you too. Now are you going to get the hint that we should be naked? Or should I take the hint that I need to try to fall asleep?"

A toothy grin spread across her face. "Turn off that lightkeeper."

Chapter 18

RACHEL WOKE TO A PAIR of lips on her forehead. She smiled and opened her eyes.

Guillen smiled back at her. "Hey, beautiful," he whispered. "Let's get going."

Her joy faded as she remembered why they had to quietly pack up and leave so early in the morning. He folded her bedding while she freshened up in the bathroom. She stared at herself in the mirror, flashing her sad eyes green. Did Magda really think she was such a monster because of something as simple as her anatomy? Rachel's natural brown eyes were welcome; but once they glowed green, she became something to hate? They'd been greeted in this little apartment with warmth and love, and in a day's time, it grew cold and they were being turned out without so much as a goodbye.

The streets were still quiet at that early hour. Guillen risked holding her hand as they made their way to the café. They sat, eating pastries on a bench outside.

"Don't worry about tonight. I know exactly where we can stay, and we'll even get a comfortable bed." He tried to cheer her up. "We've got tons of time. How about I take you to a neighboring town? You can check out those art galleries and everything you want."

She shook her head. "It's fine. I can just stay indoors. I don't want to cause any more problems. And I don't want to see that jerk at the entrance again."

"I'll take care of it; we'll go out the other way. I want to show you around. Please?"

"Why can't we just move on to the next community, instead of wasting a whole other day here?" she whined. "I just want to go."

He frowned. "You know we can't do that. We didn't get enough done last night."

"I know." She threw her head back, staring at the cloudy grey sky. "You don't think we'll get rained on, do you?"

"No, we'll be fine. The town I'm thinking of is just over an hour's walk each way; we'll have lots of places we can go to." He lifted her hand, placing a kiss on it. "And we can just be *us*, over there."

She allowed a small smile to spread across her face. They only anticipated spending one or two days at each of the ten stunt communities, depending on when they arrived and when they could rally folks for their meetings. Travel between each community was generally expected to take two to four days on foot with steady speed, and they hoped to cover ground as quickly as possible. But as it was right now, they genuinely didn't have anything to do until the meeting that night. "Alright. I like the sound of that."

He helped her up, and they walked to the opposite end of the community from where they had initially entered.

As soon as she spotted the guard, Rachel grabbed Guillen's arm. "We don't have the paperwork for this. If we show him my papers to leave, he's going to expect me to not return."

"It's okay. Don't take out any paperwork. Let me handle it. Just hang back."

Guillen lifted his sleeve to the guard and was waved through. Instead of moving on, he stood in place and struck up a conversation. He whispered and gestured with his head and hands toward Rachel. The guard shook his head. Guillen reached into his pocket, handing the guard a few things. The guard hesitantly accepted the offer, and Guillen turned to Rachel, winking. "Come on."

She approached, unsure of what to do.

"Let me see your mark," the guard ordered, and she pulled up her sleeve. "Fine. You better be back before my shift is over."

"You know I will be." Guillen grabbed Rachel's hand and guided her out.

"That was too easy," she breathed as they walked down the path, and stashed their belongings in a hedge.

He was beaming. "Sometimes you have to have the right currency."

"It was as simple as bribing him?"

"Not quite. My pockets are lighter, but I also gave him something to hold on to, something he could keep as collateral."

She furrowed her brow. "And that was…?"

"My ring."

Her eyes widened. "Like the one Nuren had? Like the one I've seen Kaylah wear? Isn't that, like, a one-of-a-kind, special thing for royals? I've never even seen you wear it."

He glanced around to make sure they were alone. He stopped and rested his hands on Rachel's waist. "You know I don't care about that stuff. But yes, that kind of ring. I keep it just in case it comes in handy. He knows my word is good—we'll be back for that."

Her very presence had already brought about more problems than solutions. "You're sure it's not going to cause trouble?"

"We will be perfectly fine. It's just a little day trip. Plus," he grinned, "you're the kind of trouble I like."

She fiddled with a button on his shirt, her heart warming. "Thank you. For doing this to cheer me up."

"Anything for you." He gave her a peck on the lips. "Come on. Adventure awaits."

***

After an hour of walking hand in hand, they approached a much larger town. The area was slightly greener, and the houses larger. Guillen wrapped an arm around her as they entered.

"No guards," she noted. "That's nice."

"Nope. Regular citizens are allowed to come and go at their leisure."

Rachel shook away her annoyance, trying to focus on the adventure of her first time in a standard Ivy city. As she'd already noticed, most structures were stone. Rickshaws and bicycles rode down cobblestone streets. She reminded herself Ivies couldn't fly; they would naturally rely on other forms of transportation that were faster than walking. After a few moments of taking in the view, Rachel made an unnerving observation. Other than little boys and elderly male Ivies, there were no men walking the streets. Only girls and women.

"Where is everyone?" The small community she'd just been in had an equal gender ratio, but none of them were considered competent to enlist in the Ivy army.

Guillen hesitated, facing her more directly. "Kaylah told you all able-bodied males are enlisted, right? Ready to be deployed at any moment?"

Her heart dropped. "Are you kidding me? This is practically a ghost town!" she whispered. "You're telling me they've drained the cities and sent them *all* to war?"

He frowned, holding her hand. "You're surprised? It's not like they all went *willingly*. It doesn't mean every city is like this, either."

The only word that came to Rachel's mind was: *millions*. She imagined the Ivy soldiers in droves. In the human world. Marching on Seeder borders. Soren wasn't holding back.

Her heart raced. "Why are we wasting our time here? We need to let Kaylah know. We need to be doing something. Not just being tourists."

Guillen raised both eyebrows. "You know we're not her only spies. She has plenty of others. Who can rift and get her that kind of intel."

Rachel took her hand back, shoving both of them in her pockets. "Yeah, but we could be doing more. We're asking people in your communities to sabotage things, to steal things. They could get hurt, Guillen. They're not trained for a fight like you and I are. Don't you feel bad about that?"

He crossed his arms. "No. I don't. I know those people, and they need to learn to be their own advocates. They know what the risks are. You and I, we're doing our part. Who else is going to be able to move through those communities without suspicion, spreading Kaylah's message, if you and I get caught sabotaging something?"

She looked down, shaking her head. Guillen gently lifted her head with his hand under her chin. "Please try to enjoy today with me? We're not just being tourists. It's good for you to see this—the empty cities, so we can inform people in the stunt communities, because a lot of them have family they love out here; the culture, so you can blend in better and even share information with your people when this is all over."

Rachel gazed into his eyes, crestfallen.

"Please," he said softly. "Just for today, set aside the noise and worries. And just enjoy it with me."

She nodded, a small smile making its way to her lips. "I'll do my best."

Guillen's face brightened. He wrapped his arm around Rachel again. "Where to first?"

"I'll let you pick."

He didn't know this city well, but he wasn't afraid to ask around. They first found an art gallery. Rachel perked up and took her time admiring the paintings. She wished Saff could be there. Despite all the chaos of war back in their village, Saff had shown Rachel some of her paintings—she was really talented.

"It's amazing, isn't it? Art is a universal language. It speaks to all of us." Rachel stood entranced by a mural with swirls of vibrant blue, green, and yellow, representing the bountiful beauty of the Green Lands.

Guillen held her from behind, resting his chin on her shoulder. "I think you're right. Beauty is universal." He kissed her on the cheek, then swayed back and forth with her.

She let out a small giggle. "You are a *completely* different person."

He stopped swaying. "I… I guess maybe I take a little more than others to open up." He removed his arms from her waist. "Am I making you uncomfortable? Going too fast?"

She faced him, furrowing her brow. "No. I'd let you know." Her face softened into an adoring smile. "I love this version of you."

He grinned and swooped in for a brief kiss. She returned with a hug before moving on to see the rest of the exhibits.

They strolled to a museum nearby. It was interesting to see art and history from an Ivy perspective: The way decades of war were represented. The way her people were depicted. Seeders were often painted with a look of stupor, or monstrous villainy. Ivies were portrayed as heroes, standing triumphant and proud above their enemies. As ridiculous and biased as the paintings seemed, Rachel was curious how they would compare to Seeder art. Other than what Saff had shown her of her own paintings, Rachel hadn't seen much of Seeder art, hadn't left her family home enough to venture to places like this.

After a while, she caught Guillen admiring her as she was immersed in everything the museum had to offer. They'd never really gone on a 'proper' date, but if they decided to call this outing one, it would have been the perfect one.

"We've only got time for one more stop," he announced after hours spent in beautifully peaceful exploration.

He guided her to a large outdoor market, teeming with bright clothes, fruits and vegetables, home décor, and tons more she couldn't see. Strong spices wafted through the air around them. They walked by a booth that sold jewelry. Unlike mass-produced items in the human world, these items were individually handcrafted. Very few of the gems were precision-cut or sparkling like diamonds. Rachel spotted a fair amount of jade.

She whispered in Guillen's ear so the vendor couldn't hear them. "Does jade mean anything special to your people?"

"I don't think so. I think it's just a common stone in the Green Lands. Is it special to you?"

"Well, to our culture, yeah. It helps harness energy; we get a charm that helps when we bloom."

He smiled. "Let's get you something. Anything you want."

She shook her head. "I'm happy to just look."

"I insist. I want to."

She sighed at his handsome face; he was clearly eager to treat her. "I already have a necklace. What about those cute jade earrings to match?"

He pulled out some money and paid for them.

She put the small studs in her ears as he beamed.

"They were made just for you."

"Yeah, well, when you—" Her voice trailed off, as did her smile. She'd been about to say 'when you come visit *my* home, I get to be the one to treat you.' But her lands were poisoned; they wouldn't be able to share moments like these back in South Fortinda. Sure, they had figured out how to heal the lands, but to do so with their current method would take years, maybe even decades, to cover the expanse of affected land.

"What's wrong?"

She forced a smile, touching her earrings. "Nothing. I love them, thank you."

Guillen took her hand. "You know you're a bad liar, right?" He smirked. "At least you are with me." He gestured with a tilt of the head. "Follow me."

He led her to the center of the market, where a violinist played live music. Lining the town square were tented outdoor cafés. In the exact center was a giant intricately carved water fountain, featuring a stone replica of the Mother Vines snaking around it.

Guillen stopped, resting one hand on her waist, offering his other hand.

Rachel looked over her shoulder at the passersby. "We can't just dance in the middle of town."

"Says who? No one here knows us. We have the time. And I want to dance with you." A smile tugged at his lips as he dared her to challenge him.

She took his extended hand and let him guide her. Another thing he was surprisingly assertive with was dancing. Not wanting to embarrass him again like she had about having servants, she didn't ask, but she assumed his pedigree probably allowed him the privilege, and possibly even the expectation, of this kind of activity.

"Are you going to tell me what ran through your mind back there, when you lost that sparkle in your eyes?" he asked.

She bit her lip. "I… Does Ivy poison affect you the same way? Like it does with humans, or Seeders, or other Ivies? Kaylah once told me Ivies are affected by their own poison, but it's different than with Seeders. And I know Seeders react different than humans."

He furrowed his brow in thought. "You know, my dear, I don't really know. If I've needed numbing for something, the nurses have always known what I am. But the numbing has some pretty nasty side effects, so I haven't used it often. Why?" His jaw dropped as if he were shocked. "Are you trying to poison me?"

She chuckled. "No. I just wanted to know because, you know … my home." She gripped his hand tighter. "I kind of imagined me repaying the favor and having you visit. But I don't know that you'd … be able to." She glanced at the large scar on his temple. Scars were a rare sight amongst Seeders, given their healing abilities. She imagined Ivies might have more, but even then, they had accelerated healing. If his body didn't heal like green folk with powers, he probably couldn't withstand his own people's brand of killer poison.

He gave her a smile, though it didn't reach his eyes. "I'm happy to be with you, one day at a time. Let's not let a mysterious someday steal from our today."

She nodded. "You're right."

He spun her around with a dip as the song came to an end. "Thank you. For a perfect day."

***

Rachel and Guillen headed out of town, hand in hand, having purchased food from the market to eat on the way. They picked up their pace as they approached the stunt community, fearing the angry clouds darkening overhead. Rachel breathed a sigh of relief when they returned to find the same guard still on duty.

Guillen handed him more money, and the guard returned the ring. "This was a onetime thing," the guard muttered.

"Not a problem. I appreciate your discretion," Guillen remarked. He let go of Rachel's hand long enough to guide her to a row of apartments a few streets down. He had her wait at the street corner while he went to talk to someone.

Returning with keys, he announced they'd be staying the night in room four. It was a clean, minimally furnished studio apartment—the stunts' equivalent of a hotel. These communities were hardly destination locations, but they had a few rooms dedicated for travelers, or visiting family members; just simple accommodations.

"One bed?" She lifted her eyebrows.

Guillen shrugged. "We could get a second room, but I'd feel a lot better if we weren't split up. You can take the bed."

She sat down on it and bounced to check the springiness. It was fairly hard, but the comforter was soft. "We'll make it work. Is it all that different from sleeping on the same floor together?" She lay down. "We have some time, right? I believe you owe me a cuddle session from last night."

He grinned. "We've got some time. I'm a man of my word." He set their packs down, as well as his knives on a side table, and crawled onto the bed next to her. She willingly became the little spoon as his arms enveloped her.

She breathed in the moment, willing time to stop. "Thanks again. For today. I needed it."

"You're welcome. We all need a good distraction sometimes." He squeezed her tight. "You're my favorite mission as a traitor and spy, you know that?"

She shook with laughter. "Oh my gosh. Who says that?"

"Hey, I was just being honest." He chuckled.

"How long until we have to leave for tonight's meeting?"

He drew a deep breath. "I'm… I'm going to this one alone."

A heaviness instantly settled in her chest. "Why?"

"Jacob and I agreed it would be for the best, just to iron things out. They already got to meet you. They understand they have Seeders backing them up now."

She stared at the wall, still in his embrace. "No one wants me there. Why did I even come?"

He let go of her, sitting up. "We need you. Just try to be patient. The next meeting will go much better. I promise."

She didn't look at him or move. Something inside her was bending, breaking.

"Are you mad at me?"

She rolled over to face him, frowning, unsure of what to say. "No. I probably would've done the same thing. Just get done what you need to."

"I won't be out a moment later than I have to." He paused, clearly hesitant. "Do you… Maybe I'll head out now in case everyone gets there early, so I can get back earlier?"

She couldn't muster anything beyond a weak nod.

"Alright. Don't open the door for anyone, okay?" He gave her a quick kiss, then strapped on his knives and patted his pockets. As the door clicked closed behind him, she lay on the bed, frozen.

The first tear hit her pillow as thunder rumbled the building. She wanted more than this. To help. To be with Guillen.

She'd felt so safe with Guillen, so happy. Now she could barely breathe—assaulted by flashbacks, that shining beacon of hope he'd given her dimming. Pain she'd held back for months now flooded in, doubled.

Why did he have to do that?

She sobbed in the empty, lonely room.

Chapter 19

RACHEL WIPED AWAY HER TEARS, getting out of bed. She blew her nose and grabbed the spare key, making sure she had Ivy money in her pocket. She wasn't going to stay in that room alone. Not alone with her thoughts.

She hadn't expected something so small to trigger her, and she couldn't blame Guillen—he hadn't even realized what he'd done. But her old demons had come calling, and she needed to walk them off. She needed … to try something different.

It took her a moment to orient herself, and she braved asking a stranger for directions. She distracted herself by stabbing her palms with her fingernails. The sky began to spread a mist as she opened the door to the community pub. There couldn't have been more than a dozen patrons, but she wanted to steer clear of them all. Rachel sat at the bar, not completely sure what she was doing. The only alcohol she'd ever had was half a wine cooler. But she was ready to try this, if it could numb the pain.

The bartender came up to her, wiping down the counter. "What'll it be?"

"What's the strongest you have?"

"Vodka usually does the trick."

"I'll take two."

"Your ID?"

She rested her head on the counter, annoyed with herself. She'd forgotten to grab her forged papers. They showed she was of legal age in the Ivy Kingdom. She quietly moaned at the unfairness. *If they're going to let you drink at eighteen, why even check? Especially in such a small community?*

"It's okay, I'll vouch for her."

A hand caressed her lower back, and she bolted upright. The slimy guard from her first day there grinned down at her. "Thought you'd stood me up and skipped town."

She tried to keep a neutral expression and tone. "No. Just got busy."

"I'll have whatever she's having."

"Full strength? For both of you?" The bartender looked between Rachel and the guard.

"Of course," the guard replied.

The bartender returned with four shots, and Rachel tried to tip one back, coughing after the first swallow as it seared down her throat.

The guard chuckled. "Full strength is pretty daring for one of your kind, especially with such a delicate figure." He rested a hand on her thigh.

She ignored him and choked the rest of it down, then moved on to the second as he threw back his first.

"I don't remember your name. Mine's Tony."

"Elizabeth."

"Right. How much longer are you here for?"

"Just tonight."

He smirked. "Then let's make it a good one. Two more for each of us."

Rachel let him talk about himself for what seemed like ages as the buzz set in. He was beyond arrogant, not requiring much from her in return. She tired of his boring small talk, tossing back the next couple of shots, her third and fourth.

After a few minutes, her vision began to blur. She turned to face Tony, wagging a finger at him. "So you, are here. Why aren't you out there? Why guard … when could be killing weeds?"

His hand rested more heavily on her thigh. "You don't find pretty girls like yourself on the battlefields out there. Do you want another shot?"

She extended her pointer finger, putting it up against her eye.

"Let's get two more for her."

She drank another one.

He gave her a lusty grin. "How about we head back to my place once you finish that last one?"

She closed her eyes, trying to focus as she clung to the counter. "I think. That I'm a *little* tipsy to walk."

He stood and moved behind her, inching his hands and vines between her legs, midthigh. "I can help," he whispered in her ear.

She squeezed her eyelids tighter, shaking her head. The room spun, causing her to grip the counter more firmly.

He quickly removed his hands and vines. "I don't think you were completely honest with me, Elizabeth." His tone was no longer flirtatious.

She registered the change and began to worry.

"I'd say palace boy is more than an acquaintance with the staredown he's giving us."

She turned to look at the entrance. Guillen marched over, disappointment painting his face.

"Mmm. Him." She faced the bar, frowning.

Tony backed up a pace.

Guillen grabbed her wrist, his voice firm. "Come on. You shouldn't be here."

Rachel furrowed her brow and yanked her wrist back. "Maybe I'm not ready." She reached for the other shot, and Guillen pulled it from her hand, slamming it on the counter out of reach.

"You're done."

Tony spoke up. "Hey now, she's free to make her own choices."

Guillen glared at him. "I know your kind. And unless you want to be reassigned to guarding the *Shadows of the Afterworld*, I'd recommend backing off." He put an arm around Rachel. "Please?" he pleaded.

Rachel slid off her stool, Guillen supporting her shaky legs.

She turned back to Tony, waving a finger in his general direction. "Thank you, Toby, fur a luffly evening. And the sshots." She swallowed as stomach acid inched its way up.

Tony plopped down on the stool, scowling. "Yeah. No problem."

Guillen ushered Rachel down the street as fast as her wobbly legs would allow; the earlier trickle of rain had become a full downpour. They were drenched by the time he got her back to their room. He sat her on the edge of the bed and locked the door behind them.

Guillen stood in front of Rachel, arms crossed, his wet hair clinging to his forehead. "Why would you do that?"

She squinted. "Are you jealouss?"

"Was that what you were going for back there?"

She scowled. "No."

"Then what was that about?"

She stared at the ground, her mind still beyond fuzzy.

He huffed. "That was stupid."

She looked back at him, brow furrowed. "I'm not an idjit. I wasn't leaving with him."

"Right." He scoffed. "Because you're clearly in perfect shape to fight off a man twice your size! You were doing a great job *all* by yourself." He shook his head. "And our mission—that was selfish."

"I'm not that drunk!" She pouted. "I wouldn't've said anything."

"Have you ever had hard alcohol before, Rachel? Because I seriously doubt you've had Ivy-distilled. Your people don't handle poison as easily, do they? You wouldn't *have* to say anything! Did you even think about the fact that you might have unknowingly started to glow or something with another shot? You don't know how that stuff affects you!"

She instantly started to ugly cry at his chastisement. "I just didn't want it. I don't wanna be heere. It'ss only abou' my body. They touch it, or they take what they want. But they don't care, 'cause I'm stuuupid. I don't want it. I just wanted you." She licked her salty tears as he frowned. She squeaked out the last part. "I just don't want it."

He sighed softly as his shoulders dropped. "Let's get you to bed. Sleep it off, and we'll talk in the morning."

She pushed herself up and balanced against the wall. Then dropped her pants.

He whipped around. "Why are you stripping?"

She tugged on her shirt sleeve in frustration. "Because. I'm. Wet!"

"Fine. Hurry up and get under the covers."

Her waterlogged shirt fell to the ground with a *splat*. She glanced down at her underwear, deciding not to bother before climbing into bed.

"Are you covered?"

"Maybe."

"Rachel…"

"Yes. Don't know why yur being prude. You've seen me half nak'd before."

He turned, scolding her with his eyes, bending over to pick up her wet clothes and taking them to the bathroom.

"Do you still like me?" She pouted as he returned, her tears threatening to make another appearance.

"Yes," he breathed gently. "You know I do." He grabbed a spare blanket and left the room again, returning with it wrapped around him. A soft *pitter patter* came from the bathroom, where he must have hung their things to drip-dry. "Go to sleep."

"Will you kiss me? I want to cuddle with you." A short candle lit the room, the flame dancing. She craved the warmth of his body next to hers.

He shook his head and sat on the edge of the bed next to her. "No. Not while you're drunk." His blanket dropped, just covering his waist and below. "I'm tucking you in, and we'll talk in the morning."

As he reached over, she grabbed his bicep—the one without the stunt mark. "One of yer tattoos. Is pretty. Whas it mean?"

"It means you should go to sleep. Good night, Rachel."

Chapter 20

RACHEL WOKE, HER HEAD SCREAMING like it had been cracked open. She grimaced and placed a hand on her head, moving healing energy to try and help. She forced herself to sit up after feeling hardly any relief.

"Did it help?" Guillen was sitting on the love seat, shirtless, in his spare change of pants. His tone and expression hinted at frustration, but weren't unkind.

She groaned. "Not really."

"Well, it's good to know you can't just zap your way out of all of life's consequences. Drink some of that water on the bedside table."

She reached over, then stopped. The blanket had slipped, revealing her bra. She snapped the covers up to conceal her chest.

"I slept on the floor. Nothing happened."

She frowned. "I'm sorry."

He scratched his knee. "Are you ready to talk?"

She eased the water off the table, guzzling half of it. "I'm guessing you're not going to take 'no' for an answer."

Guillen crossed his arms. "You guessed right. Talk. Why was it so horrible to be left alone for a whole hour and a half? So bad that you had to go drinking?"

"It's not that simple."

"Honestly, Rachel. You acted like a child. I know it hurt, the way Magda and everyone reacted, but I never imagined you'd go out and do something like that. Do you want to go home? Are you going to be able to finish this mission?"

She looked down. "I can do it. I need to do it."

"Why do you *need* to do it?"

She stared at her hands, digging her fingernails in painfully.

"I'm going to grab us some breakfast. You get dressed, and we'll talk more when I get back, okay?" He raised his eyebrows. "Can I trust that you'll be here when I return?"

She rolled her eyes. "Yes."

Guillen threw on a dry shirt and headed out. Once he left, Rachel rifled through her pack. Since they needed to travel light, her only spare clothing, other than the underwear essentials, was a t-shirt with sleeves long enough to conceal her tattoo, and some fairly short shorts. She finished her water and refilled the glass. Sitting on the bed, she rested her pounding head on her knees.

He returned with a couple of pastries and apples. They silently dug in. After a while, he tried again. "I know this is about something deeper. You said you feel safe with me; will you please just talk to me?"

She picked at her pastry. How could she ever share her demons with him? "I don't think you're the right person for this."

"I'm trying to be patient. But I care about you, and I don't want to see you bottling it up anymore and hurting yourself like this." He lifted her chin to make eye contact. "You don't need to worry about sparing my feelings, or me judging you for anything that's happened. I know what that asshole's capable of. Please just let me help you."

She leaned back against the headboard, folding her arms around her legs. Staring at the ceiling, she gathered her courage. "I spent my whole life, happy. Thinking I was something I wasn't. For a short while, I thought I had a loving dad, who I found out either hates me for who I am, or was murdered by Nuren. Nuren acted like he loved me for a decade, just to use me to kill my own people. My best friend poisoned me—for months—to screw with my head and make me feel worthless. I started to hurt myself to deal with it. My boyfriend attacked me in a hot tub and then manipulated me into trusting him." She lowered her head to look at Guillen. "That's all before I was kidnapped. How are we doing so far?"

He gently rubbed her arm. "I'm sorry."

"Me too." Tears filled her eyes, and a whimper escaped her lips. "Because it's *my fault* I ended up here. I didn't get to choose what world I'd live in. He stole that from me! He made me trust him, and then he took me here, and drugged me. And then I was stabbed a thousand times, and all they cared about was my Seeder energy. It felt like … they drained my soul with it." Her tears flowed freely, carrying with them the rest of the pain she hadn't been able to share with others. "All because I was stupid. And he didn't even rape me, but he," her voice quivered, "he touched me, and I didn't know when he would stop. I couldn't move, and he wouldn't stop!" She bent over, weeping, barely able to breathe.

Guillen wrapped his arms around her. She leaned into him, letting out the hurt that had been pent up. Each tear burned as it rolled down her cheek. They seared with the guilt of each Seeder who had died because of her stupidity in ever trusting Soren, the guilt of her mom's pain at being all alone, the guilt of surviving and being happy to any degree when other kidnapped Seeder girls weren't so lucky.

"It's not your fault. You need to remember that. It's not your fault. And you're not stupid. I shouldn't have said that last night. I'm sorry." He kissed her head. "Don't blame yourself for trusting him. He carries *all* of the blame, and he'll pay for it. I'll make sure of it."

Rachel woke a half hour later, her head on Guillen's lap. Her eyes were puffy, and her headache raged on. She sat up. "Thanks for listening." She couldn't look him in the eyes.

He held her hand. "Any time. Do you feel better?"

She leaned her head on his shoulder. "My head—not so much. My heart—maybe."

"Was the pub all about the human dad thing? Him maybe judging you for being a Seeder? And Magda? Or the other stuff, and Mr. Handsy I-Might-Break-His-Face-Before-We-Leave?"

She grinned before frowning again. "Those are both part of it. But … I was just so happy with you. You're like that one good part of my life right now. I don't even fit in with my Seeder family. My mom back home is in a Unitas safe house. Everyone in my village thinks I'm brainwashed. And … you lied to me when you promised you wouldn't."

He leaned away, visibly confused. "I lied to you?"

She sniffled. That had been what sent her over the edge, what had pulled the rug out from underneath her. "You knew I wouldn't be going to the meeting last night, but you didn't tell me until *after* we had a great day. I know you were doing it to make me feel better, but you manipulated my feelings. I don't want that." She fidgeted with her hands. "I just want the truth, even if it's going to hurt."

"I'm sorry." Regret filled his voice. "I never thought of it that way. I swear. I'll do my best to be completely upfront with you, okay?"

"Thank you. I know I'm … complicated."

"You're worth it." He paused. "What you said, about hurting yourself. Do you … still have a hard time with that?"

She examined her palms, where she'd been digging her nails in to feel the pain. It wasn't the same as stabbing herself with a needle, but she'd done it in the same spirit. She was too ashamed to look up. "I promised Kaylah I wouldn't. But I don't know if I can keep that promise."

"Would you tell me if you started again?"

She frowned, meeting his soft eyes. "I *want* to say yes. I'll try."

"That's all we can do." He wore a reassuring smile. "We try, learn, and grow, and heal. One day at a time." He cleared his throat. "And I know it's really sensitive, with … him … and what he did to you. But please tell me if I do anything, say anything, touch you, in a way you're uncomfortable with. I don't want to be that guy. I want to be with you, but not by hurting you."

She nodded, immensely grateful he was so understanding. "It really doesn't bother you that I dated him?"

He smiled again. "Does it bother you that I've dated other women before you?"

She sighed. "That's hardly the same."

"Maybe not. But I add it to the list of what I admire about you. It just shows you have great taste to ditch a crown, and slum it with the likes of me." He nudged her playfully.

She let out a small sincere laugh.

"There she is." He kissed her shoulder. "Are you ready to pack up and leave this place behind?"

"Can we cuddle for a while longer? Let my headache die down?"

"Sure."

They slipped under the covers, and she rested her head on his chest.

"So, these tattoos—you've been exposed."

"Mmm… It appears so."

"Can I see them?"

"Sure."

She sat up while he pulled off his shirt, then leaned back against him as he lay down. She traced a thin but intricate design on his arm, a band inked on his bicep. "What's the story behind this one?"

"That one has the least meaning, honestly. I just thought it looked cool. And I think I wanted to put something on my body that was by *my* choice. I got it soon after leaving home."

She gently pressed her lips to the tattoo. "Then it means something important." She rolled over, touching his third tattoo, a small one on his chest. "I recognize this one. It's the Unitas symbol, right?"

He grinned. "Yeah. Kaylah was scorched, but it's not like I walk around with my shirt off. And Craig did it for me, anyway. I got it shortly after I pledged my oath to Kaylah. A blossom and an ivy leaf." He held her hand over it. "Keeping what matters most to me, over my heart."

She stared lovingly into his eyes. Scooching up, she placed her head higher on his chest, snuggling again. He kissed the top of her head as her body moved to the rhythm of his lungs.

***

They checked out of their room after a couple of hours. Guillen strode down the street with his arm unashamedly around Rachel. They intentionally left the community from the exit Tony wouldn't be at, despite Guillen wanting to crack his skull open. He didn't want to put Rachel through seeing Tony again, and they couldn't jeopardize their cover any further.

The next community would be a day and a half away if they kept a good pace, so they'd need to find somewhere to stop for the night along the way. Guillen caught Rachel up on what the first group had committed to. Despite the rough first meeting, they'd made great progress the second night. Word was going out to people they trusted, who spread the truth about the cause and about their needs. Sabotage plans were set in place for the Ivy army supply chain.

Wanting to avoid any suspicion, Rachel and Guillen stopped in a regular town to rest for the night instead of trying to find a place on the outskirts of town to camp. Guillen got them a double-bed room, though Rachel would have been happy to share and cuddle. In the end, it was probably for the best that she stuck to her own bed, given how quickly things were developing between them. She didn't want to rush anything too much. She didn't want to screw things up with Guillen.

The next day, they arrived at Community Nine early enough to grab dinner, but too late to call a meeting with their connections. They took their food to-go, back to their room. Like the last community, only single-bed rooms were available.

"This is amazing. You should try some." Rachel covered her mouth while she talked. She'd ordered a salad with a particularly tangy dressing.

Guillen leaned forward and stole a kiss, then licked his lips. "Not bad."

She chuckled. "That's hardly what I meant."

He gave her a toothy smile as she lifted her fork up for him to try a bite.

He opened his mouth and sampled it. "Yeah. It's alright. I liked the first try better."

She shook her head and giggled. She loved this. When they'd been apart and she'd thought of this guy, one of her rescuers, she'd thought fondly of him. But she hadn't really understood what it meant to fall head-over-heels for someone. She'd told Prince Soren she loved him only in reciprocation, after almost three years of dating. Guillen had her heart completely.

They cleared off the bed after eating, and Rachel lay on her side, facing him. "I wish we didn't have to pack so light. It would be nice to have a book or something. Especially without games or a TV."

He flashed a look of confusion.

"It's a box where you can watch entertainment. Like theater."

"Okay." He slipped down on the bed, mirroring her position. "I remember hearing about that now."

He'd continued to teach her more fighting techniques in their free time, but there was only so much they could do in the cramped space of their private rooms.

"I guess I really didn't expect to do so much waiting on this mission," she said.

He flashed pouty lips. "It's pretty rough being stuck with me. Isn't it?"

She gave him a smug grin. "Yep. *Excruciating.*"

"You know, people do other things in rooms like this, if they're bored."

She blushed. "I'm not ready for that."

He shifted a little on the bed. "I meant kissing and cuddling. Naturally."

She bit her lip. "Naturally."

"Can I kiss you?"

She lifted an eyebrow. "Are we going back to asking?"

"When we're lying in bed, yes."

"Come here."

Guillen leaned over, kissing her sweetly. She pulled him in, running her fingers through his hair and nibbling on his lip. He slid closer, some of his weight resting on her as they kissed more passionately than they had before. Every inch of her tingled in waves through her body under his weight. He moved his lips to her neck. She shivered but pulled herself away from the moment.

"Guillen, stop. Please get off."

He jumped back. "I'm sorry. Did I? Was it … something…"

"Gosh, no!" She rubbed her forehead, having feared this exact thing would happen. "Please. *Please.* Do *not* think about him every time you touch me. I mean it. Sometimes, I just want to take things slower."

Guillen closed his eyes and sighed. "Right." He met her gaze. "I can sleep on the floor again."

"No, that's silly." She smiled softly. "Can you handle being the little spoon?"

He opened his mouth, but nothing came out for a moment. "Well, I… I'm not certain I know what you mean by that."

It was still cute when he'd confess he didn't understand her. She appreciated that he was honest and vulnerable enough to do so.

"Spooning?" She cradled her hands together. "Like if they're put away in a drawer together."

He pointed at her hands. "Yeah, but they nestle like that when they're the same size. You said I'd be the *little* spoon?"

She genuinely couldn't tell if he was just trying to pull her leg again, and didn't want to laugh if he was serious. "It's the inside spoon. The one being held."

He continued to look confused. "I just don't understand the logic behind the idiom. I'm larger than you, but I'd be the little spoon?"

"Do you want me to hold you? Or do you want me to stay on my half of the bed?"

He pressed his lips together. "I think I can manage being a little spoon."

Smiling, she blew out the candle on her nightstand, and they settled in for an early night.

Having to logistically explain spooning to her boyfriend had taken away some of the steam from their heated make-out session, but just a whiff of his hair—fresh mint and juniper berries—made her want to kiss his neck. But it wouldn't stop there, and she knew it.

"Do they sell decks of cards around here?" she asked in the dark.

He chuckled, perhaps sharing the same struggle. "I'm sure we can find some."

Chapter 21

GUILLEN GAVE RACHEL THE GRAND TOUR of Community Nine, introducing people along the way. It was much like Ten—basic, cookie cutter. She was curious, though, about some larger unmarked buildings on the edge of the community.

"What are those?"

"Family homes."

"But … you're not allowed to have kids."

"Behind them is the orphanage."

She frowned. "How can people be so heartless that they don't even want their own kids? Just because they don't have powers? Is it so hard to live with a human?"

"It's a shame thing. Status. A lot of families, like mine, still raise us. But not everyone."

She couldn't take her eyes off the buildings. "What happens if a couple like Magda and Jacob defy the law and have a kid?"

"They'd be punished, and the baby would end up at one of these, too."

She was relieved they would at least allow the child to live, but still… It went against everything in her family-centered Seeder culture. And any decent society.

He gave her an understanding look. "Not everyone gives up their children. At a young age, or even when they're supposed to, when they're older. Some parents try to conceal the child's condition, but it's impossible to do with our education system. It's a dead giveaway when you're in sparring classes, you know? Then the parents get punished for hiding the truth. Eventually, we all have to come here."

All she could do was shake her head.

"Come on." He wore an understanding half-smile. "Let's go refine our strategy for tonight's meeting."

***

Finding a quiet place in the community gardens where they wouldn't be overheard, Rachel and Guillen discussed what they would do to make the meeting better this time. They planned to listen more, pose more questions, feel out the concerns and frustrations of the particular group, and then lean into those.

They talked about addressing the Seeder part of the equation much more in depth, earning more attendee trust, not revealing her identity too early. And she wasn't just a representative, a witness bearing testimony. She could demonstrate her people's commitment.

"Are you sure you're okay with that?" Guillen winced. "I know we talked about you possibly offering to heal, but … I just want to make sure you're really okay with it. I think we'd still do alright if you decided not to."

"I want to help. You don't think they'll consider it pandering, do you?"

"No. I'm sure they'll be happy to be healthier. I just … don't want you to feel used." He reached a hand up to her stunt mark.

Her body … yeah… She'd already demonstrated her commitment to the cause, on her own body. The thing she was tired of people using and abusing.

The difference between using her energy to heal, and using it to power a war machine, was her choice in the matter.

She gazed into his eyes. "There's a difference between using someone, and letting them be useful. I'm here to help."

He replied with his signature grin. "Alright."

Their rocky first meeting had taught them a lot. And luckily, reworking their presentation proved successful. The room came together with much more harmony this time. Progress was made. Rachel's heart swelled at the number of people who introduced themselves after knowing what she was, even if it seemed like some did so just out of curiosity. They told the group when they could meet the next morning if they wanted to bring anyone to be healed, as long as they were absolutely sure anyone they brought could be trusted.

Guillen had some acquaintances here as well who offered to let them stay with them, but after the first experience, Rachel preferred the comfort and privacy of having their own place. They lay in bed, facing each other, beaming at the day's success. Rachel hugged herself as they chatted. They were both gushing about how the other had said just the right thing at the right time, connecting with the people. She loved being so united, so in sync.

He traced her curves, tenderly running a couple of fingers from her shoulder down to her hips. His face became pensive. "It really never bothers you? What I am?"

She flashed him a reassuring smile. "Ruggedly handsome and unbelievably kind?"

He blushed. "Yes. That's exactly what I meant."

Her smile grew to a huge grin. "It doesn't. I don't get why it would bother anyone. To me, you're normal. For almost all of my life, every guy I ever met, at least that I knew of, didn't have powers. That's the benefit of growing up in the human world."

He studied her. "That's true. But once you gained powers, can you honestly say you weren't drawn to others who shared them?"

She furrowed her brow in thought. She'd liked the prince *despite* his powers, but that had been complicated, him being the enemy. Not that Guillen wasn't the same race as the enemy... Back in her Seeder village, she had gotten attention, as did all the girls, for being a new arrival. In a society low on females, she was a hot commodity. But she hadn't been drawn to any of the guys. And then Zeus... Well, there was that.

"Think about it like ... well ... *him*." She'd rather not say Soren's name. "Once I realized who he really was, I didn't suddenly think he was better in any way, because he was a prince. Power, whether political or physical—it doesn't change who you really are."

Guillen smiled. "So, you're not just after me for my crown tattoo?"

She chuckled, then lifted an eyebrow. "Wait, is that a thing? I honestly hadn't thought about it that way. Are you a ladies' man and I don't know it? They fling themselves at you? You did once say that you were 'lucky' to have your royal ties." She winked.

He pursed his lips. "It is ... actually kind of a thing. At least in these communities. If I married one of my kind, she'd get the same level of freedom."

"Oh. That kind of sucks. Knowing people might have ulterior motives." She frowned. *Yeah, like the prince dating you, just to use you.* She and Guillen were so different, but at the same time, shared a lot of the same struggles.

She wanted to change the subject away from Soren. "Have you ever dated girls with powers? Or just those like you?"

Guillen shifted his weight. "I've dated both. Do you want to talk about our dating histories?"

Her cheeks warmed. She'd barely turned eighteen when she was back home in her Seeder village, at least according to her human-given birthday. And she'd really only dated the prince in high school.

But Guillen was almost twenty-four … and apparently had women chasing him for status. "Maybe not."

He shrugged with one shoulder. "I don't have anything to hide."

She smiled shyly. "I'm fine. What about me? It doesn't bother you that I'm a Seeder, powers and all? I feel like that's more of a stretch than me being okay with you." She realized … he might not have always thought fondly of her kind… Or worse yet…

"I mean … I could assume you like me because I'm a shiny thing, exotic. Maybe a fetish or trophy or something."

His look made his sentiments clear, a 'Really? You're kidding me, right?' kind of face. "Didn't you just say it's about personality and not power?"

Touché. "Yes. And you just clarified that the ladies can't keep their hands off of you, because of your status," she teased with raised eyebrows.

He gently poked her arm. "Before you knew who your brother Jeff was, that either of you were Seeders, you were nice to him. He was awkward and didn't fit in, but you tried hard to make him feel welcome."

She was pulled from the fun of their playful banter, disarmed by his casual mention of Jeff. She searched his face intently. "I don't remember ever mentioning Jeff to you. Or any of that."

He averted his eyes, tracing patterns on the bed between them. "No, you didn't. That was one of the stories Kaylah told me about you."

She'd known Kaylah had talked about her, but it just now dawned on her that she really didn't know to what extent. Rachel felt uneasy, and he must have noticed when he looked back at her.

"I…" He swallowed. "I just feel like I kind of got to know who you were before we met. I might have … been interested in getting to know you … but I don't want to come off … you know…"

She rolled onto her back. Kaylah had never mentioned Guillen in all their years in the human world. And she knew why, aside from the obvious undercover mission. Kaylah had already pushed her into a relationship with Soren. Just like Kaylah had encouraged that romance, she'd been pushing Rachel into Guillen's arms.

Knots formed in Rachel's stomach. She couldn't believe Kaylah had nefarious intentions, but the parallel was sickening.

"I don't know what to say," he whispered. "I'm sorry if that creeped you out. I don't mean to come on too strong."

She stared at the ceiling. "Did Kaylah encourage you to date me?"

He paused far too long. "Not like that. No. Not like a mission."

She couldn't get herself to look at him. If Kaylah could bring people together for the purpose of kidnapping (despite it being under orders), she could certainly manipulate people together for a different cause of her choosing. Rachel despised the thought of possibly being used as a pawn again. And even more, her heart ached at the thought of Guillen innocently being used that way. He might not even realize it. Kaylah could have planned this whole thing, just so the pair of them could rally people to her cause. Not that it wasn't a just cause…

She dared to ask, "When she picked who would help rescue me from the palace…" But she couldn't let herself finish that accusation.

The hurt in his voice was apparent. "I'd like to think I was chosen for an elite mission because I've worked hard for Kaylah, and *earned* her respect, her confidence in me."

She rolled away from him, hiding her face and fighting back tears. *Great. Let's mingle our struggles and personal identities.* She'd just been trying to sort through her own trauma, not realizing what her question had implied. She'd questioned his competence at something intimately personal—at least that was how he'd taken it. The layers of deception and torture in her life were like a rockslide pinning her down. It was too heavy. She may never know what a healthy relationship was.

"I'm sorry," she whispered. "I didn't mean it that way."

After a minute, Guillen blew out his candle. "Good night."

Rachel lay there in the dark, her mood sinking deeper and deeper. And also surprised to find herself getting angry with him. He was textbook perfect in being a considerate boyfriend—soft, kind, understanding, patient. But this once, she wanted him to raise his voice, demand she understand his feelings, make his position clear, *fight* with her, for her.

Chapter 22

RACHEL WOKE IN THE EARLY MORNING, having cuddled up to Guillen during the night. He was awake already.

"Sorry," she said as she moved off him.

"Don't be. I'm not." He wore a soft smile. That usual kind, soft smile.

He sat up against the wall, and she followed suit.

She gave him a sincere frown. "I'm sorry about how I asked that last night. I would never question how capable you are. I was just in my head, and it didn't come out right."

He met her gaze. "Thank you. It means a lot to me. Especially because *I* know, that *you* know, that it means a lot to me."

She gave a tiny half-smile of acknowledgement.

"About the rest…" he said.

She looked at him sheepishly. "I don't really want to talk about that right now."

He exhaled loudly.

Deciding it was best to just get out of bed and hop in the shower, Rachel started to move. Unexpectedly, he grabbed her hand. "I do."

Owing to the determination on his face, she backed up against the wall, tucking her knees under her chin.

"I'm not trying to rush you through what you're dealing with, but this has to do with me, too, and I deserve to have a say in it."

She didn't even know what to say, but she had a small sense of satisfaction in him standing up for himself, for them.

He continued, "Yes. I knew more about you than you knew about me, before we met. But the chemistry we have, the feelings I have for you, those aren't from pictures and stories."

She blushed and looked away.

"Rachel, I'm not going to patronize you by asking, because I know you. But maybe you need to ask yourself: Would you be here, doing this mission, risking your life every day, if you were with someone else? And if someone other than Kaylah had asked it of you?"

Perhaps he gave her a little too much credit. She'd have been much more hesitant to embark on this mission if it hadn't been with someone she trusted. But in spirit, in morals, Guillen was right. Even if she'd never met him, even if things had happened differently—these people didn't deserve to be treated this way. And her people deserved to stop living in fear. Even before she'd met him, she had wanted to be part of the solution.

"Why do you like me?" he asked.

She searched his face. Wasn't it obvious? "Because you're sweet, and thoughtful, and funny, and smart, and strong, and talented." She bit her lip. "And you're not exactly bad looking, or bad at kissing, or hugging, or really anything." She couldn't look him in the eyes.

"Would you stop dating me if Kaylah ordered you to?"

She furrowed her brow and met his gaze. "No. That's none of her business."

He raised his eyebrows, slightly smirking. "It sounds like you're with me because you actually *want* to be. And I personally know you were picked for this mission because of what you have to offer. And *I'm* here because I've dedicated my life to this, and I'm damned good at it. And I'm with you, because…" He paused with his mouth open. "I think you're amazing … and I like who I get to be when I'm with you."

Silence hung in the air.

"Guillen, I'm sorry. I really don't know how to do this. I feel like … I'm always going to be like this. The smallest things, intentional or not, good or bad… They take me back to places and things I'd rather forget. I don't know what I'm doing." Her eyes welled up.

He shifted to face her, leaning his shoulder and head against the wall. "The only way you learn to trust again is by trying. I don't expect you to not have moments like this. Challenge me—I don't have anything to hide. But what you *really* need to do, is challenge yourself. Tell yourself that you've learned, and that you deserve to move on. Because you have, and you do."

She nodded thoughtfully.

"You trust me? You feel safe with me?" he asked.

She drew a deep breath. "Yes." She faced him, also leaning against the wall.

"Do you feel stupid for trusting me?"

She frowned. "Um…"

"Because I could have more training than you think, on manipulation."

She searched his eyes. *No.* Looking back on Soren's behavior, she could now discern where he had molded her the way he'd wanted. She'd never sensed that in Guillen.

"You've slept next to me for, well, weeks now, if we include the first trip with Jon. Have you ever felt like you weren't safe? That I wouldn't respect you?"

She shook her head.

"I have a half dozen weapons within arm's reach right now. And I've had them every single one of those nights. I've killed for this cause. I've killed for Kaylah."

Her eyes grew wider as her heart pumped faster. She'd assumed as much, but they'd never discussed it. The man she knew was the sweetest, most gentle man she'd ever met. He was strong, and competent, and wise. But he was also a successful spy, and she had allowed herself to forget that.

"Why are you telling me this?" she asked.

Guillen searched her eyes. "Because this is who I am. Do you still trust me?"

She closed her eyes. A mix of emotions bombarded her, one of them guilt, for making any of this about her, in her doubts. "I've always trusted you." She fidgeted with her hands. "I know who you are. I'm sorry."

He reached over and took her hands. "I'm not looking for an apology. I'm just asking you to trust yourself more. When you question me, or you, or us, or anything, the only way you're going to move forward is to question your questions, and choose to take a step into the dark."

"Okay," she whispered. "Thank you."

After a moment of silence, he asked, "Can I kiss you?"

She leaned forward, meeting him in the middle. The longer they kissed, the more her worries melted away. She was in that place again, the place she felt safest, with him. She pulled back, grinning. She adored his smile, the piercing look he was giving her, seeing his bare chest rise and fall. She gestured with her head for him to lie back down. She propped up her head, lying on her side. "How about we give this a fresh start?"

"Hmm. What does that entail?"

She straddled him, a mischievous grin spreading across her face. He shifted to accommodate her, matching her smile.

"I think we just have to go back to that first kiss. And maybe it's best if, instead of starting from the beginning, we trace our way back. Just for good measure." She leaned down, getting lost in his eyes before locking lips in a kiss as passionate as any they'd shared.

Her whole body radiated her feelings for him. His strong hands tightly gripped her hips, holding her in place. She pulled back for a moment, catching her breath. She mused at how much her Seeder transformations betrayed her when she shared her affections so freely with him. He didn't need to have any powers to make it clear what he wanted.

"We have lots of time," he said. "Just ... not today."

She smiled sweetly. "I know." She honestly wasn't sure if they were talking about the same thing ... but either way, they were still on the same page. She wasn't ready to go further than this, and they needed to get ready for the day, and focus on their mission.

She sat there, tracing his Unitas tattoo as their breathing calmed down.

"I would kill for you," he whispered.

Taken aback, she met his gaze. His face showed how serious his resolve was, though his soft eyes expressed his vulnerable desperation for her.

"To keep you safe."

She swallowed a lump in her throat. That was a given. They were partners on a mission—that was part of the job description, to keep each other alive. But that was *not* what he was saying. That was the kind of declaration that told her, no matter what, even if this war took a turn for the worse, he planned to be by her side.

"And I'll keep you safe," she whispered back.

The corner of his lip curved up. "We need to move on."

After allowing herself one more moment of pure happiness in the here and now, she slid off him. "Let's go heal some people."

Chapter 23

ONLY A PAIR OF STUNTS showed up for minor healing in Community Nine before Rachel and Guillen moved on. Which was good; they didn't want to drain Rachel too much before a long day of travel, and the more people who knew her identity as a Seeder, the riskier it became for them. The handful of people present were in as much shock and awe at her Seeder abilities as Guillen and Jon had been the first time they'd seen her heal herself.

The more heartbreaking of her two patients was a fourteen-year-old boy. For his birthday, he'd been ripped from his family and forced to take the mark, assigned to this community. His arm was still red and sore.

He hadn't even been given the option of numbing like Olivia had provided for Rachel. Or a healer. He looked so confused and scared as he glanced at those around him. They were all strangers to him. She gently placed her hand on his mark, wishing she knew what to say.

He studied her face; this was no doubt the first time he'd ever seen a Seeder. "Why are you doing this?"

"Because you're worth it."

A shy smile appeared on his face, before a frown overtook it. He looked down as Rachel finished healing and removed her hand. "My mom got hurt, when they came to … well, she … um…" Tears filled his eyes. "She's in Cassa. Would you be able to go heal her?"

Rachel bit her lip, glancing at Guillen out of the corner of her eye, hoping, praying, that somehow Cassa was a regular city nearby they could stop at.

Guillen's eyes held sadness as he gently shook his head.

They hadn't come to heal. That wasn't their mission. "I'm sorry," Rachel said, her eyes moistening and warming, her heart yearning to do more. "I'm really sorry."

The boy's frown deepened. "Why not? Couldn't you fly there?"

Her chest physically hurt.

"It's Marcus, right?" Guillen asked.

The boy looked at Guillen. "Yeah."

Guillen gestured with a nod to follow him to the front of the room. "Let's chat."

Rachel hung back, standing next to the only other person still in the room—the elderly woman who had been in their meeting the night before, and come this morning, escorting the boy.

"Never gets any easier to see it," the woman muttered, her focus on Guillen and Marcus.

Wiping away tears, Rachel tried to calm herself. "It's so horrible."

The woman slowly nodded. "And you always worry if they'll make it."

Rachel's eyes widened. "What do you mean by that?"

"People can spiral."

Rachel gulped. *Suicide.* "Fourteen is too young to be taken like this."

The woman eased herself down onto a chair. "Is there a better age to have your life stolen from you?"

Rachel's own kidnapping played through her mind; it made her sick to her stomach. "No. I don't suppose there is any sort of ideal for something like this."

Guillen and Marcus sat on a large desk at the front of the room, talking. The boy continued to cry, and Guillen hugged him.

"When did he get here?" Rachel asked.

"His intake was this morning. The rest of today will be his tour and orientation. He'll start work tomorrow."

"So quickly?"

The woman gave a gentle shrug. "If you can walk, you can work. Our people have a lot of labels for our kind. The one I use? Slaves."

"Yeah," Rachel half breathed, crestfallen.

They watched on as Guillen and Marcus chatted. Marcus had wiped away his tears and was putting on a brave face. He even cracked a smile once or twice as Guillen talked to him.

"I'm glad I got to meet the infamous Guillen," the woman said. "He's a good man."

Rachel's heart swelled as she studied him. "Yeah. He's the best kind there is." She knew in that moment that it was love. She didn't even question it. There was no 'maybe' about it.

Less pleasantly, her mind drifted to the first man she'd ever professed her love to. She'd waited for him to say it first. That wasn't going to happen this time. This time she actually meant it.

Guillen lifted his sleeve to show his mark to the boy, then pointed in Rachel's direction. She blushed as Marcus looked at her with a surprised face. She didn't know when she'd tell Guillen how she really felt. She'd wait a little while, making sure it was the right time. They were good together. She promised herself she wouldn't allow doubt to creep in again and screw things up.

Guillen stood, finding a piece of paper and a pen in a drawer of the desk. He handed it to Marcus. While he wrote, Guillen approached the women in the back of the room. "Sorry, we're almost done. I know you have a tight schedule."

The woman waved a dismissive hand in the air. "It's okay. I'll tell them my old, aging body slowed us down if they complain that I took too long to give him the community tour." She winked.

He smiled, then turned to Rachel with a frown. "How are you holding up?"

She gave him a warm smile. "Better." She glanced past him to Marcus, who wiped away another tear as he continued to write. "What's that about?"

Shoving his hands in his pockets, Guillen pressed his lips together. "There's only so much we can do. I didn't want to overpromise." He looked at the woman. "Next time I make a contact that can manage it, we'll get it to his family."

She smiled appreciatively. "That's fantastic. That will make a big difference."

Rachel narrowed her eyes in confusion. "A letter? I thought family could pretty much write or visit whenever they wanted."

"When his mother fought back?" the woman replied.

Rachel's heart deflated. "Yeah, how bad was it?"

Guillen's hand moved as if to reach out and hold hers. Before he touched her, he quickly recoiled and shoved it back in his pocket. "Um ... It's hard to know. It's probably not as bad as he thinks it is. Extractions can be chaotic when the parents fight back. And when they do, visiting and communication privileges are revoked for a while. Depending on how bad it was, it could be a month, could be a year."

Rachel couldn't do anything more than shake her head. The lines blurred between people like Guillen, Soren, and the spectrum in between. How could a society get to this level? She'd never understood it in her human history classes, and she didn't understand it now.

Still at the front of the room, Marcus folded the papers he'd written on. "So, we're finding a way to smuggle it to his mom?" Rachel asked.

Guillen shrugged. "We'll hand it off. But yeah." A smug grin grew on his face. "You'd think by now that I'd learn my lesson on illegal activities. Spy. Smuggler."

Rachel shared his grin. If they had been alone, she would have kissed that smug face and added one more word—sexy.

Heading back to the front of the room, Guillen rejoined Marcus.

Rachel double-checked with the woman to make sure Marcus understood he couldn't speak of this meeting to anyone, and that he'd keep his tattoo covered at all times, as it shouldn't have been that healed for weeks or even months.

Guillen gave Marcus one last hug, handing him something. They approached the women, and Marcus gave Rachel a half-smile. "Thank you."

"You're welcome."

"Alright, come on. We need to hurry," the older woman said, putting an arm around his shoulder and thanking Rachel and Guillen.

After the door shut, Rachel and Guillen were left alone, reading each other's faces.

"You…" she said, unable to form a sentence.

He smiled, his eyes squinting a little. "You."

It only made her smile more.

He finally reached a hand out, intertwining their fingers. "We need to get going. We'll have all day to talk on the road."

She nodded. "But I'm not leaving without at least one kiss."

He pulled her in, giving her the slowest, softest kiss known to mankind or green folk. The kind that literally takes your breath away, that makes you physically weak. He pulled back. It was like torture, leaving it at one.

"I wish we didn't have to hide 'us,'" she said.

A look of longing crossed his face as he squeezed her hand. "I promise you: someday, we won't have to be a secret. And that will be the best day … ever."

***

After presenting her exit papers, Rachel safely left Community Nine. A few minutes later, Guillen exited and caught up to her. The back highway was often empty, and therefore their main travel route. It was mostly used by stunts, prison transfers, and unsavory characters with their own agendas.

After ensuring no one was in sight, Rachel took Guillen's hand. Her mind lingered on the boy they'd just left behind. "I still wish I could have done something more."

"I know." Guillen's voice was filled with similar regret. "His family's city is hours out of our way. We'd lose a whole day, at least."

She gave his hand a squeeze. "It is what it is. Better something than nothing." She thought back to the last part of their interaction. "I saw him put something in his pocket. What did you give him?"

A grin formed on Guillen's face, but he kept looking forward. "A birthday present."

She raised her eyebrows. "And that was…"

He cleared his throat. "One of my knives."

She wasn't really sure how she felt about that. What the old woman had said, hinting that some chose to take their own lives, made her uneasy. But it wasn't like stunts weren't allowed kitchen knives. "Isn't he a bit young?"

Guillen looked down, shaking his head. "His childhood is over."

She'd known that, but it was still a punch to the gut. She tried to lighten the mood. "Well, I'm a little jealous now."

He turned his head to face her, an eyebrow raised.

She splayed a hand on her chest. "I thought *I* was the only one special enough to be gifted a Guillen knife."

He chuckled. "Only *very* special people get one of those. I have a few to spare."

"Hmm." She released his hand, moving closer and putting her arm around him. "Hopefully there aren't *too* many special people along the way, or you won't have any weapons by the time we get to Community One."

He chuckled again. "The gentleman I have custom make them is along the way. He knows to have some ready for me."

After just a few more minutes of striding along the path, her mind turned back to Marcus. She didn't know what all they'd talked about, but seeing the relief on his face, after how hard he'd been taking his first morning there… She was an expert witness of how something as simple as a few minutes in conversation with Guillen could make all the difference in the world. "What was it like for you? When they came for you?"

Guillen hesitated. "They *didn't* come for me," he answered softly.

Rachel cocked her head. "I thought you were allowed to live with your family until you were eighteen, as an exception, and then you were forced to go."

He opened his mouth, but nothing came out for a moment. "I had to get my mark at fourteen, just like Marcus. But yeah, eighteen—that was an option for me. An option I didn't actually take." He gave her a quick side-glance. "I still had the tutors, but I left on my own, at sixteen."

Her chest hurt. Moving out at sixteen to go live on his own? And somehow, he'd decided manual labor was preferable to living with his own family. She had a clear view of his scar. "Because of your mom?"

He took a deep breath. "That's the short answer."

"I'm sorry you had to go through that."

He slowly nodded. "Me too." He shrugged. "But then, sometimes I realize I'm not that sorry. You know?"

She lightly kicked away a pebble in her path. "No. I don't know."

"Just…" He stood taller, wearing a pensive look. "If my mother wasn't who she was back then, then I wouldn't be me. And if I wasn't me, I probably wouldn't be that close to Kaylah. And I wouldn't have been as driven to help out. And I never would have met Marcus, or you."

Rachel smiled, her cheeks warming. She could hardly agree that she was somehow okay with his mom being abusive, even if it had eventually brought them together. But she understood what he'd meant by it. "I wish I could say that about my life—that I'm at peace with my past. I mean … not that I'd obviously give you up."

He grinned, leaning down and planting a kiss on her cheek. "I've had years to process all that. You get a lot of time to think when you're working with your hands on the job. *Your* wounds are still healing."

Her heart full, she stopped walking, turning and gazing into his eyes. "I am *so* lucky. And…" *Is this the right moment?*

Guillen cleared his throat, throwing a sideways glance down the lane. No, this wouldn't be their moment. They quickly moved apart, and she strode forward at a quicker but natural pace while he stayed back, fiddling with his shoe.

Note to self: nowhere public.

She fought resentment as she passed a small group of travelers. They nodded, and she reciprocated. Sometimes, she and Guillen struggled to follow their routine, but they'd agreed to do better— they could only be acquaintances in public.

What were we just saying about life bringing us together?

After a few minutes, Guillen caught up to her, only grabbing her hand again after a few glances to ensure the coast was clear. "Sorry. What were you saying?"

She pursed her lips. "Um … Just that I'm lucky to be here with you."

He gave her hand a double squeeze. "Not as lucky as I am."

Chapter 24

COMMUNITY EIGHT RECEIVED GUILLEN and Rachel well. Rachel was happy to have one of the guards join them for the meeting—one of the guards who served these communities because they actually wanted what was best for these people. Guillen had known him for years. Chatting with the guard gave Rachel a huge boost of confidence. He was able to report how Unitas sentiments were spreading throughout the 'regular' communities, as well. Perhaps not as swiftly—those people weren't as oppressed; they didn't have as much to motivate them. But there were plenty growing tired of splitting up their families and losing people in a war they found themselves decreasingly passionate about.

When Rachel and Guillen made it to Community Seven, they had some time, again, to tour the area before their evening meeting. They stood in front of the family housing and orphanage.

"I know adoption isn't just a magic wand you can wave at couples that can't have kids, but have Magda and Jacob considered it?" she asked.

Guillen pursed his lips, reluctant to answer.

She sighed heavily. "It's never that simple, right?"

"It's a rare defect. Orphanages are positioned in every other stunt community. It's luck of the draw. Magda and Jacob were assigned the wrong place as kids. And we're sometimes allowed to move to a different community for something like work needs, but it's rare. It requires a new tattoo, more paperwork, and a significant reason."

She balled her fists, her jaw clenched. She'd never understood how people grew up thinking themselves so much better than others.

He took her hands, easing them open. "That look you get—when you're indignant, when you're scorched like this—it's one of the reasons I love you."

Her muscles relaxed as she looked into his soft blue eyes. "You love me?"

His mouth hung open. "I guess it wasn't the most romantic way to say it. But yes. Is that too soon?" He gazed into her eyes with a look of hope.

"No." She smiled. "I just kind of hoped I'd say it first."

He grinned. "Then never mind. I retract my statement. I do not love you yet."

She chuckled. "I don't think it works that way." She swallowed. "I love you, Guillen."

"I love you too." He held her hands just a moment longer before letting them go.

They barely had time to grab a quick bite before attending their meeting. It killed her—the glances they exchanged, keeping their distance in public after their moment. They just had to get through their meeting, and then she could be with him.

***

He closed the door behind them as they returned for the night. Locking it, he turned and leaned back. "That. Went. Great."

"It did." She smiled and fidgeted with her hands. Their propositions in this meeting had been met with minimal resistance, but her mind was already back to the moment they'd shared earlier.

He radiated happiness. "And I'll say it again—I love you."

Her smile widened. "I really love you too. I just don't know that I'm ready … for some things to change yet."

He stepped forward, setting his key down on the side table next to her. "I didn't say it with expectations. We can take our time."

"Thank you." She blushed, giving him a hug.

After getting ready for the night, they sat on the bed, playing cards they'd picked up. They were different from a standard deck in the human world, and he was teaching her his favorite games.

She thought back to their conversation earlier in the day. "You've said 'scorched' a few times. That means 'pissed,' right?"

His face showed confusion and disgust. "What does being angry have to do with urine?"

She covered her mouth, laughing.

He read her face, bunching his eyebrows. "Is 'piss' not universal with Seeders and humans?"

Rachel struggled to stop laughing, but successfully managed, instead wearing a huge smile. "Yes, I guess you're right. Piss means urine. But when you say you're 'pissed' or 'pissed off,' it means you're upset."

He shook his head. "I still don't get the connection."

"Honestly, I don't even understand that myself." She realized it was her turn, and placed a card down. "Scorched is better."

Guillen studied his hand with a smile. "I guess we'll add that to the list to remember."

"Yeah, I suppose I haven't used that one, since you haven't given me that horrified look until now."

He chuckled. A minute later, he spoke again. "I forgot to tell you—I'll be leaving during the night. We should be getting an update from Kaylah. I made a contact." He played a card. "I know you don't want to be left alone while I head out on official business, but—"

She looked up. "I get it. Sometimes the fewer people involved, the better. Thanks for letting me know so I'm not worried."

"Thanks, honey." He smiled; she grinned back.

"I was wondering … about the orphans," she started.

"Yeah?"

"When you first explained to me the restrictions on your kind, you sounded like you wanted to have kids." And that was all before she'd seen him with the boy, Marcus.

Guillen shrugged. "Well … there are a lot of factors involved, aren't there?"

They exchanged a knowing glance. This war, their societies, and physiology. There were a lot of what-ifs. Seeders were incapable of having kids with other races, not even with their own kind without powers.

"Yes. In an ideal world, I think I'd like to have kids," he continued. "If the laws changed. But they haven't yet. And even when they do … it's not a deal-breaker. I've lived my whole life with the expectation that I couldn't."

Frowning, she set down her playing cards. "But once your people have equality, you shouldn't have to sacrifice that part of yourself. I'm not trying to be presumptuous, but you know what I mean."

He acknowledged his understanding with a lift of the eyebrows. "What about you? Do you want kids?"

Rachel shook her head. "Not the Seeder way. That's way too many kids for me, even if I had closer bonds to my family back there to help out. I always kind of imagined a couple, though. Back when I thought I was human. So, I guess it's all or nothing, for my kind."

He looked back down at his cards.

"Would you ever consider adoption?" she asked. "One of those kids? Or even an Ivy or Seeder with powers, orphaned from this war?"

He read her face. "Yes. I would."

She smirked. "You would make a great dad."

He gave a shy smile, looking down at his hand again. "And anyone in your life is lucky to be there."

They finished the game, and Guillen shuffled the cards. His face looked as though he were lost in thought. "Talking of sacrifices and … well … you know, if things…" He twisted his lips. "What about you and your powers?"

She narrowed her eyes. "I'm not following."

"Don't you get another power if you choose to be with one of your own kind?"

"Oh … that." She hadn't thought about the fact that she'd never get the ability to throw darts if she never paired off with a Seeder. A sinking feeling in her gut brought her gaze down to the bed they were sitting on. She wanted to say that it didn't matter, that it was trivial. But she hesitated. Sometimes, back in the Unitas camp, she'd been paired to train with a male Seeder, and had extended energy for darts. She'd gotten annoyed more than once that all she could do was provide extra power, that she couldn't do the aiming herself, that her part was so passive.

"I don't expect an answer right away," Guillen said. "Or the one you think I want to hear. I want your honesty as much as you want mine."

She glanced up, pressing her lips together, nodding. They continued to play in relative silence. It ate at her. Was she being selfish? He was willing to sacrifice something he wanted and could only get elsewhere, but she wasn't? She tried to shift her perspective. They were talking hypothetically, anyway. In the future. A future where a Seeder and Ivy could actually even be together. A future where they both made it out of the war alive. What could darts do for you when there was no war to fight? Make glorified pushpins?

"I could live without them," she said.

He remained silent as he finished his turn. "You're sure?"

"Yes. You don't have to have everything, to be happy. Look at you—you're amazing with your knife work. You don't need vines."

He looked her in the eye, seemingly skeptical. "Give it some thought. I find people often come to resent crutches, and would usually prefer to have fully functioning legs, if given the choice."

She frowned. "I don't see you that way."

He smiled, but it didn't reach his eyes. "I appreciate that. But my birth defect wasn't a choice. We're talking about you forfeiting potential."

It hurt, the way his truth pierced. But at least he wasn't holding back. She had to ask herself about her checklist of life goals. She obviously hadn't been obsessing over it, and she hadn't even chosen the Seeder life. She could do without darts, but part of her wondered if he was right—that it might nag at her down the road, leaving a box unchecked.

An outsider might just say the easy solution would be to have a quick fling with another Seeder to get those powers. But that wouldn't be fair to a Seeder—he'd be mated to only her for life. Infidelity amongst Seeders was extremely rare; the bond made other romantic and physical relationships unfulfilling. She wouldn't be able to enjoy Guillen the same way afterward.

After finishing another round of their game, she was more confident in her answer. "If I had to choose between you and darts, I'd choose you."

He smiled softly. "Okay."

***

Rachel opted to stay up late and spend more time together, until Guillen had to leave for his rendezvous, then she promptly passed out in bed.

She woke in the morning to his handsome face resting peacefully. She didn't move, not wanting to wake him, unsure of how long he'd been out.

Her mind drifted to darker times, when she'd woken up in the prince's arms. Someone she'd thought loved her. Someone who, aside from being an evil, warmongering liar, had also cheated on her. He'd dated his fiancée for years behind Rachel's back. Rachel tried to imagine the woman—if she was as horrible as he was, or just naïve, like Rachel had been. Rachel grinned, hoping she'd left him with a nice scar after he'd assaulted her.

Her trust had been violated repeatedly, by several of those closest to her. Why did it come so easily with Guillen? She didn't have an ounce of doubt that he was who he claimed to be. She didn't worry that he'd lost his way during the night and landed in another woman's bed.

"You okay?" His groggy voice pulled her from her memories.

She smiled, breathing in the quiet moment. "I am. Really." She moved closer and gave him a kiss. "So, this is what it's like to wake up to someone you love?"

"Mmm. I guess so."

"How late were you out? What kind of news is there?"

His smile faded, and he broke eye contact. "Not great."

Her heart beat faster. "Just tell me." She sat up, leaning against the wall.

He sat up to join her. "Everyone you and I know is safe. Okay? Let's start there."

"What's that supposed to mean?"

He bit his lip. "Another one of the girls at the palace died."

She wanted to cry, but tears didn't even come. At this point, that kind of news from the palace was exhausting, disappointing, and hopeless. She leaned forward, resting her face in her hands.

He rubbed her back. "I'm so sorry. I wish we could have gotten you all out of there at the same time."

She sat up straight. "You don't get it. It was hell back there, and it was just a few days for me. Those girls have been there for *months*! We need to be doing more!"

"We will. I promise. And there's more. It's not all bad news."

She closed her eyes. "Please at least tell me it doesn't get worse."

"No. I think that's the worst of it."

"What else?"

"Well … Kaylah is safely still at the camp. But … the camp is under siege, and the word will be going out today throughout our kingdom about her part as a traitor. She's been named, as well as accomplices like Jon and Olivia. Kaylah's wanted alive. The others … wanted dead."

Rachel nodded as a couple of tears made their way to the surface. "Do they know about you? About us? Our mission?"

"No. We're still safe, from what we can tell. Barely anyone knows what we're up to."

"Why would Soren finally be changing the story?"

Guillen shrugged. "He's desperate. Losing another girl weakens their attack. Acting like Kaylah was a prisoner wasn't enough. He wants her back. He wants a win."

"He doesn't *seem* desperate." She rolled her eyes. "We're hardly a threat, just letting the rest of the girls rot."

Guillen shook his head. "You know we can't just march there and get them out. I don't mean to sound heartless, but people have to understand the number of lives it would cost to rescue just one of those girls right now, with his fortifications."

She met his eyes. "Would you feel the same way if you'd rescued someone else, instead of me?"

Hurt shone in his eyes. "That's not fair."

She lowered her gaze. "Keep going. I'm assuming there's more."

"Seeders have openly and publicly embraced Unitas," he shared in a more cheerful voice. "Your leaders sent a formal declaration. We're going to do this." He waited a moment. "That's the last of it."

She took a deep breath while he cautiously held her hand. She ought to have felt more triumphant about the success, something she'd been key in, but her heart and mind dwelled on the palace.

"I love you," he said. "I'm going to keep you safe. And we're going to win this. You just keep being your wonderful self. What you and I are doing—we're making a difference."

Her heart was still heavy. "I just wish it was more. I love all the free time with you, and getting to see your lands, but isn't there a way we can move faster?" She wished she could rift from community to community, but catching a breeze in Ivy skies would be a death sentence, even if it were possible to rift within the Green Lands to another location internally. And besides, she didn't know how to rift from the Ivy side; she only vaguely knew the portal locations from Seeder airspace. And Guillen still couldn't rift, even from the ground. "Can't we call earlier meetings, instead of waiting around all day?"

"I know you want to go faster, but it's crucial that our work continues unnoticed. We can't disturb people's work schedules."

She leaned back, faster than she'd intended to, smacking her head against the wall. She winced. "Then let's get going. No more sleeping in. We can travel through the night, sleep outside on the way, if it will get us from place to place faster."

"Okay. We'll see what we can do."

They promptly got up and dressed for the day, setting out for their next destination.

Chapter 25

SAFF AND DEVIN DEPARTED THEIR TENT, walking hand in hand to training practice.

"This should be interesting," he said with a smile.

She nodded with a matching grin. "Who would have thought?" Despite the daily demands on her energy, time, and heart, this was a place where Saff had grown comfortable. She still missed being back home in South Fortinda, where most of her family helped keep the village going and fought to keep their portion of the border safe. But anywhere with Devin was home. And both of them had learned important lessons in trust and forgiveness. Not just with each other, but with the Ivies they associated with on a daily basis.

After a short walk, they met up with their sparring group for advanced training. Twelve Seeders were paired with twelve Ivies, preparing for future tactical teams, when the time would come that they were ready to advance on the palace.

Saff was paired with a female Ivy. While modern Ivy culture usually relegated their women's powers more to nursing roles, Kaylah willingly took volunteers to train in combat. Saff shook hands with her new partner, Flora. Flora's waist-length burgundy hair hung down in braids, and she couldn't have been more than eighteen.

"Let's check out those darts first," Flora said, stepping back and extending a vine from her wrist. She coiled it into a flat disk, holding it out in front of her as a shield.

Saff hesitated. All of her Seeder training thus far had involved dart-throwing at targets, never a living person. "You sure you're ready?"

Flora lowered the shield to reveal her face, wearing a crooked smile. "I'm ready, but maybe you're not?"

Saff accepted the playful taunting. Ivy vines and leaves were less sensitive to pain than even Seeder blades. Her strikes wouldn't physically hurt her partner, as long as they landed in the right place. Saff balled her fist, centering her energy, then flicked her wrist to launch the darts. Three projectiles landed in the coiled vine shield. One made it halfway through, having found its mark between the edges of the vine.

Flora lowered her shield, eyes wide.

Saff grinned. "Keep it tight, or they'll sneak through."

Flora cleared her throat, plucking out the darts. "Right. Yeah. Let's try that a couple more times."

They later moved on to hand-to-hand combat, leaf-tips and blade-edges blunted to avoid any significant damage. Saff snuck a glance in Devin's direction every once in a while to see how he was doing.

Flora was attempting to take Saff down with different vine-wrapping techniques as Saff got distracted by Devin's exercise with his partner. Devin's counterpart had balled up the end of his vine and was swinging it around as a flail. The dulled leaf edges made it less menacing, but Saff had to hand it to the Ivies—Seeders could fly and throw darts, but when determined, Ivies were no less lethal.

In Saff's moment of distraction, Flora tried something new. Saff startled at a couple of quick pricks in each of her forearms, then the surrounding areas went numb—both hands and lower arms quickly lost all feeling.

"Hey!"

Flora reeled in her vines, backing up and folding her arms. "You seemed preoccupied. What can you do now?"

Saff scowled at her, shaking her arms as though that would somehow bring the feeling back. She stood with her mouth agape, realizing how impotent she was at that moment. Numb arms. She couldn't rift, or catch a breeze, extend blades, throw darts … anything, really. "It's not exactly a fair challenge, though, is it? None of your females will be guarding the palace."

Flora casually studied her nails. "You never know. Either way," she oozed pride, "you have to admit, we have a great teacher."

Saff had to concede she was right. Kaylah, Ginger, and Olivia had not only taught their women in camp how to be more efficient nurses, and how to heal the Seeder lands, but tactics like these— which would be incredibly effective. They didn't need to expend enough poison to make an opponent unconscious; just enough for a simple local numbing could get a lot done.

Saff looked down at her arms again. She had to be able to do *something*… Just like she'd learned to master the separation between her energy and emotions, she surmised she could still force a change, even if she couldn't physically feel it. Focusing on just one arm, she pushed her Seeder energy down. She kept pooling it there, willing it to do what she wanted. Soon enough, her right blade extended, and she glanced up. Flora was ready with a shield and a smirk.

With an uncomfortable lack of feeling and control, Saff swung her arm, striking at Flora and landing a solid slice into her vines. Gaining a little more courage, Saff struck again, cutting through the edge, and leaving a gash in Flora's arm.

Flora flinched, sucking in air through clenched teeth.

Saff gasped. "I'm so sorry! I didn't know it was sharp. I can't really control it while numbed! Let's heal that for you."

Flora instead extended a fresh vine, puncturing herself near the wound. It stopped bleeding, and she poked around it, appearing to no longer be in pain. "We'll heal when we're done. Let's keep going."

After another hour of both experimental and established fighting strategies, Flora and Saff sat down to hydrate and heal.

"You're pretty impressive," Saff said, her glowing hand finishing up the job on Flora's wound.

"Likewise." Flora smiled.

Saff took a swig from her bottle. "If you don't mind me asking … why did you join Unitas? And why fighting, not just healing the land?"

Flora cracked open a water bottle of her own. "I had *two* boyfriends break up with me, choosing to join a human-world detail." Her tone changed. "Then I had a brother killed in the war."

Saff frowned. They both hurt for brothers who had died on the battlefield, and for all they knew, it could have been in the same battle, against each other. "One of my brothers was killed, too."

Flora nodded. "There's too much of that. It shouldn't be this way. And … when I learned I could really help, not just sit at home, doing a regular job … I came with my friend."

Saff smiled. "I appreciate you. I hope someday history will see Kaylah for all she's really done for both sides."

"Same." Flora took a drink.

Saff shifted sitting positions on the hard-packed dirt. "So, how did you learn about Unitas? Who recruited you?"

Flora pointed her water bottle in the direction of some of the others still sparring. "The friend I told you about."

There were dozens of Ivies living in the Unitas camp by now, and Saff hadn't met them all, but she vaguely recognized the girl Flora pointed out. Her friend, a shorter girl with shoulder-length black hair, sparred with a Seeder Saff had spent more time with.

"Her name's Raven," Flora said. "She's actually the one who was initially recruited. I'm just a tagalong."

Devin and his partner joined the girls, both of the guys a little bloody.

Saff gave Devin a disapproving look. "I see neither of you listened about keeping sharp edges to yourselves." She first set to healing the Ivy male's cuts.

Devin smirked. "We decided it wouldn't feel realistic if we weren't actually at risk of getting hurt."

Saff rolled her eyes. "Well, next time, you should pair up with Flora. She's got some surprise moves up her sleeve." She winked at Flora, and Flora chuckled.

The group chatted a bit about the different techniques they'd practiced, while Saff finished healing Devin. Eventually, Raven and her fighting partner also joined them. They all exchanged handshakes before Saff and Devin got up to go.

"I'll walk you to the border?" he offered.

"I'll take it." She straightened her shirt.

He wrapped his arm around her, and they headed to the edge of camp. "Doing alright after all that healing?"

She poked him in the ribs. "You're lucky I have meetings today, so I don't need all of that energy."

"Mmm... I'm glad we get to do this together. I wouldn't have it any other way."

She leaned into his embrace. "Ditto. Better together. Which is why I'm glad they're not holding us women back next time. Or the Ivy women. We need to stop hedging our bets."

He nodded. "There's no doubt about it; you ladies are impressive."

She took a slow, deep breath. "Can you imagine how things could be by the time we're old enough to have a clutch of our own? If the lands were healed enough, or we were allowed more space in the Neutral Woods to raise our kids ... *together.*"

"I think about it every day."

Kaylah and her accompanying guards approached to meet up with Saff.

Devin stopped and pulled Saff in for a hug. "Find me for dinner?"

She squeezed him tight, then stole a peck on the lips. "Camp protection detail, right?"

He nodded. "I know. Be safe—I will be. Same goes for you."

***

Saff and Kaylah walked out of camp through a narrow neck of the Neutral Woods. They passed several Seeders without powers working on reinforcement walls to keep the passageway open. Despite the siege on the Unitas camp, war council leaders often had their attention occupied with official Seeder lands. The Seeder border walls—the protective barrier thickets—were still failing under the constant attack of Ivy soldiers and the War Vines.

Saff spotted a friendly face. "Zeus, what are you doing out here?"

He lowered a hammer, wiping his brow. "Hey, good to see you. Just doing my part. I'll go back to checking on my cleanup crew soon."

She smiled. "That's great. You guys are doing awesome work." She and Kaylah felt awful for drawing attention to Arcadia, which had previously been undiscovered and untargeted by Ivies. But they had needed to open the cave outside of their border walls, and this rocky terrain afforded them those options. After Unitas's camp location had been compromised, the entire village went to work, helping to build fortifications. In a way, it was good for them to not be so isolated. The goal was to integrate them back into regular Seeder society someday anyway, when enough of the lands were healed.

"Any, uh, word? About," Zeus awkwardly fidgeted with the hammer, "well, in general. People, places, things?"

Saff hid a grin. He was definitely asking about Rachel. "No big news to report, sorry."

He nodded with a half-smile.

"We can't be late for our meeting. But it was good to see you."

He resumed his work while Saff and Kaylah continued on their way.

Saff cleared her throat. "Look at that—he's still interested. And his kind are inching their way into regular society. That makes him even more dateable."

Kaylah laughed. "And I'm sure *many* Seeder women will swoon over that deep voice and those muscles. Rachel will not be one of them."

Saff rolled her eyes. "You're so sure of yourself."

Kaylah grinned. "On some things. I'm good at picking up on what people want and need. That's probably why Eric and I moved so fast. Once I got to know him, I knew he could be the one."

A wave of guilt washed over Saff, that she could be there and have Devin's support while Kaylah and Eric were still separated. "So, I have questions for you."

Kaylah ducked under a tree branch. "Go for it."

"I was just paired up with Flora."

"Ah, yes. That one's a quick learner! Her friend, too."

Saff chuckled, remembering how panicked she'd been with numb arms. "Yeah. You really don't think we'll have female Ivy opposition, even at the palace?"

Kaylah shook her head. "Nope. Guards and soldiers are all male."

"But why? That's pretty stupid. You told us once that Ivies were lied to about their own powers, and that you could teach them. But wouldn't even the palace have a secret stash of competent women with skills like this?"

"Hmm, that is a *very* complicated story."

"Give me the abridged version."

Kaylah linked arms with Saff. "Well, let's first talk about our viewpoints on women. Both of our societies are matriarchal, but how we're treated and how our powers manifest themselves are different. We have the head matriarch, the queen. All of your fully-rooted women are considered matriarchs in their own rights. Let me ask you a question—even without the extra chemical arts, why aren't our women trained as soldiers and assassins, according to what *you* were taught?"

Saff shrugged. "Because you're physically weaker, and your leaves aren't as sharp."

"Yes. The 'weaker' sex. At least some would see it that way. But in a matriarchal society, as in many others, I'm sure, we're also the 'fairer' sex. Some would say we should be revered and protected. So, either way you look at it, people can justify sidelining us. And unlike Seeders, we have pregnancies pretty similar to humans, so we don't just ship women off to war with child."

"Okay. But those that are not pregnant…"

"That's where it gets stickier." Kaylah nodded politely at a group of workers, and they reciprocated. "The hodgepodge of information we're going off of is a collection of your stolen archives and our *hidden* archives. At least that's what I think. I think some of those books were censored, though some may not have been. Either way, I'm fairly certain the general public doesn't have access to those books regarding just my people. My uncle dug those out from some pretty deep vaults."

As gravel crunched under their shoes, Kaylah continued. "The energy your people wield is identical to what we do. Not necessarily the quantity, but the makeup is the same. I think our chemical abilities are more varied, and it's widely accepted that the chemical composition of even our most basic 'poison' varies. That's how true nurses in the profession are sorted out—people prefer their poison to that of others when needing medical help. The main reference I'm teaching these girls and women from was written by Sanath Fulgrum. Do you know what Sanath is known for?"

"Uh … No…" Saff barely knew anything about the internal workings of Ivy society and its prominent citizens and leaders.

"Publicly—nothing," Kaylah said. "In medical journals— quackery. Someone obviously found it curious enough to store her notes in archives, and for that, we're grateful. Humans used to think they could cure all sorts of sicknesses with bloodletting and, well…"

Saff twisted her lips. They both knew what Kaylah was implying, but Saff wouldn't dare utter it—leeches. She still remembered the last time she let that one slip from her mouth, out of habit. It was undeniable that the term fit in a lot of ways, in relation to Ivies and the ways their powers worked, but that didn't excuse the use of it. And it still stung the way Rachel had censured her. Saff's only experiences with Ivies before Kaylah had been filled with assassins, soldiers, and pain. And she'd never been a racist in the human world. She made a concerted effort after that, to be extra careful.

"Anyway," Kaylah said. "We're always learning more about ourselves. Sanath believed there's a spectrum of powers, that we possess discernable channels for different abilities, and that the crude poison we use is actually a combination of them. It made sense to me when I read it, and I began experimenting. Just like our vines, some things come natural to you guys, like your eye glow, right? But I'm guessing you might have never learned to rift or catch a breeze if no one had taught you."

Saff smiled. "Yeah, that's safe to say. But imagine the first person who realized they could commune with the wind and decided to give it a try!"

Kaylah chuckled.

"So, that's what you meant, by your people being lied to? That some doctor's theories were hidden?"

Kaylah frowned. "I wish it were that simple." They were now just yards away from the Seeder Outer Wall. "Long story short, I can't prove all of my theories. But our people talk about having had extra powers before the wars, and that your people did something to weaken us."

Saff scoffed. "Like what? Our powers don't work that way. We don't know how to do anything to you but physical harm, like—"

"I know. But when you don't have contact with the enemy, it's easy to lie and fashion a scapegoat. Then again, maybe I'm reading into things, and it was a genuine misunderstanding. You yourself misunderstood the reason for your ability to wield extra energy, right?"

Saff nodded. Reaching the stone doorway that led to the other side of the thicket border wall, they waited, surrounded by several more guards.

"Princess." The one in charge gave a polite nod. "Saff."

The women reciprocated.

"Anyway," Kaylah continued, speaking a little quieter. "Do you know how Germans and the Japanese teach their students about World War II?"

Saff shook her head.

"Honestly, me neither. I should have studied that. But we all take unique perspectives. I guess, look at the US. Most people call it the 'Civil War,' while some still call it the 'War of Northern Aggression.'"

Saff rolled her eyes again.

Kaylah shrugged as they opened the door and filed into the stone tunnel lined with lightkeepers. "Your people call what we did 'The Great Poisoning.' Do you know what Ivies call it?"

"No."

"Well, it sounds pretty bad." Kaylah glanced at their guards as they waited for the last locked door to open. She leaned forward, whispering in Saff's ear. "The Great Cleansing."

It churned Saff's stomach. "You mean like racial…"

Kaylah raised her eyebrows. "Kinda. Like I said, it sounds bad. The fact that very few details are taught to the public tells me some things are censored. But we had to have a heck of a lot of poison stored up to be able to poison all of your lands at once. We're talking *vats* of it into your soil and waterways."

Saff gave a polite smile to the guards as they were permitted past the border wall. "Thank you for your service." The daylight was refreshing, as was the whistle of nearby songbirds, but she was still queasy from the conversation.

"Our women stored up that poison for *decades*. If our poison isn't metabolized, it stays potent. The way I've heard it taught, 'The Great Cleansing' was more of a spiritual-type movement. Supposedly, just like your women go to temple wells to deposit energy, ours lined up to 'rid themselves' of the impurities of poison. Somehow, if they could make regular deposits, they would 'cleanse' themselves, and prove us the superior race. The more vitriolic and potent the poison one could fashion, the better the person became."

Saff scrunched her eyebrows. "Really? And they didn't realize they were just stockpiling a weapon?"

Sighing, Kaylah straightened her bun. "I genuinely don't know. The fact that those deposit sites have all been torn down, and the way it's taught… Not everything lines up for me. Maybe they knew it was a weapon and then dressed it up out of shame. Or the public really didn't know, and there was backlash when they found out, so the truth was buried? Either way, the attack was carried out, and I surmise those who still remembered or tried to use any former channels of chemical arts were silenced. Your people got blamed for us losing nebulous powers." They stopped short of entering the council meeting building. "Maybe we actually did lose our understanding of how to do more, after decades of only being laser-focused on one thing. We'll never know."

Saff frowned. "What will you teach your people after this is all over?"

Kaylah tucked her hands into her pockets. "That's something your leaders and I have discussed, and will continue to discuss. We agree that we hope to both be as truthful as possible. The aftermath of war is just as ugly as the process of being in it."

Saff gave her a fake smile. "On that happy note, let's not keep them waiting."

Kaylah chuckled, throwing an arm around Saff's shoulder. "On that happy note…"

Chapter 26

SAFF AND KAYLAH SAT WITH a dozen Seeder leaders, in a village near the edge of Seeder territory and the Unitas camp. Both women were still utterly exhausted from the efforts just to keep their camp safe. The leaders only looked mildly less worn-out.

"You're really sure there's not a way to stretch your protective borders?" Kaylah asked. "That would allow us to focus our efforts on what we really need."

The head council leader shook her head. "No. It's absolutely out of the question. You know as well as I do that those walls were constructed before The Great Poisoning. We haven't built one in a century. It would require a *massive* amount of energy—energy we don't have to spare. We can't divert our resources like that."

Kaylah rubbed her forehead.

The councilwoman spoke again. "I do still think it would be better to move Saff and Devin's training to be safely behind our borders."

"No," Saff said. "We'll escort the girls home as quickly as we can, but we need to be there to greet them. And the camp needs as many strong people as possible, and we're willing to put in the extra work." They were the new line of defense for the village without powers now, and the cave.

"We still don't even know if the cave strategy has been compromised," the councilwoman reminded them. "We haven't seen any attacks, in either world, trying to use one of the caves."

"Not yet," Kaylah snipped.

"Speaking of caves." The woman stacked some papers on the table. "A lot of your plan hinges on intrarealm rifting between them. How is that coming?"

"I'm almost there. I can feel it. I was going to ask if I could take another look in your old records."

The councilwoman nodded. "Yes, you can be escorted there any time."

"Thank you."

A knock sounded at the door, and a messenger stepped in. "My apologies. You asked for this update the moment it arrived." The messenger handed Kaylah a letter.

She opened it and smiled. "Perfect timing. We could use some good news. It's…" She surveyed the room as if to ensure the information was safe with those in attendance. "It's from Rachel and Guillen."

Saff sat up in her seat.

"They're safe. Still undiscovered. They're picking up speed and doing well. One of our outposts just got a shipment from some of the communities they've already rallied in."

Everyone was happy to hear the news and further details. At the meeting's conclusion, Saff and Kaylah left together.

"I'm glad to hear things are going okay over there. And that she's still in one piece." Saff frowned. "I can only imagine what the news of that last girl at the palace did to her. If things go south, you still think Guillen will be able to keep her safe, without any powers?"

"He will. I wouldn't have sent her over there with anyone I wasn't confident in. They'll keep each other safe."

Saff bobbed her head thoughtfully. "You encouraged her to like him. Knowing what she's been through with your family and people, do you really think that's a good idea? I still … worry."

Kaylah tilted her head. "I've known them both longer than you. I love them both. They're good for each other." She smirked. "And I'm not usually a matchmaker, but you can't deny I'm good at bringing people together."

Saff laughed. "*That* I will absolutely agree with."

They stopped walking but continued to chat.

"Why is the cave-to-cave strategy so important to you? Are you willing to support an attack if you can't figure it out? Once Guillen and Rachel have made enough progress?"

"We *really* need that element of surprise. If we have to, we could try to send enough of our troops through this cave to the human world, then slingshot them back to that cave. But I haven't been able to get that one to work yet, in any capacity. And it would waste a lot of time and energy. It's not that I'm not open to different ideas, we just need a breakthrough to ensure a quick win once we advance on the palace. I want as few lives lost as possible."

Saff held her hands up. "I'm not the strategist. I'll leave that to you and the council. Why did you request to go back and look at the old records? You really think there's something we missed?"

Kaylah pursed her lips. "I don't know that we were looking for it when we were there last. Do Seeders teach old history?"

"What kind of old history?"

"Like where we come from? Were the Green Lands here first, and those that left became human? Or was it the other way around?"

Saff shook her head. "No. I've never heard that taught. Though Devin and I have speculated before."

"Ivy kids grow up on all sorts of lore and fairy tales. I've sent for some books to be smuggled here for us to review. I think the humans came first. From the way our stories go, a group of people stumbled on the energy of the Green Lands. There are stories of caves, and the ancient language, rifts, travel, transformation and discovery. Even jade is included in the stories, though we don't incorporate it into our powers the way your society does."

"That sounds cool." Saff wished she had more time for studies. She and Kaylah had barely shared any time on research lately. "But that's a lot of hope, basing war strategy on bedtime stories."

Kaylah gestured widely at the sky. "Growing up in the human world, wouldn't this whole place seem like a fantasy to you?"

Saff smiled, sensing the Seeder energy in her heart. "Yeah. It's like a work of fiction."

"And I remember having to read human fairy tales—a lot of those are based in truth. I haven't been wrong yet, have I?"

Saff took a deep breath. "You're pretty clever. I'll give you that. I was a nearly-straight-A student in high school. You must have been one of those five-point-oh students."

Kaylah laughed. "C-average. Not that my real parents knew that. Ginger and Nathan helped me fudge that truth while I focused on learning all of this."

Saff glanced down the path. "Are you heading back to camp?"

"No. I'm going straight to the libraries. Please let Jon and Ginger know. And give everyone my best."

"Will do." Saff hugged Kaylah. "Stay safe, *Princess*." She smirked, having started to annoy Kaylah, addressing her by that title.

Kaylah grinned and rolled her eyes. "Try and keep the camp in one piece until I'm back."

***

As the sun rose in the sky the next morning, Saff set out from her tent toward the Unitas garden to grab breakfast for herself and Devin; he was on a walk with Heather.

The sunrise was too beautiful to neglect. Pulling her mind from the training ahead, and the murmur of constant battle at camp borders, Saff strolled toward the quietest place she could think of—the canyon's edge.

Detouring from her original destination, she soon found she wasn't the only person with that idea. Kaylah sat on the cliff's edge, her feet dangling over, peering at the painted sky. As usual, two guards accompanied her, standing several paces back.

Saff approached one of them. "Is it okay if I go sit with her?"

The man she'd approached stood tall with crossed arms. "Your Highness, are you—"

"Stop calling me that!" Kaylah snapped.

Okay. Maybe no chat today… "It's fine. I'll go."

Kaylah looked over her shoulder. "Oh." Her tone softened. "Do you need something?"

Maybe it was best to leave Kaylah alone to think in peace, as she was clearly having a rough morning. Then again, maybe she needed someone to talk to. It wasn't like she had a whole lot of personal support now that Rachel was gone. She'd earned loyal followers, but that wasn't the same. Nathan and Eric were still in the human world, and the only other close friend Kaylah had in camp was Ginger.

"Unless you want to be by yourself, I just came to enjoy the sunrise for a minute before getting to work."

Kaylah gestured at the massive expanse of the canyon. "I don't know, it's a bit crowded." She winked.

Saff sat down by her. Oddly, she was still a bit afraid of heights when not flying. It was a little nerve-racking to dangle her legs over the edge. "You okay?"

Leaning back, Kaylah raised her chin to the sky. "Of course I'm okay. I'm always okay."

"Riiiiight…" Saff bit her lip, unsure of what to say. "Why do you hate it so much when people call you by your title now?" Kaylah hadn't seemed to hate it when they'd first met. And she had made it clear she wanted to be queen, but she wouldn't accept people calling her 'Your Majesty,' either. She didn't seem to genuinely mind being called 'Princess,' though, which added to the weirdness. But then again, Saff had never held an official title like that.

"Because it reminds me what I should be, if I'd been brave enough. If I'd had the guts to kill my parents before Soren did, this would all be over, and I could actually be making a difference right now."

Saff frowned. Kaylah was right. If she had assassinated her parents instead of defecting, creating Unitas, trying to negotiate and make an alliance with the Seeders, all of this could be over. Ben might even still be alive right now. "Look at this camp, though. How many hundreds of years has it been since our people occupied a place together and weren't killing each other?"

Kaylah raised a skeptical eyebrow. "Right... This is *wildly* successful. Every other day, there's at least one argument that has to be broken up. We're doing *so* good, just because we're not murdering each other." She glanced over her shoulder again, in the direction of camp. "And I don't sleep all that well, worried when the next betrayal will be."

Picking up a small pebble with jagged edges, Saff turned it in her hand, running her thumbs over the textured surfaces. "Baby steps." She eyed Kaylah. "I don't really know that I've seen suspicious activity. Have you? I mean, I'm always a bit paranoid, but it's not like I've stumbled upon a secret meeting planning Unitas's downfall..."

Kaylah shrugged, gazing across the canyon. "Hard to say. For all I know, *you* might still want me dead, and plan to shove me off this cliffside."

Saff leaned forward, staring down toward the base of the canyon. The river that cut through it was just a thin line from this high up. "I have a feeling I'd fare a lot better, being able to catch a breeze. People might get mad if I shoved off the leader of Unitas."

Kaylah grinned. "I appreciate your forbearance."

After a minute of silence, Saff soaked in the moment—the sky brightening, the faintest of breezes stirring the air. Moving a hint of energy to her bicep, she chucked the pebble as far as she could across the canyon. How much energy would it take for it to actually make it to the other side?

"You know, I've been giving a lot of thought to what I want to do with my life," Saff said.

Reaching to her side, Kaylah also grasped a nearby pebble, studying it. "Yeah? Change of career?"

Saff softly sighed. "I just don't know. I love learning and teaching, but maybe that's not the best use of my time. Maybe I should actually do more fighting, making use of my extra energy abilities."

Kaylah didn't respond. She instead chucked her pebble into the canyon.

"I mean, why not use it to keep our people safe, right?"

"I suppose. I'd kinda hoped that we'd have unlocked more secrets about our powers by understanding your extra abilities."

Saff slowly nodded. She'd been trying to sort through that herself, but on a more personal level. "I'll be honest." She hesitated, not sure if her relationship with Kaylah was at that level yet. "Well, it's like pulling back the curtain and... I don't know... I guess it's petty, but it was a little deflating finding out I'm only special because of a freak accident. Not really all that special."

"Mmm... I would argue that Spiderman is still pretty cool. He didn't sign up for a spider bite."

Saff almost laughed, being compared to a comic book character.

Kaylah twisted her lips. "Your leaders still haven't been able to find any girls your age who can wield as much power as you can."

"Really?" That brought a smile to Saff's face. She didn't expect a fan club, but who didn't want to feel special?

"Yep. Really. By all rights, you should have fallen into a coma and never made it home." She furrowed her brow. "I thought I'd once read something on it that made sense, but the books and scrolls kind of contradict themselves on the topic."

"Hmm."

"Plus." Kaylah shifted, tucking one leg up under the other. "I'd say you're pretty special in Devin's eyes. I see the way he looks at you when you're not watching."

Saff's cheeks burned. "He's better than I deserve."

Kaylah blew out a puff of air, turning to fully face Saff. She crossed her legs, her face more serious. "I don't know what to make of this sometimes."

'This' what?

"When this is over, could you see yourself visiting my kingdom?"

"Ummm…" Saff hadn't really asked herself that question. "Well, no offense, but I doubt it would be safe for a while, right? Unless you're talking about a guarded visit at your palace or something? Not everyone will be on board."

Kaylah pursed her lips, nodding. "Say it's safe—tension has calmed down. You come to visit my kingdom to check out the sights, to do some trading or something."

Unsure what Kaylah was trying to get at, Saff searched her face. "Well, if it's safe, I mean, we have a lot of rebuilding and restructuring of our own society to do. And I don't know how your economic system works, or any of the sights to see, and you still have to fix your own Mother Vines so it's not a wasteland, right?"

Kaylah shook her head, a look of disappointment crossing her face. "You act like you want to be my friend, and we talk about unity, but you can't even fathom crossing the Neutral Woods to be there."

Saff's jaw dropped. "No, it's…" She turned to better face Kaylah. "I'm not outgoing like you." She gestured to the camp. "I couldn't do this like you are. I like working one-on-one with these girls I mentor. I already told you I practically grew up as a shut-in, one that liked just hanging out with family and a small group of friends. It's just … intimidating." Looking down, she picked up another tiny pebble by her foot, pinching it. "And I'm not as carefree as you are. I like checklists, and prioritizing, and…"

Kaylah continued to stare at her with a calculating expression. "Maybe I could allow for some differences there, but do you know what I really don't get?"

"What?"

"You met Guillen for two seconds, and you still dislike him. It's hard for me to get behind someone who judges the people I love."

Knots of guilt twisted in Saff's stomach. Maybe it wasn't fair how much she worried about Rachel's safety because she was with an Ivy without powers on her mission. Ben could have been twice as strong as Guillen with his Seeder energy, and he'd still been killed in this war.

But it was more than that. "I worry about Rachel. And it's not just that I worry about her physical safety, or even her emotional well-being, because you're right that I don't know him. But…" She choked down her remorse over her own mistakes. "There's more than one way to lose a person."

"What are you talking about?" Kaylah seemed rightfully confused.

When they were making up, Devin had confessed to Saff that he *had* actually considered moving out, even if it was only briefly, when they'd been fighting. She'd abandoned him. In marriage, you didn't just live for yourself. She'd been completely inconsiderate of his grief over Ben's death, and how her actions had made Devin hurt that much more. For the first time since she'd met Devin, she'd had to genuinely face the reality of possibly spending her life without him. During their many heartfelt conversations since making up, they'd promised to be better about communicating with each other.

"I'm not opposed to Rachel being with an Ivy, if that makes her happy. I just see her getting along with more Ivies than Seeders, and I feel like she's pulling away." Just the thought of Saff's few years of living in the Green Lands, of getting to know her family and village, made her long for home. "I love my family, and our village, and so many things about our culture. She's not even giving it a chance."

"Does it matter who she's with, or where she's at, if she's happy?"

Questions like that had made Saff face a lot about herself that she didn't like much lately. Sure, she'd never really liked drama or gossip, but she wasn't exactly a saint. She was slower to forgive than others. She tried to give people the benefit of the doubt, but she also sometimes struggled to put herself in others' shoes. Saff was having to learn all of this the hard way.

Saff rocked her head side to side. "I know. I should trust that she knows better than I do about what would make her happy. But she's also having to figure a lot out right now." She palmed her pebbles and pulled her legs up, hugging them. "It's not like I judge you and Eric for being together. Honestly, sometimes I think about how amazing it is that you discovered cave rifting, and I think of how much closer I could still be with my friend Zach, if we'd had the ability to rift multiple times a year back when I came of age."

Zach was another person she'd lost. Not completely, but he'd faded from her life. And she'd had to let him. She was married now. He was out there dating humans. She couldn't expect him to carry on the rest of his life getting mysterious letters from an old friend he'd once had a crush on, hiding them from future girlfriends or a wife. That wasn't fair. But if they'd had Unitas a few years ago when she first brought Zach into the green-folk equation, he would have been just like Eric, there to help the revolution in a heartbeat.

But he was just another person lost to Saff.

Losing people sucked. Change sucked.

Kaylah continued to eye Saff, not saying anything. Saff wasn't sure what else to say, sensing Kaylah's judgment of her.

"Why am I the bad guy for loving my people?" Saff asked. "I think there's nothing better, in either world, than being married to another Seeder. Genuinely. And I know that sounds bad, but I wouldn't expect you to understand that—no one could that doesn't experience our mating bond. I'm proud of my people's culture and way of life, and ethics. And I feel like you and Rachel judge me for that. What's wrong with enjoying being around people like me?" Loving her own people didn't mean she hated others.

Kaylah gently shook her head. "I think it's great to have national pride. I do. Maybe someday, if you ever visit, you'll come to appreciate our rich culture, our symbiotic relationship to the Mother

Vines, all of that." She pressed her lips together. "Obviously, I'm not proud of a lot of things, too. There are more than enough unforgivable things, and a ton of growth that needs to happen. But the majority of my people are just doing their best."

Saff had to concede she was curious, that it could be a fun adventure to learn more about Kaylah's culture someday.

"What I don't understand is how you can be so blind about your own people's shortcomings," Kaylah added. "You're a smart woman. How often do you think a conflict is one hundred percent one side's fault? You don't think your people provoked any of this?"

Saff looked down. It was true that she'd never been taught anything that pointed at Seeder guilt in the 'years of parting.' Seeders were always the victims. But it stood to reason that those stories may have been coated with generalizations.

"Because as much as I know my people are in the wrong," Kaylah continued, "I do believe your people did their fair share to drive my people from their homes. Ivy history lessons may be steeped in lies, half-truths, and propaganda, but *your* people can be pigheaded, intolerant, and difficult."

The souring turn of conversation was unsettling for Saff. This didn't sound like inspirational Unitas ideology.

"So, we're judging our whole nation based on the actions of people hundreds of years ago?" Saff asked.

Kaylah clicked her tongue. "I find it's still relevant if they passed on their mindset to future generations."

Maybe Saff was just being defensive, but this conversation was starting to wear her patience thin. As much as she'd come to like Kaylah, Kaylah was still exhausting to work with at times. Granted, Kaylah probably thought the same of Saff.

Not sure if it would help or hurt, Saff dared to ask a question that had festered for more than two months now. "When we were at the safe house in the human world, you spoke of your parents, but I've never heard you talk about them since your brother killed them."

Kaylah picked at her fingernails. "What about them?"

Kaylah had said that her parents 'probably weren't as sinister' as Saff had thought. "I'm just curious about your relationship with them. What they were like. How you're doing."

Slowly nodding, Kaylah drew a deep breath. "Our relationship was complicated. I lived so many years away from home, and was lied to so much… There's definitely resentment there." She frowned, now examining the ends of her hair. "And every time I'd try to bring up something that matched the Unitas ideals… They were so disappointed."

She looked up, meeting Saff's gaze. "I knew I'd have to take things from a different angle. But truly, in my heart, I don't think they were the worst parents out there. My mother was often absent, but I wouldn't describe her as tyrannical … exactly… I think my father genuinely loved her, but followed her lead. You always kind of wonder when it comes to relationships of people in positions of power, you know?"

It clicked for Saff as to why Kaylah was so drawn to Eric. Eric was a safe harbor. Human celebrities fell into two categories. They either married other celebrities and became power couples, or they married Average Joes, not having to deal with the complications of how their relationship would be used as a career display piece. What would a royal position, Ivy wealth, and the power that came with it all, do for a human who couldn't even cross into the Green Lands? She didn't have to doubt his motivations. It was sweet.

"So," Saff tried to tread lightly, "maybe they weren't the realm's worst parents. But … you always attribute the fault with this war to your Uncle Nuren, that he was the mastermind."

Kaylah sat up straighter. "Yes. Without him, things would have continued in the stale old way they used to. Duke is an earned title; as my father's brother, he didn't have any birthright to it." Kaylah spared a glance at the camp. "In private, I used to call him Rasputin."

Saff choked on a laugh. "Like the cartoon villain?"

Kaylah narrowed her eyes slightly. "Seriously? Rasputin was a real person. My uncle would sometimes say that all it took for success was 'lots of work, a touch of luck, and enough charisma to woo the world.'" She rolled her eyes. "Honestly, I know he put in the work studying our archives, learning about psychology, and all of that, but really, I think he just weaseled his way in by catching my mother when she was weak after leaving—" She stopped abruptly, looking away as if she'd said more than intended.

"She was weak after leaving what?"

Standing, Kaylah dusted her pants off. "What? Sorry, I'm just a bit out of sorts today. Rough night's sleep."

Her sudden change of demeanor was discomforting. Saff stood to join her, letting the pebble she'd been holding drop to the ground.

Kaylah cleared her throat, looking at the guards standing a ways away. "We should get going."

"Wait," Saff said. "What was that about?"

Pulling her hair into a ponytail, Kaylah put on a more convincing act. "What? Oh, yeah, crappy night's sleep. Sorry, that's why I was a bit grumpy. Anyway…"

No… That isn't good enough…

"Kaylah…" Saff said, almost in warning.

Glancing past Saff, Kaylah smiled. "Oh look, your husband is coming to collect you. I guess we really do need to go. Thanks for the chat." She took a step toward the guards, but Saff cut her off.

"What are you not telling me?" Saff studied her face intently. "Your uncle, strategy, your mom. You may not be the queen in title, but you are in powers. Are you keeping something from our leaders?"

A smirk overtook Kaylah's face. "A girl's allowed an ounce of privacy now and then. And heaven knows, she's got to keep a secret or two up her sleeve." She winked.

Saff's heart ached as though she'd been betrayed. "*You* asked me to keep an eye on people in camp that were acting suspicious.

What's happening right now is about the most suspicious thing I've seen."

Kaylah sighed, putting up her hands. "I'm just saying, some secrets are worth keeping. Ginger has this stroganoff recipe that I'd never divulge in a million years." She did a chef's kiss. "Mind-blowing."

Saff stepped closer. "This isn't a joke," she whispered.

"Hey, Saff," Devin called on his approach. "What are you doing all the way out here?"

Saff glanced over her shoulder; he was quickly closing the gap between them. She turned to Kaylah, urgency in her voice. "Don't do this to me. Don't play mind games. Just tell me what's going on. Don't undo the trust we've been working on."

Kaylah looked genuinely hurt. She locked eyes with Saff. "I have no intentions of hurting you or your people, okay?" she said softly.

Devin's arms slid around Saff's waist from behind. "Good morning, Kaylah."

Kaylah responded with a bright politician's smile. "Right back at you. Thanks for your hard work, both of you." She shot a glance across the canyon. "Sorry I have to go, but I have a meeting with Arcadia's leaders to attend to." She rested a hand on Saff's shoulder. "Thanks again for a good chat. I appreciate you."

As Kaylah and her personal guards walked away in the direction of the rope bridge, Saff's breathing picked up, her eyes glued on Kaylah.

What the heck just happened?

Chapter 27

DEVIN SQUEEZED SAFF TIGHTER, kissing her cheek. "I thought you were going to meet Heather and me back at the tent for breakfast."

"Yeah… It was a pretty sunrise, and I got distracted."

"You ready for breakfast now?"

She stood there in a daze. She hadn't felt this betrayed since she'd discovered her family had lied about her identity all of her life. And the tough thing was that she didn't even know right now if Kaylah *was* betraying her, betraying them.

Was Kaylah just being flippant and callous? What had she genuinely been upset about? What was she hiding? Maybe Saff was being paranoid, but it felt like more than that. Kaylah had gaslit Rachel for years, making Rachel doubt her own reality. Saff had dealt with that as well. Her stomach churned, a bitter taste lingering in her mouth.

"Saff?" Devin said. He was now looking at her from the side, concern painted on his face.

She blinked. "Um… Just…" She shook her head. "Kaylah's acting weird. I think I'll talk about it with the council leader when she comes to visit tomorrow."

"Okay…" He raised an eyebrow. "If you're really this worried, we could catch a breeze and go speak to one now. You look really rattled."

Swallowing, Saff considered it. What did she have to go off of? 'Kaylah said something about her mom being weak and her uncle being evil, and then she clammed up'? Maybe it was just something Kaylah was ashamed of, and Saff had read it all wrong. "No." Saff shook her head again. "I'm probably just losing my mind. I'll bring it up with the councilwoman tomorrow."

Devin smiled. "Okay." He grabbed her hands. "So … breakfast before work? We're kind of running behind."

Wearing a small smile, Saff nodded. "Yeah, sorry."

They started walking back to their tent, hand in hand.

"Heather got food from the garden after we got back, and I had to come looking for you."

"Sorry. I let the time get away from me."

He squeezed her hand. "No big deal."

"How was the walk with Heather?" Devin had been spending a decent portion of his limited free time with his sister. While Saff didn't always love sharing him, she fully understood their need. Devin was as great of a brother to Heather as Ben had been to Saff. Heather wasn't back to her bubbly old self yet, and no one expected her to be. Walks between brother and sister were uplifting to both Devin and Heather as they worked through their grief.

"Good walk. It was a beautiful sunrise, wasn't it?"

"Yeah, it was."

Devin stopped several yards short of the tent, facing Saff. "I have a proposal."

She slid her hands onto his waist. "Let's hear it."

"You and me, alone time tonight, away from this chaos."

Saff squinted. "You want to go on a date night in the middle of camp being under siege?"

He sighed, reaching up to her neck. His fingers gently dug in, massaging at the knots in it. "We never did get to properly celebrate our one-year anniversary. And you are so tense."

She frowned. "I'd rather be tense, than past tense, if the camp security walls fall." They were both working twelve to sixteen hours a day between training and security detail.

He matched her frown. "Do we or do we not plan to sleep tonight?"

She gazed into his deep brown eyes. "Obviously, we will."

His eyes shot up, looking at the Outer Rim, the mountains beyond the canyon. "It'll take a half hour to catch a breeze. That's all. We'll probably sleep a lot better without the constant noise around here…"

Of all the things she wanted to expend energy on, fighting his sweet notion wasn't one of them. "Okay. I'll let camp security know we'll be gone for the night."

He beamed, giving her a peck on the lips.

***

Saff surprised herself with how giddy she became throughout the day, the anticipation of their getaway building.

Before dusk, she'd done as required and reported to the camp security that she and Devin would be gone for the night, returning first thing in the morning. A head count was done every night, with each Unitas camp member accounted for.

She'd gotten off work earlier than Devin and had set to packing a few things for the night.

Devin entered the tent, looking utterly exhausted. "You ready for this?"

Saff looked him over. "No blood. That's good." He usually helped with camp security against the Ivy army stationed outside of camp, after his duties as a trainer of newly returned girls.

"Yeah. Mostly hammers and nails today as we worked to rebuild the southern section they keep tearing down. And a little dart action during an attack."

She grasped the hem of his shirt, pulling him in close. "Well, that would definitely explain why there's no blood, but you're worn out."

He puckered his lips expectantly.

She leaned forward, caressing his lips. Deciding she could spare some energy, and that he could definitely use a boost, she pushed Seeder energy from her heart, the warmth traveling through her neck and up to her lips.

Seeder energy kisses, also referred to as love kisses, were utterly intoxicating. They'd learned that lesson quickly with a close call in the intimacy department back in high school when they'd experimented with their first energy kiss.

Devin held her even closer as they kissed, not allowing an inch between them. After a minute, she cut off the energy transfer and leaned back. Her eyes were warm, and his were glowing too.

"I only expected a normal kiss," he said, catching his breath, his hands still holding her tightly.

She smirked, wrapping her arms around his neck. "I figured you could use a top-up before we catch a breeze."

"I can't lie—there are perks to having a mate that has more energy than the average Seeder girl."

"Oh yeah?" she asked playfully. "Is that why you married me? You just want me for my power?"

"It is in fact the *only* reason I married you," he answered coolly.

Saff giggled. "You ready to go? I packed some snacks and blankets."

"Mmm. Give me another kiss like that, and we might as well stay in this tent."

She frowned. "You're the one that talked me into this adventure." She raised her eyebrows in challenge. "And your argument was about getting *sleep*."

His eyes still glowed green. "Do you even know me? Those words will never leave my lips. '*Only* sleep'? There will *always* be hope for more." He wore that look of adoration that always got her. There had never been anyone other than Devin in her heart, not really, not in that way.

Devin stole a quick peck on the lips, his eyes fading to deep brown. "And I will *always* enjoy your company, even if it's *only* sleeping." He winked, and released her.

"Okay." She snatched up the satchels she'd packed, handing one to him. Not wanting to weigh them down, she'd only included the bare necessities. "You know where we're going?"

"Yep." He pulled on his satchel, tightening the straps. "After Kaylah invited me to camp, I talked to some of the families in Arcadia, and asked about the surrounding area. Shouldn't take more than half an hour."

Ready for a change of scenery, and wanting to set out before all light was gone, they headed toward the canyon and caught a breeze out of camp.

***

It didn't take long to reach the mountainside Devin had been told about. As night fell, they hadn't gotten too much opportunity to take in the scenery, but it was already refreshing to be away from camp. Ivies couldn't fly up there and attack them. No one coughing in a nearby tent would wake them up.

They decided to explore a little in the dark before picking a spot to spend the night. To keep themselves from tripping, they each pulled out a lightkeeper, tapping a finger to the quartz dome and cupping a hand on top to spread the energy out.

Devin led Saff by the hand through a maze of trees and bushes, seemingly knowing where he was going. "I wish I'd been able to bring your paint set from home," he said.

Oh, how she craved to paint. It had always been her favorite thing to do when she was stressed—to step back, retreat from the chaos, and create a world of her own that brought a sense of calm.

After a few minutes, a familiar soft white noise grew louder, but Saff couldn't put a finger on it. "What is that?"

"You'll see."

Soon enough, the source of the noise was within sight. A waterfall, majestically flowing into a quaint little pond. A smile spread across Saff's face.

She took a cleansing breath, allowing the constant stress to pour out of her in an exhale. The light cast by their lightkeepers shimmered across the pond. "It's beautiful. Thank you."

"It really is." Devin nudged her arm. "It might be cold this high up in the mountains, but we could manage that … if you wanted to skinny-dip." He hummed playfully. "Just like when we were dating and you talked me into it."

Her jaw dropped. "I did not! *You* talked *me* into it!"

"That's *not* the way *I* remember it."

She turned to him, intentionally shifting her blue eyes to bright green. "Then you, sir, remember wrong."

He chuckled. "I vote we agree that we talked *each other* into it."

Devin was still capable of making her blush after four years of dating and marriage, even if no one else was there to overhear the conversation. "Fine. Maybe we talked each other into it." She laughed. "But I am pretty tired, and tomorrow's just another day. I'd rather not take a dip in freezing cold water right now."

"Works for me," he said. "Before we pick a spot to sleep, though, there's a part two to this surprise."

"Okay…"

He held a finger to his lightkeeper. "On three, we'll turn them off."

She followed his instructions, hovering an extended finger next to the lightkeeper she held.

"One. Two. Three."

They both swiped their fingers on the edge of the thin jade disk on the bottom, calling the Seeder energy back into the stone. As the light dimmed, the pond came to life.

Saff stood with her mouth agape. Bioluminescent moss on trees and boulders radiated bright green. A soft pink glow emanated from patches of fungi scattered amidst the trees. Purple pinpricks drifted through the air, winking in and out as they passed between trees.

"The special purple ones," she whispered in awe. Purple lightning bugs were the rarest type in the Green Lands; she'd only seen them once before.

Saff hadn't been the most voracious bookworm back in the human world, but she'd read enough fiction over the years to know that the secret fairy princess *always* felt out of place growing up, which hinted that there was something special about her.

But Saff wasn't a secret fairy princess. She'd felt perfectly at home during her years growing up in the human world. And other than her unique ability to wield extra energy, there wasn't anything spectacular about her. She had twenty-three siblings—just like every other Seeder. She'd sprouted on the first day of spring—just like every other Seeder.

Recalling her prior conversation with Kaylah, the good parts of it, Saff smiled wider. Someone thought Saff was special. What was it Kaylah had said? 'I see the way he looks at you when you're not watching.'

It was too dark to see Devin's face right now, and she didn't want to ruin the wonder of the moment by turning her lightkeeper back on. Saff reached out a hand, finding Devin's waist, and nuzzled up to him. "I love it. And I love you."

"Same, love."

For several more minutes, they stood in quiet contemplation. The Green Lands realm was beautiful, but few places compared to this sight. Beyond its physical beauty, it spoke to her on a higher, more spiritual level. There was a reason most Seeder girls answered the call of their energy once bloomed—it was part of them.

Ivies didn't bloom. They didn't have delayed development of their powers. But even they described the energy of the realm as addictive. Though, Saff surmised, they probably didn't feel it this deeply. After all, Seeder women held the most energy and power in this realm, so much so that it imprisoned them when they reached full maturity. How much more was Saff connected to this place because of her extra energy?

To her left, Devin yawned. "Yeah, I'm beat. Hand me your pack, and I'll set up the blankets over in that clearing we passed."

Devin laid out the thin blankets, and they cuddled up in the dark, watching the purple lightning bugs dance around, whispering as they discussed their days and the latest news via letter from their families back in South Fortinda.

Both worn out, their sleepiness doubled by the soft noise of the waterfall nearby, they quickly gave in to sleep, happily in each other's arms.

***

Saff woke, a little startled at first, forgetting she wasn't back home in their cottage or in their Unitas tent. Devin wasn't cuddled up to her anymore. Her eyes darted along the horizon, searching for him.

Nearby, a twig snapped, and she twisted to see what had caused it.

"Good morning." It was Devin, holding a mounded handful of burnt-orange sweetberries. "Did I wake you?"

Saff rubbed her eyes, yawning. He rarely woke before her. "No. I'm good."

"Great. I thought I'd supplement what you packed for a proper breakfast before we head out."

She smiled. If they could take a full day here, a week, a month… Maybe someday, when things calmed down.

They dug in, munching on the berries he'd picked, as well as oranges and nuts she'd packed.

Saff eyed Devin with admiration. "Do you know why I love you so much?"

He scratched his chin. "Because I sweep you off your feet and bring you to gorgeous locations?" He chomped down on a berry. "And I bring you tasty things?"

"Nope." She popped an almond into her mouth.

He arched an eyebrow high. "Then it must be my godlike physique. 'Cause we both know—human, Seeder, or Ivy—no one's got anything on this. You got lucky."

She laughed. "Nope."

Devin narrowed his eyes playfully. "Hurtful."

"Do you want me to tell you?"

Holding up a finger, he popped a few more berries into his mouth. "It's because I can cook and garden better than…" He cleared his throat, very clearly implying Saff. "Well, better than some people."

She grinned. "Well, it certainly isn't for your humility."

He chuckled. She'd always loved his confidence. And he wasn't wrong about being handsome, but then again, who didn't think their partner was attractive? Even if they weren't 'conventionally' attractive?

Her face softened. "But I'm serious."

He shifted his seat. "Okay. Tell me why you love me so much."

"Because…" The thought almost instantly brought tears to her eyes. "Because when we were fighting, after I was stupid and left for the human world without you, you were so quick to forgive."

Frowning, Devin shook his head. "We barely talked for *weeks*. I don't know about 'quick to forgive.'"

She wiped away a tear. "Yeah, no, I guess I didn't word that right. What I mean is—you forgave me *before* anything good came from my actions. You didn't forgive me just because you found out Kaylah and her people were doing the right thing."

"Saff," he said softly. "My love for you isn't conditional. Never will be. I gave you all of it, years ago."

How much of that was the Seeder mating bond talking? She'd stopped questioning that a while ago. Did it matter if your attraction was ten percent dimples, thirty percent sense of humor, twenty-five percent shared beliefs, and thirty-five percent natural chemistry? Or any other combination?

"I love you too." She smiled. "And I know I'm lucky to have you." She sighed, picking through the small bag of mixed nuts. "Sometimes I feel sorry for you. Kaylah's helped me to see how much of a control freak I can be."

Not two seconds later, Devin busted out laughing, slapping a hand to his mouth, his eyes wide.

That stung, after their super-sweet moment.

"No, don't take it that way," he blurted, then pleaded with his eyes. "You know I love you the way you are."

It wasn't like he hadn't listed off his reasons for loving her, but it still hurt a little to be laughed at when admitting one of her own flaws.

"It's, um, well … a Ben thing," Devin explained.

Her heart ached, just hearing his name. Like Heather, Saff had buried herself in work, distracting herself from her grief, but Devin usually found it comforting to share memories of Ben.

"He kind of swore me to secrecy," Devin said.

"What?" What kind of secret would Ben have shared with Devin about Saff?

Devin grinned. "Before your bloom, when you thought he was just a foster brother… Well, it wasn't exactly a secret you two didn't get along."

Saff frowned.

Devin still wore a perma-grin. "He told me you were uptight. He didn't know I had a crush on you. He called you a control freak, and…" Devin pressed his lips together, stifling another laugh.

Saff searched his face. "Just tell me."

"You know how much you hated how he left toothpaste all over the sink?"

She bunched her eyebrows.

"Once he realized how much that annoyed you, he started doing it on purpose."

Her jaw dropped. "What a jerk!" She instantly felt a surge of guilt for speaking ill of the dead, but it quickly subsided. She laughed along with Devin. If Ben had been there to see her face, he would have *lost* it. He would have laughed his head off. Maybe it would do Saff some good to talk more about him, instead of avoiding it.

As they polished off their meal, they shared a few more fond memories of Ben. After packing up their things, Saff dreaded returning to camp. While this little jaunt had been a welcome reprieve from the everyday crazy, it made it that much harder to want to get back to it.

Pausing briefly to take in the daytime scenery, they stood by the pond, watching koi swim. With her mind still on Ben, Saff bent over and picked up a smooth, flat rock. She ran her thumb over it. Skipping rocks had been her favorite activity with Ben after returning to the Green Lands. Raising a hand to her neck, she touched the jade charm she always wore. While it no longer served a purpose with her powers, she still kept the carved sun symbol to her skin like Devin had first instructed her to.

Maybe it was weird, but it might be cool to have Ben's name etched into a rock like this, as some type of memorial, especially since she hadn't been there for his burial.

Turning the grey rock in her hand, she smiled. "Love you, Ben." Taking a step back, she aimed and shot the rock at the pond. It skipped four times. With each skip, her heart felt a little lighter.

Devin kissed her sweetly on the head. "Ready to go?"

"Yeah."

After a few minutes of hiking to the clearing they'd landed in, they communed with the wind, catching a breeze back to camp.

Landing, Saff held out her hand for Devin's pack. "I'll return these to the tent. Would you check in with camp security?"

He handed her the bag. "Yes, ma'am." He kissed her again. "Are you still going to track down the councilwoman on her visit today? To talk to her about Kaylah acting off?"

Saff hesitated. She'd contemplated that exact thing on their half-hour flight back. Hadn't Kaylah proven herself, after all? She'd killed a soldier to get them safely to Seeder borders once. She and her people had helped bring home countless Seeder girls through Ivy rifts and the rifting cave, getting them home quicker and safer than they could do on their own.

But how much of it was an act?

While disappointed in herself for doubting Kaylah after all the work she'd done to try and form a friendship between them, something nagged relentlessly at Saff.

The assassins who tried to kill or kidnap Saff years ago had let Nuren's name slip. But her family had never reported it to a higher council. They hadn't been required to, as nothing about the man ever surfaced. They'd concluded it might have just been a figment of Saff's imagination, the fevered whispers she'd heard while fighting to stay alive, and to not fall into a coma.

But they had been wrong.

What would have happened if Saff's family had taken that threat more seriously? Perhaps there would have been a manhunt and Nuren would have been caught before the War Vines were ever formed, ever activated, ever hurt a single soul.

With her heart and mind at odds, Saff made her decision. Kaylah had probably just had a bad day, and Saff had likely been reading too much into it. But she wouldn't be the weak link.

"Yeah. I'm going to talk to the councilwoman when I can find her. Just ... out of an abundance of caution."

Devin nodded grimly. "Yeah, probably a good idea." He grabbed her hand. "Thanks again, for a perfect night."

Saff grinned. "You didn't even get any action."

"But it was with you. Ergo: perfect." He winked.

She shook her head. "Get out of my face before I kiss yours."

He chuckled, giving her hand a squeeze before releasing it. "I love you. See you after work."

"Love you too."

Chapter 28

THE OFFICIAL WORD HIT THE Ivy Kingdom with thunderous shock: the princess was a traitor, having taken part in her own parents' murders. She was wanted alive, to answer for her crimes. Circulating rumors about Unitas were being censored—they still sounded like a ragtag, pathetic group of dissenters.

The news was received at Guillen and Rachel's next meeting with mixed results. But overall, it actually seemed to be working in Unitas's favor within the stunt communities.

A small group of Unitas hopefuls gathered in the community room of Six, ready to hear the presentation. Rachel perched on the edge of a table at the front of the meeting room while Guillen began. This group was especially dirty and gruff, having lived hard lives in mines.

"Our people deserve equal rights. That's what we're here to discuss tonight," Guillen said.

"What would *you* know about that?" a man asked, jumping right in.

Guillen raised his eyebrows. "About what?"

The man crossed his arms. "You act like you know how we feel, but do you? Last I checked, your tattoo didn't have a number. How's life without needing documents to travel? What other nice privileges do you get?"

Rachel frowned, glancing at Guillen. He remained silent.

The man continued. "When you're done pretending to be one of us and saving us, do we worship you then? Or do we need to start doing that now?"

Guillen nodded, looking down. Rachel swallowed hard; she'd never seen anything get to him this way. She stood up, addressing the man, not hiding the harshness in her voice. "I'm sorry. Have *you* ever worked your full-time assignment *and* spent all your free time fighting for others' rights? No. You haven't." Guillen worked harder than anyone else she knew.

The man was not impressed. "It's easy to tout superiority when you're born into privilege. I heard he gets loads more free time than we do."

Rachel hesitated. That was true. Guillen had already listed off the crazy restrictions placed on stunts, and also the exceptions his birthright afforded him. He *did* get four times the allotted vacation time that regular stunts did. But he didn't squander it. All of that, in addition to extra time like this, created through the use of bogus orders fabricated by Unitas, had been spent fighting for their rights.

"The question is simple. Do you want more freedoms, equal rights? Or not?" She pointed at the belligerent man. "Because this is your chance to make it happen. It would be a shame to waste the opportunity to make a difference because of your pride. Whether it's a member of the royal family, or the person sitting next to you, or heck … even a Seeder, why does it matter what they've gone through, if they're willing to help?"

The man rolled his eyes as Guillen cleared his throat. Rachel glanced back at Guillen, and he threw her a quick appreciative look before continuing with his pitch.

*****

The community gathering room cleared out, and Guillen pulled out his keys to lock it up. "You go first, and I'll be a few."

Rachel cocked her head to the side. "Yeah?"

He wore a forced smile. "Just going to take a short stroll, get some fresh air before turning in for the night."

She nodded. "Do you want company?"

"No. You know the drill. Leave separate. Arrive at the room separate."

She hesitated, but gave him a quick peck on the cheek and left the building for their room. She ached on his behalf. She hadn't considered how others might view him with jealousy or anger for his place in the royal family. He wasn't fully accepted in 'regular' society, and even amongst those like him, he didn't always fit in.

Arriving back at their room, Rachel got ready for the night. She sat on the edge of their bed for several minutes, festering over the interaction at the meeting.

Guillen knocked to announce himself, and unlocked the door. She wanted to get up and hug him, but wasn't quite sure what he needed.

He smiled softly. "Hey."

"How are you?" she asked, trying to read his face after he locked the door behind him.

"I'm good. They're on board, after all." He sat down in an armchair.

Rachel got up and sauntered over, sitting down on his lap. "Your condition is rare. How many people in this kingdom have a crown tattoo?"

He met her gaze. "Well … there's me. And Lewis. Lewis is…" Guillen squinted at the ceiling in thought. "Eighty-something at this point. He lives as far away from the palace as physically possible while still being in our kingdom." Guillen grinned. "That's a perk, too. Once you're too old and broken to work, those of us close enough to the queen in the royal bloodline are graciously allowed to live in *any* community we like."

She gently ran her fingers through his hair. "Just the two of you?"

He shrugged. "That's it right now. We got lucky."

Rachel bit her lip. "That must be hard. Not knowing where you belong."

He wrapped an arm around her. "I know where I belong. With Kaylah in Unitas. And here. With you." He smiled.

Rachel frowned. "You know what I mean. To be part of the royal family," she glanced at the scar on his temple, "but not really being accepted for who you are."

He met her gaze.

"And then to—"

He raised his eyebrows. "To sometimes be rejected by society's rejects?" He rested a hand on her knee. "It comes with the territory. I'm the bastard product of privilege and disappointment."

Her frown deepened. "Don't ever describe yourself that way. That's not who you are."

He sighed. "I've accepted who I am. And I've told you before— I don't want pity. Least of all from you." He shook his head and shifted in his seat. "A lot of people have it worse than me. I can't complain."

She read his face. "Yeah, people have it worse. But there's *always* someone that has it worse. That doesn't mean you're not allowed to feel hurt sometimes." She grabbed his hand. "I love that you make the most of what life has given you, and you try to stay positive. But don't compare yourself that way. Just because someone else hurts worse, doesn't mean you're not hurting. You have a right to your feelings."

Guillen looked down, shaking his head.

Perhaps Guillen wasn't *always* openly expressing how he felt, but she'd started to pick up on his mannerisms. That contemplative look, then a slight shake of the head—she'd even found herself doing it. It was often followed by direct eye contact and a small smile that expressed more than words could. It said 'you get me' or 'how did I get lucky enough to have you in my life?'

"What?" she asked.

He looked up, smiling. "I love you."

She met his smile with one of her own. "I kind of love you a *little* bit, too." She held a hand out, pinching the tiniest bit of air between her thumb and pointer finger.

He narrowed his eyes. "Just a little bit, huh?"

She gave him a toothy smile, widening the gap between her fingers to as wide as they would stretch. "A lot bit."

He squeezed her hand. "How about I get changed and we call it an early night?"

After a quick smooch, she crawled into bed, under the covers, while he got ready. Once he joined her, she slid over to cuddle. A candle still flickered behind him on the nightstand.

"Thanks for having my back tonight," he said.

She planted a soft kiss on his Unitas tattoo, resting a hand on his exposed chest. "I'll always have your back."

"Always?" he whispered.

What kind of promise was she making? She responded with the only thing her heart would allow. "Always."

He pursed his lips. "I, uh, I think that guy got to me so much because ... you know, he was right. It hit close to home. When I first moved away from my family home, I made plenty of mistakes. I wasn't perfect back then." He gently ran a finger across the curve of her shoulder. "Well, not like I'm perfect now, but I learned a lot from my messups."

Rachel furrowed her brow. "You were sixteen when you moved out on your own. No one expects a sixteen-year-old to be perfect."

Guillen raised a skeptical eyebrow. "No? I guess we grew up in different worlds." He let out a breathy chuckle. "I suppose we technically did. But there was plenty of pressure to not disgrace the family name any further. To not make myself a target. To just fade away and be forgotten."

"I'm sorry." A bitterness rose up her throat. "I love that my mom didn't pressure me to get straight-As or anything like that. And neither did Nuren. But why would he care if his stepdaughter was an idiot?" His piercing words still rang in her ears sometimes, the things he'd said as she'd been strapped to a chair, War Vine leaves drilled into her arms, sucking her Seeder energy dry. He'd called her livestock. Why would it matter if a cow had any brain cells before it was sent to slaughter?

Guillen rubbed her shoulder again. "Do you want to talk about it?"

She snapped out of her thoughts. "No. Not tonight. But thanks." She smiled. "I'd like to hear more about your escapades."

His gaze shot to the pendulum clock in the corner. "Yep, it's bedtime."

"Hey!" She scowled playfully. "You've got to give me *something*. It's only fair. You *did* have a jumpstart on getting to know me because of Kaylah."

"Fair enough." He wrinkled his nose. "My messups cover the gambit. Stupid mistakes with girls. Co-workers. Friendships. Guards."

"Uh-oh. Trouble with guards?"

"They don't all treat me the same, right?"

"Yeah, I've noticed that." Some seemed more afraid of Guillen, others resentful, some neutral.

He shifted a bit. "Let's just say Kaylah and I … conspired… I kind of called in a favor once. In the end, it accomplished what we needed, but came with mixed results. Rumors circulated amongst the stunt community guards. They've got their own little club. Some are terrified of me because they now think I have more pull at the palace than I actually do. Some hate me because of the fallout from what Kaylah and I arranged. Some don't care."

She studied his face. "But you don't want to elaborate on what you did?"

"Um…" Guillen rubbed his face. "It involved an ex-girlfriend."

"I see…" She still wanted to know, but it was obvious he wasn't ready to share, and it wasn't like he'd demanded to know about any of her dating history.

Taking a deep breath, she smiled. "Well, now I know you're not perfect. I think I'll still stick around."

He gave her an appreciative grin.

"After all, there's no such thing as a perfect person." She walked a pair of fingers up his chest, to his lips. "But I do think that every person out there has someone that's perfect *for them*."

They locked eyes.

"Why are you this way?" he whispered.

Even when he said the wrong thing, he could say it the right way. It hadn't been said as an insult. Not with the softness of his voice. Not with the desire in his eyes. Not with the way he swallowed, as if holding back. Sharing a bed, it was no secret he wanted more, but he'd never crossed the line. He knew she needed to heal before taking things to the next step.

But staring into his eyes in this moment… She might be there.

After another swallow, with the silence hanging thick between them, Guillen waved the white flag, breaking eye contact.

"How about I be the little spoon again?"

She fought a smile, her cheeks warming. "I can manage that."

***

Once they drew closer to Community Five, Guillen rented Rachel a room in a nearby regular community. She couldn't pretend to be a fellow stunt in Five, not with their mark tattooed on her arm. Before Rachel and Guillen embarked on their mission, Guillen had scouted the sentiments of each community. This one seemed to be more hostile toward Seeders; he'd take a different approach here.

He dropped her off before making his way to that night's meeting.

"Remind me why I can't stay here with you?" he asked, before stealing another kiss as they sat on the sofa.

Rachel moaned. "I wish you could." She straddled him and gazed into his eyes. "I love you so much." She nibbled on his ear.

He shifted under her. "Okay. That's my cue. If I don't leave now, then I won't leave at all." He got up and stole one last kiss before heading out. "You have plenty of money, right? And you'll be alright alone?"

"I'll be fine." She smiled softly. "Don't worry about me."

Soon after Guillen took off, Rachel decided to go for a stroll. She mused on what it would be like in the Green Lands when there was peace—how tourism would look, if it ever got to that point. Sure, these communities weren't as beautiful as Seeder lands, but that would change once Kaylah had control. And it held its own kind of charm over here, anyway.

Rachel found a nice little outdoor café to eat dinner before heading back to her room for the night. She expected Guillen to be back pretty late. This town was eerily, though not surprisingly, as empty as the previous 'regular' one she'd toured before. Remembering Guillen's words, Rachel focused on enjoying her chickpea, lentil, and carrot stew. She was halfway through her meal when she overheard a couple of women gossiping behind her.

"I still can't believe it. It's not right."

"But what did you expect him to do? I don't think he can default to the next in line, not until she's out of the picture. It doesn't work that way."

"Yeah, but naming himself king? And his bride, queen? She has *no* power over the Mother Vines. She's not even royal."

"It's just temporary. Once she's dead, I'm sure he'll set things right. We can't be weak without a proper leader while this goes on."

"Yeah. I guess you're right. But it's still weird."

Rachel pushed her wooden bowl aside. It couldn't be interpreted any other way. Soren had gotten married. He'd claimed the throne. He was showing his power-hungry colors.

And that might be just another misstep caused by his pride. If others of his kind shared these girls' sentiments, he may have crossed the line, even by their estimation. Like Kaylah had said—royal birth didn't automatically mean your people would stand behind you. You needed loyalty. And what he considered to be a show of strength...

Rachel wore a smug grin.

"Are you finished here?" her waitress asked.

"Can I get the rest of this to go? And one of your best desserts?" She placed a few more coins on the table to pay for the to-go glass jar and food wrapping.

***

Rachel took her food back to the room, sorting through her emotions. Yes, she was happy to hear Soren's people disapproving of the 'king' and his latest blunder. But she had so much emotional trauma tied to that man, and his new queen. Rachel knew nothing about the woman, not that she hadn't thought about her. Sometimes Rachel made herself sick thinking about her. But her curiosity always stopped short of asking Kaylah or Guillen. She couldn't unknow that. She didn't want to compare.

Rachel had come to think of Soren's bride as the 'other woman,' but perhaps it was really her that was the other woman, if this new 'queen' was his primary interest. Or maybe it didn't really work that way. Maybe his bride had known about Rachel, and she could only be the 'other woman' if she had been in the dark about his relationship with Rachel on his mission. It mattered little, but Rachel sorted through the complex emotions as best she could.

She had hoped to stay up late enough to see Guillen get back for the night, but realized she'd passed out when the click of the door opening startled her awake.

"Hey, honey. It's just me," he whispered in the dark.

She reached over, her hand feeling and grasping a striker. She lit a beeswax candle, and he sat down on the edge of the bed.

She squinted against the light. "Hey, handsome. How did it go?"

He frowned hesitantly.

"How bad?"

"No, actually, the meeting was surprisingly amazing."

"That's great." She smiled.

"There's just some news that might bother you."

She furrowed her brow. "What?"

"Soren."

"Oh. The whole marriage and calling himself a king thing?"

Guillen raised his eyebrows. "So, you heard? You're taking it better than I thought you would."

She slid her hand into his. "I'm doing great. I gave myself time to process it. And I'm happy he did it. From what I hear, he's shot himself in the foot."

Guillen's face lit up. "Yeah! They were *all* sorts of scorched tonight. If there was a community I was worried about, with the exception of the two closest to the palace, it was this one. We needed this win." He leaned over and stole a kiss.

It warmed her heart to see him so happy. "I'm glad you're back. Did you get a chance to eat?"

"Not much. I'm famished."

"I brought you back some leftovers, just in case. And a dessert to share."

He stole another kiss. "You are going to spoil me."

Rachel got out of bed, giving Guillen a quick hug. "You eat up. I was going to take a shower; that way we can leave first thing in the morning."

By the time she came out, he'd finished eating and was organizing his things.

"I think I'm going to follow your lead before we turn in. Then we'll break into that delicious-looking treat over there?"

A few minutes later, she leaned in the bathroom doorway, brushing her wet hair. He stood at the sink, brushing his teeth, shirtless.

"Was the water cold?" she asked.

He spat out the Green Lands equivalent of toothpaste—crushed, dried mint leaves and a special kind of abrasive fiddlehead fern. "It's fine. I don't mind it that much."

"I love you."

His smile reflected back at her in the mirror. "I love you too."

She sauntered up to him, setting her brush down. Her stomach in knots, she wrapped her arms around his bare midriff. "I … want to be with you."

His reflection's gaze met hers. "What do you mean by that?"

She blushed. "You know—what I said the other day I wasn't ready for yet. You … and me … and … stuff…" She knew how stupid she sounded, but couldn't bring herself to actually say the words.

He grinned. "And stuff?"

She bit her lip. "Are you going to make me spell it out?"

"No. But I do love watching you squirm." He chuckled. "And you know how to sell it like it's sexy. '*Stuff.*'"

She leaned her head against his shoulder and laughed.

He faced her, holding her by the waist. "Are you sure you're ready for that? I'm not in a rush."

"Well, I … unless you're not. And if that's the case, I can respect that."

"I'm ready."

She smiled. "I am too."

He took a deep breath. "I know you don't want me asking, but this doesn't have anything to do with today's news, does it?"

She shook her head. "No… I've kinda been wanting to ask you all day."

"Okay." His voice was soft and mesmerizing.

She fidgeted with her hands. "I just, uh… I haven't done this before."

He grinned mischievously. "You say that like it's a bad thing."

She shrugged. "It's just … you're older, and … stuff."

He raised his eyebrows. "More stuff, huh?"

She traced his abs while smirking.

"If you're sure, then my answer is yes. And I'll tell you a secret— we'll be figuring this out together."

She looked up and searched his face. "Really?"

It was his turn to blush. "Really."

Rachel pulled Guillen in for a hug, savoring the warmth of his skin. She shuddered as he moved his hand up her shirt and slowly pulled it over her head. He gave her a knowing look—he recognized that bra, the same one he'd accidentally seen her in months before. She embraced him again, more skin now touching as she lingered in his arms. He nuzzled her neck, his soft lips slowly descending.

A loud and quick knock at their door pulled them out of the moment.

"Why?" she whispered. "Why does the universe hate us?"

Their uninvited visitor knocked again with urgency.

"Who knows we're all the way out here?" Her frustration mingled with fear.

"Only William. And he'd only come if it was important. Stay put; I'll check it out." Guillen grabbed a shirt and pulled it on, covering his Unitas tattoo.

Rachel stayed in the bathroom, deflated, as Guillen left her side to open the door.

"William, what's wrong?" he asked.

"It's the princess!" William hissed.

Rachel's eyes shot wide open. She bent down and snatched up her shirt, throwing it on. She brought her energy back in to appear normal. Guillen leaned back to check if she was fit to be seen. "Come inside."

The man named William entered and sat on the couch while Guillen locked the door. Rachel shyly leaned in the bathroom doorway. William, a portly man with greying hair, looked shocked to see someone else in the room.

"Sorry, this is, um…" Guillen blanked, gesturing to Rachel. "Elizabeth. She's safe to talk around. She's close to Kaylah."

Rachel tugged on her sleeve, making sure her tattoo was hidden. Even with a friendly, she wasn't going to risk giving that up in this area.

"She's gone missing."

"What?!" Guillen blurted.

"She just … went missing from the training camp."

Rachel covered her mouth. "How long has she been gone? We don't know if she's at the palace?"

"No. We haven't been able to confirm yet. And we aren't sure if he'll claim it. He probably wants Unitas to think she's abandoned them."

"Is there doubt?" Guillen asked.

"It's too early to say. There's been tension in camp. Some people are bound to think she's double-crossed us. The royal family is known for elaborate strategies…"

Guillen looked at Rachel. "You know she wouldn't do that, right?"

Rachel shook her head. "No, I know she wouldn't. I just hope she's okay … and that my people still trust in the cause."

"Is anything being done to get her back?" Guillen asked.

"I don't know; I have very little information. Once she's at the palace … it's going to be near impossible, with how things stand."

Guillen ran his hands through his hair. "Alright, I'm taking a detour. I know what I need to do." He turned to Rachel. "I can pay for you to stay here for a while. Stay hidden. I'll try and get someone to you soon, to get you out."

She furrowed her brow. "What are you talking about? I'm not just sitting here! Where are you going?"

Guillen glanced at William, then back to Rachel. "Let's talk." He grabbed her wrist and led her outside. "I love you," he whispered. "But I can't take you."

She scowled. "Take me where? I'm not just here as a girlfriend, remember? I'm an initiated member. I've trained enough."

"If Soren has her, he wants her to control the Vines. If she doesn't cooperate, he may just kill her and move on to the next heir."

Wait a second… She looked into his eyes. "The next heir is… How many sisters did the queen have? Kaylah doesn't have any sisters."

He raised his eyebrows, his face grim. "The next queen is my mother. And then my little sister."

Rachel's heart dropped. "Guillen. I don't… I mean…"

"I'm going to go make sure they're okay. Convince them to go into hiding. If they're out of reach, he doesn't have an easy alternative. It'll keep Kaylah safe until we can get her out."

She nodded, still in shock. "But why don't you want me to go?"

"Honey, it's dangerous. And ugly. It's so much closer to the palace. And that's not what you signed up for. I can handle it."

She narrowed her eyes. "That's a shit excuse! I'm coming. I promised Eric I'd watch out for her. I may not have the same training, but I owe her this."

"No!"

Rachel clenched her jaw, fuming. The light of a candle flickered to life in a neighboring apartment at their escalating argument.

"Why can't someone else go?" she whispered. "Someone … that can rift. They'll go faster."

He shook his head, his voice low. "You don't know my mother like I do. She's not going to easily betray the palace. I need to go. And I need to get going before he realizes what we have. If he hasn't already."

"Unless you tie me up, I'm going with you! We take care of each other."

He stared at her, pursing his lips. "Fine. For now. But if things get dicey, I might take you up on that threat, to tie you up for your own good. I really don't think it's worth the risk."

Chapter 29

EXHAUSTED, HAVING USED UP HER Seeder energy, and having been summoned for a meeting, Saff shuffled across the Unitas camp. *How could this possibly get worse?* She'd never really wanted to be a soldier; she loved teaching. But she was having to take more time from training new girls to help with camp border patrol. With Unitas's location compromised, and the War Vine attacks being significantly weakened on official Seeder territory borders, Soren's army had rerouted an obscene number of troops to take on the camp.

After her and Devin's excursion into the mountains, Saff's worries had mounted about reporting Kaylah's behavior to the council. What if it had really meant nothing, and Saff's words to the council member eroded the trust they held in Kaylah?

But Saff couldn't shake the weight of responsibility to report the behavior. The problem, however, was that the councilwoman assigned to Unitas never showed up for her regular visit that day.

And that night, all hell had broken loose in camp. Kaylah had gone missing, and that was just the half of it.

Saff sighed as she approached her intended destination, Ginger's tent. She pulled back the door flap and cautiously walked in. Ginger sat in a chair, staring at a corner of the tent, pensive and worn out.

"You called for me?" Saff said.

Ginger drew a deep breath. "Yeah. Please sit down. Let's talk."

Saff took a seat facing her. "Talking is about the only thing I'm good for right now."

Ginger frowned. "We need to discuss what's going on. We need answers."

"And you think I have those?" Saff asked, exasperated.

Ginger shrugged. "I don't know what to think anymore."

Saff didn't either. The way Kaylah had gone missing was disturbing. As usual, she'd had guards stationed outside of her tent—two of them. One Ivy, one Seeder. Both were missing. During the surge of aggressive attacks on camp that night, most camp members had been pulled to the borders for fighting. No witnesses had come forward about seeing Kaylah or her guards going missing.

There were, however, plenty of witnesses who had rushed into action when Kaylah's tent, as well as the patch of emergency exit rifting trees, had all lit ablaze.

A few trees remained unharmed, as well as some of the books and scrolls in Kaylah's tent, but many of the ancient books were irreparably lost, reduced to smoke and ash. No bodies had been found.

Ginger pursed her lips, the dark bags under her eyes accentuating her frustration. "My people can't help but worry they're risking their lives for the wrong cause. You can't pretend things aren't suspicious with your leaders and the current circumstances."

Saff's jaw dropped. "You're kidding me. Seeders are somehow at fault? Don't pretend Kaylah hasn't hurt my people before. That she hasn't let people she supposedly cares about get caught in the crosshairs."

Ginger's eyes narrowed, and she stabbed a finger onto the desk she sat at. "Where are your leaders right now? When we need them? *My* people are completely cutoff. *Your* people have made sure of that, haven't they?"

The rifting cave security had been doubled, and the Seeders had chopped down the remaining rifting trees in camp, fearing more betrayal, more deserters.

"We can't exactly rift into your territory for a meeting. *Your* council can send someone through the cave. Or catch a breeze over the troops. But they're *not*. They're ignoring our requests."

Saff sat up straight. "They're a little busy right now!"

Right after Kaylah went missing, a messenger had arrived bearing news from the council. With the War Vines not working as well, missing the energy of the extra kidnapped Seeder girls, Ivies had converged on one weakened point, in the thousands. Maybe even tens of thousands. For the first time in known history, a portion of both the Inner and Outer Walls had fallen, in sickeningly close proximity to Saff and Devin's home village.

It made her physically ill. She had no word from home. From her family. They'd discussed Devin returning to help back home or to at least get an update on their loved ones, but concluded the camp needed him more, and they couldn't justify the time spent traveling.

Ginger shook her head. "They could give us *something*. They've all but abandoned us."

"Abandoned? Their focus is to save lives. And if Soren's people get their hands on even one or two of our fully-rooted matriarchs in their raids, we're screwed." The War Vines weren't as effective as they'd previously been, missing more girls to power their attack, but they continued to break down and weaken the Seeder border thickets. If Soren got his hands on another Seeder girl, especially a powerful matriarch…

Ginger rubbed the back of her neck. "The facts remain. She was supposed to be guarded. We're not getting a lot of help. We're cutoff."

Saff nodded. "The facts *do* remain. Kaylah knows how to take care of herself just fine. And she hasn't really fulfilled her promises, has she?"

"Like your council, she's been a bit busy." Ginger glared. "*My* people aren't blind to the fact that *your* people are impatient, and might consider pivoting their strategy and keeping you out of the loop on that."

Saff crossed her arms, ready to keep going at it. But this was getting them nowhere. "When did we go back to 'your people' and 'my people,' Ginger? This isn't what Kaylah wanted. I know you love her, and I do too." She frowned. "It may have taken me longer to get there, but I believe in this cause. And I know you do too."

There were only three possibilities: Kaylah had double-crossed Unitas and the Seeder people, Seeder leadership had abandoned the cause and double-crossed Kaylah, or Soren's forces had found a way in to take her.

Ginger sighed, studying the ground with a slow nod.

"We've got people searching in both realms, right?" Saff said. "I know things are touchy. I know we all want answers right now. But we need to give them time to find out what really happened."

"Yeah," Ginger whispered. "We should hopefully hear back from palace insiders soon, on whether Soren has her."

Saff fidgeted with her hands. "Hopefully. If we even have any insiders left on our side."

Ginger rubbed her face with her hands. "Business as usual. Protect the camp, the community without powers, the cave. And sit here … waiting for news. And for something to change…"

"Yeah." Saff's heart was heavy. She *wanted* to believe it had been Soren; she couldn't bear to imagine Kaylah or the council betraying Unitas.

Saff's mind was muddled. Partially from physical exhaustion, partially from the tax on her Seeder energy, and partially from the stress of having taken her first lives. Then again, was it *her* kill, or Devin's, if he had thrown the darts, boosted by Saff's energy?

Splaying her hands on her thighs, Saff tried to think straight. "Can we just go over the logistics again?"

They discussed the events of the night Kaylah had gone missing, both doing their best to not take offense when the loyalty of their people was called into question. They discussed motive and opportunity.

Saff outlined her thinking first. "There could be multiple reasons for Kaylah to turn."

Perhaps Kaylah had found something in her research that didn't sit right with her, prompting her to bail. Or she'd intended to set the camp up to fail from the beginning. Or Soren had snuck in a spy with an offer she couldn't turn down. If she'd abandoned Unitas, it would make sense that she would light fire to her own tent to cause confusion and to destroy the ancient research. The fire would give her a distraction while she and her Ivy guard took out the Seeder guard, disposed of the body in the canyon, and snuck out through a tree rift. But it was odd that they would have set fire to the emergency rifting trees in camp as well. Would Kaylah have been vindictive enough to her own Unitas Ivies to imprison them in camp, knowing they'd fall to either Soren's forces, or the Seeders upon her betrayal?

"None of that is true," Ginger asserted, teeth clenched but her tone civil—barely. "And if she'd discovered anything like that to make her turn on us, she would have discussed it with me, too."

You could cut the tension in camp with a Seeder blade. It was spelled out on everyone's faces. The only reason most of the Unitas Ivies hadn't defected at her departure was likely because they had nowhere to go anymore. They'd staked their lives on this cause. They wouldn't return to their kingdom to be executed as traitors. They couldn't seek refuge in Seeder lands with the existing hostilities. And they couldn't physically leave anyway, with the emergency exit trees now gone, all exits from camp guarded, and the rifting cave well-manned.

The only reason Seeders didn't take on their Ivy counterparts in camp and wipe them out, or detain them, was simply because they were needed in the fighting to keep Soren's forces at bay.

Reluctant or not, begrudgingly or not, both sides of Unitas still needed each other. They didn't know how to deactivate the rifting cave Kaylah had set up, and they couldn't just abandon it to Soren's army. There was nowhere to evacuate the Seeder men without powers to, other than marching them into the mountains somewhere, for some unknown amount of time, with the vines of the Ivy army at their heels.

Unitas was an island in this war right now, and they needed to hold the line and take care of their own while the main Seeder territories managed their weakened borders in the bigger picture.

"So…" Ginger tapped her fingers on the table. "If the Seeder council betrayed Unitas…"

They explored that option as well. Perhaps Kaylah had stumbled upon some darker truths in the history of Seeders that they'd hidden from their people. They'd needed to shut her up. Perhaps they'd been disappointed that she hadn't yet delivered on half of her promises thus far, and were ready to dissolve their alliance. Either way, the same motives for the fires that night loomed as possibilities—destroy evidence, create panic, cut off Unitas Ivies from retreat.

The Ivy guard that night could have been a casualty at the bottom of the canyon somewhere, while the Seeder one had carted Kaylah away, perhaps through the cave, even. But that would have required several guards to look the other way, and would stand to have more witnesses, as the cave was farther to travel to. How many people would have had to conspire for that to happen?

"The logic doesn't hold up," Saff said.

If the Seeders had carried this out, why wouldn't they have sent more troops to protect their own village, and the cave? They could have sent troops in to sweep the camp clean if they'd wanted to end this experiment; they wouldn't have needed to steal Kaylah away in the middle of the night. Then again, their resources were stretched thin with the border walls failing.

Suspicion waxed and waned between Saff's heart and mind, in her attempts to be logical, but in the end, this *didn't* smell of Seeder treachery.

Seeders wouldn't intentionally abandon their sons and brothers without power, and they wouldn't be so heartless and underhanded. Saff could understand Ginger's doubts, though. It wasn't like they'd sat around a campfire singing songs and sharing smiles with council members from the beginning. It had been a rough road. But they'd been giving Kaylah so much more freedom in her strategies, orders, and research.

"It *had* to be Soren's doing, right?" Saff asked.

Kaylah had to have been taken against her will … somehow. But if Soren's forces had found a way to sneak into camp and sneak her out, why hadn't they just wiped out the camp altogether in a bloodbath? It had to have been more stealthy than that. Other than the two missing guards, no one else had gone missing, and it stood to reason that more than one or two guards would have been needed to take her hostage and keep her quiet.

And assuming Soren's people had dragged her back to the palace, how could he even manage that without the cave or on foot? They'd probably used the emergency exit trees, but Ivy rifting wasn't as simple as running a vine down the spine of a tree and shoving someone through. There was a mental component to Ivy rifting. The rifter had to know their destination as they created the rift, and the only being they could pull through one was a female Seeder, not another Ivy. It didn't add up. How could Soren have forced Kaylah to open her own rift to a location of his choosing? No matter her faults, Kaylah was made of tougher stuff than that.

None of it made sense. Which was likely what the culprit had been going for. It was infuriating.

Saff shook her head, trying to clear it. They weren't getting anywhere. "Have you noticed Kaylah acting off lately?"

Ginger leaned back in her seat again. "Off? Not really…"

"Because I did. She clammed up when we were talking about her Uncle Nuren and her mom. Something about a weakness he took advantage of?"

Furrowing her brow, Ginger wore a contemplative look. "No. You mean like a weakness in the queen's powers that would have been passed down to her? Something that would have made her vulnerable to kidnapping?"

Saff stretched her legs out, slumping a bit in the hard chair. "Maybe? Ivies can't rift into this camp because of the coordinates she scouted, but they can rift out. Maybe something … like the royal line has a defect…?"

"Absolutely not."

Something kept tapping Saff in the back of her mind, urging her to keep searching. It tapped. It knocked. It pounded. Her focus shifted to the emergency exit trees time and time again. The culprits could have set more tents on fire if they'd wanted to cause confusion. And they hadn't successfully burned all of the trees down to cut off Unitas Ivy retreats. Maybe they'd just flubbed that part, but that would have been rather sloppy, given how well-timed and silently this had all been carried out.

And then something clicked. Something Kaylah had once brushed off. Something Devin had mentioned after she'd gone missing.

Nathan… Kaylah's Ivy guardian from her mission in the human world. Saff had once asked why he was always in the human world instead of in the Unitas camp, and Kaylah had brushed that question off.

But Devin had seen Nathan in camp shortly after Kaylah's disappearance. According to Devin, Nathan had practically been marched into camp, toward the emergency rifting tree patch, and onlookers had been shooed away. Everything had been chaotic, so they hadn't known what to make of it. But Nathan hadn't stayed in camp. He'd been sent back to the human world again.

Eyeing Ginger, Saff clenched her teeth. "Why isn't your husband here?"

"Because your leaders think he's best suited to working for Unitas in the human world."

Saff narrowed her eyes. "Why? What skills does he have that would justify him being stationed there? I bet you and Kaylah would have loved to have him here in camp for support."

Pressing her fingers to her lips, Ginger averted her gaze.

Saff's stomach knotted. She'd never suspected Ginger and Nathan of malintent. "Why was he in camp right after she went missing?" Her tone was deep and threatening. "Ginger?"

"'Need to know' information, Saff," Ginger said quietly.

"I need to know. Neither of us are leaving this tent until I know the truth." Saff wasn't playing more Ivy games. She wasn't afraid of taking on Ginger, even in her current worn-out state.

Ginger met her gaze, visibly worn down. "If I told you, your leaders would take my life."

Saff's eyes darted, searching Ginger's face. How had the Seeder leaders come into the equation again?

"Why would my people kill you over a secret?" Saff glanced at the closed tent door flap. "If they know whatever secret you're keeping, then I have no reason to tell them. You can trust me."

Ginger kept her mouth closed, barely shaking her head.

"Do you know where Rachel is right now?" Saff asked.

"Of course. She went back to your home village."

It sounded as convincing as any lie Ginger had told before, and in line with the lies Saff had been repeating, to keep Rachel and Guillen's mission a secret.

Kaylah usually brought Ginger or Saff to the council meetings, but they couldn't spare them both. The council now knew that Saff was in on the secret of Rachel and Guillen's mission.

"How about where Rachel's *really* at? And who she's really with? The mission they're on?"

Ginger looked surprised.

"Right. Kaylah entrusted me with that secret, too. Something no one was supposed to know. It's time to bring me into the equation. And I swear, I won't say a thing."

Nervously tapping on the desk, Ginger stared at Saff in silence. Finally, she opened her mouth. "Your leaders keep us separated because if he doesn't do his job, if he lets them down, they've threatened to kill me. It keeps him in line."

That didn't make any sense. He was just guarding the human-world rifting cave right now, or so Saff had thought…

"Doing his job? What's so special about his job?"

"He's a whisper."

That meant nothing to Saff, but before she could ask, Ginger elaborated.

"It's a rare gift. 'Whisper rifters.' Probably our kingdom's best-kept secret."

"And what does a 'whisper' do?"

Ginger was still hesitant to speak, wringing her hands. "It depends who you ask. They're said to be able to hear the whispers of a traitor from miles away, to be able to walk through solid walls, to be able to kidnap your children through a rift, to be able to read your soul, steal your energy, and have five times the strength of a normal Ivy."

Saff's mouth hung open. "Excuse me?" *Some kind of ridiculously overpowered Super Ivy?*

Ginger rolled her eyes. "From what we can tell, the tiniest fraction of that is actually true. That's why they're such a secret, kept even from our own people. That's how the queen and king keep their subjects in line." She blew out a puff of air. "There's a common saying, that 'the Mother Vines have eyes and ears.' It's ridiculous. We have spies planted throughout our cities, reporting to law enforcement about those who would dare oppose the queen and king."

Her heart racing, Saff could only imagine Rachel's situation. "Does Guillen know to look out for them?"

"Yes," Ginger answered confidently. "And he's being careful. The communities they're in aren't managed the same way as regular Ivy society."

That brought little comfort. "So your monarchy spies on your own people. What can whispers actually do, if they can't do all of those things?"

Ginger sighed. "It's nebulous. Whispers are steeped in mythology. The rumors and fairy tales that circle the kingdom either lead you to stay in line, because you're paranoid one might come after you, with all of these ridiculous claims about their powers, or you're branded as a fool for believing they even exist. It's the perfect balance for a secret weapon. They're like Bigfoot, or the Loch Ness Monster."

She stood, clasping her hands. "You're either too proud to believe outlandish fairy tales, or too paranoid to be disloyal to your queen."

Saff tried to take it in and make sense of it while Ginger paced the small tent.

"Their powers, as far as we know, can include more energy and strength, as well as reading a tree, and ... third-party rift creation."

"What do those last two mean?"

Ginger pursed her lips. "To read a tree means that a whisper can sense the location a dying tree was used to rift to. It's a way of tracking deserters or anyone else they want, as long as the tree is fresh. It's said they can sense the last whisper of life in that tree as it dies, giving up the coordinates."

"Okay..."

Sitting back down, Ginger crossed her legs. "That's part of why Kaylah and Olivia didn't join Rachel's party after rescuing her from the palace. They rifted out on the palace grounds, hoping they'd be followed, leading their pursuers away, so they wouldn't search for Rachel and the others on foot."

So many questions ran through Saff's mind. "What about that last one you mentioned? Third-party whatever?"

Rubbing her temples, Ginger hesitated. "It's entirely possible that there are a gifted few who can … open a rift like Seeders do."

Saff furrowed her brow. "In the air?" Could these whispers fly, too?

"No. They can open a tree rift for someone else."

The weight of the truth slammed down on Saff. "Kaylah could have been forced through a rift to any location they wanted, against her will. And if…" She searched to put the pieces together. "If your husband can read a tree, they could have covered their tracks by burning the tree she'd been forced through?"

"Yes," Ginger confessed, a look of defeat overtaking her.

Saff's ears burned. "Why did you waste my time blaming Seeders, when you knew good and well it was an Ivy whisper this whole time!"

Ginger glared. "You're forgetting one key thing here. *Your* people are keeping it a secret, aren't they? But your leaders know some of us Ivies in Unitas know the truth behind the whisper gift, and *your leaders* could have taken her, and burned the tree themselves to incite suspicion."

Saff couldn't believe that. It sounded like the kind of lie you tell yourself when you're in denial. That theory was too much of a stretch, given they'd agreed this was most likely Soren's doing.

But the question remained. Why were the council leaders keeping this ability a secret? Why was Unitas keeping it a secret?

"What are they making your husband do with his gift?"

"He helped Kaylah secure the location for camp. He tried to read the burned trees. And before the cave was primed, he monitored other Unitas Ivies who were running Seeder girls back home, so we could prove our trustworthiness, and so none of them were led through a rift to the palace, should we have a traitor."

That was all great. And understandable. "So he spied on Unitas Ivies to gain Seeder trust. Why hide it? I'm sure they would understand. Seeders would, too. We should be using this gift more, not shoving it under a rock."

Ginger grabbed a water bottle, unscrewing the cap. "Like I said, it's rare. We only have five known whispers within Unitas. And we still know so little about the gift. My husband only divulged his secret to Kaylah and me over a year ago."

Saff recalled the shock of seeing Kaylah's tent half-burned, still smoldering. She'd ached at the years of history they'd lost in the books and scrolls destroyed. "Is the information about whispers in one of the lost books?"

"No." Ginger took a sip of water. "Like I said, whispers are steeped in myth. They're off the record. Men like my husband were picked at a young age, and molded in their education. They didn't even know they had the gift. Because of their gift, and their skill in sparring practices, they were singled out to train as assassins." Ginger puckered her lips. "Once they're in assassin training, their whisper skills are nurtured, in secret. Under the threat of death and the death of those they love, they're not allowed to ever discuss it. Assassin training takes them away from their families. They're privately tutored, not even allowed to know other whispers. It's a burden of isolation, knowing that for the rest of your life, you'll keep this secret, and serve at the beck and call of your queen and king, answering to their every whim, betraying your own people."

Saff could sympathize with Ginger. The levels of deceit within Ivy society rivaled the level of brutality they'd aimed at the Seeders. "I don't get Kaylah. I understand that these men might not easily give up their secrets, but she talked about being honest with her people, about not covering up the ugly truth in history."

Screwing the lid back on her water bottle, Ginger spoke softly. "People can only handle so much at once. She plans to sort out whispers and their exploitation, but you can't bury people in an avalanche of truth all in one go. Because when you do, they stop seeing the person trying to save them. They'd see Kaylah as just another queen in the same family line of manipulators and liars." Ginger's eyes glistened with tears. "I'd rather not have my daughter taken to a guillotine because people couldn't see her for what she is."

Saff's heart went out to Ginger. Sometimes, she forgot that Ginger and Nathan had half raised Kaylah in the human world as her surrogate parents. They loved her. They weren't just regular Unitas members to her.

The two sat in silence, the hopelessness, and grief, and questions still looming. Saff explored the possibilities, the strategies at play. An idea sparked, a glimmer of hope. Even if Unitas only had a handful of whispers…

"Hold on. Kaylah and Olivia rifted away from the palace after rescuing Rachel? Kaylah said the Mother Vines and War Vines restricted rifting within the protective border there."

Ginger waved a dismissive hand. "We can rift out. Just not in."

"Oh." That was disappointing. "I guess the palace barrier isn't *exactly* the same as our thickets."

And then the disturbing reality of the implications crushed Saff. She forgot how to breathe entirely. "Ivies can't rift into our lands because of the protective thickets. I'm guessing not even whispers can…?"

"Correct."

"But if *both* of the walls are compromised… If *both* of them fail…" Saff's eyes blurred in her despair, her mental map dotting with dozens, even hundreds, of rifts opening in the middle of their villages. Raiding whispers could tear away matriarchs left and right, taking them back to the palace to hook up to the War Vines. The War Vines that had done inconceivable damage with just a half dozen teenage Seeder girls, barely rooted. The War Vines that only one person in the realm, in the world, could control—Kaylah.

Unitas had five whole whispers in their pocket. How many did Soren have?

The air had grown cold and thin. Saff panted. This could be catastrophic. Seeders and Unitas were doomed. Looking at Ginger through blurred, warm, glowing eyes, Saff was overcome with rage.

"Why the hell would my leaders keep this a secret? My people deserve to know the threat they're facing! I have family fighting tooth and nail to keep our village safe!" She didn't care if her yelling was too loud, if someone outside of the tent overheard her.

Ginger tried to shush her.

"No! I'm done with this. It's one thing to lie to growing Seeder girls about their identities, so they get to live normal lives while hiding from assassins. It's another to lie to an *entire nation.* They deserve to know." Saff stood, unable to bear this. "I may not be a war strategist, but hiding a massive threat from your own army is the stupidest thing I've ever heard!"

Shooting up from her chair, Ginger crossed the tent in two steps, standing between Saff and the tent door. "Think for one second. Step back for a moment and just look at yourself. You are panicking."

Saff studied her face. *Maybe I wouldn't be panicking if people would just be honest. If my family knew what they might be facing.*

Ginger's voice was firm but quiet. "If your people understood the possible threat posed by whispers, what could they even do about it that they aren't already?" She paused. "Hide all of your women in the human world? Can't do that. Wouldn't even want to, because they're needed for healing and charging your borders. Knowing *this* truth would do nothing but stamp out the barely there hope they cling to. Knowledge of the full threat can be empowering, *if* something can actually be done about it, but we have *nothing* to mitigate this. You are *one* panicking Seeder right now. Do you want millions more to join you?"

Saff's cheeks wetted as she stood there, helpless, her knees threatening to buckle. Never had she been more gutted, more devastated, more hopeless. "I understand."

"Good. Because even if you don't care about *my* life, I don't know that your leaders would take kindly to you knowing something you shouldn't."

"What can I do?" Saff whispered.

Ginger sighed. "Help me keep the peace? Keep a lookout for suspicious activity?" She lightly rested her hands on Saff's shoulders. "We're not even sure that Soren knows the truth about whispers, okay? He may not realize what he has. Kaylah's parents never told her, and she was their heir."

That gave Saff the tiniest speck of hope. Maybe they were overthinking the threat. But the only other alternative was Seeder betrayal or Kaylah deserting them.

"If it was a whisper that took her, they may be someone we're not aware of," Ginger added.

Saff searched Ginger's eyes. "Right... Only one Ivy guard went missing." It wasn't likely that only one traitor had pulled off Kaylah's kidnapping. They might still have a spy in camp. "What whispers do we have on our side, aside from your husband?"

"Three are in my kingdom, undercover. The only other one I'm aware of is Jon, one of the guards who helped in Rachel's rescue. They were all former assassins. All former or current palace guards."

It made sense. *Keep your toolbox close.*

Saff swallowed hard. "Yeah. I'll do everything I can: Keep up morale. Try not to jump to conclusions. Look for odd behavior."

"Good. We just have to hold the line, wait for word, and ... we'll see what we need to do once your council members reach out again."

Saff nodded, dazed.

"And even if Soren has Kaylah..." Ginger pressed her lips together, looking like she might cry. "She wouldn't betray us."

Shoving her hands in her pockets, Saff looked down at her shoes. "I wish I was as confident in that. It's easy for us to imagine we'd be brave in our last moments, or through torture, but no one really knows until they're there." She looked up as tears streamed down Ginger's face.

Saff gave her a hug. "I'm sorry. I shouldn't have said that."

Ginger squeezed her tighter. "But you're right."

After a while, Ginger finally pulled back from the hug. "Thank you," she said with a weak smile.

"Ditto. You and I were here from the start. We need to keep Unitas going."

Ginger nodded. "I'll send word if I get any updates."

"As will I."

Ginger returned to her chair as Saff opened the door flap to leave.

Turning to ask Ginger one last question, Saff hesitated. "I know this isn't the most tactful thing to ask right now, but if we suspect a whisper took Kaylah, are you *absolutely* sure your husb—"

"Don't. You. Dare," Ginger growled. The fire in her eyes matched the fierce redness of her hair.

Saff opened her mouth to elaborate. She understood that Ginger might not want to consider the possibility that Nathan may have betrayed Kaylah. Under duress. Under old orders from Kaylah's real parents that he'd never truly abandoned. After all, he *had* kept this huge secret from his wife for over two decades…

The venomous rage embodied in a single stare caused Saff to close her mouth. She would have sported that look herself, if someone had questioned Devin's integrity that way. She would go to bat for him, just like Ginger was for Nathan, especially after the way Seeder leaders were using Nathan for his gift, dangling Ginger's life in front of him.

"I… I'll see you later." Saff turned and left the tent.

***

Walking back to her own tent to rest up and allow her energy reserves to recharge, Saff was lost in thought. She couldn't even risk confiding in Devin this time.

"Hey, stranger. You okay?"

Saff looked to her right. Flora closed the gap to walk alongside her. Gashes covered her arm and face, but she still bore a smile.

Saff frowned. "You look like I feel. Camp protection shift over?"

Flora nodded. "No more fun and games, huh?"

"Something like that."

Flora pursed her lips. "Any updates? What are your thoughts about what's going on?"

Everyone was waiting with bated breath for word from Unitas spies at the palace, as to whether Kaylah had ended up there. "No updates, yet. We need to continue on without her, until we hear more. We have to believe in Unitas. What about you?"

Flora nodded, looking straight forward. "I agree. Maybe it's just selfish thinking, but I can't allow myself to imagine I gave up everything back home to just have your people betray us, or to have *her* betray us."

Saff glanced at Flora's injuries again. She wanted to reach out and heal them. It wouldn't take long. But she'd expended all of her energy on darts.

Flora must have read her mind. "It's fine. I numbed them and got them to stop bleeding. I'm sure I can track down someone around here to help out. Maybe at the far healer station." She smiled. "It's past your tent; that's where you're headed, right?"

Saff nodded. "Yeah. Water and some sleep. If you can't find someone, check back with me in a little while."

Flora put her arm around Saff's shoulders. "Sounds like a deal. I'll drop you off."

This was what Unitas was supposed to be. Normal people, just trying to do their best, and seeing past their differences.

"How's your friend doing?" Saff asked. "What was her name?"

"Raven. She's good. She just finished protection detail a little before me."

Saff smiled. As long as they could keep working together, there was still hope.

Chapter 30

GUILLEN BEGRUDGINGLY AGREED TO HAVE Rachel join him. He wasn't even telling William what their plan was; he wanted to keep this one close to his vest. He told William he'd report his progress with their contacts as he could along the way.

Guillen and Rachel threw their stuff together and set out on the road in the middle of the night. While the trip would normally take several days, if following traditional roads, Guillen would be able to significantly shrink that timeframe. He knew every shortcut, where to find connections along the way, defensible places to rest, where to avoid scrutinizing eyes.

They stopped to rest for short periods, just long enough to allow Rachel to try and heal their aches and pains, take a brief nap, and be on their way. As they got closer to the 'royal region,' as he called it, the scenery became greener, brighter; the homes—bigger.

Splurging on a room for the night, they allowed themselves to finally get a full night's sleep.

Rachel woke the next morning with Guillen's arm around her. While she normally loved his embrace, she couldn't help but be annoyed. Multiple times a day, he was still trying to talk her out of continuing with him. It was pretty much the only thing that cut through the silence between them. The day before, he'd threatened to leave her during the night and go on his own. It hadn't exactly ended in a screaming match, but voices had been raised and less-than-kind sentiments shared.

She rolled her eyes and slid out from underneath his arm, getting out of bed. She took a seat on the couch in their room and stared out the window. When he stirred in bed, she glanced in his direction; he rubbed his eyes and sat up.

"I'm ready to go," she said.

He closed his eyes and shook his head. "Please. For me. Stay."

"I told you I don't like being lied to. And having you withhold things from me. You keep mentioning 'dangerous' and 'messy' and all this other crap, but you won't elaborate. Either you think I'm a liability, or … what? It's not like this is a girlfriend thing, and you're afraid for me to meet your mom." She huffed. "We're doing a *great* job pretending we're not an item right now, anyway."

"I know you want to help," he replied in the same tone he'd used the last few days, one with a bit of an edge to it. "And it frustrates you that you can't save the realm single-handedly. But this one is on me."

She scowled. "Don't patronize me."

"You want to know why?" His brow furrowed. "My father, while not likely to be home, is not exactly reliable. And my mother… She's always found the Crown's methods distasteful and wasteful. Note that I said 'distasteful'—not 'deplorable,' not 'despicable.'" He ran a hand through his hair. "She's unpredictable. She's lukewarm. She wouldn't be the kind to *plan* to hook you up to the War Vines, but she's loyal to the kingdom, to a fault."

"So, force her to come! Gag her if you have to."

He glared. "I'm sure her loyal guards and servants are going to let us waltz out of there with her tied up. The moment Kaylah's dead, she has the right to the throne. You don't think they've ramped up security at their manor in this chaos?"

Rachel tilted her head. "You think you need to convince her. I'll what? Sour things? Even if she thinks I'm one of you? I can't be there to help keep them safe after you've done the job of leading them away? I can play a lot of roles in this, and you're wanting to dismiss them all."

He clenched his jaw. "She could turn on me. On us."

The way he'd said it gave Rachel pause. She studied him, worried. "You don't think your mom would turn on Kaylah … do you?"

He rubbed his eyebrow with a knuckle. "No. I don't think so. At least not easily. I think, that if push came to shove, she'd take her place, under Soren's influence. But she's not eager to rule."

"Then it can't be all that bad."

"She's the kind of woman who beat her own son, and hasn't lifted a damn finger to stop this war!"

Rachel frowned. He had to be overreacting, but his feelings were born of pain, and he had a right to them.

He looked at the ground as if ashamed. "And she hates Seeders."

"I won't be going as a Seeder. We've made it through half of the communities without problems, right?"

"I don't care. She's smart. And maybe someone from the palace will recognize you as we get closer. A million things could go wrong."

"You're right. They could. And I signed up for that. And unless you can honestly say to my face that you *genuinely* believe I'm more of a liability than an asset…"

"You're not a liability. I just don't want to have to worry about you at the same time."

She sighed, facing him directly. "I need you to trust me. Believe in me. That when it comes time, I won't let you down. Guillen, I love you. But this is bigger than that."

He gnawed on his bottom lip. "Let's get going. We can be there before nightfall."

***

Guillen's family lived little more than an hour from the palace by train, but Rachel and Guillen still wouldn't risk taking a train, especially in the royal region. Based on reports he'd gotten throughout the last year, his parents and siblings continued to have minimal interaction with the ruling family. Soren had never respected his aunt much, and she wasn't one to interfere.

Guillen prepared Rachel on what to expect. He assumed only his mother and sister would be at their manor, with guards and servants. He described his mother as tall and thin with warm brown hair but none of that warmth in her personality. His little sister was prim and proper, as a lady of her station ought to be. Rachel could tell how much he regretted that he didn't visit more, for her benefit, and how much he loved her, by how he spoke of her.

"She's clever and witty." He smiled. "A bit precocious." He frowned. "She's in a tight spot, having to live with my mother. But she has a good heart."

Rachel looked forward to meeting his little sister. Not so much his mother.

As Rachel and Guillen drew closer to the home he'd grown up in, they talked about strategy and switching up their cover stories. He wanted to keep Rachel's identity a secret, but couldn't come up with a reason for why she'd be there as a co-worker, or a friend, and they certainly wouldn't mention Unitas right out of the gate.

It felt like a frivolous way to spend their time, but Guillen insisted they stop in the nearest city and freshen up with nice new clothes. It was odd for Rachel to wear a fancy dress, but they needed to make a good impression to try to win his mother over.

Rachel chose a cream linen dress with bright embroidery—a much more sophisticated style than the stunt clothes she'd been wearing for their mission. Guillen must have approved, judging by the grin he wore when she came out of the dressing room. She couldn't deny how nice he looked, too, in more formal Green Lands attire—a comfy-looking dark brown linen suit.

Before getting too close to the property, they ditched their travel packs in a bush to reclaim later. Rachel's nerves were all jumbled as they passed several guards at the property entryway. Down a long lane flanked with huge hedges, they finally arrived at the door to the mansion, and Guillen knocked. The butler recognized Guillen right away, bowing. He guided them into a large sitting room. So far, it had gone a lot more smoothly than she'd feared. Her palms were a bit sweaty after passing so many guards, but she and Guillen could handle this.

Rachel caught herself with her jaw down, taking in the exquisite décor of the sitting room. She hadn't seen any fancy rooms in the palace, just basic, tucked-away spaces. As a room meant for audiences, this was the nicest thing she'd seen in the entire Green Lands. Chandeliers and tatted curtains draped from tall ceilings. Wainscoting and murals covered the walls.

Guillen observed her, a small smirk on his face. He took her hand and gave a reassuring squeeze. A cold, hard metal met her skin—he wore his royal ring for the first time. She was intrigued to see him in this environment, even though it hadn't been one of her reasons for coming along.

A rather ill-tempered-looking woman entered the room with a wineglass in her hands. "Guillen, what are you doing here?" Her skin was youthful, but the sour face she wore detracted from her beauty.

"Hi, Mother. Just a short visit."

"Who's this girl?" She sat down without offering a hug to greet her son, instead taking a sip.

He slid his arm around Rachel. "This is Elizabeth, my girlfriend. She's from Community Five. I thought you should meet."

His mother eyed Rachel, scrutinizing her from top to bottom. "I see she must be enjoying your stipend."

Stipend? Money? Did she just assume I'm a gold digger? To a stunt?

Guillen's mother was clearly less than impressed. "A bit foolish to waste your meager week off coming all the way here, and unannounced." She looked at Rachel, but not really. It was more like looking *past* Rachel. Speaking to her, but in a way that sounded more like she was talking *about* Rachel, rather than *to* her.

She turned her gaze fully on Guillen. "Is she pregnant? I'm not willing to petition Soren for an exception so you can keep that kind of baby, if that's what you're asking."

Rachel bit her tongue and concealed her rage, conscientiously cramming every last speck of her Seeder energy into her heart, locking it up to keep her cover, and hide her true feelings on the discussion at hand.

Guillen replied calmly, as if his mother hadn't just insulted them both, and his kind. "No, Mother. Just a simple visit. I know I don't come around often, but I try to for the important things. And she's important to me. That's all."

"Hmmph. What is it you do, Elizabeth?" The way she said either of their names sounded like their very names were somehow insults.

Rachel forced a smile. "It's nice to meet you, ma'am. I work in textile."

"Hmmph. Wouldn't expect someone like you to do or know any better," she muttered, then drained her glass of wine.

How odd would that feel, if it were true that Rachel actually did work in textiles as a stunt? Her persona could very well be the person who slaved away making some of the ornate fabric in the room, or the very clothes on this woman. The class difference hit Rachel like a punch in the gut. Guillen's mother certainly didn't try to hide her opinion of her guests, and why should she? Rachel was only a gold-digging crown-chaser. But then again, this horrid woman probably didn't care enough about her own son to think that way. She didn't at all give off an air of concern, only ample insults.

"Your father's not around, if you were hoping to see him."

"That's fine." Guillen glanced around the room. "Is Catrina here?"

She stood and poured herself another drink from a carafe on a nearby gilded table. "Yes. I think I saw her running around here somewhere."

"Do you think we could move somewhere more private, perhaps the library, to speak?" he asked.

"This is private enough, I'm sure." She waved her hand, gesturing at the room. "Do you see anyone else here? I'm quite comfortable, thank you." She sat back down.

Guillen tensed.

"Such odd news from the palace, isn't it?" his mother said. "I'm assuming you've heard about Kaylah?"

Rachel's heart skipped a beat.

"It's hard to say," Guillen replied coolly. "One hears a lot of things. What's the most recent news?"

"Well, Betsy's son, Ayden—you remember him, right? He's been promoted at the palace. A good boy—nothing to be embarrassed about with him. He said they've rescued her. Of course, Soren sent out word that she turned on the people, but I can't imagine her doing that. She's such a sweet and capable girl. I'm sure they'll set it right and she'll take her place, putting an end to all of this."

"So, she's at the palace?" Guillen asked.

"Isn't that what I just said?" his mother drawled.

Rachel dared to speak up. "You'd like to end this war, ma'am?"

She furrowed her brow at Rachel. "That's an odd question. All it's doing is disrupting our way of life. We were all quite happy a couple of years ago before my sister let Nuren practically take over, the imbecile." She rolled her eyes. "And all that work, all this fuss, for what? He gets himself killed, and the weeds walk out with a couple of their useless rejects. Stupid idea from the beginning." She shook her head, raising her glass in their direction. "And if you ask me, it's enough to want to take our lands back, but to bring that filth over here, on our soil…"

Every ounce of Rachel's focus went into concealing her energy further, concealing her feelings. She couldn't react. And she'd known ahead of time that this wouldn't be sunshine and daisies, but she hadn't been prepared for a personal attack like that. She was aching to hear Guillen speak up. Just something, *anything*. For him, for her, for her people. Some sort of censure; this vile woman didn't deserve to consider herself so high and mighty.

Guillen reacted calmly. "Has Soren reached out to you throughout all of this?"

"Why should he?" She scoffed. "They messed this up. He and Kaylah can mop up their own mess." She swatted a dismissive hand in the air. "We've obviously attended the funerals, but that's all."

A girl walked in, looking a couple of years younger than Rachel, sharing Guillen's eyes.

"I thought I heard your voice!" She lit up. "What are you doing here?" She ran over to Guillen. He stood and gave her a huge hug.

"Hey, Sis. Just visiting. Stay and chat with us."

"Guillen brought a girlfriend home."

"Elizabeth, this is my sister, Catrina. Catrina, this is my girlfriend."

Catrina raised an eyebrow. "Girlfriend?" She extended a hand to Rachel. "I'll have more questions about that later."

His mom finished her second glass of wine. "He says there's no baby."

Catrina looked back up to Guillen, questioning with a glance.

He finally let out a hint of frustration. "She's not pregnant. It's just a visit."

Catrina sat down opposite them.

With scrutinizing eyes, Guillen's mom addressed him again. "You can't possibly be upset about us drawing that conclusion. You show up unannounced with a girl… And after that whole debacle with your pregnant ex-girlfriend?"

Guillen's jaw dropped.

Rachel couldn't resist the urge to want to hear more about the rumor. It *had* to be a rumor, after all. Guillen had never slept with anyone, and he was *not* the type of guy to have a secret baby out there somewhere.

"How did you even hear about that?" Guillen asked his mother.

Rachel's veins turned cold. *What? It's true?* He'd lied to her...

His mother arched an eyebrow. "You don't think the family hears about your escapades when you drag Kaylah into your shame? When she oversteps her bounds of authority to do you a favor? Her pity has always been wasted on you."

"It wasn't like that," Guillen protested.

Rachel was queasy. Guillen had told her he'd had Kaylah help with an issue that involved an ex-girlfriend, but hadn't elaborated. Rachel hadn't imagined it involving a child... She went to pull her hand out of Guillen's, but he grasped it tighter.

He met her gaze directly. "It's *not* like it sounds," he said emphatically.

What was she supposed to say in that moment, with his mom and sister watching on? She and Guillen weren't there for dating drama.

"So, Guillen..." Catrina shyly spoke up. "What, uh, what brings you on this visit?"

"We were just talking about our dear Kaylah," their mother answered. "Now that she's back home, I was saying, we'll get everything sorted out. And get her properly married off. She may have dawdled on accepting suitors to this point, but it's not right to lead without someone at your side. There's far too much work for it to be done alone."

"I don't know, Mother." Catrina seemed hesitant. "I was talking with Sarah, and I'm really starting to think Kaylah may have done the things they said. Why else would Soren claim the throne, unless he didn't think she'd be fit to lead? She *did* seem kind of soft about the weeds, if I'm honest." She frowned, timidly straightening her dress skirt. "Then again, it doesn't really make sense that he's calling himself that. Maybe he can't bring himself to…"

Her mother threw her a glare. "We've discussed this. I'm not *crawling* to him, asking for the position. If he finds her guilty, then I'm sure he'll do what needs to be done and reach out."

Sitting up straighter, Guillen took a deep breath. "Either way, I don't think we need to know Kaylah's intentions right now. That will sort itself out. But now that you're both here, we need to discuss the real reason for my visit."

He glanced around the room—there were still no guards or servants lurking about. His mother looked thoroughly unamused.

"You two aren't safe," Guillen said. "And I'm here to take you away until things calm down. We need to leave tonight. Quietly."

Catrina shrank back in her chair, visibly concerned, but still skeptical.

"Why would you say something like that?" His mom appeared disbelieving. "No one has a need to hurt us. Should I call for the guards?"

"No!" He paused. "Soren may want to hurt you both."

They both looked shocked.

His mom shook her head. "I know you're bitter that you're not as good as the others, but honestly. Picking up a few knives hardly makes you a valuable army man. Why would anyone confide something like that in you? About your own family, no less."

"I heard it from his own mouth," he lied convincingly.

"Why?" Catrina's voice was filled with worry.

"You know as well as I that he just got married. If he's named Beata as queen, then he intends to kill the downline."

Rachel was surprised he'd brought that up. They thought Soren would be willing to torture and kill his way down the line of heirs to have one be a puppet for him, but this strategy also made sense—he may not intend to place a puppet queen at all, instead wanting to reassign the allegiance of the Mother and War Vines to his bride.

Kaylah had told Rachel how Ivy queens were made, how Vine allegiance could be retrained. Kill the queen and the next five downline heirs, and that unique power could be reassigned. The thought ran shivers down Rachel's spine—Soren and his bride, recognized as legitimate rulers.

Guillen continued. "Let me get you both somewhere safe, and we'll sort things out. We'll be able to go over questions later."

The surly matriarch moved her focus to Rachel. "If your story is true, what's with her? Is she going to knit us a shawl to keep us warm where you're taking us?"

"She has lots of training with blades, too. She's here to help get you out safely."

"Consider me unimpressed," she muttered. "If what you say is actually credible, then all we need to do is alert the guards, and they'll be competent enough to ensure our safety."

"Shut up, Mother!"

Rachel jumped at Guillen's outburst. Catrina sat with her jaw on the floor.

His mother glared. "How dare you!"

"Ma'am." Rachel tried to do some damage control, putting on her best diplomatic tone and resting her hand on Guillen's knee. "I'm sorry, he's just worried about your safety. The reason we can't rely on others is because they may be compromised. Please allow us to see you to somewhere comfortable, to make sure you'll be okay. If it turns out the information is incorrect, we'll return you promptly and ensure no one even knows why you were gone."

She narrowed her eyes at Rachel. "I suppose you do sound *somewhat* competent."

"Mother, please," Catrina pleaded. "We can just go away for a day. You know Guillen wouldn't come around unless it was important."

"Yes, please. Just a day," Guillen echoed. He and Rachel were *definitely* willing to lie to get what they wanted, as long as his mother and sister would come quietly.

"Fine. We'll pack some bags and treat it like a little getaway. We'll discuss it in more detail before we go. And I'm going to need to approve the conditions of the place." Her lip twitched in revulsion, as she looked at Rachel again. "I'm not willing to stay in a substandard hovel, like that awful apartment you have."

Rachel couldn't fathom having to spend any more time with this wretched woman, but it may be the only thing that kept Kaylah alive. She focused on her breathing. In and out. Calmly, smoothly. And hopefully, miraculously, they'd soften this horrible woman's heart and shut her prejudiced mouth enough to make it all tolerable.

"We'll make sure you're well taken care of. Please pack quickly, and quietly."

Chapter 31

GUILLEN'S MOTHER, FORMALLY CALLED LADY VERA, and Catrina left the room to go pack a bag each, while Guillen and Rachel stayed in the sitting room.

He gave Rachel a relaxed smile. "I'm sorry. You were right. You did amazing!" he whispered. He leaned in for a kiss, and Rachel moved her head to dodge, crossing her arms.

"What?" he asked.

She huffed, shaking her head. Every glance and insult from that woman had etched deep, on multiple levels. Maybe it was the pent-up energy in Rachel's heart, fighting to get out. Or how tired she was from their journey to get there, or how frustrated she'd been for days about Guillen having dismissed her in this strategy... Rachel's logic wrestled with her emotions, and logic didn't win this time. "You didn't want me to come because you can't stand up to your mom."

Guillen narrowed his eyes. "Are you kidding me? I warned you about her, and I needed her to come willingly."

She rolled her eyes. "It's not like you had to spill your guts, but you couldn't speak up and put her in her place, even once?"

He scowled. "I tried. You saw how well that went. You need to stop taking this so personally."

She was just as frustrated with herself for getting upset, as she was with him. She pursed her lips. Maybe it hadn't been the personal insults. Maybe it had been the implications. She hadn't cared whether or not Guillen was a virgin, but he'd claimed to be. And then the whole pregnant ex-girlfriend bomb... "They both seem to think you're likely to come home after knocking up some random girl. I'm sure that will be interesting to unpack later."

His mouth hung open in obvious contempt. "Really? I shouldn't have to defend myself about that! Kaylah could vouch for every detail of what really happened. Either you love me and trust me, or you trust a self-centered lush that knows practically nothing about me." He stood and strode to the edge of the room.

She instantly regretted the accusation. And hated herself for flying off the handle. She walked up to him. "I'm sorry. I need to not let it get to me." Hadn't she promised to not allow her trust issues to get between them again?

His stare bore a hole right through her. "Integrity means a lot to me; you should know that by now. I don't need you adding to the mess of this. I get attacked enough around here, without someone, who I thought cared about me, making things worse."

"I really am sorry." She reached for his arm, and he shrugged her off.

He shook his head. "I'm patient, aren't I? I understand how it feels to work through crap. But I don't do it at the expense of others. You need to grow up. I'm not a walking mat."

She frowned, holding back her tears and Seeder energy. If she could so easily ruin things with Guillen, the perfectly patient partner, she didn't stand a chance. She shuffled back to the sofa, wilting as she sat down.

"I'm going to make sure they're okay." He walked out.

A few minutes later, he returned with both women.

Rachel surveyed the three of them. "Where are the bags?"

Two men appeared behind them, holding said baggage.

"These are the two guards who will be assisting us. As we go on our short *day trip*," Guillen announced, sharing a look with Rachel. This was not what they had planned.

"I insist," Lady Vera said. "I don't care what you two say. They're coming with us."

"Well, I… Uh…" Rachel grappled to help right the situation.

"Sir, I'd like to briefly discuss security details in private, if that's alright?" one of the men said to Guillen.

"Yes, Richard, of course." Guillen flashed Rachel a glance, as if asking her to carefully watch his mom and sister.

Hair on the back of Rachel's neck stood at attention as she started to panic. It was just supposed to be the four of them. They'd take them away, and if necessary, actually tie them up, until Kaylah could be freed. Taking along two more unpredictable elements might cripple them.

Rachel thought back to when she, Saff, Ginger, and Kaylah had run into Ivy soldiers on their return from meeting in the human world. They had originally spared the soldiers' lives, because they could. While Kaylah had eventually killed one before they made it to Seeder borders, Saff and Rachel had allowed the men to live at Kaylah's request, and because they outnumbered them, and couldn't leave the men to rat them out. Things might not go so smoothly this time; getting just his mom and sister to cooperate was going to be a daunting task on its own.

She ran through different scenarios while waiting for Guillen to return. He was smart—he'd know what to do. But he wasn't the first to return from the discussion.

In fact, he didn't return at all.

The guard reappeared, bloodied and scraped, carrying a dripping knife in his hand.

One of Guillen's knives.

"What did you do to him?!" Rachel screamed. "Where is he?!"

The guard pointed the knife at her. "That traitorous cripple doesn't matter anymore." He barked to the other guard, "These three are coming with us. We're taking them to the palace!"

Rachel threw a panicked glance at Guillen's mom and sister, who looked equally shocked.

"Excuse me!" Lady Vera protested.

The guard next to them extended vines to restrain them when they didn't immediately comply. "M'lady. Miss."

From there, Rachel's next few breaths, her next few moments, all played out in slow motion. Rachel studied the bloodied man, suppressing her Seeder energy, just like she had so desperately trained to do back in the human world when she'd been poisoned.

He still might not know I'm a Seeder.

The man quickly surveyed his injuries; Guillen hadn't gone down without a fight.

Rachel reached for the knife Guillen had once given her, unsheathing it as she slid it out of a pocket in her dress. She pointed it at the man, taking a defensive stance.

He flashed her a look of annoyance, and then amusement. "All of you heaps of compost are the same, aren't you?"

Good. A stunt community guard had once uttered that insult. Guillen's assailant still thought she was an Ivy stunt.

The guard dropped Guillen's knife. With a soft *thud*, Guillen's blood stained the rug at the guard's feet.

Guillen had trained Rachel for this, how to use a knife. But the guard's vines were reaching toward her, and fighting hand-to-hand wasn't her strength with a knife. She didn't have good range for throwing it, and didn't stand a chance of aiming decently with how hard her heart was beating.

But that hadn't been her plan anyway. The knife had done its part.

Jumping back from the man's approaching vine, she held her hands in the air. "I'm sorry. Okay. I'll come. Please don't hurt me!"

"Good. Smarter than your boyfriend."

She fought images of Guillen lying dead somewhere, or bleeding out. Keeping up one hand in surrender, she bent a knee to place the knife on the ground.

As the man stepped forward and wrapped his vine around Rachel's upheld wrist, she stood, concealing her free arm behind her back.

"Come on, your other wrist."

That was never going to happen.

She wasn't the most book smart. She wasn't the strongest. But she'd been poisoned for months. She'd fought tooth and nail to squeeze out any energy during her training in the human world, and if that had done anything for her, it had made her capable of powerful bursts of energy, now that she had no poison hampering her, now that she was rooted in the Green Lands.

Decisively, she thrust her energy into her concealed arm, flaring and sharpening her Seeder blade. Before he knew it, she'd swung her arm forward, slicing clean through the vine restraining her other wrist, and had lunged for him, her eyes now bright green with rage.

A gasp escaped his lips as she barreled into him, her energy strengthening her arms. Off-balance, he fell, taking Rachel down with him as he shot his vines around her body.

Tussling on the ground, he clenched his jaw, reaching his hands up and choking her. The razor-sharp leaves on his vines stabbed her flesh as he pulled her in tighter, limiting the mobility of her arms.

She yanked an arm forward with all the force she could, before his hold would become too tight, fighting to put her blade against his neck. She grunted at the embedded leaves dragging through her flesh. She closed her eyes and focused all of her energy. Her blade now touched his throat. Ignoring her own pain and struggle for air, she pushed.

And kept pushing.

Seeder's blades didn't have as many nerve connections as the rest of their bodies, so she couldn't feel it all, but she could feel enough. She felt the downward movement. She felt the sickening sensation of her blade sinking in. She felt herself hit something bone-hard. And she felt her attacker stop moving.

Rachel peeked to confirm it was over, though she had already known it was. She could breathe, and the vines were looser. She heaved, catching her breath and trying not to vomit on the spot. Behind her, Lady Vera and Catrina had just finished taking down their attacker.

Rachel yanked the embedded leaves from her arms and leapt up, yelling for Guillen. She sprinted in the direction he'd left in. Standing in the front entrance, she looked around. "Guillen!"

No answer.

She darted down the nearest hallway, then turned a corner. "Guillen!"

Still no response as she ran back to the entry room. His mom and sister now joined her, calling his name.

Maybe they went outside? Her eyes shot to the front door. *No. There are guards stationed out there; there would have been an audience.*

Instantly, she loathed being in such a large house.

Taking a moment to gather herself, she scanned the floor. Droplets of blood, down the hallway.

She dashed back down the hallway, tearing open each and every door. Dizzy and frantic, unsure how many she'd opened, she finally found him.

Guillen lay on the ground, in the middle of a large library. He wasn't moving.

"No! Please, no!" She ran to him, his mom and sister trailing behind her.

She threw herself on the ground next to him. He was still alive. Grimacing, he struggled to breathe, clearly in agony as he clutched his side. Blood pooled around the injury.

Rachel moved his hand and pressed both of her own onto the wound. She put her body weight into it, to help stop the bleeding, and all of the energy she was capable of summoning, into healing him.

"Please, don't leave me. I love you. Stay with me." Her voice shook. "Please!"

Tears poured down her cheeks as she weakened. Having already exerted herself to save her own life, she was struggling to heal him. She reached into her core and accessed every last drop she could. The last thing she saw was his face, as her arms buckled, and she lost consciousness.

***

The tap of light footsteps on wood accompanied a soft feminine humming as Rachel woke. She opened her eyes, quickly finding her bearings. Catrina paced the room—a bedroom, perhaps a guest room.

"Where is he? Is he okay?"

Catrina startled. She pointed to the wall. A mumble of voices filtered from the other side—one was male.

He was alive. Rachel closed her eyes, starting to cry. Nothing else mattered. He was alive.

Still drained, she forced herself to sit up on the bed, hanging her legs over the edge. "Where am I? What happened?"

"You, uh … passed out. Saving my brother's life. We're still at our manor."

Rachel shook her head. "That's not safe. We need to go."

"It's okay. They're working something out next door. You just need to recuperate." She pointed to a glass of water on the bedside table. "He said being hydrated helps with your kind's healing and energy like it does ours."

Rachel grabbed the water and drank. "Thank you."

Catrina pressed her lips together, nodding. "Well … thanks for keeping him alive."

Rachel frowned. The cat was out of the bag now… And the fact that other servants or guards hadn't finished the job already, was a miracle.

"You, uh … were pretty intense back there," Catrina continued. "We just poisoned our guard until he passed out, but you… That was brutal."

Rachel couldn't hide a resentful scowl. "We don't all have the luxury of poison, do we? And there were two of you; I had to fight on my own."

Catrina shyly shrugged. "I didn't really mean it as an insult. I mean… I can't get that horrible image out of my head. But … you saved Guillen, and that's what matters."

Rachel was tired of pretenses. These women didn't deserve any courtesies. "Yeah. Well, he wouldn't have needed saving if he wasn't so insistent on protecting you and your horrible mom."

Catrina nodded once more. After a few moments of silence, still pacing the room, she spoke again. "Is it true what you said? That you love him?"

Rachel met Catrina's gaze. "I do."

She pointed to Rachel's arm. "You have our stunt mark. How did you guys even meet? I don't understand why a wee—" She looked away. "Why a Seeder would be over here, pretending to be one of his kind."

"It's a long story." Rachel took another sip of water. "And … you're surprisingly calm about all of this."

Catrina fidgeted with her hands, glancing back at the door. "I'm more like Guillen than my mom. She's a bit crazy."

That's one way of putting it. "Let me guess—she'll come around?"

"Probably not."

Rachel chuckled and then winced in pain. "At least you're honest."

"Is it also true what he said about Kaylah, that she's the leader of the dissenters?"

"I wouldn't put it that way, but yes." Knowing a little about their family dynamics now, Rachel pondered how she could best win Catrina over. She could be a good ally, once properly educated. "How do you feel about Soren?"

Catrina's lip curled. "He's always creeped me out, and he's a real jerk to Guillen. And really, everyone."

"I dated him for almost three years in the human world."

Catrina's eyes widened. "You're *that* girl?"

Rachel narrowed her eyes. Jon had once said that no one outside the palace knew about Duke Nuren's plans. "How long have you and your mom known how Nuren powered the War Vines? A guard told me no one outside of the palace knew about it."

Catrina rested her hands on her hips. "We may not attend many palace functions, but I'd like to think we're not *completely* out of touch. We heard rumors. It was confirmed to my mother at his funeral." A flash of guilt crossed her face as her hands dropped. "I, uh… I don't know *how much* my mother knew about the details. I didn't really understand what all was going on until a few minutes ago. I'm sorry. I just meant, you know, that I knew Soren spent a lot of time in the human world on a mission, dating a Seeder."

Rachel nodded. "Anyway, yes. I'm *that* girl. Alive, thanks to your brother. He's a good man. And Kaylah's amazing. They're not dissenters; they're good people that just want this war to stop. And to give people like Guillen equal rights, like they deserve."

Catrina sat down in an armchair, wringing her hands. "I love Guillen. He's different, but he's family. I'm glad … that…" She forced out the words, as if she spoke against her own will. "That he found … someone … who cares about him. The way he deserves." She looked down. "I've never heard him talk about a girl the way he does you."

Rachel allowed a smile to cross her face. Catrina had a long way to go, as did most green folk, to accept their kind of relationship. At least she hadn't reacted like Magda. Rachel decided to lean into Catrina's love for her brother.

"He deserves to live a happy life. I'm not stopping until his kind are free to do that."

Catrina returned a warm smile.

The door popped open, and Guillen appeared. He was shirtless, with a bandage wrapped around his midsection. He winced as he strode over to Rachel. She forced herself to stand up, and he gave her a kiss on the forehead. She wanted nothing more than to hug him, but it didn't bode well that he was bandaged up.

"I'm so happy you're okay." His eyes were bloodshot. "Thank you. I love you. I'm so sorry."

She frowned, staring at the bandage. "You're still hurt. Let me see it."

He shook his head. "No. I'll be fine. It's just a flesh wound now, and we need you to focus on healing yourself."

She took his hand. "I'm really sorry about what I said. I know who you are, and it's not those things."

"It's alright. We'll figure it out." He glanced back; his mom lingered in the doorway. Her face still sour, she didn't appear to have softened any, compared to Catrina. Guillen turned back to Rachel. "We need to talk about making a change."

Chapter 32

GUILLEN ASKED FOR SOME PRIVACY to talk with Rachel. His mom and sister left the room and promised they'd wait in the next room over.

Guillen and Rachel eased themselves down on the edge of the bed, both in rough shape.

Rachel glanced at the large bandage covering his injury. "Let me see it," she demanded.

He took her hand. "It's really not that bad. We had the family nurse finish stitching it up. My body can handle it. I'll be fine on my own."

He was pale, likely from blood loss. She wasn't going to drop it, but she changed the topic for now. "Why are we still here? We need to go. Soren could have people on the way. How can we be sure there aren't more servants or guards that would betray us?"

He replied calmly, "You're right, we need to go. But we have it under control, for now. After you passed out, other servants tied up the other guy. We've addressed the staff and put our own spin on it. It's precarious; but for now, we just need to focus on you getting your energy back."

She found little comfort with all of the variables. At least it was obvious Guillen's family hadn't betrayed him, but their staff's loyalty was clearly unreliable.

He must have sensed her anxiety. "This is the home I grew up in. I know, at least amongst the older staff, who's more on my side. If I'd known my mother was going to insist on guards like that, I would have suggested a different security escort. I have the ones I trust making sure no one leaves."

"Okay."

"I need you to heal. I…" He swallowed hard. "I need you to do something that I can't. I need you to regain your energy enough to take my mother and sister away." He rubbed her hand with his thumb. "I'm asking you to take them to Eric for safekeeping in the human world."

Rachel matched his frown. That had to be a hard request to make. Guillen was a proud man… And now, having been stabbed by his own weapon. Having to ask someone else to use powers he was born without. Having to subject Rachel to close contact with his mother. She could only imagine what was running through his troubled mind and aching heart.

She squeezed his hand. "I'll take them."

Tears coated his eyes. "Thank you."

She tilted her head ever so slightly. "But what will *you* do? I need to know you'll be safe back here."

"I'll be fine. I'll regroup with my contacts. Make sure they know Kaylah's at the palace. We'll get her out as soon as we can, and I'll get word to you as quickly as possible."

She nodded as she processed his request. The whole time, she couldn't shake the dead man's haunting eyes. "I just… Give me some time to rest up. How long can we risk it?"

He kissed her hand. "You'll be fine. Do what you need to. I'm going to walk the perimeter, keep an eye on things, and make sure everything's okay. Try to conserve your energy. If something happens, your knife's right over there." He gestured with his chin to the side table, wearing a far-off look. "Still clean. Guess you didn't need it after all."

The way he'd said it—defeated, as though somehow the knife he'd given her represented his heart, as though somehow any of this was *his* fault—hurt more than any of her physical injuries. "I did need it."

"Right, well, I need to go monitor things. I'll check in in a little while." He kissed her forehead, then clenched his jaw as he stood, clearly still in a great deal of pain. She wished that at the very least, someone like Olivia could be there, someone aptly trained in the Ivies' new numbing methods.

The room fell silent when he left. Rachel finished the glass of water and lay back down. Healing and energy restoration happened a lot faster with proper hydration and rest, but she couldn't fall asleep, despite how thoroughly exhausted she still was. The events played out in her mind as she stared at a small chandelier on the ceiling.

She'd killed a man.

It had been justified. It had been done in self-defense. It had been to save the man she loved, and his family, and Kaylah, and the Unitas movement. Morally, she was in the clear.

But that didn't dull the horror of what she'd just done. She surveyed her arms and hands. They must have cleaned her up a little while she was out; she wasn't completely covered in blood.

She lay there, silently crying. Maybe Guillen had been right— she shouldn't have come. But then again, he'd likely be dead if she hadn't. There was no way to know how it would have played out without her.

She'd taken a life.

She'd been trained to protect herself. This was war. But she'd never had to really fight. She'd been healing, and negotiating, and sharing energy.

Could the man have been turned, convinced to join Unitas? Did he have a family? Her mind shifted to Guillen. Was this whole thing her fault? What could have distracted him so much that he let his guard down? Her stupidity, their argument. He'd almost lost his life because she couldn't keep it together for a single hour. She'd almost had two lives on her conscience, and one of them meant more to her than the world.

Guillen quietly came in after a while to check on her. She rested on her side, staring blankly across the room. He slid a chair over and sat next to her, now wearing a loose shirt.

"You should be sleeping." He rubbed her cheek lovingly.

"Yeah, I can't sleep right now. Sorry."

"How are you feeling?" He frowned.

"I'm getting better."

"How long do you think until you'll be able to guide them through a rift?" he asked, cringing, likely bothered by still having to ask for help.

"I don't think it takes much. I've never felt that drained when being assisted by an Ivy through a tree rift."

He gave her a hesitant smile. "That's good."

She stared at him with an unyielding expression. "But I'm not going until you're completely healed."

He narrowed his eyes slightly. "I told you—I'm fine."

"You're still in pain. Let me see it."

He took off his shirt and carefully removed the bandages. He was out of the woods, as far as she could tell, but it was far from a simple scrape. His family nurse had done a decent job of stitching it up, but that didn't mean he was alright internally.

She moved a hand over to heal it more, but he intercepted her, holding her hand instead.

"No. We can't waste more time. You know this isn't that bad."

She pulled her hand back and hugged herself. The other nicks and bruises he'd sustained in the fight—those she could overlook. Not this giant wound. "I'm not changing my mind."

"I know you love me, and you're worried, but you need to remember this is bigger than us. Think of Kaylah. Look at the big picture."

A dark storm swirled in her mind as she clenched her teeth, and fresh tears formed. She could barely breathe, her chest tight, her anguish choking her. "Right now, all I care about is you. *You* are *my* big picture." She started to dig her fingernails into her arms, simply trying to keep it together. Trying to keep some semblance of self-control. Trying to find some way to just … make it through this.

"Rachel… I…"

She whimpered, and her voice shook as she cried freely. "I can't leave you again without *knowing* you're okay. I can't handle it."

His mission was dangerous enough. He could get an infection. And she didn't know all the details of how Seeder healing worked. With that serious of a wound … if he took a tumble, would it rip open? And this was All. Her. Fault. If she hadn't lost her cool earlier, he wouldn't have been distracted, wouldn't have gotten hurt.

Desperation bubbled up inside her. He opened his mouth as if to protest once more.

She whimpered again; she'd never been able to ask for help. Not with this. It was her shame. It was her private torture. It was why she'd turned to the Ivy pub, when she was trying her best to keep her promise to Kaylah about not hurting herself any more.

But she didn't know how to cope, how to manage another moment with him not being safe. Visions flashed before her eyes, of his dying body, lying on the floor in a puddle of blood. She increased the pressure of the grip on her own arms, as if it would somehow help her better grasp on to hope.

Forcing out the words took everything she had. "*I. Can't.*" She sniffled. "*I'm. Not. Okay.*" She stared into his eyes with meaning, with a look that had to be capable of carrying the rest she couldn't say out loud.

I need help.

I'm drowning.

I can't do this on my own.

His brow furrowed, then his gaze landed on her fingers digging into her skin, and his eyes flared wide open. "Okay! Okay!" He carefully removed her hands from her arms and held them. Her own skin and blood were now under her fingernails. He looked terrified. "I'll let you heal me first. Okay?" His eyes welled up. "We'll get through this."

She started to hyperventilate. That had been the hardest thing she'd ever done—calling for help from her personal prison. And he'd understood.

Guillen held their clasped hands in his lap, studying them. He may not have known what to say, but he could be there with her.

Her breathing eventually calmed, and he looked her in the eye. "I love you, Rachel. How can I help?"

She didn't really know. "Just … buy me some time. And maybe get some more water."

His handsome face was still riddled with concern. "Okay. I promise. We'll be safe long enough to take care of it. If I go get water, will you be alright?"

She searched her mind, and slowly nodded.

"I'll be right back." He left the room and promptly returned with a pitcher of water. A minute after he came back, someone tapped on the door. He got up and thanked whoever it was that handed him a large ceramic bowl and some towels.

He sat down again and asked warily, "Can I clean you up a bit?"

She clenched her jaw and looked down, nodding again. He dipped a towel in the bowl of water and gently wiped at her arms. They still hadn't healed from the Ivy attack; she had only added to the damage. He then took her hands and dipped them in the bowl, one by one, cleaning underneath her fingernails. She hated it, but she loved him more for his kindness.

He dried off her hands and drew in a deep breath. "How is your energy?"

"I have enough to try."

"Alright." He raised his eyebrows. "But if you have to do it in more than one session, that's fine. Don't take yourself too far like you did the first time."

"Okay." She carefully moved a hand to his side. Having somewhat calmed down, she channeled the hints of Seeder energy that had rebuilt. His eyes darted around her face, monitoring how she was doing. She started to get dizzy, but she was *so* close to being done.

"Honey, take a break." He removed her hand.

She closed her eyes and focused on breathing. He was right; she was too close to passing out. That could lose them valuable time. Glancing at the wound, she was frustrated with how close she'd gotten.

He poked near it with his fingers. "It's practically gone." He read her face. "But we can wait, and finish it up."

She averted her eyes, fully knowing her demand was irrational, but grateful he was considering her feelings.

"I'm going to take care of these. You drink some and rest up." He picked up the dirty towels and bowl before leaving.

Rachel balled herself up in the fetal position, still unable to fall asleep. She wished she could be back home, her human home, with her human mom. Samantha would be doting on Rachel like when she'd been sick as a child. Rachel wished she didn't have to ask this of Guillen.

She pushed the swarming chaos away by focusing on the immediate future. She'd take his mom and sister through a rift to Eric. They'd place the women in a safe house. Then she'd return to the Green Lands. Rachel frowned—she couldn't just rift back to the Ivy Kingdom. Whatever Guillen did next, he would be far from her. He would be moving on to more dangerous territory, changing his focus to the palace. She hoped they'd done enough with their mission, having only hit half of the stunt communities. They were far from accomplishing what they'd wanted to, but she knew wars were never tidy. There were always contingency plans. She just hadn't thought of this one.

Not much later, Guillen rejoined her—sitting in the chair again, caressing her hand, simply being there.

"I think your sister might not be horrible," she offered.

He smiled. "She's pretty great. Not perfectly enlightened, but I already see a shift in her from this."

Rachel failed to smile. "I guess *something* good came from all of this, right?"

He squeezed her hand, giving her a look of encouragement.

"Aren't you worried about the rest of your family coming back while we're figuring this out? Where are they?"

"We'll be fine. My brother is plenty busy with the war; I don't think he visits much. And my father… Well… It's not really acceptable for him to get a divorce in his position, but he doesn't stick around here long. If he popped in before we left, I think he'd be okay. He was the reason I was allowed to grow up at home."

Guilt over this whole fiasco weighed her down. "I'm *really* sorry. For treating you like I did. You're the best thing to happen to me, and I don't know why I acted that way."

"I forgive you. I'm sorry I didn't take it well. Let's move past that."

If only it were that easy to dismiss her screwup. "I'm sorry I got you hurt," she whispered.

"What?" He furrowed his brow. "How did you get me hurt?"

"You told me not to come. And I forced you into it. And then I distracted you before you went out to talk with him."

"Rachel…" he scolded lovingly. "No. Don't blame yourself for that. I just… He… It's not your fault. You take the weight of the world on your shoulders, but you shouldn't. Please try to let this one go. It wasn't your fault."

She bit the insides of her cheeks. She wanted to believe him, but he could be lying, or refusing to admit the truth to himself.

"Can I try to finish it?" she asked, throwing a glance at his midsection.

"Have you had enough time?"

"Yeah. It won't take much for what's left."

He nodded, and she set to work again, healing. She got a bit woozy, but stopped once she was satisfied with her work.

"Thank you," he said. "Good as new. I had someone retrieve our packs, so I have my tools to take out the stitches myself. Boy Scout here." He winked.

She cracked a tiny smile. That had been a magical moment for her, too, as a handsome stranger with kind eyes once removed her stitches in the darkness of a cave after he'd helped rescue her from the palace.

"Do you think you could get some sleep?" he asked.

"I haven't been able to."

"Would it help if I lay with you?"

She nodded. "Probably."

Chapter 33

KAYLAH WOKE TO A HAND covering her mouth, that of one of the guards who was supposed to be keeping her tent secure during the night. Another Ivy stood at the end of her cot, vines wrapped around the neck of a hostage, hands restraining her arms.

"Get up, and stay quiet," the guard ordered.

Still groggy, and now terrified, Kaylah tried to assess the situation. Her guard had already wrapped her wrists tight with his vines, so she couldn't extend her own. The hostage, a girl Kaylah had gotten to know well from training her here in camp, was on the verge of tears. "Please, Your Highness," the girl pleaded.

Kaylah slowly sat up, dazed, starting to panic.

"Let's go have a chat. Scream, and you both die."

He tied a gag around Kaylah's mouth and pulled her up. Her mind raced. *Where are they going to take us? Where's the Seeder guard who was stationed outside?*

Allowing them to push her out of the tent, she bought herself time to plan how to get both herself and the girl out of this mess. They passed tent after tent lit by lightkeepers and flickering candles, but no one was outside, available to give aid. *How late is it?*

Kaylah screamed to get someone's attention, but the gag muffled her voice.

"Shut up," her guard growled, slapping his hand over her mouth to quiet her further.

The shouts of battle on the border of camp were so loud. How could she have slept through that?

As the men marched their hostages forward, Kaylah's mind raced. She kept scanning the horizon for help, but no one was walking around camp at this hour, likely sleeping or in battle at the border.

Assessing the situation, Kaylah was surprised they hadn't even gagged the other hostage. *Why aren't you screaming?* She mentally pleaded for the girl to snap out of her daze, to not be so afraid, to be willing to sound the alarm.

And she'd need to do it soon. As they approached the emergency exit trees, for some reason not guarded at the moment, it clicked as to why they'd brought a hostage. They intended for Kaylah to rift to a new location.

Are the traitors not whispers, then? It stood to reason they had a way of contacting someone on the outside, to confirm Kaylah had rifted to the location they were trying to force her to, and if she didn't, they'd kill this innocent girl.

Kaylah's heart broke. How much was one innocent life worth? One loyal follower sacrificed in the name of keeping Unitas together? Queasy, she accepted the girl's fate. If Kaylah walked through a rift into Soren's clutches, this all would have been a waste. She was *so* close to figuring things out.

They stopped at the trees, and Kaylah desperately tried to catch the girl's eye. *We might survive, if you would just scream!*

"Alright, the rift, hurry it up," one of the men said, glancing around.

They hadn't even told Kaylah where they expected her to rift to, not that she would… Plus, her wrists were still bound.

Instead, they released the hostage, and she reached out a vine, drawing it down a tree trunk. It cracked, opening a rift.

Wait, what?! Perhaps Kaylah was still too dazed from being woken from a deep sleep, or being drugged, or both, but the logic didn't add up. They were sending *both* girls through a rift, with no assurances? When had they even told the girl where they were supposed to rift to?

Kaylah shook her head violently, yelling as loudly as she could through the gag, pleading for the girl to raise the alarm, to not go through, to do *something*.

The girl turned to Kaylah with a somber gaze, stepping back from the tree. "Thank you for the extra training, Your Highness. My apologies." She nodded at the guard holding Kaylah hostage.

Kaylah's eyes grew wide in the split second it took the guard to release his vines and shove her right into the rift.

A rift created by a whisper rifter. Created by a *girl...*

***

Kaylah stood in the dungeon, shackled to the wall. *How could I be so stupid?* She'd only ever identified a handful of whisper rifters, all palace guards. All former assassins. All men. But a girl? Why had she not even allowed that possibility to cross her mind?

Just as sickening as being held hostage in the dungeon of the palace she ought to be in charge of, was the realization that Unitas had at least two traitors in their midst. Only the solo Ivy guard traitor had created a rift of his own and followed after her.

There wasn't a single chance this was going to end well.

The cell door creaked open, and with zero surprise, Kaylah was greeted by her older brother, Soren. A menacing smile accompanied his green eyes and dark brown hair.

"What did you do to my Seeder guard?" she asked.

"Come on. No 'hello'? That hurts. After the lengths I went through to *save* my little sister." He looked her over from top to bottom. "I'd offer a hug, but you seem a little tied up right now."

"What the *hell* did you do to him?"

Soren rolled his eyes. "You and I both know I have no need for male weeds. Can't milk them for energy on the Vines, can we? And I certainly have no need for witnesses, either."

She had guessed as much.

"I know—you're disappointed. I am too. I would have preferred to nab a female Seeder, as well, while we were at it. I have plenty of use for *them*."

Kaylah huffed. "You were dropped on your head as a child."

He leaned back against the stone wall, crossing his arms. "In fact, I'd prefer to have *several* more female weeds. It's shocking how much we're struggling to get them. How well concealed they are. How many high school students in the human world are going missing."

Kaylah smiled. "Sounds like Uncle would find you a bitter disappointment."

Soren crossed the room, slamming his fist into her gut. She reeled in pain, losing her breath and almost losing her last meal.

He glared, inches from her face. A signature spark of rage rose in his eyes. "I will murder you. Slowly. And with great joy."

She clenched her teeth as she steadied her breathing.

After a minute, he backed up against the wall again, staring her down. "Speaking of Uncle, his study is shockingly empty. Any thoughts on that?"

Kaylah stared right back at him, tight-lipped.

He searched her face. "Yeah, well, none of your spies we've killed have given that one up—yet. So, I guess we'll just keep torturing the staff, one by one, until we find who misplaced those."

She frowned. "What have you done to Kyas and Rian?" If Soren could kill his own parents, she didn't know how far he would be willing to go. They had little brothers, now parentless.

Soren swatted dismissively at the air. "The runts are fine. Servants are taking care of them."

She knew him well enough to actually believe him, for now. "Thank you."

He scoffed. "Don't make me change my mind." He pursed his lips. "How's Rachel? That one hurt a little. You bring a girlfriend home to introduce her to your parents, and then your little sister has to ruin *everything* by stealing her away."

Kaylah scowled. "Somehow, I don't think she saw it the same way." She glanced closer at his lip—there was no scar from where Rachel had bitten him in self-defense. "It's a shame. Someday when I see her again, she'll be disappointed to find out you didn't get a scar. I thought she bit clean through, and there were stitches." She sneered.

He met her challenge with a smile of his own. "Mother loved *one* of us. The one she *wasn't* disappointed in, she granted extra permission to. She let me take a weed off the Vines long enough to recuperate, and then heal me."

"How much did she love you when you murdered her and Father?"

Soren's ever-mercurial temper rose again. "That's on you!"

"How do you figure?"

He jabbed a finger at her. "You're the one who screwed this all up! You messed up the plan. You didn't even understand all of the plan, but you managed to royally screw things up. All you had to do was play your part." Soren shook his head. "If you wanted to roll around in the weed patch and disappoint us all, you could have at least not killed Uncle."

That was a huge relief, in a somewhat-odd way. She had been right in that decision, to make sure and take out Nuren as soon as possible. "I'm not sorry I disappointed you. And I'll continue to. I won't help you with the Vines, and I won't help you find more Seeders. I won't help you with *anything*."

He grinned. "I think you overestimate yourself."

"I won't be a puppet queen."

Soren raised his eyebrows. "Who said anything about you taking your place as queen? Your coronation ship has sailed."

She searched his face. "Then you'll what? Kill me and move to work with Aunt Vera? I doubt that."

He chuckled. "Work with that hag? I don't think even *she* can stand herself. I have no need for her, either."

Kaylah's heart sank. The next in line—Catrina—was a sweet girl. "You'd really take out the line for a succession change? For Beata?" They'd literally announced their engagement the same day he kidnapped Rachel.

He sighed, clasping his hands in front of himself. "You can guess all day and get nowhere. I'm here," he pouted, "for a family reunion." He took a deep breath. "And for answers. I'd like to know how to find weed girls, what you're doing with Uncle's research, and any other little tidbits that can end this thing. I don't want this war to go on any more than you do."

She looked him straight in the eye. "Go screw yourself."

He straightened. "I get that you think I'm the bad guy here. But you lost yourself in the human world. Why else do you think you were kept in the dark? We knew we couldn't really trust you. When you were in the human world, you learned to be weak. You focused on dating airhead humans you met at animal shelters, and making buddies with the weeds." He pointed to himself. "I learned a thing or two, myself. And that includes loyalty, dedication, and pride for my kingdom. And doing what it takes to get the job done. You're no one's hero, Kaylah. Not even for the weeds, anymore."

It hurt—he was right. She hadn't been able to crack as many things as she had wanted. She'd been *so* close on her research. But it hadn't been enough. And certainly wouldn't be from a musty dungeon. Saff had been too busy to help most of the time. Camp was under siege. Rachel was somewhere along the path with Guillen. *And they probably don't even know I'm here.*

Soren glared with a look of genuine contempt. "You've always been ungrateful for what you were given. For the mission you were assigned. Whining to come back home."

She gritted her teeth. "I was a little girl, forced to live in the human world away from my home."

"You were offered the opportunity to prove your worth to your people as a strong leader at the time of a breakthrough." He huffed. "And once I was established with Rachel, you could have come home, but you didn't."

That was also true. She'd finally been allowed to call it quits on her assigned mission in the human world. Her uncle and brother could have handled Rachel without her, though not as easily. *But I couldn't leave Rachel alone.*

Soren pulled Kaylah's dagger from his pocket, using it to clean under his fingernails. "Do you know why we needed someone else to manage Rachel in the first place?"

Kaylah didn't answer. Did the details matter?

"It was enough that you questioned Mother and Father on their policies, but then…" He clicked his tongue. "Words matter, Kaylah. How often did you start calling them 'Seeders' instead of 'weeds'? As the humans say: when you raise a cow for slaughter, you don't give it a name."

What was Kaylah supposed to have done? Not try to change her parents' minds as a girl, and just skip to assassination? And she'd always tried to keep up the ruse of calling Rachel and her family weeds, and every time she scolded Soren for his behavior, warned him about taking things too far with Rachel, it had always been under the guise of his actions jeopardizing the mission.

But it hadn't been enough. *She* hadn't been enough.

A sinister grin overtook his face. "I do very little in life without purpose. Other than ensuring the mission was a success, do you know why I volunteered to be stationed in the human world?"

"Clearly," she drawled, tired of his gloating, "because now you're the one who gets to claim success for infiltrating a Seeder network and establishing the War Vines."

He wrinkled his nose. "Small perk, though appreciated." He pointed Kaylah's dagger at her. "Because I knew Rachel was such a close friend. What an opportunity to screw with you! Every time I touched her, messed with her head, made her feel bad about herself… It hurt you, too. Two for the price of one. The black eye you gave me for attacking her in the hot tub… I'd do it again, ten times over, just to see your reaction."

It took everything Kaylah had not to cry. Everything she'd ever tried to do was wasted, had only hurt those she'd tried to help. Rachel wouldn't be coming to free her from the palace, like Kaylah had done for her just months before. Unitas would fall. No one would be coming.

Curiosity still nagging at her, she studied his face. "How did you even know about whispers? And that girls can be whispers?"

He narrowed his eyes. "That hurts, doesn't it? That I've always been two steps ahead of you in this. That Mother and Father never even told their heir… I'm frankly surprised you even know about whispers at all."

Kaylah was going to be tortured, and was going to die; there was no way around that truth. She probably ought not to fuel Soren's rage, but perhaps it might bring *some* satisfaction before she died.

"I learned about whispers when I made my first kill. Do you know who that was?" she asked.

Soren seemed intrigued. "Do tell."

She wore her own grin now. "I confirmed their existence when I caught one of Uncle's spies following me." She prepared herself for the blow, possibly the end. It had been one of Soren's best friends in the human world, one of his assassin buddies who had gone missing. "You should have heard Teagan *scream* as I slit his throat."

Soren's eyes darkened; his jaw set. And just as quickly as that look came, it passed, giving way to another smirk. "Didn't think you had it in you. I told him to be careful when I sent him to watch you."

Soren won again. She'd always assumed her uncle or parents had sent a spy to make sure she wasn't up to funny business.

"And yeah… Girls as whispers. That's funny you'd assume they couldn't be. The Vines have eyes and ears, after all." He turned the dagger in his hand, examining it. "Like I said, I do very little in life without a purpose. And I do love my women."

Kaylah gaped. "That girl is one of your whores?"

He feigned offense. "Slut shaming? She prefers the term 'lover.' Frankly, I always appreciated Uncle's motto: All you need for success is lots of work, a touch of luck, and enough charisma to woo the world."

Soren flicked at the dagger's edge. "Oh boy, sharp. I bet that means less pain, and definitely less damage." He extended his arm and stabbed the dagger against the stone wall a few times.

Kaylah winced in anticipation with each *clang*.

He reexamined it. "That'll do the job." He approached her again.

Kaylah's heart rate skyrocketed as she eyed the beat-up dagger.

"I want weeds for the Vines, and want to know what's in Uncle's research. Question and answer time."

***

A half hour later, Kaylah's face was covered in a mix of sweat, tears, and snot. She stared at her arm. Blood dripped from where Soren had carved the word 'traitor' on her forearm. Soren threw her dagger on the floor, on the opposite end of the cell, then stood back to admire his work.

"That was a disappointment," he said, tilting his head. "I've got places to be and things to do, so I guess we'll leave it like this for tonight."

She couldn't say anything; she was still trying to catch her breath.

"How about this? Scream loud enough," he winced, rubbing his own ear, "and the guards will hear you and know you're ready to give us something. Give me information that leads to at least one fresh weed girl, and I'll let her heal you before going on the Vines." His voice was cool, confident, casual. "I consider that more than a fair offer."

"I won't help you," she whispered, her voice shuddering.

He drew a deep breath and let it out. "I think we've learned an important lesson today. You do better when it's other people in harm's way. I can work with that." He glanced down at the dagger with a hint of recognition, then laughed. "Wait a second. That's not standard royal issue, but I thought I recognized the pattern of the handle from somewhere. You got it from that moron cousin you take pity on."

She frowned.

"Carrying around his little knives, compensating." Soren grinned. "What community does the compost pile live in?"

She did her best to steady her breathing. Guillen had been living in Community One. And she didn't know how soon he and Rachel would be there for their campaign.

In the absence of her reply, Soren continued. "That one's easy enough to find out. Until we bring him back, it's a servant a day. Maybe I'll start with the nurses. I knew I should have killed the disobedient nurse who went missing when you took Rachel."

Kaylah struggled not to cry again. She didn't want anyone else hurt on account of her and her failed plans. She hoped camp was at least still intact, and that he wouldn't find Olivia and actually bring her back to torture her to death in front of her.

Soren studied Kaylah in silence, narrowed eyes calculating. "I'll give you till the morning to decide. We could put aside our differences and do what's right for our people—a brother-and-sister team. If you still want to be queen, working with me, then I might really consider it. We can tell our people it was all a misunderstanding, that it was really the weeds who got Mother and Father. But if you can't come to your senses by then, that choice will permanently be gone. And I have a feeling you're going to regret your choice when you find out what comes next."

He looked down at his hands, shaking her blood off, then met her gaze with cold eyes. "One more thing. I owe you this, from high school."

Kaylah flinched, closing her eyes for the inevitable blow. It was swift to follow—the punch to her eye, payback for the shiner she'd given him less than a year ago, when he'd bragged to her about attacking Rachel in the hot tub, just for the fun of it. She kept her eyes closed, only whimpering when the door latched shut.

***

Soren woke her early in the morning on his promised visit. He beamed. "Hey, you! Did you miss me?"

She swallowed hard, ready for round two. Two of whoever knew how many.

He arched his eyebrows. "Answer time. Queen? Yes or no?"

"Yes. I want to be queen."

He narrowed his eyes. "Really? Okay…"

"When your body is cold and dead."

He put a hand to his heart, smiling. "That's more the Kaylah I know. Glad you haven't lost that can-do spirit. So, no to the queen part. A little disappointing, but that's par for the course, as the humans say. No little tidbits to even earn a healing?"

Kaylah gritted her teeth. "You can torture and kill every servant in this palace, and it wouldn't equal trio Seeder lives you'd take by having one of them on the Vines. That's going to be a no from me."

He sighed, gesturing at her. "See, I can't even work with this anymore. I still kinda want the public to go back to liking you for my plans. But then again, I wouldn't have to retract my accusations if they thought you were crazy. And I can still work with crazy."

"Yes, you're crazy."

He smirked. "I love these conversations. But sadly, I'm short on time today. Let's remember the terms before we get started. Weed girls equal healing. Other info might do well, too. Either might save a servant a horrible death." He extended a short vine tendril, sharpening a leaf. "Here's the thing—if we're going to go this route, I'm okay with scars. I think it would actually be kinda cool to do scars. But..." He raised an eyebrow. "They really ought to be nice-looking. So, you should try not to move too much."

Her breathing sped up as he approached her face.

"Oh, yeah, and if you move too much, I might get your eye. I don't see any need for you to be blind."

In no time flat, he'd sliced a diagonal line into each of her cheeks. Her wounds stung once her salty tears seeped down into them.

He examined his work. "Yep. I think it's a good start. You've always been vain, anyway. I was going to rub some mud into it to help it infect and scar," he grimaced, "but your face is already pretty gross from yesterday, so we'll see how this goes."

Soren stood up straight. "Nothing?"

"Go fall in a ravine."

He frowned. "Such harsh words for a groom on his wedding day."

Her eyes widened.

"That's right, I didn't tell you." He beamed. "Today's my big day. Sorry you're not invited. I know that's in bad taste, but you're not really dressed for the occasion." He prodded around her black eye. "Not the right colors."

"Well, congratulations," she said wryly. "You and Beata deserve each other."

"Thanks. That's big of you. I'm crazy about her."

Yep, crazy is definitely one of the words I'd use.

"Anyway, not much time to spare. Obviously, I'm busy."

"Don't let me hold you back."

He winked. "Don't worry, I won't. Since we're congratulating me, you should also congratulate me for becoming king today."

She read his face, not sure how to feel about that. "So, you're killing the downline after all, and naming her queen?"

Soren rolled his eyes. "I didn't say that. I'm only going to say this once, so you should savor it—you were right. Our kingdom should make some changes."

There had to be a catch. There *always* was with Soren.

He sat on the ground, crossing his legs. "Who says we need a queen to lead?"

She stared at him, unamused. "Our laws, traditions, and the dictates of our powers?" It had only ever been named a 'kingdom' to mirror human examples, but Ivy kings had always been consorts to their queens.

He wagged a finger at her. "Yes and no. If one of us is going to change how this kingdom works, anyway, I'm betting our people will more happily follow *my* lead. I learned a thing or two from the humans, just like you did." He shrugged. "Who says power over the Mother Vines means you should be entitled to rule the kingdom? Why couldn't that power and responsibility be relegated to a different title, say … a priestess? Isn't that great? We can still be a sibling duo and make this work."

Kaylah glared. "You're out of your mind. I don't care what you call it. I still won't help you."

Standing up, he dusted himself off. "I think priestess sounds cool. And it goes with the scar vibes. With how quick we heal, everyone will know they're intentional, ritual. A sign of your penitence. I'll issue a pardon. How many scars you end up with, and how many people die in the process, depends on you. I'm okay with head-to-toe scars. You can even be a slutty priestess, so we maximize the square space. But once your mind goes, from the screaming— that of yourself and others—I have no use for you. I need you to appear lucid in public. If I have to kill you, that would be a shame.

But I'd do it, and then take out the old hag, and poor innocent Catrina is next on the list. Choose wisely."

The tiniest slivers of hope Kaylah could cling to were that Unitas could figure out what she hadn't been able to with her research, that they could continue to keep Soren from getting his hands on any more Seeder girls to power the War Vines, and that Soren would make a misstep somewhere, that he'd miscalculated something. Because right now, he had this in the bag.

"You don't understand our people as well as you think you do," she said. "They won't tolerate your brutality for long. They would never accept a king in lieu of a proper queen. Never."

He tucked his hands into his pockets. "No? People forgive heaps of brutality in the name of war. I think when the truth comes to light, people will soften. Sure, you have the rarest gift in the Green Lands. But it's not like I don't have my own gifts."

He really was an arrogant prick. "Stupidity doesn't count as a gift."

He chuckled. "That's a little weak, even for you. Strength comes from loyalty. Take an oppressed and exploited group of people, and give them hope, and you become their savior."

She furrowed her brow. Oppressed and exploited? Stunts would *never* follow Soren's lead willingly. And Rachel and Guillen were already securing their loyalty by explaining her goals to restore their rights. "Sorry to inform you, but stunts hate you."

That garnered a look of confusion. "Who said anything about *them?*" He stuck up a fist, lifting his pointer finger. "Royal birth—check. Strategy—check. Connections—check." He lifted a finger with each point, ticking off his list. "Unique gift that the majority of the population doesn't possess—check."

Why did he think he was so special? "What gift?"

He looked at her like she was stupid. But maybe she had been, because that last piece snapped into place. "You're a whisper?"

Soren teemed with pride, opening his arms as though he'd just cut the ribbon at a grand opening ceremony, as if presenting himself with an award. "Not the only gifted one in the family."

Crap. That might tip the scales.

Unable to resist patting himself on the back, he breathed in the victory. "Your face tells me you know exactly where this is headed."

And she did. She'd spent enough time talking with Nathan and Jon to understand the plight of whispers, their forced lifelong servitude to their queen and king, betraying their own people as spies. They wanted out. They wanted camaraderie, to be allowed to even discuss their gifts with whom they wanted, to use those powers when *they* wanted to, if at all.

'When the truth comes to light, people will soften.' He had their parents' resources, likely a list of all known whispers in the kingdom.

She had a handful.

"Free them from their shackles," Soren said. "Promise them power, and position, and wealth. Promise them a leader who understands what it's like to be one of them." He reached for the door handle. "I wouldn't even *have* to be one of them. They're so desperate, they'd just need to *think* I was."

Her mouth hung open. "So you're not."

He winked. "I didn't say that. Whether true or not, those words would never come out of my mouth. But it kills you not to know, doesn't it?"

He'd always loved his mind games.

Soren pulled the cell door open. "Oh yeah, normally you gift the bride and groom. But your hands are a little tied up. So, I'll throw you a bone this once. No servant screams today; I think it would put Beata out of the mood. But tomorrow's a new day." He hesitated before leaving. "You *could* offer me a wedding gift, actually. If you led me to Rachel, I'd promise to not even put her on the Vines. I'd just keep her for myself." He smirked.

"You're disgusting. I'm sure your bride would love to hear that on her wedding day."

"What she doesn't know won't hurt her." He winked again. "Plus, kings sometimes have concubines. I think I could wear her down. Love ya, Sis." He exited and closed the door behind him.

Kaylah fell numb, everywhere except the pulsing ache in her arm and eye, and the sting of her fresh wounds. She'd wanted to do right by her people, those with and without powers. She'd wanted to do right by the Seeders, and the humans caught in the crosshairs.

Fresh tears rolled down her cheeks as she thought of Eric. She loved him more than anyone. He was in the human world, and she would never see him again. She would never see *anyone* again. Except for innocent people forced to die in front of her until she broke or Soren ended her.

Staring at the battered knife still on the ground, she wondered if it was even worth it to try to hang on to hope. She'd never follow Soren's stupid plan, but perhaps she should have bided her time. She should have gone about this all a different way—killed Nuren, *and* her parents. But in secret. Then she could have taken her mother's place and *slowly* changed things. But what she could have done, and should have done, were immaterial at this point.

Frowning, she considered Rachel. Despite Soren's declarations, there was a part of him that actually did like Rachel, in his own perverted way. She wasn't just a Seeder. She was a trophy, the one that got away. And if he caught up to Guillen on his mission, he'd also catch up to Rachel. Rachel had already been through enough hell.

Is this what she felt like, captive in this palace—hopeless and alone?

Chapter 34

THE MAN'S BODY WENT LIMP, lifeless, under Rachel's weight, and by her hand. She kept her eyes closed for a moment. Panting, she dreaded the next moment. Opening her eyes, she expected to see the guard who'd just attacked her. Instead, she saw the face of the man she loved—dead. She'd just murdered him.

Rachel wailed, pleading for him to come back. She'd made a mistake. She'd killed the wrong man.

"Rachel!"

Her eyes snapped open; a hand gently covered her mouth. Guillen was behind her, lying on the bed, holding her.

"It's okay," he whispered. "It's okay. I'm right here."

He removed his hand from her mouth and stroked her hair. She started to sob as the bedroom door cracked open. Catrina peeked inside, clearly concerned about the screaming. Guillen spoke up again, a little louder, as if addressing both Rachel and Catrina at the same time. "It's okay."

He stayed cuddled up next to Rachel as Catrina left the room, easing the door shut behind her. Rachel had finally been able to find some rest. But the nightmares were back, with a brand-new horror at their disposal. She groaned at the unfairness. Guillen placed a sweet kiss on her head, and she shifted, trying to get herself to fall asleep again.

The next time she woke, it was much less traumatic. Her eyelashes fluttered as she remembered where she was. Her heart warmed at Guillen's touch. They breathed in unison. She didn't want to go, but it was time.

She turned to look at him. Awake, he gazed into her eyes with pure adoration. "I love you."

"I love you too. Thank you. Again."

"You never have to thank me for the pleasure of your company." His lips twitched into a warm smile.

She sighed heavily. "I'm ready to go."

"Are you sure? You're still pretty beat up. We could take them where we were originally planning, and give you another day to heal. Then rift out."

Rachel frowned. "No. You were right. I can't be selfish. And we'll all be safer over there." She paused. "And I'm not waiting until the last minute when there's a dozen soldiers cornering us. I need to know you got out of here cleanly."

He pulled her closer, squeezing tight. "I never want to let you go. But the sooner we take care of this, the sooner I get to see you again."

They slowly got out of bed and made sure she could stand on her own. He held her waist. "I want to be there for you. And I'm sorry we have to rush you like this." He caressed her cheek. "I may not know Eric, but he sounds like a good guy. Can you promise me you'll talk to him … if you … need help? And Saff, when you get back to your side?"

Rachel had no idea what she was capable of anymore. But she could try. She nodded.

He held her tight. "I'm going to miss you so much." Finally releasing her, he leaned down and kissed her. It was gentle and sweet, but not just a simple peck. For a fleeting moment, Rachel lost her will to continue in this war. They could run away. They could carve out a space for themselves, a cabin in the Neutral Woods, and be happy and safe—together. They'd both already sacrificed enough.

As their lips parted, she knew it couldn't be that way. She drew a deep breath. "I'm ready."

They walked to the neighboring room. Catrina hopped up from a chair when they entered. Lady Vera sat, looking unimpressed still. "Are we *finally* ready?"

Guillen scowled. "Yes. She's ready to save your selfish life."

Rachel tried to hide a grin of satisfaction. She wanted to say a thing or two, but it would have to wait. The moment they were safe with Unitas, those floodgates might open. But now wasn't the time.

They went out to the lush gardens surrounding the mansion. They were beautifully manicured, their perfume filling the air.

Rachel and the others found some appropriate trees—pines—for Ivy-type rifting. She shared the coordinates they were aiming for in the human world with Guillen's mom and sister. Kaylah had shared the location in her last message to them, so they could quickly reach out to Eric in just such an emergency. The Ivy women easily visualized it. It was briefly discussed who Rachel would be going through with.

She'd rather saw off a leg than be paired with Guillen's mom. The thought of having that woman touch her with vines, puncturing her skin for energy to get them both through… It was visceral, repulsive. But if, heaven forbid, something should go wrong, she should be with the next heir to the throne.

Just before leaving, Guillen gave his sister a hug, then Rachel.

"Here. Give this to Eric when you get there." He handed Rachel a sealed envelope, and she tucked it into her pocket.

She pulled him close, breathing in the moment. They said another round of 'I love yous,' and then he held her at arms-length. A lot could be said or repeated. Nothing was certain, nothing guaranteed.

"I'll stay safe if you will," he said with a grin.

"Deal." She gave him one last kiss before turning and standing next to his mother. Lady Vera glanced at Rachel's arm in disgust as she wrapped a vine around it. The Ivy women each opened a rift; Rachel looked over her shoulder for one last glance at Guillen. He had his hands shoved in his pockets, his face fighting to keep it together, trying to force a smile.

And the women walked through.

***

The moment they arrived in the human world, the warmth of the Green Lands no longer lingered with Rachel. It was colder here. She would take longer to recharge with less ambient energy. She was on borrowed time until she'd have to return. Catrina and Lady Vera stood still, as they'd been instructed to, looking decently concerned.

"Hold it," one of the guards ordered. There were *a lot* more guards than Rachel had anticipated, though it made sense with Kaylah having gone missing.

Nathan, Kaylah's human-world deployment guardian, bounded up from the line of mixed Unitas guards at the cave. "Rachel?!" He looked both surprised to see her, and horrified at her appearance. She'd only taken a quick glance in the mirror, but she was bruised, sliced, and diced. It wasn't pretty. He cautiously greeted Guillen's mom and sister with a bow.

"Yeah," Rachel said.

A handful of other guards approached, closely following Nathan. Rachel didn't recognize any of the others, and was uneasy about an audience with this mission.

"Could I talk with Nathan in private for a second?"

"No."

Reading the tension in the group, Rachel calculated what to do next. She didn't know who was privy to the details of her and Guillen's mission, she didn't know what details they had about Kaylah's disappearance, and she wanted as few people as possible to know who she was tucking away for safekeeping. "I have details I need to discuss with a member of the council." She wanted someone she could trust on her side. "A member of the council and Nathan. No offense, but the council wouldn't want a dozen guards hearing what I need to report."

The guard eyed her. "Fine. The four of you: follow me."

Nathan, Rachel, Catrina, and Lady Vera all followed after the guard, as the rest fell back to their positions.

After only a few minutes of walking, they reached a small log cabin, and the guard ushered them in. The senior Unitas guard on duty was inside, focused on paperwork. Once the guard who had guided them there left, they all took a seat except for Nathan.

"How can I help you?" the senior officer asked.

Rachel's palms began to sweat. He wasn't a member of the council, at least not one she recognized; she wasn't sure what she was safe to say around him, or what he knew. "I, uh, I was on a mission for Kaylah, for Unitas. It had ... problems."

The senior officer scanned her. "You look it."

"Well, it was classified. Um... Do you know what happened to Kaylah? And are you able to help me put these two women into a safe house?"

The man flipped open a book. "Name?"

"I'm Rachel Lyzasdotter."

He found her name. "Yes, I see you on the list as an anticipated user of the rift cave. And these two?"

A Seeder would obviously be in charge in the human world for Unitas, and it was clear he didn't recognize Lady Vera and Catrina, despite their high station in Ivy society.

"Can't I talk to someone on the council?" Rachel asked.

He was less than thrilled to have his authority questioned. "I have their full authority when in the human world."

She hesitated.

Nathan cleared his throat. "This is Lady Vera, next in line as queen after Kaylah." He gave her another small bow, which she only met with a contemptuous glance. "I don't quite recognize this young lady," he confessed.

"This is Guillen's sister, Catrina," Rachel said.

"You don't say!" Nathan perked up. "I remember you now. You were a little thing when we last met. Before we were stationed here."

Catrina blushed.

Since the cat was out of the bag, Rachel gave the briefest description of her mission with Guillen, and the guards' betrayal at his family manor. "We need to keep them safe. But they're not exactly on board, if you know what I mean. I need Eric—now. And as few people as possible to know about this, even amongst us. But we'll need extra security on-site."

The man nodded and pulled out his phone, stepping outside to make a call.

"Any updates?" Rachel asked Nathan. "On Kaylah, perchance? Last I heard, Soren had her at the palace."

Nathan frowned. "That's the latest I've heard, too. We just got word from one of our remaining spies at the palace."

"How's your wife?" Rachel asked.

"Ginger's good. Worried, of course, but good. She's at the camp, trying to keep everything together."

The man reentered. "Okay. We have someone ready to escort you to a safe house."

"Alright." Rachel stood. "Could it just be Nathan that takes us there?"

"No." He shot a glance at Nathan. "Nathan won't be privy to the location of where you'll be heading."

Rachel frowned. Seeder leadership had been slow to warm to Kaylah, but now they distrusted Nathan? "Why? I trust him more than a stranger I don't know. He wouldn't jeopardize things."

Nathan gave her a tiny downtrodden shake of the head. "Don't worry about me. I'm doing what I need to for Unitas."

***

Rachel broke the awkward silence of the car ride. "Thank you for the ride."

"No problem," the male Seeder said as he took a right turn on the outskirts of a nearby town. "And always happy to meet new Ivies in the cause."

Lady Vera stared out the window. "Hmmph." She still hadn't deigned to speak to a human or Seeder.

The rest of the ride was fairly quiet. After at least a good half hour, they pulled up to a house Rachel didn't recognize. "I thought we were going to be dropped off at Eric's safe house."

"This is it. After Her Highness went missing, it was best to move his location as well."

Rachel frowned again, but she found a spark of hope in seeing Eric again, and hopefully finding out more about how Unitas was progressing.

As she reached for the door handle, something on the street put her on edge. "There's a guy in that parked car. Just sitting there..."

"You're fine. It's extra security."

She sighed in relief. "Thank you. This is going to make a difference."

He grinned, staying in the car while the others got out. "Unitas."

Rachel guided the women to the front door and didn't even have to knock before Eric pulled it open, ushering them in.

"Let's get them settled, then we can talk," Rachel instructed.

Eric nodded in agreement.

A couple of guards stationed at the safe house appeared from a stairway and guided them up to spare bedrooms. Lady Vera and Catrina were assigned a room with two beds.

Catrina sat down on the far bed, bouncing nervously with tight lips.

Lady Vera surveyed the room disapprovingly. "Intriguing."

With every highbrow mumble and scowl from the woman, Rachel's distaste for her grew. *This* would be that moment she'd waited for. Rachel stood straight. "You are a *horrible* woman! I don't care who you are! You don't deserve to have children, especially not one as great as Guillen. So be grateful for your pathetic life, and shut the hell up!"

Lady Vera glared at her. Catrina stilled, stunned. With them being so close to the Crown, Rachel doubted either had ever had such a candid opinion shared freely. It felt good.

Rachel closed the door, leaving them there, and then turned to Eric. His eyebrows were raised, and it looked like he was fighting a grin. The guards side-eyed her like she'd lost it.

Eric told the guards he'd show Rachel to her room and that they were fine from there. He and Rachel returned downstairs to the living room, where he had a first aid kit ready on the coffee table.

"I know you can heal, but they said you were in pretty rough shape. So, I figured it wouldn't hurt … as a precaution?"

"Sure. Maybe just some disinfectant until I can regain my strength to finish healing."

He pulled out some alcohol wipes. "It looks like you've had quite an adventure. Bruising on your neck, looks like good old-fashioned strangulation. Not much I can do about that. I recognize the Ivy puncture wounds. What caused this other pattern?" He pointed to the crescent-shaped injuries on her upper arms.

She looked at her arms, disgusted with herself. "I'd rather not talk about it."

"Sorry, yeah. Bad day, obviously." The alcohol stung on her wounds as he cleaned them.

"Thanks. Oh yeah, Guillen gave me a letter for you." She mused at the irony as he opened the envelope. A human and an Ivy, an Ivy and a Seeder. Two relationships that couldn't work. And the men she and Kaylah loved would never be able to meet, both trapped in their own worlds. She studied Eric's face as he read the letter.

"Do you mind if I read it?" she asked, wanting to know what Guillen hadn't told her. Did it disclose his plans?

"I … think he'd want me to keep this private. Nothing to worry about. Some of it I already knew, like Kaylah."

She couldn't imagine how it would feel to be so isolated here in the human world while everything played out in a completely different realm. "How are you handling it?"

He wore his best brave face. "She'll be okay. I have to believe it."

"I'm sorry I couldn't keep her safe."

He shook his head. "You were on your own mission; I couldn't blame you. And she's strong." He shifted in his seat. "So... Guillen explained why you brought them here. You think it'll keep her safe?"

Rachel rubbed at a dried blood smear on her dress. "I do. It's something. The only thing we can really do until an extraction is worked out. Guillen was brilliant to think of it so quickly."

"Speaking of..." Eric tapped the letter on his leg. "Sounds like Kaylah was right about you two."

Rachel's cheeks warmed. Kaylah had talked about her and Guillen to Eric? Kaylah had no idea how far they'd come in their relationship, but she'd encouraged it... Guillen certainly hadn't written a love note about her to Eric, but maybe he'd mentioned that he loved her and asked Eric to make sure she was safe.

"He's amazing." She smiled, though with longing. Her heart was back there, in a completely different realm right now.

"Then I'm glad you found someone good for you." Eric's eyes darted to the ceiling. "Though, if things work out, it sounds like you might have a rough go of it with your future mother-in-law." He laughed.

"Oh ... gross..." She grimaced. "That never even crossed my mind." She shook her head. "We're far from that. And frankly ... he may forgive her for what she's done, but I never could. After I go back, I'm staying as far away as humanly possible." She paused. "Not that I'm a human... Hmm ... you know, it's funny how sayings change meaning." She chuckled.

Eric met her chuckle with a friendly smile, cleaning up the first aid supplies he'd used. Seeder healing did a fantastic job of repairing damaged bone and tissue, though it wasn't as helpful against infection, so it was for the best they'd gone the extra mile, as she hadn't been able to heal herself right away.

Despite Eric's offer to show Rachel to a room where she could rest and clean up, she wanted to talk more first. They discussed progress with Unitas; there had been a boatload that Rachel hadn't been privy to while on her mission. She'd almost completely forgotten the human side of the equation, how hard Eric and the others had been working on behalf of the green folk from this side of the rifts.

Despite Eric's kindness and dedication, he quietly expressed frustration at the way Seeders were handling things, that they'd even consider that Kaylah, and by association, *he*, might be a traitor.

"Honestly, sometimes I'm not sure if I'm at this new safe house for my protection, or as a hostage."

Rachel's heart ached. "I thought we were doing well. I had so much hope after spending time with Guillen." Granted, Magda and Jacob, and Guillen's family wouldn't exactly become Rachel's BFFs, but she'd met plenty of Ivies who had given her hope along the way.

Eric rubbed his hands together, keeping his voice low. "I get that they're being overly cautious, but your leaders know ... things... It's just as likely that *they* did something with her as it is that Soren had her kidnapped."

The finger-pointing was getting old. So was the war. If Rachel could snap her fingers and make it all go away, she'd do it in half a heartbeat. "What do you mean, our leaders 'know things'?"

Pursing his lips, Eric hesitated. "I can't talk about it, but... Jon, and Nathan..."

Rachel furrowed her brow. "Yeah, what's with Nathan?"

Footsteps creaked above, making their way down the stairs.

Eric and Rachel craned their necks to see.

Catrina timidly poked her head around the corner. "Am I interrupting?"

"No, you're fine. Come on in." Eric offered her a chair.

"This is Guillen's sister, Catrina. Third in line to the throne. Catrina, this is Eric, Kaylah's…" Rachel panicked. What was he by now? Still a boyfriend? Had they made other plans? Lady Vera had mentioned Kaylah should have suitors in the Green Lands…

He acknowledged his precarious position with a glance in Rachel's direction. "I'm the human Kaylah dated in high school. How can we help you?"

"Well… I… Um… Guillen asked a favor before we came. He wanted me to get to know you two." Catrina shrugged. "So… I'm just here to talk, if that's okay."

Eric and Rachel shared a warm smile.

Chapter 35

CATRINA SHIFTED UNCOMFORTABLY IN HER SEAT. "That was a car, right? Earlier?"

Rachel's eyes widened. "Right, I forgot. You really haven't been around here. Yeah, that was a car. I imagine there's a lot that's different for you already."

Catrina gave a cautious smile, but sat awkwardly, as if she didn't know what to say.

"I'm going to be blunt, and I hope you're okay with that. 'Cause I'm really tired, but I like you, okay?" It was time Rachel spoke her mind with Catrina, too. She was sweet, but anyone who referred to her people as 'weeds' still needed to learn a thing or two.

"I know you think you're better than us—a human and a Seeder. Just because you're royal, and you're an Ivy. But all that means is we might look different when we transform, that we have different abilities. If you love your brother the way I think you do, you should be able to get over that and realize the Unitas movement is one worth joining."

Rachel paused. "And the humans—sure, they don't have powers, like Guillen … but that car ride… Wasn't that neat? It would be kind of nice to travel that quickly in the Green Lands, wouldn't it? Different doesn't mean bad."

Catrina looked down into her lap, and Eric sat silent.

Rachel cocked her head to the side. "Sorry. I could be a lot more tactful. But like I said, I'm tired. I should go lie down to heal up and prepare to leave, sooner than later."

"It's okay." Catrina gave a half-hearted smile. "I'm willing to hear anything you have to say. I told Guillen I would."

Rachel loved Guillen more than before, if it was even possible. He couldn't come to the human world, but he was still pushing forward the movement. Where was he that very moment? She refused to worry. He'd be safe. He'd be out there working on getting Kaylah back.

"Just remember I said I liked you first, okay? I'm open to answering questions about anything Seeder, and about how your brother and I met, if you still want to learn more. Maybe in the morning? If you don't have any burning questions, I'm going to head to bed. Eric would be great at explaining Unitas to you."

Catrina said she'd be okay with talking to Eric while Rachel turned in for the night. She stayed in the living room while Eric showed Rachel to a room with a single bed and en suite bathroom, and offered her the necessities.

Going through a rift, she couldn't bring her things with her that she'd been carrying around. Rifts allowed only a limited volume through, in relation to the Seeder or Ivy's body mass. Rachel surveyed her dress and rolled her eyes at the coincidence. The last time she'd been attacked by an Ivy, she had also been in a fancy dress. Neither experience had been worth dressing up for. Perhaps she would never wear a dress again.

"Thanks again, for taking us in," she said before Eric left the room.

"No problem. You know I'm always here for you."

She wrung her hands, figuring she might as well warn Eric. "I … might have nightmares. I'm sorry if I wake you up." It was going to be hard without Guillen there.

"I'm sorry, Rach. Here, I didn't give you a proper hug." He opened his arms, and she happily obliged.

Rachel frowned as she realized what she'd just done in the living room, that she'd slipped on something she'd promised to keep a secret. "Sorry I told Catrina about you and Kaylah. I promised you two I wouldn't tell anyone you were back together, so you'd be safe."

He shook his head. "No worries. I was technically the one that said it. And Guillen's note said he was certain she could be trusted. And, honestly, the Seeders were half of the concern, anyway, back when we asked you to keep that one under wraps. But I'll let Catrina know to keep that tidbit from her mom." He shrugged. "I guess it's just nice to … talk about her."

Rachel gave him another long hug. He'd all but given up his family, friends, and foreseeable future plans for Kaylah and Unitas. This had to be immensely difficult for him to trudge through alone.

After a few more minutes of catching up, he left Rachel to the quiet room and the solitude of her thoughts. She appreciated Eric. He was Kaylah's Guillen. She did worry about him, though. Rachel hadn't had someone who loved her that way, when she'd been held captive at the palace. And while Soren's torture wouldn't be the same with his own sister, she had no doubt Kaylah was enduring something at his hand. Eric had to be hiding a world of pain. She also worried how it would affect the network if Kaylah didn't make it out. Eric wasn't the oldest member, but he was pretty central to the human side of Unitas. How long would he stick around if she was gone for good?

Trying to force it out of her mind, Rachel took a shower and lay down, carefully setting her knife and jade earrings on the bedside table. Despite the lack of Green Lands energy, and how cold the empty bed was without Guillen, the comfort of being in the human world afforded her quick rest. The nightmares came, but she didn't seem to disturb anyone during the night. Instead, she woke with sore teeth. She shrugged it off. At least she didn't have to be ashamed in front of the others.

Leaving her room, earrings back in place, dressed in fresh clothes, Rachel was surprised to be the first up. She'd gone to bed first, but it was already pretty late in the morning. A note from Eric on the kitchen table caught her eye.

Stayed up late chatting. Muffins on the counter, juice, anything you want. Save some room for bacon when I wake up.

She poured herself a tall glass of orange juice and sat in the living room, peeking out the blinds. There was a different car parked outside, a change of security detail. After waiting awhile, it was time to do some healing. The self-injuries had to go first; she couldn't handle any more questions. Since the Ivy cuts were in the same area, she cleared them up at the same time. She'd recharged enough that her glowing hands took care of the task without leaving her too drained.

Eric finally got up, clearly wiped out. He stumbled his way to the kitchen, a good host in a comforting refuge. If memory served Rachel right from her experience in a similar safe house months earlier, he wasn't a half-bad cook, either.

"How late did you stay up?" she asked as he reached for a pack of bacon in the fridge.

Eric yawned. "I think around four?"

"Holy crap! Were you talking with Catrina the whole time?"

"Yeah. She's pretty golden." He tore the plastic open. "I think she could be a great ally for Unitas. And she's lived an interesting life. You guys should chat sometime."

"Yeah. Maybe someday when I see her again, we'll have time for that." Rachel pulled out plates to set the table.

As the bacon finished cooking, Catrina emerged from her room.

"Hi, Rachel. You're looking better." She smiled warmly, then turned to Eric. "Is that smell the stuff you were telling me about?" She closed her eyes and breathed deeply.

Eric and Rachel laughed. "It'll blow your mind."

He set a plate of bacon down, and offered to make up anything else he had on hand, but Rachel declined; she'd be fine with anything premade, particularly with how tired he was.

The three of them sat around the kitchen table and munched on the bacon, nibbled on some muffins.

Rachel turned to Eric. "When do you think we could call me a ride to get back to the cave?"

Catrina furrowed her brow. "You're leaving so soon?"

"Yeah. I'm not really very helpful here. I should get back and see how I can help with our camp and Kaylah's rescue."

"I just… I wanted some more time," Catrina confessed.

"With me?" Rachel picked up another piece of bacon. "We can chat a little, and I'm sure we'll be able to talk some other time."

"No. I mean…" Catrina looked at Eric. "I want to go."

Rachel shook her head. "No. You two are meant to stay here. Guillen trusted me to bring you here. Where would you even go?"

"Give me more time today to talk to my mother. She doesn't have to believe in your cause. She just has to be willing to help the right family members, and care enough for her kingdom. She grew up in that palace, before the newest renovations. I think she could help."

Rachel froze, midchew. She hadn't given that a single thought. If nothing else, if Lady Vera was willing to provide insider information … that could be *immensely* useful. Rachel wasn't a fool. Lady Vera couldn't be trusted, so she'd still need to stay with Eric for safekeeping. But if she could be useful in some way…

"That's a hard sell," Rachel said. "But I can give you a few hours to talk to her. She's still in your room?"

Catrina nodded. "And I know I'm not really useful, but I want to come."

Rachel sighed. That wasn't what Guillen had asked her to do.

Eric raised his eyebrows with a gentle glance at Rachel. "It might be safer to split up the heirs, anyway. Just in case. I understand they've increased camp security since…" He looked down and bobbed his head. "Just … I think your leaders would agree it's for the best."

"Please?" Catrina begged. "I want to help."

Rachel read her expression. Guillen's eyes were framed by Catrina's kind face. Rachel considered her plea to come with her. Eric had a good point.

"If you come, realize you may have a guard escort everywhere," Rachel warned. "Go see if you can reason with your mom, and we'll talk about you coming."

Catrina piled a plate with half of the bacon, and shoved another slice into her mouth, thanking them and bounding up the stairs to her room. It was by far the least ladylike thing Rachel had seen her do thus far.

Eric chuckled. "Should I make more? I forget to make an extra pack when we have bacon virgins in the house."

Rachel pointed at him, equally amused. "You know what, I'd normally turn you down, but I think I could use some extra bacon to make things better. Got any chocolate for breakfast, too?"

"Ooh … chocolate for breakfast." He put up his hands. "I won't judge. I've got hot chocolate, chocolate bars, and chocolate ice cream. What'll it be?"

A flashback to the Ivy pub imparted a bitter taste in her mouth. *What'll it be?'* Had Guillen been so upset because his mom had a drinking problem? Whether or not that was the case, it had been a stupid mistake.

"Never mind on the chocolate." She forced a smile. "Let's just do the bacon."

While Rachel impatiently waited for Catrina to work her magic, she reflected on the first time she'd been in a safe house like this, with Saff, and how the roles had been reversed in a way. She was in charge this time, instead of Saff.

Catrina was a good egg; Rachel could feel it. If, heaven forbid, Kaylah didn't make it out, Rachel imagined skipping over Lady Vera and forcing Soren out of the palace, then putting in Catrina as their new queen. Of course, it was a little morbid, mentally plotting the imaginary assassination of your love's mother … so Rachel moved on from that line of thinking.

As the day stretched on, Rachel finished off her healing. The huge bruise around her neck would draw unwanted attention. She took some time to call her human mom, Samantha, which was a godsend. She didn't tell her about any of the traumatizing events, or about her mission in any sort of detail, but she told her about the man she loved. It helped. The conversation was only tainted by the reminder that, like Eric, her human mom would never get to meet Guillen. But at least her mom was still safely in Unitas custody, one less person to worry about.

Catrina finally emerged from their room by early evening. "She's … stubborn. A little more time?"

Rachel shook her head. "I need to go. If she changes her mind, Unitas can reach out to us on the other side."

Catrina looked hesitant. "And me?"

"You really want to go?"

She nodded. "I want to see what it's like, what Guillen is risking his life for. And maybe I could come back and share that with my mother."

Rachel relented. "Alright. Let's do that."

Eric had been kept up-to-date on their cave trials, and shared the details with Rachel while they waited for a Unitas escort to pick the girls up. So far, it seemed neither Seeder nor Ivy had found a way to do more than one round trip a day. They still had energy stores to be able to use their other abilities, but something kept them from being able to expend it all on multiple rift trips in a short amount of time. The effects of fatal root rot on the Seeder women, associated with frequent travel to the human world, were still unknown. Though, as Saff had experienced months prior on her second visit in one year to the human world, it didn't seem cumulative.

Their ride pulled up, and they said their goodbyes. Rachel sat in the back with Catrina. This would be Rachel's first time leaving the human world through a cave. She appreciated the ease of it, and not having to rely on an Ivy.

After a short meeting with the Unitas supervisor, Rachel and Catrina were given permission to return to the Unitas camp, but only through a Seeder-created rift made by one of the guards, to ensure neither of them 'accidentally' rifted somewhere they ought not to.

Catrina was in obvious awe at the concept of cave rifting.

Crossing through the rift, Rachel breathed in the energy of the Green Lands, glad to be free of worry of root rot, glad to be back to work.

With a guard in tow to accompany them, Rachel's first order of business was to find Saff. They made their way up the canyon wall with the rope ladders that had been constructed to aid Ivies, and Seeders without powers, up to camp.

Camp had grown and changed so much since Rachel had last seen it, but Saff's training was in the same place, more or less. Saff immediately dismissed her training class and ran up to hug Rachel.

"You're back! All in one piece!" she breathed in relief.

Devin was working nearby and greeted Rachel as well. She introduced Catrina, and Devin offered to take her on a tour so Rachel and Saff could talk about official business.

There hadn't been any news on Kaylah yet. Unitas was still talking about strategies. Saff broke the news to Rachel that another one of the girls at the palace had died. Rachel hardly reacted. Those girls had to be so drugged up and drained at that point … they died from exhaustion, and had probably died inside long before that. Unitas didn't just need to rescue the last remaining Seeder girl, or Kaylah, from the palace. They needed a swift and final strike. Especially with the War Vines being weaker now with only one Seeder girl powering them.

"Why don't we just take our armies and march over there?" Rachel asked. "We still have the numbers…"

~

Saff sighed. "It's … too risky."

Rachel's shoulders slumped, and Saff had a pretty good guess as to how she felt. Rachel had been one of those girls stuck in the palace, enduring torture every day. And she was unfailingly loyal to Kaylah. But it wasn't that simple. The Mother Vines created a protective border around the expansive palace grounds. Even if the War Vines had never been created, the Mother Vines were a formidable barrier. Add to that the whispers hardly anyone knew about… Ginger had clarified to Saff that the mythological rumors of possible powers held by whisper rifters had obviously been exaggerated. Even the Seeder leaders balked at the claims that one of those men blessed with the gift could possess the strength of five men. None of the whispers in Unitas were even twice as powerful as their regular Ivy counterparts, but they *did* exhibit more strength. Marching Unitas and a large portion of the Seeder army across the Green Lands would leave the severely damaged Seeder borders too vulnerable.

They needed something more.

Saff pulled Rachel into another hug. "Trust that we're doing our best, okay?"

One thing she would never voice to Rachel, was some of the strategies discussed in meetings Saff had still been permitted to attend on occasion. If they could hold out long enough, and the last Seeder girl in Soren's custody died, a march on the palace would be much more feasible; the War Vines would have no one powering them. But how long would the remaining girl last? And how long would Kaylah?

"Are you going to be staying in camp?" Saff asked, pulling back.

~

Rachel yearned to be by Guillen's side, but that was a nonstarter. For now, they were on separate paths. She choked down the ache and worry in her heart. "Yeah. How can I help?"

Saff led Rachel to a heavily guarded tent. In the middle was a large table overflowing with all kinds of books and scrolls, in various stages of aging, coated with ashes. Next to the table sat a large chest.

"How do you feel about research?" Saff asked. "Maybe you can make out something useful to figure out Kaylah's plans, or why she went missing. Maybe something we missed." Saff shook her head. "I've spent so much time training… We just…" Her voice was full of regret. "Who knows what we lost for good in the fire? Kaylah and I did a little research, but didn't really have any breakthroughs, and now…" She gestured to the wooden chest. "They just packed it all away in there. Some of the pages are super brittle, and there's no organization. It's like we're starting at square one. *Less* than square one."

Rachel frowned, the singed pages bearing the odor of fire and heartache. "Yeah. I can help."

"Awesome. I'll stop by to join you when I can. Devin and I have limited our training to teaching the newly returned girls to catch a breeze home. They're continuing their training back in their home villages, so when there's a lag in returns through the cave, I've been trying to sort out this mess."

"Do you believe the reports on Soren having her?" Rachel blurted. "You don't think she left Unitas, do you?"

Saff shook her head with certainty. "No. I've spent enough time with her now, to trust her." She bit her lip, looking down. "I've had my doubts—it could've been someone from *our* side that took her."

"Really? You think we'd do that?"

Saff scrunched her eyebrows. "Not really. I was just exploring all the possibilities. Despite any tensions in camp or meetings, I don't think our people would have done it. And the last report was from a palace insider. It doesn't sound like the Ivy people know yet that they have her. Plus, there's… Well, it's just a lot more likely that an Ivy kidnapped her."

No one had been able to explain to Rachel how they'd taken Kaylah. She didn't voice an additional concern that plagued her thoughts, not wanting to stress Saff out further. But what if their sources were all wrong? What if the 'confirmation' that Kaylah was being held at the palace had been intentionally fabricated? What if they had a double agent amongst them? What if Soren had had the foresight to plant that information with Lady Vera as well, knowing someone from Unitas might come for her? "Do you know who the information is being passed to and from?"

Saff shook her head. "Not from inside the palace. But from what I understand, your friend Jon has been doing a lot of back-and-forth with information."

Rachel smiled. He could be such a porcupine on the outside, but she'd come to see the sweet gummy bear hidden in the center.

"Do you trust him?" Saff asked.

"Of course! He and Guillen saved my life."

Saff silently nodded, obviously suspicious. "I just… I promise I've been playing nice with the other kids."

Rachel couldn't help but smile again.

"But he's pretty high on the list of suspects in Kaylah's kidnapping."

He couldn't be. Not after all he'd sacrificed to help Rachel and Kaylah, and Unitas as a whole. "Kaylah and I would trust him with our lives."

~

Saff didn't respond. When had she and Rachel ever agreed on their suspicions? "Did Kaylah ever say something to you about Ivy queens having a weakness, or your stepdad having some kind of strength or weapon?"

Rachel's face scrunched in confusion. "What? Um…" She looked away, pensive. "No, I… No."

Tucking her hands into her pockets, and shooting another glance at the table full of books, Saff decided to let it go. She didn't even remember the suspicious wording Kaylah had used. Maybe she'd meant nothing by it, despite Saff's hopes that it had meant something that could win this war, that could explain Kaylah's disappearance.

Saff frowned. "Did you hear how many spies we've lost at the palace?"

Rachel shared a frown. "No."

"He's probably dismissed or killed off half of the palace staff, trying to weed out the disloyal ones. We might have the advantage with them struggling to find new girls to put on the Vines, but if we lose our remaining spies in the palace…" She pulled Rachel in for a tight squeeze. "Either way, I'm glad you're back." At least she had one less person to worry about now.

~

Rachel enjoyed Saff's hug, especially given how stiff and awkward things had been on her departure from camp. She processed the fact that Soren was hunting down their spies, recalling some of their interactions from the years they'd dated. He had a temper. He was … a bit off. *He's like a spoiled toddler having a tantrum.*

Rachel pulled back from their hug. "I'm glad you guys are okay here. And that camp's doing so well. I … worried."

Saff swallowed hard. "It's been rough. But once they plugged the main border breach, they sent word and lots of backup." She gave a faint smile. "I'm glad to be back to helping the girls more, and helping with the research."

Rachel looked past Saff. "So, no idea at all how this is organized?"

Saff walked to the table, pointing to a couple of stacks. "I've gone through these already. Granted, that doesn't guarantee I haven't missed something… Kaylah talked about studying our jade charms, and trying to get our cave to open to the one by the palace. I wish she had figured it out before she was taken—we could really use it right now."

"I'll take a look. Maybe some fresh eyes could help. I think Catrina can be trusted; I can keep an eye on her while we work on it."

Saff hesitated. "I don't know her. So that judgment call is up to you and the new council member assigned to camp. Who knows, maybe Catrina could help with Ivy fairy tales." She chuckled.

"What do you mean?"

"Oh." Saff straightened a stack of books. "Something Kaylah said once—that Ivies have more stories about Green Lands origins. She wanted to get some books to compare, but I don't know if any of these are what she was looking for."

Rachel squinted at the stacks. Hopefully Catrina was ready for another late night.

Chapter 36

SAFF ENDED UP JOINING Rachel and Catrina for a late night, poring over the books and scrolls Kaylah had collected and smuggled. Questions bombarded the trio. There were several piles, dozens of bookmarks, but they had no idea where she'd left off.

They asked themselves why jade would matter, what unique properties it held. Seeders used it for energy distribution between their temple wells and border walls, and to dampen and hide their girls' blooms in the human world, to keep the process safer.

Why had they never been able to rift between different locations in the Green Lands? And why wasn't the name of the other cave working?

They studied for hours; exhaustion was setting in. Saff finally retired for the night, and Catrina's energy was waning from her previous long night of chatting with Eric.

Catrina and Rachel claimed a tent for the night. While they couldn't fully obscure Catrina's identity amidst the Ivies in camp, she did her part by styling her hair differently, and wearing Seeder clothes. They hoped she could be mistaken as a doppelganger. Despite how humble the clothing and accommodations were compared to her norm, Catrina graciously followed along with all of it. The primary condition of her permission to stay in the Unitas camp, and to participate in research, was that she would be watched at all times. They surrounded the tent with guards, and both girls slept soundly, safely.

The next morning, Rachel sat on her thinking boulder while Catrina slept in. She breathed in the freshness of the Green Lands. None other than Zeus spotted her and climbed up; she was surprised to have a visitor so early.

He looked as handsome and muscular as ever, armed with a huge smile. "I'm glad you're back! Think you'll be staying long?"

Rachel gave him a soft smile. "I don't know. I hope not. I mean … no offense."

He chuckled, claiming a spot next to her. "Got a taste of some adventure back home, and back here is too boring now, huh?"

"Something like that. I've just got a lot on my mind."

They sat quietly for a while, side by side.

"I'm guessing you won't have any free time to … go out anytime soon?"

She fidgeted with her hands. "You're a great guy, Zeus."

"But you're seeing someone?"

She gave him an apologetic frown. "I'm sorry, I am." She considered consoling him, explaining it had nothing to do with his lack of powers. But that kind of explanation would probably have the opposite effect. If she could love an Ivy without powers, why couldn't she a Seeder without them? And she hadn't *officially* been working with Guillen anyway—her cover story still included her spending time away from camp back in her home village, not behind enemy lines.

Zeus pursed his lips, nodding. "I, uh … thought I saw a guy leaving your tent with you after we hugged goodbye."

"No, he…" She rubbed her face. Both of the guys she'd kissed had had the opportunity to check the other out. *Great.* "Yes. I'm dating that guy. But it wasn't like that at all. We were just friends back then, okay?"

"It's alright." Zeus nudged her. "You're a nice girl. I just didn't get enough time to win you over before you left."

She didn't dare correct him, that he'd never really had a chance with her heart. "How's the progress coming along—clearing the poison behind our borders, growing the flowers?"

"It's incredibly slow, but you have to hand it to them—these Ivy women are working long hours. Before Ivy troops cut off our land access, we'd been able to carve out a path, and a small patch of land, where my kind can survive." He beamed. "The first time in a normal village *in over a century*. A handful of them have been there for over a week without any ill effects."

"That's fantastic! I'm so proud of you guys."

"Thanks. I just kinda wish I'd been trapped over there, instead of over here." He wrinkled his nose. "Feel a bit useless now."

She could empathize, but it was encouraging to hear him stepping out of his comfort zone in his little corner of the realm. "I know they're working on reclaiming that stretch of the woods. We need both you, and more Ivies, over there to help."

After another minute of small talk, she announced that she needed to get on with her day. She stood and offered him a hug.

He accepted, then flashed her one more friendly smile. "Let me know if you need anything with what you're working on. I'm happy to help."

"Sure thing."

As she descended the boulder, she couldn't help but think about Jon. He'd left camp for recon a while back, so she wouldn't get to shoot the breeze with him again as she had before her mission. She smiled as fond memories of Jon replayed in her mind. He'd cracked a smile a time or two after she'd met his callous comments with sarcasm. He'd sacrificed love and a respected career to help Seeders, the enemy.

As much as it annoyed Rachel that Saff and their leaders questioned Ivies like Jon, she could understand that struggle. She herself had once told Guillen that she'd 'earned' her trust issues. Where did one draw the line between caution and paranoia, when they'd been hurt and betrayed?

Several yards before she reached her tent, Rachel ran into Saff.

"Sorry I can't join you," Saff said. "I really need to get back to my girls. But come find me if you need anything, okay?"

"Definitely. No problem."

Saff tilted her head to the side. "Before I head over, I just wanted to see how you're doing. We didn't get to catch up much. You seem different."

Rachel playfully tucked a fist under her chin. "Is that good or bad?"

Saff laughed. "Good. I think. More mature."

"Thanks. I guess. There were some … uh … intense moments while I was out there. I'm sure it would help to talk about it, but it's too much to unpack right now."

Saff gave her a warm smile. "I'm here for you, when you're ready."

Rachel scooped her into a hug. "I really appreciate it. It was rough."

~

"That guy you went with, Guillen. Did he keep up his end of the bargain and keep you safe? Did he treat you right?" Saff released Rachel, eyeing her. Her worries about Rachel had only increased after hearing how much Soren was hunting for spies. And once Kaylah had gone missing, she feared Soren might torture information out of her, like the fact that Rachel was roaming around in his own kingdom.

~

As far as Rachel was concerned, she still blamed herself for the attack on Guillen and herself. "Yes, he kept me safe." She couldn't hide a longing grin as she felt her earrings, as the weight of his knife rested in her pocket. "He treated me right. He helped a lot."

Saff crossed her arms. "I've seen that look before. I'm guessing Zeus's visit wasn't to rekindle something?"

"No. Definitely not. I know you don't like that Guillen's an Ivy. But I love him."

Saff rocked her head back and forth. "Well, I guess I've done some growing up of my own while you were away. The more time I've spent with decent Ivies, the more I've found myself caring about them. I still need to introduce you to my sparring partner, Flora." Saff poked Rachel in the arm. "But if Guillen's really worthy of you, then I might be okay with you two being together."

Rachel dramatically wiped her brow. "Phew! Now that we have *your* approval, I'll bring him home for dinner sometime."

Saff gave her a wink and headed out.

Rachel returned to her tent.

Catrina sat on her cot, dressed for the day. "I wasn't really sure what to do with you gone, since there are all of those guards outside. And you need to be there for any of the research."

"I'm so sorry! I should have left a note or instructions or something. Are you up to doing more reading?"

Catrina was happy to have something to do. They looked at the stacks of books and each picked one to focus on. Only a few minutes in, Catrina spoke up. "What do you suppose this means? She had a bookmark at this page."

Rachel looked. "Oh, that. The jade charms we use, when we're going through our bloom—they prepare them for us, and it helps so the change isn't so hard in the human world. I guess we don't really need them over here, so maybe someday when the poison is cleared up, and our girls don't have to flee to the other world, they'd be obsolete."

"What do you mean by 'prepare' them? Is that what these symbols mean?"

Rachel furrowed her brow, studying the page. "Maybe. Honestly, I've never asked about how they're prepared. If you think it matters, we could ask."

Catrina shrugged. "I don't know. Doesn't hurt to find out."

"Okay, well…" They could ask the guards outside, but Rachel would rather work with those she knew well. "Let's go ask Devin."

They grabbed the book and headed to Devin's training area. He readily gave them a minute of his attention.

"How do you prepare our charms when you spot our bloom?"

Devin straightened his shirt. "We bring over jade from the Green Lands. I'm not sure if the stuff from the human world would work, too. But we take some of ours, shape it into a smaller stone, and then carve the sun symbol, like the one here." He pointed to a drawing in the book. "You have to place it against your skin for it to work."

"It's just that simple? Carve it and wear it? What about these symbols? Do those mean anything to you?"

He shook his head. "No, sorry. I don't know the old symbols."

Rachel pursed her lips. "Let me see. Kaylah talked a little bit about how to pronounce them. Ex-pe-dee-oh?"

Devin's eyes lit up. "Yeah, expedio. I've heard that referenced. I guess I forgot that part. Before the jade leaves the Green Lands, the matriarchs transfer energy into the stones. That's something they say in the process. I've never seen it done, but I've heard about it."

Rachel loved learning all of the neat tidbits of her Seeder culture, but still didn't see how this helped. "Okay. So … jade. From here. Energy, the right word, the right carving, skin contact. And it controls the energy?"

"Sounds about right."

"What about the other symbol on this page?" It was a swirl. She read the description. "I think this one is labeled 'cogo.'"

He scratched his chin. "I don't know. Sorry. I've never seen it used or heard that word."

Not the breakthrough they'd hoped for. "No problem, thanks for your help." They said goodbye, and the girls started strolling back to the research tent. Rachel stopped, turning to ask one last question. "When you say Seeder matriarch, you're talking about a mother, right? A fully-rooted woman? Not just any of us?"

"Yeah."

Rachel and Catrina returned to the tent. If they were looking for a needle in a haystack, maybe this meant something, even if it was just a small part of the equation.

"Unitas is Latin." Rachel attempted to bring Catrina up to speed. "Maybe cogo is, too. What I wouldn't do for the internet right now."

Catrina gave her the same kind of confused look Guillen sometimes did.

Rachel smiled. "You should spend some time in the human world; it would really open your eyes. The internet is a place to look up information. Anyway, cogo … and the symbol, it's just a basic sun and swirl."

"Maybe it's as simple as it seems." Catrina drew in the air with a finger. "The sun radiates; the rays shoot out from the center. The swirl keeps it in, so maybe it stops it from leaking?"

Rachel wrinkled her nose, skeptical. "I don't know about that. Everyone talks about the charms we get 'suppressing' or 'dampening' our energy. Doesn't that mean it's keeping it in? Bottled up so it doesn't leak out? That would mean the sun keeps it in."

Catrina plucked up a new scroll, carefully laying it flat on the table. "I could be wrong."

Rachel spent a painful amount of time finishing that book and the next without any seemingly useful clues.

Lunchtime rolled around, and they could both stand to stretch their legs and grab a bite. Rachel and Catrina, accompanied by two guards, strolled to the rudimentary camp kitchen next to the garden. They basked in the sun at a picnic table, munching on a platter of jicama and asparagus with an herb dip.

Catrina people-watched as they munched. Rachel's curiosity got the better of her. Guillen still hadn't talked all that much about his childhood, but he'd obviously felt awkward talking about having grown up with privilege. "What was it like growing up with servants?"

"Umm…" Catrina met her gaze, having just grabbed another jicama stick. "Well, I don't really know what it's like to *not* have them." She dunked her jicama into the herb dip. "Guillen said it was a bit hard to transition to living without them." She looked down shyly, her voice hushed. "Then again, he wasn't treated the same growing up because he wasn't an heir, and because, well, you know. And then when he moved to those communities…"

Trying not to frown, Rachel grabbed another steamed asparagus spear and took a bite. "He loves you."

Catrina gave her a soft smile. "He's a good big brother." After another bite, Catrina hesitantly added, "And what my mother said about, well, back at our manor, the baby thing… It wasn't his." She snapped a jicama stick in half. "You looked pretty shocked when my mother brought that up."

Rachel studied her plate. "Thanks. I believe him." She still felt cruddy for questioning him, for getting jealous, for giving his abuser a second of credibility before allowing him an explanation. She still didn't know the whole story, but Guillen had honestly been the slower one to open up about his past struggles in detail. If she couldn't trust him, who could she?

For the rest of their lunch, they chatted about lighter topics, mostly surrounding new cuisine Rachel had tried in the Ivy Kingdom, and which dishes Catrina thought she ought to try someday. While the textures used in Seeder cuisine were more to Rachel's liking, the spices Ivies used were incredible.

Fully recharged and ready to tackle more books, they moseyed toward the research tent. On their walk back, Rachel couldn't resist the call of a specific tent in the distance, blackened and abandoned.

"Can we take a look at Kaylah's tent?"

The guard shrugged. "Sure."

The closer they walked, the more knives twisted in Rachel's gut. The tan fabric draped from sturdy wooden poles. A third of the fabric had burned away. The guard explained its surprisingly messy state. To put out the flames, dirt had been shoveled onto it. Once they'd extracted the valuable books and scrolls, the remains of the tent had been doused with water for good measure. Mud coated the outside of the tent.

Rachel and Catrina ducked inside. There was a thick layer of dried mud in here, too.

"There's nothing of value in there," the guard said.

Scanning the tent, Rachel easily confirmed that. Kaylah's cot was missing, as well as the table and chest—everything had been removed with the exception of a water bottle and a singed blanket half-stuck in the mud.

"Where's her stuff?" she asked.

"Other than the research, her personal belongings are being kept in Arcadia."

Rachel nodded absentmindedly. "And we're sure—"

"Nothing that would help with your research."

Sighing, she sat on the dirt floor, tucking her knees under her chin. What had run through Kaylah's mind when it all happened? Had she been panicked? Had they started the fire when she was still inside? Was she still alive right now?

Catrina stood with her hands folded in front of her. She surveyed the roof, a good portion of it missing, allowing daylight to fill the area. "It's weird to imagine she's our queen now, and that she was living in a place like this." She reached out and touched the fabric of the tent. "Granted, I'm sure it looked a lot better a few days ago."

Lost in thought, Rachel drew the Unitas symbol in the dirt. That was one of the things she loved about Kaylah, wasn't it? She had her own kingdom, but wasn't above roughing it in a tent. Between her looks, wit, and position, she could have had her pick of *any* suitor in her kingdom, but had fallen in love with a 'lowly' human. Kaylah had become a beacon of hope—not just for Seeders; she was already a woman of the people for Ivies. She'd never be the kind of ruler to harshly dictate and be unrelatable.

But could it be enough? Wistfully, Rachel drew a heart around the Unitas symbol. While her mind jumped to Guillen and his tattoo, her heart actually reached out to his people in that moment. What if Rachel should have gone back to Ivy territory to keep up their campaign? Perhaps she still could… What if their mission could do more than slow Soren's attacks and prepare for a smoother transition when Kaylah took her place on the throne? What if they could get the Ivies to actually revolt and take Soren down? Not a ragtag group of dissenters in Unitas, but the whole kingdom?

It was a wish. A dream. Unitas was already campaigning in regular towns, much like Rachel and Guillen had done in stunt communities. Combatting Soren's propaganda was too tall a task to expect a full-on revolution in time for Kaylah and the last Seeder held captive in the palace to come out of this in one piece.

Resigned to that, Rachel took one last contemplative look around the tent. Wanting a piece of Kaylah with her, no matter how silly it seemed, she grabbed the neglected water bottle and then reached down for the ruined blanket. Perhaps she wouldn't take the blanket back to her tent with her, but tidying up the spot a little felt more respectful.

A good chunk of the blanket was buried in mud. Rachel tugged on it, but it didn't budge. After handing the water bottle to Catrina, Rachel grasped the blanket with both hands, moving energy to her biceps and fingers. She yanked it. The mud resisted giving up its captive, though Rachel was stronger. She had it almost all out when she discovered the real weak point—the blanket itself. With one last pull, the blanket ripped. Before Rachel could react to commune with the wind and catch herself, she landed on her back. Without skipping a beat, she laughed.

"You okay?" Catrina looked down at her, wide-eyed.

Rachel nodded. "Super graceful, right?"

Catrina wore a grin. "Something like that. Maybe you *are* right for Guillen. He was a bit clumsy growing up."

It was hard to imagine that, given his skill level with blades, but Rachel loved hearing anything that had to do with him. She pointed at Catrina. "I like having you around. I expect to hear all of the dirt you can give me." She stood, brushing off her backside. "Speaking of dirt…"

Rachel folded the sad blanket, then knelt down to get a better position for the shred left in the mud. Another quick tug freed it, and to her shock and surprise, it freed something else. Something that had been buried in the corner of the blanket, under inches of soil and mud—a scroll.

"Hey!" Studying it with narrow eyes, Rachel tried to piece together the information on it. Luckily, it had been buried deep enough for the ink to be preserved. The scroll had a few drawings on it. One of those drawings included the sun symbol she and Catrina had been researching earlier. "Hmm."

"What is it?" Catrina asked.

This scroll had modern English on it, making it easier to sift through. It described the blooming process, the different changes the Seeder girls went through in the human world. Rachel hadn't knowingly experienced many of them—her bloom had been completed peacefully with the jade charm on. But a lot of it sounded like it had come right out of Saff's journal. The pain, the surging energy, and the inevitable coma, if the charm wasn't used at all. A diagram showed the human body with wavy lines coming from it. After scouring the entire scroll, Rachel finally realized how the charm worked. It wasn't like she'd imagined. It didn't just bottle up the energy to cloak it.

It's like a balloon.

Not that a Seeder girl would physically pop like a balloon—that was both gruesome and silly to consider. But the intensity and pressure of their powers coming in, the magnified energy, was all too much when blooming in the human world. It caused them to overload. The sun charms slowly 'let out some of the air.' They dispersed some of the energy. Rachel shook her head. Of course it meant that. Kaylah had already explained the trade-off when using those charms in the first place. She'd described the negative side effect as 'dulling their ultimate potential.' Some of that dispersed energy, once siphoned off to protect them during their bloom, was gone for good.

"You're right," Rachel said, meeting Catrina's gaze. "The sun sends some of the energy out, so the swirl probably keeps it in."

Catrina's lips twitched into a triumphant grin.

"You can say it. 'I told you so.'"

Catrina's smile grew. "That would be undignified of me. I'll just leave it at 'you're welcome.'"

Rachel rolled her eyes, wearing a smile of her own. "Come on, let's get back to work."

Heading back to their study tent with the scroll and water bottle, Rachel found renewed hope.

The swirl keeps energy in. Or… maybe concentrates it? Condenses it? But why would we condense energy?

Ducking back into the tent, she set the new scroll aside and kept searching for clues. By the time dinner approached, Rachel knew exactly what she needed to do, if for no other reason than to shut her curiosity up.

"I know we just got here, but how about we make a super quick trip back to Eric's? You can see if your mom's had a miraculous change of heart."

Catrina was willing to follow Rachel around on the adventure. Nathan and the other guards in the human world were surprised to see them back so soon, and rushed them to Eric's place at Rachel's request.

"What's up?" Eric asked as they sat down in the living room of the safe house. "They didn't give me any updates."

"Nothing yet. But…" Rachel scrunched her face. "I need to ask you some personal questions." She made sure Catrina had already gone upstairs, so she and Lady Vera couldn't overhear.

"Okaaay…" Eric said.

"You and Kaylah. I know she has a lot of grand ideas about what she wants. One includes bringing our unbloomed girls home. They're essentially humans. Has she ever talked about that with you? It's… I just wondered … what you guys had in mind for your relationship when this is all over…"

"It's a pipe dream." A sad longing tinged his voice. "Their stories talk about humans discovering the Green Lands centuries ago. So, we hoped we could find a way in. But I think that's even more complicated than your unbloomed Seeders, because all of you were at least born with that in your genes—the energy. Or hatched, or whatever, over there."

Rachel sat straighter, silently putting the pieces together. "You're right. Our powers are latent, dormant, we Seeder women. You don't think that…" She asked for his phone and did a quick search. "Cogo. Condense. We might waste some time, or we might make history! Do we always have a human stationed at the cave for security?"

He furrowed his brow in confusion. "Yes. Always, at least one of each of our kinds."

"Great. I'll be in touch." She radiated her excitement.

Their driver prepared to take Rachel and Catrina back to the cave. Unfortunately, Catrina hadn't made much progress with her mom, though they couldn't expect too much. Now that Catrina had been in camp, the Seeder guards at the safe house wouldn't allow her to speak unsupervised with Lady Vera, fearful she might pass secrets to her and they'd somehow make their way to Soren's forces.

As soon as Rachel and Catrina got back to the Green Lands, they went straight to Zeus's garden—he'd been bummed out by not being able to help more right now, and his village wasn't all that much farther from the cave than camp was.

"Well, hello!" he said, setting down some pruning shears.

"Sorry, I'm in a rush, and you said you'd be willing to help if I needed it."

"Yeah, anything."

"I need jade, someone that can carve it, a matriarch, and … you, if you're willing to try something out." Rachel grinned, her hope building.

Chapter 37

THEY RAPIDLY PUT TOGETHER EVERYTHING Rachel needed for her experiment. Her mind was running a mile a minute, feverishly connecting the dots, seeing the chain reaction this discovery could cause. Jade was blessed with energy by a Seeder matriarch, using the newer word 'cogo.' The swirl was carved into it. All they had to do was see if Zeus had latent energy—the son of a being with powers, sprouted in a world full of energy.

Rachel brought Zeus and Catrina to the cave entrance the next day, practically bouncing on the balls of her feet. "Okay, I think just holding it will be fine, but hold it tight in your hand, so the symbol makes contact with your skin at all times while you're going through."

"You really think the swirl symbol would work for him?" Catrina asked. "I still think the sun symbol would better fit your theory. If he has hidden energy, wouldn't you want to use the sun one to draw it out? Not make it hide more?"

Rachel sighed, now starting to doubt herself. "I was thinking maybe his energy is already dispersed in his body, and it needs something to pull it together, to make it stronger. Maybe even drawing in external energy?"

Catrina shrugged, and Rachel continued.

"Well, we have this one made, and we came all the way out here. Let's try it first." Her personal blooming necklace was still in South Fortinda where she'd left it, but if this didn't work, Saff would probably loan hers, or they'd get another one made up.

Zeus glanced between the girls warily. "You're really not all that sure what's going to happen?"

"I, uh… Well…" Rachel hesitated. Saff had endured pretty significant pain when experimenting with her powers and rifting. But Saff had also once posed a rather curious question about green-folk abilities—about whether green folk could sense the energy within each other. They'd dismissed the idea a while back, because Saff's close call had been with an Ivy assassin *before* she began her bloom. But Kaylah had commented that maybe some people could sense that hidden energy better. Maybe they were right?

Rachel looked Zeus over. Just like any of the guys with powers, he was once a seedling, one who had sprouted like any other Seeder. But once he grew into more of a standard human form, any uniquely Seeder abilities ceased. He was like any unbloomed girl, but his abilities had been stunted. She cringed just thinking of that label, but there had to be something inside him still.

"I'm confident you'll be fine." She hesitated once more with added guilt. "You'll probably just keep walking, like all the girls that have experimented at this cave, when they've tried to go more than once in a day. None of them experienced anything harmful, but I wouldn't blame you if you didn't want to go."

He puffed out his chest. "I want to go. Just wondering if I should have thought up some clever last words, just in case."

Rachel gave him a smile. "I'll be right behind you."

While Ivies could only form a rift for themselves, or make it large enough to accompany a linked female Seeder, Seeders had always been able to form a rift for more than just themselves.

Brothers and fathers accompanying their girls home did it all the time in the air. Rachel surmised that all Zeus needed was this charm and someone else to open the doorway for him. She stepped forward and opened a rift in the air at the cave entrance.

He took a deep breath and walked forward—disappearing from sight.

Rachel squealed, throwing a glance at Catrina. They shared a smile. "I won't say anything undignified," Rachel said.

Catrina giggled and remained with her guards while Rachel quickly followed after Zeus.

Rachel was greeted on the other side by half a dozen guards and an extremely stunned Zeus. She bit her lip and tears came to her eyes. "We did it! We really did it! Zeus: Welcome to the human world!" She jumped up and down and gave him a hug. "I promise you'll get the charm back to go home, but let me try something first."

"Okay…" He handed her the stone, and she asked the guards for a human volunteer. Maybe, just maybe, there was latent energy in these humans no one knew about. They opened a rift at the cave entrance, and the human volunteer walked forward—and kept walking.

She frowned. "Okay. I knew that one might be more of a long shot. Thank you for being willing to try."

She handed the charm back to Zeus and rubbed her temples. Humans couldn't do it. At least not this easily. But Seeders without powers, they could! Bringing back unbloomed girls was still irresponsible—they had nowhere to take them with how slow the poison cleanup was, and they couldn't contribute to their own safety. But this discovery, in and of itself, could win them the war. This was the thing that was going to tip the balance.

She asked to borrow a cell phone and called Eric. Despite the Seeders' caution with Eric after Kaylah went missing, he was still a strong ally. He was tech-savvy and had been one of the first humans in Unitas. His work was monitored more closely by Unitas, but he continued to help with their programming, hacking, and tracking efforts. Eric picked up the phone after a couple of rings.

"Do we have any that have *started* the blooming process," Rachel asked, "that would be ready to go home tonight or tomorrow?"

"Uh … maybe? Did … you figure it out? They can't go through that kind of pain by just taking off their charms to finish the change; you know that."

She was still grinning ear to ear. "I haven't figured out humans. But I can get Seeder girls home, without the pain."

He agreed to reach out to his contacts; he'd send someone over to the camp once he could find anyone willing and able.

It was getting late, so Rachel escorted Zeus back home. She asked him to do whatever was necessary to have several more charms just like it made up, ASAP. She needed to run back and talk to Saff and Devin, but before she could go, Zeus grabbed her hands.

"Thank you, Rachel. I know this means a lot to our people, but it means something personal to me, too. It opens a whole new world of possibilities." His eyes and smile were trained on her. "I knew we were meant to meet for a reason."

She squeezed his hands. "Then I'm glad you got the honor of being the first. In this world or that one, you're bound to meet the right girl for you. You've got a lot of potential." She gave him a bear hug.

She ran off to Saff and Devin's tent to share the update, leaving Catrina at their sleeping tent along the way. Both Saff and Devin were excited to hear the news. They realized the implications, if they could actually get partially-bloomed girls back faster. So far, only fully-bloomed girls could rift, even with the new cave rifts. But if they came back earlier… It took almost as much time for a tempered bloom to happen, as it did for them to train and rift. They'd cut their time in half. They could have twice as many girls with energy returning, quickly!

After a few minutes of excited chatter with Saff and Devin, Rachel returned to her tent, apologizing for leaving Catrina alone. Catrina had been supportive, but not exactly giddy about this discovery after Rachel and Zeus returned to the Green Lands. Rachel hadn't expected it to be a big deal for Catrina. It really didn't mean as much to her, personally. But, in a way, it did.

"Do you think it would work for Ivies without powers, too?" Catrina asked.

"I … don't know. I know some of our stuff works across species, but not everything. Maybe…"

Catrina gave her a hesitant smile. "I'd love for Guillen to be able to go somewhere new. Start fresh. Not have people hate him."

Rachel frowned, an image playing through her mind of Guillen leaving her to follow his dreams of spending time with humans. "Yeah. We'll definitely try it when we get a chance. Let's head to bed."

It took Rachel eons to fall asleep. Between the adrenaline and her thoughts … it didn't come easy. She thought of Kaylah, praying she was alright, and wishing she could share the news of their accomplishment. She thought of Guillen, and the implications of the discovery she'd just made. Catrina was right—he deserved a chance at human life. Even if the war was won in a day, it would take *years* for his society to alter their ways. He shouldn't have to wait a single day to be treated fairly. And if Magda and Lady Vera were any indication of the way people felt … they would have a rough go at it, trying to have a relationship publicly.

Rachel's heart sank. He loved her—he would choose Rachel. She couldn't go live with him over in the human world. Nothing in their research had indicated any changes to that knowledge of their limitations. But could she be so selfish as to ask him to stay…

Shortly after she finally found sleep, Rachel was woken by a messenger.

"Sorry, Eric thought you'd want to know right away. He said he'll have two waiting nearby, in the morning."

Excitement entered the tent, while any hopes of sleep exited. She volunteered to help patrol the camp during the night, to keep busy. When it was barely dawn, she went to Saff's tent.

Saff emerged, yawning. "You know, Rachel, I love you, but sometimes a woman just wants to spend some more time with her husband in the morning."

Rachel blushed. She may not be married, but she knew that desire. "Sorry… I've been up all night and couldn't wait."

"Why all night?" Saff scrunched her eyebrows. "You're already worn down from a round trip yesterday. Sit down, crazy woman."

Rachel chuckled. "That's exactly it—I can't go. It hasn't been a full day for me. But I picked up a second charm from the craftsmen, and I need someone to take them through. The girls should be there any time."

Saff smiled warmly. This would be her second trip through the new cave, and the first time alone. "I'd be honored."

***

Rachel paced impatiently. Catrina joined her at the cave, much calmer than Rachel. "They're probably just taking a while to get there, even with those cars."

Rachel cupped her hands over her mouth once Saff arrived with two girls. The girls' faces were plastered with the usual amazement of first-timers to the Green Lands. They were promptly ushered to camp, where Devin was waiting for them.

The girls sat on a pair of chairs, clearly intimidated to be in a new place, with new people and a growing audience.

~

"Hi, I'm Devin. We're all excited to get to know you. They told you about the change and everything, right?"

The girls nodded. One had been wearing the charm for a month already, the other, just a few days. Saff was now holding on to their original charms—they'd had to take them off so the new ones would work for a rift. It could take hours for them to really feel sick, as she recalled from her own unfortunate blooming. She prayed they were right about it being different back home in the Green Lands.

Within no time, the girls' eyes, hair, and skin began to glow. The one who had been further along in her blooming changed faster.

"This is how it's supposed to be, right? This is okay?" one asked, fear growing in her eyes.

"You're not hurting?" Devin asked.

"No…"

"Then you're just fine." Devin shared anxious glances with Saff, then offered the girls water to drink, in case it could help. He'd only ever actually seen the change in his wife, midway through the process, and it had been brutal. The fact that these girls were this lit up, so quickly, and feeling *nothing*…

A half hour into the change, the one who was farther along was so bright that the observers were beginning to squint. Almost as quickly as the change started, it faded away. Once she was down to just yellow hair and glowing green eyes, Devin coached her about channeling her energy—from her heart to her hand. A ball of light rested in the palm of her hand. He then asked permission to access it. Devin hovered his hand over the girl's and flicked his wrist at the ground. The darts produced were phenomenal. *Every* Seeder who had gathered to watch now stood with their mouths open.

"Wow," Devin whispered in reverence.

~

Rachel grinned triumphantly. *Definitely more powerful than Saff, and probably anyone in living generations of matriarchs.* "Give me a couple dozen girls to bloom in the Green Lands, and we'll see how powerful they can make our walls. If that's all they do, from the safety of the temples … how many people can we spare for a march on the palace? How quickly can we end this thing?"

~

Saff shared a knowing grin. Every risk they'd taken, every sacrifice—it had been worth it. "We need to get the word back to Eric. Let's bring them home. And make a home they can be safe in."

"I'm going to see how those charms are coming along," Rachel said.

"Rachel," Saff scolded. "Sleep."

Rachel smirked. "I'll try. First, charms."

***

After checking their progress on making more charms, Rachel relented and decided to give sleep another go. Catrina followed her back to their tent, not having much choice in the matter.

"Wasn't that cool?" Rachel exclaimed. "No living Seeders have gotten to see that before, but you got to." Her excitement had her almost bursting at the seams.

Catrina scrunched her face. "Yeah, I guess that was interesting."

"Not easily impressed, huh?" Rachel lay down on her cot.

Catrina fidgeted with her hands. "It … actually kind of worries me."

Rachel sat up. "Why?"

Catrina bobbed her head back and forth, easing herself down onto the edge of her own cot. "Your people are already pretty powerful. Each of our peoples have limitations, but … what you just showed me, that looked like *a lot* more."

Rachel frowned. "They teach a lot of propaganda in history classes, even Kaylah admits that. I know your people feel like you were wronged, but we're taught differently. What the actual truth is, maybe we'll never really know. Just because we're more powerful, doesn't mean we're going to harm your people or try to take over." She considered something else Kaylah had once said, about their dirty nickname and Ivy fears of Seeder overpopulation. "I think weeds are just plants in unwanted places. That doesn't mean they're bad, or not pretty. Honey bees still like them, right? We just want to be safe and left to live our lives."

Catrina looked at the ground, digging her heel into the packed soil. "It's easy to dream like that, but power corrupts. Look at my brother, his kind. They don't have any, and they're treated like scum."

"Hey." Rachel gave her a half-smile. "I *do* think about your brother. A lot. I'm well aware he doesn't have powers. And I do. And we should be enemies. But what have I done to him or for him, with those powers?"

Catrina nodded. "I wish more people … were like you."

That melted Rachel's heart. She wanted nothing more than to give Catrina a hug, but she had a feeling Catrina wouldn't be fond of that, not yet. "Have some faith. My people have men like that too, and we don't treat them like Guillen, right? It's not just me."

"You're right. It's actually kind of nice over here. The way people talk to, and about, each other." She threw a glance at a notebook in the corner of their tent. "Anyway, I should let you sleep. I'll quietly look over our notes again."

Rachel lay back down. "Thanks for the chat. I like you too, remember that." Her smile faded. "One last thing… We probably shouldn't mention this development to your mom. I don't imagine she'd take the 'more power' thing well."

Catrina pursed her lips, flipping open the notebook. "No. I don't imagine she would."

Rachel added that to her to-do list—make sure the new girls remained a secret. They'd already made an irresponsible display today. What if a spy let Soren know about these new girls? Even without Kaylah's help, the War Vines were primed and awaiting replacement girls to power Soren's now-shrinking advantage. He would lust after that energy. He would do anything to have it.

Chapter 38

PARTIALLY-BLOOMED SEEDER GIRLS trickled into the Unitas camp with increasing speed. Councils met. Plans were formed. There was finally hope on the horizon, and not just to end the last hellish year.

This would be the one to end it all.

Rachel found it hard to hear the various strategies discussed in meetings she, Saff, and Ginger were invited to, but they had to be prepared for anything. What if Kaylah didn't survive? Seeders would no longer be content to slink back to the human world with split families. And Lady Vera didn't seem like a suitable replacement once Soren was out of the picture.

They did discuss occupation, as a last resort—to do what they had to, just until peace could be organized. They talked about what they would do if Kaylah had indeed betrayed them. Either intentionally, or under duress. Her life hung in the balance.

While they couldn't implement many of the battle tactics she'd previously shared, in case they had been tortured out of her, her ideals were still on the table. They would rescue Kaylah, the Unitas leader, and continue to work with her to heal their lands and societies. The remaining Seeder girl in the palace would be saved, the War Vines destroyed.

But no matter what the results were, the means weren't pretty. The Seeders could fly to the palace, saving themselves several skirmishes along the way. But it would still take some time and require breaks, no matter what part of Seeder territory they left from. Ideally, they could fly and shoot darts, but it was nearly impossible to do so simultaneously. To add to that, despite efforts like Jacob's back in Community Ten, more and more archers were popping up in the Neutral Woods amongst Soren's forces.

Most of the Seeders' options were hand-to-hand. All of them bloody. All possible confrontations ended in significant loss of life to break through Soren's troops protecting the palace, and those crawling throughout the woods. And all it took was one scout and one tree, for Soren's troops to be alerted of Seeder movements.

Rachel stressed the cave strategy, that it gave them the element of surprise, located on the border of protected space around the palace that Kaylah had described—which made Ivy rifting near the palace impossible, and Seeder flight above it, near impossible. They could distract Ivy troops with the main attack, and then send in a smaller team much closer on foot from the cave. The council reminded her that no progress had been made on that account— they couldn't wait forever.

With Soren down from six to just one Seeder hostage powering the massive War Vines, the Seeders would be able to shift some of their focus in training and fighting, spending less time protecting their border walls.

As the council discussions came to a close, a messenger arrived.

The leader of the meeting read the latest update with a grim expression. "Their one hostage will soon turn to four."

Gasps filled the room.

She went on to explain, "One of our safe houses was compromised. They've taken three. We're not sure where they're at right now."

Rachel's jaw dropped. "Is … you-know-who safe?" *And my mom?*

The leader nodded. Even in camp and on the council, they entrusted very few with the information about Lady Vera and Catrina. Few knew they were even in custody, or their true identities, or where they were being kept. "We're confident on that safe house for now; it's disconnected enough. But we're looking into how this breach happened."

The names of the kidnapped and their Unitas protectors—now dead—were read off. Rachel's mom was still safe. Going by the breath of air that whooshed out of Saff, she didn't recognize the names, either. She had significantly more people to be worried about after giving Unitas her and Devin's host family names to help in the cause.

Rachel could give a sigh of relief, albeit the tiniest of sighs. Though, her anxiety still rose about a breach in their safe houses at all. Soren had seemed barely competent at stepping into his parents' and uncle's shoes. But he'd just reminded Unitas how serious he was.

The leader explained the situation, that the girls were midbloom with charms on. From Rachel's experience, they didn't hook them up to the War Vines until the girls were actually rooted, which could take months … unless they removed the charms. Her stomach churned at the torture. Could they drag someone in a coma through a rift? Would they be as efficient on the War Vines if they were in a coma?

Unitas prioritized retaking a strip of Neutral Woods between camp and Seeder borders, to allow for passage on foot again.

A quota was set. After a certain number of freshly bloomed girls returned and were trained on the walls, the march would begin. They were done waiting.

***

Much to Rachel's relief, word had gotten back from Guillen. He was safe—for now. She'd had a horrible nightmare about him again, two nights prior. This time, Eric was in the dream and finally let her read the contents of his private letter. In it, Guillen left her a goodbye note, in case he didn't make it out alive. It soured her whole day, and she almost stormed through the cave, just to rip the letter from Eric's hands to make sure it wasn't true.

But Guillen was safe—for now. He was busy rallying support, still undiscovered. If the cave failed, maybe Guillen could still find a way to help sneak people closer. Either way, they needed a new tactic other than just marching up to the palace. It had been breached twice already; Soren wasn't likely to let anything slip a third time. They needed a new option. They needed the help of someone who grew up in that palace.

"You're sure she won't budge? Honestly, just some kind of map would help," Rachel pleaded with Catrina on behalf of Kaylah, the Seeder girl who had been tortured there for months now, and the three new girls—she was desperate.

"No." Catrina shook her head. "She used to like Kaylah, but she doesn't support her now that she knows what she's fighting for."

Rachel bunched her eyebrows, exasperated. "So, she'd rather have Soren be a fake king?"

"No. She hates that, too."

Rachel threw her hands up in the air. "Then, what? I thought she didn't want to rule."

"Also a no."

"Well, she has to go with one of the three options, doesn't she?"

Catrina bit her lip in thought. "Honestly, I think she'd prefer *I* be queen at this point."

Rachel stopped pacing the research tent. "But doesn't that mean both she and Kaylah would have to die first?"

"No."

Rachel stared her down, eyes wide open. "What do you mean? The queen controls the Mother Vines. When Kaylah's mom died, the control went to her. It follows the matriarchal line, right? How can you skip a generation?"

"The queen can choose," Catrina stated, as though it were common knowledge. "She can abdicate and assign that power to the next in line. It can't be taken from her, and it still has to follow the line. That's why Soren can't just kill Kaylah and have his wife control them." She rocked her head side to side. "If Kaylah *did* die, which I don't want, then it would fall to my mother, but she could give it to me willingly."

Rachel drew a deep breath, more than a tad annoyed. "How is it possible no one ever mentioned that?"

"I doubt you know a lot of things about our royal ways." Catrina gently raised her eyebrows. "And I'm guessing if Kaylah never mentioned it, it's because she intends to rule."

"Would *you* want to rule, if given the choice?"

Catrina shifted in her chair. "When you're this close to the crown, you grow up imagining it. But when you're fourth in line, you know it's not likely. I would do it, but only if Kaylah weren't an option."

An idea sprouted in Rachel's mind. She and Catrina rifted over to the human world again. Catrina waited with the cave's guards while Rachel talked privately with Eric. They strolled the woods near the cave, but only after the on-duty Unitas supervisor gave her a stern and direct order to watch what she discussed with Eric.

"Thanks for coming all the way out here. I just figured it would save us some time, and I wanted to talk in person," Rachel said.

"No problem, seriously. I get stir-crazy in that place." He laughed half-heartedly. "Especially with that high-and-mighty 'guest.'"

"Yeah, sorry. She's a pill."

Eric tapped a tree trunk with his shoe as they passed. "She doesn't hate me as much as Seeders, but she still has *no* respect for a human like me. She's hopeless. I'd recommend transferring her to another safe house if she weren't such a valuable political refugee."

"Speaking of that. You're sure the network is still safe?" Rachel stopped to face him. "Those girls."

He gave her a look of dismay. "Yes. Practically no one knows where Lady Vera is. And we're adding extra security." His nostrils flared. "Plus, now that they don't have to worry about *me* being the leak…"

If that wasn't a kick-'em-when-they're-down moment, Rachel didn't know what was. The woman he loved—the woman he'd sacrificed a normal life for—was missing, probably tortured or dead right now. And *both* the Seeder and Ivy leaders of Unitas (excluding Ginger) had voted to curtail Eric's participation. Having been central in coordinating safe houses from the beginning, he was a prime suspect for the latest girls' kidnappings. Either that, or they were punishing him for the leak because they supposed Kaylah might have given information to Soren under duress, or willingly.

The fact of the matter was—Soren might have just gotten lucky. At least that was what Rachel kept trying to tell herself. It wasn't like his assassins hadn't continued roaming the human world in search of more Seeder girls.

Aching inside, Rachel tried to remember what Guillen had told her about taking too much blame on herself. "Are we doing enough to secure the caves? Could we have a traitor that would bring those girls through, bloom them over there, and then turn them over to Soren?" She'd gone over the possibilities constantly. Either Soren was planning ahead and waiting out their blooms, to force them through a rift like he had with her and the other five… Or he could force their bloom by removing the charms—she cringed at the torture that strategy involved. Or … maybe their latest bloom discovery was known already by a spy. Maybe he knew their potential, his spies would get their hands on the charms, and they'd go through the caves. Or, worse yet, perhaps they knew by now how to make their own cave rifts.

Rachel was rattling off all of her suspicions, starting to hyperventilate.

"Rachel." Eric stopped her, holding her head in place with both hands, getting her full attention. "Calm down."

She focused on her breathing as his friendly eyes calmed her.

"First of all," he countered, "you can't stop trusting everyone. They could only make a new cave with *two* Seeders *that have their powers,* assuming they even knew how to." He stared into her eyes, as if to emphasize his logic. "And they'd need the new charms, which are *well-guarded.* Remember that Soren's family has been working on this for *years.* He's probably just waiting out their bloom here, okay?"

She swallowed hard, looking at the ground as Eric removed his hands. "They're not holding back on troops. He's serious. And you don't know him like I do. He'd force the change." She huffed and shook her head. "Heck, if they slipped into a coma from the change, then he wouldn't have to waste any poison to subdue them."

She looked up to see him frowning.

"You could be right about that," he said. "But still—we've got the cavalry out looking for them. And I refuse to believe they'd have the added benefit of a Green Lands bloom, okay?"

She nodded, conceding the fact that their cause would have to be riddled with a lot more traitors to pull that off. Soren probably didn't even know taking off their charms early gave them a boost in energy capacity, even when done in the human world, like with Saff. Unless he'd gotten information from Kaylah…

Despite fighting it, Rachel began to cry. "I miss her. I just… I'm done with all of this."

His eyes misted over as well. "Me too." He pulled her in for a hug. "We're in the final stretch; I can feel it. We'll get to see her soon enough."

She stood in Eric's arms for a couple of minutes, grateful her best friend had good taste, that she'd found someone so considerate. Rachel lingered longer—Eric needed this too. It had to be hard to be stoic through all of this, so disconnected and helpless.

When they pulled apart, she sniffled and gave him a reassuring smile. He wiped at a tear on his cheek and shoved his hands in his pockets.

"About Kaylah…" She wrung her hands. "And you… I'm going to have to dive back into sensitive territory."

He chuckled. "At this point, my life is your life. Unitas. Out with it."

"You and Kaylah. What were the plans? If she could figure out a way to get you into our realm? And if she couldn't? Did she discuss abdicating?"

Eric blew out a puff of air. "If we can figure it out, I planned to join her. I don't know what all that looks like, and we know it might be rough. Her people aren't likely to easily accept a king, or whatever I'd be, that's human. Not right away. But I have been taking college courses on politics and economics and stuff."

Rachel smiled. "Does that mean you two are engaged?"

He blushed, his eyes darting around. "Yeah. I asked. She said yes. It's just not public, for obvious reasons."

She beamed. "I'm happy for you. That's *so* great. And I know that it's helping her fight over there."

He flashed a sad smile. "Thanks. That makes me feel better."

She gave him a sympathetic frown. "And … what were the plans if she couldn't bring you over?"

"I really don't want to think about it," he said, his tone dejected, reaching out to touch a branch on a nearby tree as they passed. "I can't imagine her leaving me, but I also couldn't forgive myself if she turned her back on her people. We toyed with the idea of reorganizing things so she played a much less significant role. So she could spend more time over here."

Rachel nodded thoughtfully before responding. That sucked. That kind of life was no couple's ideal. It was worse than being married to a trucker or pilot, because at least *they* got to enjoy each other's company at a mutual home. Kaylah was to be the queen of half of the Green Lands, and she fiercely loved her people and culture. Eric may never be able to fully be part of it. Rachel ignored the avalanche of guilt headed her way as she wished the charm that worked for Zeus had worked for humans as well.

Shaking away the cascade of negativity, Rachel transitioned to the main reason for her visit. "I brought Catrina today because I think the two of you can get Lady Vera to talk. We need to know how to get inside the palace. Every possible entrance. Especially the ones Soren wouldn't think about."

Eric lifted an eyebrow. "How?"

A grin formed on Rachel's lips. "Let's manipulate that bitch."

He poorly stifled a laugh—Rachel rarely swore.

"Catrina is *certain* that her mom would prefer Catrina ruled, out of the options available, instead of Soren, Kaylah, or even Lady Vera herself. If we can get her to think her daughter will be queen if she helps us … we're as good as gold. Tell her Kaylah wanted to turn it over. Tell her Kaylah's dead. Tell her we changed our strategy. I don't really care. Just get me those locations."

Eric smiled. "We'll make it happen." They began walking back to their original meetup point. "What if we can't manipulate it out of her? I'm not a soldier, but plenty in Unitas are… What if we needed to … take it further? Hurt her?"

Rachel's stomach knotted. No one liked Lady Vera, least of all Rachel. But Guillen had forgiven her on some level for her abuse in his childhood. And Eric was asking if they could rough her up? Rachel stared at her feet. "That's not really fair to ask me, you know?" She met his eyes, and he gave an understanding frown. "I'm not the one that calls the shots, though. So … just… You didn't bring it up with me, okay?"

Eric nodded. "We'll obviously try with Catrina first."

They strolled in silence for a while. Rachel considered his question further. What was one person, compared to the millions in the Green Lands? One *rotten* person, compared to just Kaylah? Wasn't this problem still in existence because Seeders had hedged their bets for so long?

"Unofficially, Eric?"

He glanced her way.

"I didn't say 'no.'"

He nodded again, squinting with determination. "One way or another, we'll get it done."

***

Rachel went back to Kaylah's books while Eric and Catrina sorted out Lady Vera, hopefully. She felt pulled to Kaylah's notes in particular, trying to pick up where she'd left off. Saff had said Kaylah had thought she was close to a breakthrough.

One paper had columns of names, with the first column listing all of the Seeder village names. They all ended with the same letter; Rachel had only previously thought the trend poetic. But seeing them listed on a piece of paper made it stick out. Fortinda, Siqendra, all of them—they ended with the letter A.

There was a column of Ivy rift locations; they ended in a different letter of the alphabet.

A third column listed human-world rift names. Again, they all shared an ending letter.

A fourth column had the names of the newly activated cave locations. Scribbled at the top of the paper were the old symbols Rachel had seen scratched into the cave wall in Ivy territory, near the palace. The translation—it ended in a different letter altogether.

Kaylah had underlined the ending letter.

Highlighted it.

Circled it.

She'd had it at the tips of her fingers, so close. She'd known it had meaning.

If the rift didn't enter or exit a known Seeder, Ivy, or human-world location … what was the fourth option? Could there be … another realm?

Rachel shook the idea from her head. No one had ever mentioned anything like that. No stories, no fairy tales, no history books. It had to mean this was the kind of thing they were looking for. The fourth ending meant it was intra–Green Lands. But how to work it? Nothing they'd tried had shown any promise. They'd even tried rifting to the old palace cave using the new swirl charm, hoping that was all it would take since it condensed energy, and maybe they just hadn't put enough energy into their attempted rifts.

Rachel dreaded the thought of having to find another preexisting cave that magically connected to it. Or having to create one, like those they were now using in the human world. There was no time to play around with that.

***

Rachel woke with a sore neck, having fallen asleep while reading. Catrina had woken her up, teeming with pride. "It took all day, but guess what my mother gave us?" She practically danced around the tent. "Let's get my cousin back!" She opened her eyes wide and added with some drama, "The one who's nice to my brother, and *much* better prepared to lead than the rest of us in the family."

Rachel chuckled, rubbing her neck with a hint of a glow to her fingers. She was beyond grateful that Catrina's 'sweet girl / youngest child / only heir' charms had worked on her mom, and that they hadn't been forced to try anything else. "That's great! Really." She cracked her neck. "Look at this page with me. I'm assuming the council has the palace plans already?"

"Yes. First thing before I came here."

"Great. Now we have to do our part. We're on the clock. This paper's about the cave. And you know Ivy fairy tales…"

Catrina looked it over, and Rachel explained what she'd surmised so far.

"Why did she draw the sun and swirl symbols?" Catrina asked, pointing to the paper.

The old language name had been written on the paper; in front of it was the sun, then a dash. Behind it, a swirl.

"I'm sure she was just doodling while trying to put it together," Rachel said.

Catrina raised her eyebrows, skeptical. "But she didn't seem to know the swirl symbol meant anything."

"You're … right…"

Rachel closed her eyes, reminding herself what that cave looked like. It had been so long ago. And it had been dark. And she'd been traumatized. And distracted by a handsome man, who was starting to distract her all over again as she remembered his distraction… She opened her eyes. "I didn't think anything of them. They were just like doodles on the cave walls. They were smaller and weren't weird like the other symbols, so I just filed them away as nothing special."

Catrina tilted her head to the side. "Anything else you forgot from the cave that you might remember now?"

Rachel tapped her fingers on the table, double-checking her memories. "No. That's it. If there's something else, I didn't notice it."

Saff popped her head in the tent. "How's it going?"

Rachel smiled. "Come join us, Miss Four-Point-Oh."

Saff chuckled, sitting down. "Those grades don't matter in the Green Lands. And my theory about using that swirl charm to get to the other cave didn't pan out. But I'm happy for a breather. What's up?"

They ran through the details with her.

"Okay." Saff nodded thoughtfully. "If the symbols mean something, maybe we just need to think the associated words before and after the location name?"

Catrina wrinkled her nose. "But the words don't mean anything without the jade, right?"

Rachel sighed. "True."

Catrina sat down between them. "You keep asking about fairy tales, our origins. Let's go over those again."

They pulled out a fairly thick book that an Ivy in Unitas had smuggled into camp for Kaylah. It was half burned. Some of the pages were completely lost, but several were partially legible, though not enough to make sense of anything.

Focusing intently on each page, Catrina read out loud the fairy tales and poems, one by one. She had to pause and correct herself several times.

"You really know those well," Rachel remarked. "Especially for having half of the pages missing."

Catrina shyly looked back down at the book. "Yeah, I spent a lot of time in my room reading as a little girl."

Saff wouldn't have known the significance of that, having never met Lady Vera, having never heard how Guillen came by the large scar on his face, but Rachel did. She would have hidden in her room a lot as a child, too, if one of her parents had been like Lady Vera.

~

Catrina cleared her throat and continued to read the Ivy fairy tales, filling in the gaps.

The one in particular that pulled Saff in wasn't a story about how botanical beings had come to be—despite how fantastical those stories were. It took place before that—how the Green Lands had been discovered in the first place. Or more appropriately, how *rifting* had been discovered. Discovered, not necessarily created. Just like Saff with the story, green folk had been pulled in—literally.

"Green Stone, Green Land, Green Eyes—that was the order, three.
Push and Pull of the earth, like Ebb and Flow of the sea.
Rich Soil and Air shared by Green Folk, all Kin:
The Temptations and Prizes that Pulled them In."

Saff loved poetry thanks to her English classes in high school. Hearing those words, it finally made sense to Saff why normal human electronics didn't work in this realm, and why there was turbulence after passing through a Seeder rift to the human side. She smiled. "That's awesome! I think I get it."

Catrina and Rachel still seemed confused by the mysterious grand revelation.

"Green stone—Jade. It was crucial to the discovery. Like we've used it to get Zeus and our girls back. Push and Pull. The sun symbol disperses, dissipates; it *pushes*. The swirling symbol gathers, collects, concentrates; it *pulls*."

As it clicked for Rachel, a lightkeeper lit in her eyes. "It's like a friggin' magnet!"

Catrina squinted. "Like, we need one of the symbols on the special jade, on each side?"

"I think that's *exactly* it!" Saff could barely contain her excitement. "And if we want to end up at the cave by the palace, to be *pulled* there, we need someone in that cave with the right jade."

Chapter 39

RACHEL AGREED WITH SAFF'S SUGGESTION that they discuss their hypothesis with Ginger, as she'd been left to pick up the pieces after Kaylah's disappearance. Ginger was doing her best to liaise.

Rachel gave Ginger a huge hug once she and Saff entered Ginger's tent. They'd hardly gotten any time to chat in passing.

"How can I help you young ladies?" Ginger asked with an exhausted, forced smile.

Rachel and Saff followed her, sitting down. They explained the need to get someone to the cave.

Ginger nodded thoughtfully. "Guillen's network is all on standby, in close proximity to the area. Once we get him—"

"No!" Rachel blurted. Visions of him lying on the ground, bleeding out, danced on her heartstrings. "Anyone but Guillen."

Ginger sat back. "Why? Kaylah trusted him to get you there and back safely."

Rachel shook her head, her chest caving in. "Your kingdom is empty. Our walls are barely even at risk of a breach again with only one girl left on the Vines. Their attacks have calmed down. Where do you think those soldiers are? Protecting Soren as he cowers in the palace. That cave is inside the ring of protection from rifting. They'll be guarding that whole perimeter he'd have to cross."

Ginger gestured at Rachel with her hands. "Isn't that why we need that cave so badly? Because it'll bypass the vast majority of Soren's defenses?"

"You're assigning him a suicide mission!" Tears pooled in Rachel's eyes. "Anyone but him. I love him."

Ginger scanned Rachel's face. "If it's not him, it's someone else's loved one. And if you love Kaylah, too, you want the best person there to make it happen."

Rachel looked down, sniffling. "He's not invincible. He almost died. I barely healed him in time."

Saff quietly reached over and squeezed one of Rachel's hands.

"Did Kaylah ever tell you when she first dedicated herself wholeheartedly to this movement?" Ginger asked.

Rachel looked up, wiping away tears. "No."

Ginger gave her a soft smile. "Or who her first recruit was? Over four years ago?"

"I have a feeling you're going to say Guillen," Rachel half breathed.

Ginger nodded. "Sometimes, I think they recruited each other. I don't know him well, but when Kaylah finally brought Nathan and me into the loop, we knew he was key in this. Guillen knows those woods and mountains likely better than anyone. He knows the risks. Let him do this."

Fighting more tears, all Rachel could muster was a whisper. "Yeah."

~

While Saff empathized with Rachel, Ginger's logic *was* a bit of a stretch. "But … how?" Saff asked. "Guillen's network can't be that huge, that they can bust through a line of Ivy soldiers we ourselves are afraid to take on, just to get inside that cave."

Ginger distracted herself, stacking papers on her desk and straightening them. "Like I said, he knows those mountains."

"But … how?" Rachel echoed. "He never talked about spending time in those mountains… And when they rescued me, Kaylah made a diversion, and the palace hadn't been expecting the rescue."

Ginger still wouldn't look up. "It'll be fine. Just trust me."

Saff may not have picked up on her parents' lies to her over the years as they'd concealed her true nature as a Seeder, but she'd fine-tuned her lie detector since then. "Ginger." Her tone was threatening. "What are you hiding?"

"You always assume the worst, Saff." Ginger finally met her gaze.

"Maybe I'm just good at detecting BS. Is this something else our council would be shocked to hear if I brought it up in one of our meetings?"

Ginger's countenance turned dark. "Don't shoot yourself in the foot. You know too much already, and the only reason you're permitted into *any* planning meetings is because *I* bring you."

"I'm permitted into meetings because Kaylah started inviting me, because I'm trustworthy."

Leaning forward, Ginger looked Saff squarely in the eyes. "And who sits in Kaylah's stead now?"

"You and Kaylah *promised* you never lied to our council. If you're hiding something from them…"

"We never lied. I never lied about that. That doesn't mean we told them *everything*."

Saff couldn't help but think Kaylah and Ginger played fast and loose with the definition of 'truth.'

"Kaylah's always had a contingency plan. Guillen's working on that right now."

Rachel piped up, her face veiled in disappointment. "Soren said that once, after he… He always had backup plans for his backup plans."

"Rach, don't equate them," Ginger said softly. "They may have been trained by some of the same people, but they're not cut from the same cloth."

"If you can trust anyone, Ginger, it's us," Saff pleaded, gesturing to herself and Rachel.

Ginger shook her head. "I swore an oath." She focused on Rachel. "I can't promise things will work out the way we want, but Guillen will find a way to get that jade charm to the cave for us."

"Or die trying," Rachel whispered, hugging herself.

Ginger gave her a reassuring smile. "Let's give him a chance. And once he has the jade stones, he can make his way to the cave. Once he's safely arrived there, we'll have all the pieces we need." She turned to Saff. "And for once, please let my people carry out part of Kaylah's plans without mucking it up in some way."

***

The first wave of Seeder troops was already set to head out that morning. Jon, who'd somehow still retained Seeder leadership trust, pocketed the new charms and intel for Guillen, rifting out to take them to Guillen on a regular run for information exchange with spies in the Ivy Kingdom.

And now the Seeders marched. And waited.

Jon returned just over twenty-four hours later. The stones were in Guillen's hands—it was up to him.

Saff, Rachel, Catrina, and Ginger found time to meet. There was still a lot they didn't know. This was a long shot. While they had sent a stone with each kind of symbol, their nearby cave wasn't named with the same letter. For now, at least, it might just be a one-way trip.

They were going to give Guillen three days to make his way to the cave, before trying to rift through from the Unitas camp side. Catrina was transferred behind Seeder border walls for safekeeping; Rachel gave her an awkward hug, promising she'd look out for Guillen.

As a last-minute strategic addition, the Unitas camp was to be emptied of all nonessential occupants; only Seeders well trained in battle would be left behind. They planned to set up their strongest troops to fall back and maintain protection of the cave location and Arcadia. It would free up more hands and draw Ivy troops in for an ambush.

Saff worked to pack up her and Devin's belongings while he helped harvest the camp garden before their retreat.

"Saff?" a familiar voice called outside of her tent.

"Flora? Come on in."

Flora entered, and Saff gave her a smile. Instead of reciprocating, Flora held her hands on her hips. "Do you know what they're making us do?"

Saff stopped folding a blanket. "Um… No? Who's 'they' and 'us'?"

"Your leaders, us Ivies. It's a load of crap!"

The strategy had been discussed at the last meeting Saff had been invited to, so she couldn't pretend she didn't know what Flora meant. The list had been all but decided upon as to who would be allowed to try rifting through the cave. Fearing further deception, and having never discovered who the traitor or traitors were in camp, the Seeder war council had struck most Ivy names from the list. Instead, the male Ivies would be broken up and reassigned to Seeder wall protection duty, closely monitored. Ivy females were all being reassigned to healing Seeder lands while troops marched on the palace.

"It's just a change in strategy, okay? It's not a permanent reassignment," Saff reassured her.

Flora frowned. "Are we giving up on Unitas? Because this is what it feels like to give up."

That hurt to hear, but Saff could see how Flora would read the situation that way. No, they weren't joining together at the cave, storming the castle in a blaze of glory, hand in hand. But they also hadn't given up on their alliance with Kaylah, even if things were shaky. They just couldn't risk their cave strategy, or *any* strategy, making its way to Soren's spies, whoever they may be.

"We're not giving up. I *promise*," Saff said emphatically.

Flora studied her face. "Then at least let me fight with the guys." She crossed her arms. "No offense, because I love that I got to make a new friend, even if it was a weirdo Seeder like you," she grinned for just a moment, "but I didn't come here to make friends. And I didn't come to heal your lands."

"Flor—"

"No." Flora held up her hand. "Hear me out. I will fulfill my queen's promise to your people to come back and help heal your lands when she's on her throne, but that's not why I came. I left my family, my friends, my entire life behind to follow her and to learn. I've sparred with you and others in camp at every available chance. Raven, too. We've both devoted countless hours to fighting our own people at the edge of this camp. We're as good as any of your soldiers, so don't pretend this is fair treatment for all we've done."

Needing to keep her knowledge of whispers a secret, and wanting to not be kicked out, Saff had been rather silent at council meetings lately, even if she didn't agree. But in Flora's shoes, she would have felt the same.

Flora continued, "Look at it my way. What happens if this keeps dragging on? Or your people lose and, well, somehow don't all die."

That was a little bleak and insensitive.

"What would become of us women who joined Unitas? We would be slaves in your lands for the rest of our lives, forced to cure the poison in your soil, one day at a time." She pointed at Saff. "Don't you dare tell me it would happen differently."

Saff didn't skip a beat. "You're right." She held no doubt that, at minimum, Seeder leadership would demand reparations via the Ivy women already working on their behalf, if things went sideways.

"Good. Then we're on the same page. We're not stupid, either. If we're closing up shop here in camp, that means something's changed. And if we're not giving up on Unitas, that means," she raised an eyebrow, as well as her inflection, "special strike teams that some of us have been training for?"

Saff couldn't hold back a hint of a smile. She liked this girl. "I can't discuss strategy, but I'll see if I can be a squeaky wheel about letting you fight instead of being assigned to poison duty, okay?"

Beaming, Flora gave her a hug. "You're my favorite Seeder, by far." She winked. "Make sure *both* Raven and I get reassigned, if you can."

Not a minute after Flora left the tent, Devin returned.

"There's the woman I love." He wrapped his arms around Saff, pulling her onto their cot.

She laughed. "Lying down for a nap is counterproductive right now."

He nuzzled her neck. "Who said I wanted a nap?"

She laughed again. "You have got to be out of your mind."

Devin scoffed. "Who's gonna suspect us of anything in our tent in the middle of the day?"

Saff pulled herself closer, resting her forehead against his. "In the middle of the day? When we're supposed to be evacuating camp? I think someone might come by for a head count when we're not accounted for, and they're not likely to announce themselves before peeking in."

Devin huffed, melodramatically flinging his body back on the cot. "War, always coming between me and my love!"

She grinned. "Yes, I can see how you passed your acting classes with *flying* colors. It is in no way astounding that you were picked to go to the human world as one of my protectors."

He chuckled, then drew a pensive breath. "It's weird, isn't it? Leaving camp?"

It had already been over two months since Saff had seen her home, or other family members. "Yeah, it is. I doubt we'll ever see this place again." Either because they'd be back home in South Fortinda, rebuilding after a successful attack on the palace, or they wouldn't return because they'd been killed in the attempt.

Saff and Devin had made it on the short list for the cave rifting attempt. Devin was as good of a soldier as any Seeder out there, but the crux of the choice had been Saff. Seeder matriarchs couldn't rift anymore, not even through the caves, just like Kaylah had suspected. Aside from the newest Seeder teen returns, who had barely any training, Saff was the most powerful female Seeder in the Green Lands capable of going with this strike team. She could pack a punch, and she was willing. Devin was her husband, her mate.

"What was it you told me in high school? You didn't want to fight with me? You wanted me by your side?"

They shared a warm smile. "Yes." He leaned over and stole a peck on the lips. "And hopefully we do come back to this area. We have a second honeymoon in the mountains on the books, don't we?"

"It's a date." She got lost in his dark brown eyes for just a moment, wishing she could share more about the secrets she'd been entrusted with. But this time, it was her turn to keep a few secrets, to keep those she loved happy, blissfully unaware of the potential danger that lurked around them, a threat they couldn't do anything about, even if they knew the truth.

She broke eye contact. "Well, I need to go see a man about a horse. Do you mind packing the last of our things?"

"Come again?" he said as she stood. "No horse beasts in this realm."

Saff winked, adjusting her jade necklace. "Okay, I need to see an Ivy leader about a squeaky wheel. It won't take long."

***

Saff found Ginger in her tent, also organizing her things. "How goes the packing?"

"Oh, you know…" Ginger stuffed some clothing into a pack. "Getting there."

"I have a favor to ask."

"Favor, huh? Favors often come with strings attached."

"Nope, not this one. Not really."

"What is it?" Ginger placed her pack into a wooden chest and closed the latch.

"I want you to convince the council to let Flora and Raven come on this mission."

Ginger perched on the chest. "That's going to be a no. We don't know how small that cave is, or if this strategy will even work, and we can't risk one of them leaking that information to a spy."

Saff rubbed her face with her hands. *Why can't we ever agree? Even when I'm advocating for Ivies, I can't win!* Sure, she'd been too busy for a lot of things lately, but she'd kept her promise to Kaylah to keep her eye on other members of camp. Especially after Kaylah went missing, Saff had put extra effort into scrutinizing her peers. These girls didn't have a sketchy bone in their bodies. Not to mention, they had been accounted for the night of Kaylah's disappearance, with witnesses vouching that they'd fought by their side during the Ivy army's attack. And, while they hadn't been paired up with Raven in training, Saff and Devin had broken bread with the friends together. He would have agreed with her judgment call.

"They don't have to understand any of the strategy until we have them in the cave on this side. They won't tell anyone. And we know neither of them is a whisper."

Ginger rolled her eyes. "Of course they're not."

Only men were whisper rifters. Unitas just hadn't been able to identify the one unknown whisper amongst them. Granted, it had probably just been the one Ivy guard who had gone missing the same night Kaylah had, and he'd fled through a rift, too.

"Exactly. They're good fighters; even Kaylah thought so."

"They might be good, but they're young."

"So am I. They're barely younger than me."

Ginger crossed her arms. "You're not a standard Seeder, though, are you? Those girls don't have extra powers or capacity to wield energy like you do."

Saff picked at her fingernails. She'd still been struggling to reconcile the truth about her energy, and about her future, and about who she wanted to become. "You know, I didn't earn this extra energy. I wasn't even born with it." She glanced up. "I only have it because I didn't complain about how sick I was when I hadn't been wearing a piece of energy-infused jewelry for too long, and because my brother saved my life before assassins could take it." She shook her head. "These girls are like me, and Rachel. Right place, right time. Or maybe wrong place, wrong time. But the right skills and motivations."

More than anything, the way that Flora had seamlessly called Kaylah 'my queen' had pierced Saff. "You wouldn't stop Kaylah from going. And frankly, I remember, just hours after meeting me, a certain redhead telling me her story, about how she'd always wanted to learn to fight but no one would train her. And how delighted she was to finally get the opportunity when she became a protector and host parent to her future queen." Saff lifted her eyebrows high. "These girls want to fight for their queen. They've been trained."

Ginger shook her head, wearing a knowing smile. That redhead had been her. "I don't know about you." She pointed at Saff. "I don't know if you're brilliant, or manipulative, or brilliantly manipulative."

Saff tucked her hands into her pockets, shrugging. "You can call me narrow-minded, or whatever you want, but I just feel like honesty can go a long way. They're an asset in a fight. Soren doesn't have any female guards or soldiers. He won't see it coming. They'll diversify our team."

"I'll see what I can do."

"Thank you."

Chapter 40

SEEDER TROOPS MARCHED ON THE PALACE.

In an unprecedented move, a legion of Seeder fathers and brothers—having still been stationed in the human world to protect their daughters and sisters—rifted home to fight, entrusting their unbloomed girls with human hosts and Unitas safe houses.

The camp ambush proved successful, and all that was left to test was the cave.

According to all of their knowledge, a rift either worked, or it didn't. Green folk didn't experience any accidental misdirects, or serious injury. Their hope, and expectation, was that the new cave strategy would work the same way. If they disappeared through a rift, they'd assume it worked as advertised. They didn't have a way to instantly confirm.

An elite group was assembled for the cave strategy, held back from the main march. If their theory didn't pan out, they'd still be able to get to the palace, but it would set them back, taking at least another day to get where they needed, risking having to sneak the group in closer like Guillen was doing with the charms and a small group of allies.

They gathered at the cave entrance at Tonoru, the rope bridges and ladders cut down, camp abandoned, and Seeder soldiers holding the line at the top of the canyon against Ivy forces.

Saff nervously squeezed Devin's hand as she surveyed the group. While Heather's specialty was healing, she'd devoted herself to further training after Ben's death. Healing *and* fighting.

Ginger, and surprisingly, Jon, were in charge of the Unitas Ivies chosen to be on the elite team. Nathan was still sidelined in the human world, but Jon had apparently earned enough Seeder trust through his loyalty, hard work, and intel.

One more male Ivy who Saff hadn't gotten to know well was permitted to join. The fact that Flora and Raven were also there at the cave made Saff proud. She struggled with a pinch of guilt, because it kind of felt like irresponsibly taking Rachel to the human world to meet Kaylah again. But these girls weren't traumatized, new-to-the-Green-Lands pupils of hers. They were young, but they were soldiers.

Reluctantly, Saff was forced to accept that the council had approved Rachel to go as well. Despite Rachel's raw talent in sparring, and the fact that she was now eighteen, and the fact that Saff *knew* she needed to stop trying to protect Rachel and allow her to make her own choices, it wasn't easy to let it go.

"Hey, love?" Devin whispered in her ear as final instructions were being given at the cave.

Saff pulled her gaze from the group. "Yeah?"

"I might need that hand." He kissed her on the cheek.

She loosened her grip, making sure her energy was in check. "Sorry. Yeah."

~

Rachel stood at the entrance to the cave, gathered with just under two dozen others, mostly Seeders. Her anxiety peaked. *What if this doesn't even work?* They'd built up their hopes, but they didn't even know when those symbols had been etched into that cave on the other side of the realm. Was it after the palace had been built there, in the mountains? Would the Ivy protective barrier now prohibit even a cave rift? Seeder rifts, Ivy rifts, and the combined cave rifts all worked a little differently. And what if the cave was compromised? What if Kaylah had given it up under torture? One of their safe houses had been compromised… And just as sickening was the thought that it might not work because Guillen had died trying to get the jade stones there.

Staring at the cave entrance, Rachel tried not to let the mounting fear grow, or at the very least, not to show it. She had no way of controlling the tightness in her gut, or the sweat on her palms. *There's only one way to find out if this will work.*

After the briefing, Jon volunteered to be the first to try. Rachel found some comfort in that. He and Guillen had been her escorts, her rescuers, when she'd been tortured at the palace. They'd found refuge in that cave. Now, she hoped and prayed that she, Guillen, and Jon could reunite and find strength there again.

Jon extended a vine, running it along the rocky cave floor. A rift formed. Holding the jade charm, he stepped forward. As he breached the rift, the surrounding air rippled, shimmered, and then took him from their sight.

The group erupted into cheers. Rachel exhaled her relief, and was afforded the honor of going next. It felt different—warmer, thicker—going through this type of rift. She was greeted on the other side by relative darkness. The darkness of a familiar cave.

Jon had moved off to the side, and there were a couple of other men at the back of the cave where she and Jon had emerged, right next to the etched symbols. Rachel gave Jon an excited hug.

Jon even hugged back this time, smiling. "Back where we started, huh?"

Rachel matched his smile.

"Rachel! Jon!" Guillen rounded the corner, swooping Rachel up into a firm squeeze.

She could finally truly breathe again.

"I missed you so much!" Guillen said, his tone echoing her own sentiments. "And you did it! That's amazing!"

She held him tight, not wanting to let go, burying her face in his neck. "I missed you too."

That part of the cave was starting to get crowded as more arrived, so they moved their reunion further out.

Between the Unitas group following Rachel, and the men Guillen had brought with him, there wasn't any privacy. Rachel and Guillen couldn't have cared less. He took her to the side and laid a reunion kiss on her. They were both safe. And they were both about to risk their lives again.

"I can't believe you led everyone to the cave without being detected." She surveyed him. He was *completely* dusty and fairly sweaty, with a bit of a nasty scratch on his forehead and arm, but otherwise without injury. "You really are like a shadow, aren't you?" She held his face between her hands, gazing into his gorgeous blue eyes. He even had a little scruff on his face.

"You doubt my skill?" He raised an eyebrow, wearing the sexiest grin she'd ever seen.

Her heart pounded against her ribs. "Never. But how did you even do it?"

He pulled her into another embrace, whispering in her ear, "Tunnels."

Her eyes grew wide as she pulled back. "Wait, what?"

"When Jon and I rescued you and brought you here, you only ever checked out the *left* chamber of the cave, right?"

She nodded. Jon had told her to.

"The right side is narrower, but it keeps going."

Rachel furrowed her brow. "Seriously? And Kaylah knew that the whole time?" It was actually insulting. She almost punched Guillen in the arm right then and there. "Why have we waited? Why didn't we sneak people in that way, weeks or months ago?"

"It's not like that." His voice was soothing. "There are actually a lot of caves and tunnels like this in the Green Lands, especially in this region. I think they're lava tubes? Not really sure. But she's had people secretly scouring the back mountains for a while now. That's what I've been helping with since you left. The right channel of this cave looked like it experienced a cave-in, so Kaylah hoped we could find the right tunnel and clear it, connecting to here."

"So, you just had to find the right one? How long have you known about them?"

He pursed his lips. "We just got here four hours ago and secured the opening. But yeah, I knew this was in the works for a while."

She couldn't pretend she wasn't disappointed to just now be finding out about this.

He held her by the waist, looking her directly in the eyes. "Do you remember us talking about the coffee cup clue she left you in that cabin? About why Kaylah separated those clues? Why she hadn't just given that code to Jon or me to give you?"

Rachel's shoulders slumped. "Because then it couldn't be tortured out of you."

He gave her a half-smile. "Sometimes, when it comes to strategy, it's best if the left and right hands are a bit out of sync."

Rachel shook her head, admiring Kaylah. She really hadn't lied about being trained on strategy. She'd been working from two angles, not even knowing they would need to come together. "And you just barely discovered the right tunnel?"

"We've been narrowing it down, but it's slow work, with more than one cave-in. We'd been working in teams for safety. When we got word of this deadline, we worked through the night and had to split up. We couldn't play it safe."

"Is… Is everyone okay?"

Guillen winced. "There's still half a dozen of us unaccounted for." He moved a hand up, tucking a strand of her hair behind her ear. "But let's stay positive. They might still find their way out and join us before we know it."

She could only imagine what it would feel like to be lost in the depths of a tunnel or cave all alone, or to suffer a slow death crushed by a cave-in. She prayed that his optimism came to fruition, that they'd all find their way here safely.

After hugging Guillen once more, Rachel didn't leave his side as they introduced each other to different people, everyone discussing their training and expertise. Basic plans had been made ahead of time, but final strategy would be hammered out in the cave between the two groups.

A bit of a shocker to Rachel, and apparently a large portion of the group, was news of the existence of a group of Ivies known as 'whisper rifters.' The Unitas party was warned to watch out for each other, and to anticipate that many of the guards at the palace might be stronger than they would normally expect of a regular soldier.

"Okay," Guillen whispered in her ear, "*Now*, I'm not keeping anything from you, and I won't ever again."

She couldn't even be mad. She just leaned her head on his shoulder, savoring his warmth. Most of the others in the cave were too busy with their own preparations to pay them any attention, but a couple of people from the Seeder side did a double take.

Jon, Ginger, and a pair of experienced Seeder generals led the discussions. Anyone with experience in the palace gathered into one group, reviewing drawings of the place. It was tight quarters, so Rachel didn't at all feel guilty about being in Guillen's arms as they discussed such important matters. It gave her strength and calmed her nerves.

Unitas took their time planning. They wouldn't attack until it was dark outside, and they wanted to make sure they weren't missing anything important. Their latest update had the earliest deployed Seeder troops engaged in battle nearby. They could provide backup to hold the palace after the strike teams secured their targets.

As the main Seeder march seemed to already be pulling more Ivy troops from the palace, Unitas decided to take the palace in two groups. Having a couple dozen people there, they would split their infiltration attempts between two entrances. They aimed for one that seemed more structurally vulnerable, and one they only knew about from their new insider knowledge. The second attempted entrance was in a neglected part of the palace that even Jon had never seen.

They broke for lunch, dispersing a smidge. Rachel sat on Guillen's lap as they ate sunflower oatcakes.

Guillen was chuffed that his sister and, unknowingly, his mother, had been helpful with this part of the mission.

"Thank you for taking care of them," he said. "And I'm really happy to hear Catrina came around so quickly. I thought she might."

Rachel smiled. "You should be proud of her. She made a lot happen that we couldn't on our own."

There was an awkward silence between them as they sat there. What did you say to the person you loved, when you were both about to put yourselves in mortal danger?

Rachel's eyes rested fondly on Saff and Devin. Everyone was at risk, but she was sure these two could cause some damage. Devin had years of combat training under his belt, and Saff had come far, and was so powerful.

~

Saff's heart hung heavy. This was the first time she would be in the middle of a battle. Even at camp, she'd fought with darts, not in hand-to-hand combat. And while they prayed for a quick and stealthy win, there were no guarantees. But she was happy to have her husband by her side. She leaned into him, squeezing his hand.

She exchanged a smile with Flora. During a break in planning conversations, they'd stolen a moment to chat. Flora was understandably jittery, but excited. She confessed that Raven was a lot more nervous. Not wanting someone that might chicken out at the last minute, Saff had suggested that Raven stay behind in the cave to guard it instead. After Flora returned to discuss it with Raven, Saff decided perhaps that hadn't been the best advice to offer. Raven glared at Saff, no doubt resenting the suggestion. If looks could kill…

Saff glanced over at the other team. Heather was in conversation with a male Seeder she'd be working with. Both Devin and Saff had had a hard time accepting Heather coming on the mission, but she was determined.

"What are you thinking?" Devin asked.

"Mmm." She leaned into him more. "Just nervous. What's new?"

He rubbed her back. "We'll be okay."

Maybe it was just the calm before the storm, or the adrenaline pumping, but her mind didn't reject that.

"I know." She turned to him, smiling. "Tell me something about yourself that I don't know."

"Something you don't know?" He held her hand, playfully intertwining their fingers, tickling her palm. "I don't know, love. Um…"

He took another moment to mull it over. "Okay… I … still think about how I almost lost you in high school. Every day." Regret filled his voice. "I don't know if I'll ever fully forgive myself for letting you get hurt. I could have said something. I should have."

Her heart went out to him. She'd only asked as a fun distraction as they waited for their attack. "I forgave you years ago, as well as my parents. You know that."

He bobbed his head back and forth. "I know. Sometimes it's easier to forgive others than yourself."

She didn't know what to say to that. "I love you, no matter what."

He cracked a reassuring smile. "In this cave, that palace, or anywhere, in any world, I've got your back."

She squeezed his hand. "Ditto."

Devin shifted on the cool stone floor. "Your turn. What don't I know about you?"

She hadn't prepared anything ahead of time, but it came to her quicker than she'd expected. Unable to stop herself, she actually let out a soft chuckle.

"Oooh, a good one."

A couple of soldiers looked at them, and she blushed.

"No, it's stupid."

He poked her in the ribs, and she squirmed a little. His voice was playful. "No, no, no. Now you have to tell me."

She bit her lip, trying to think of a new one, but she couldn't. "Fine. It's *really* stupid. But, since you mentioned our high school days…" She couldn't look him in the eye. "I know you, and my human parents… I *know* you were picture-perfect in giving me space to choose which world I'd live in, and … between you and Zach." Her mouth opened and closed like a guppy gasping for a cool drink as she tried to form words. "I just… I never blamed you for not being willing to sacrifice your identity as a Seeder, especially after moving here and meeting our families. I get it. But part of me was always kind of … hurt … that you never once *actually* asked me to give everything up, to choose you."

His reaction was spot-on with what she'd anticipated. "You're kidding me, right?" He lifted his eyebrows, his voice quiet enough to not disturb others. "Girls are impossible to please sometimes!"

Her cheeks grew warm. "That's why I never said anything. I know it's silly, or vain, or … too romanticized."

Scratching his chin, he shook his head. "I was never subtle. I was *pretty* dang clear that I wanted to be with you."

She felt that much more stupid. Why would she have brought up such a silly girlish notion in such a serious moment? "I know. Sorry." That was like a human girl getting a dozen long-stemmed roses and then saying 'Sorry, but I think sunflowers are better.' *Take the stupid roses and appreciate the gesture.*

Perhaps she shouldn't have brought up Zach vying for her heart back in the human world, either. Devin really wasn't normally the jealous type, and he'd thoroughly apologized for what he'd said when they were arguing, about her revealing green-folk secrets to Zach. She could understand why he'd done it, that sometimes people lashed out when they were caught up in their emotions, but maybe the mention of Zach at all during this particularly tense situation had been the wrong move.

Frustrated with herself more than Devin seemed to be with her, Saff reached into her pocket, opening a small satchel of mixed nuts. "Want one?"

"No, I'm good." He focused on the cave wall, a contemplative look painted on his face.

"Are you mad?"

He gave her a half-smile. "Of course not. Just thinking."

She kicked herself even more, shoving a couple of cashews in her mouth. After chewing in silence, surrounded by chattering co-conspirators and allies, she swallowed, then picked up a hazelnut.

"Saff?" Devin finally said, studying her face.

"Yeah?" She set the hazelnut back down.

His face was sober and vulnerable in a way she rarely saw, almost like on the day he'd proposed, but this time his expression carried something more akin to hurt, rather than nerves. "Choose me."

Something within her knew right away what he meant. He wasn't mad about Zach, or about a petty girlish dream. He wasn't mad at all.

Her heart sank instantly to her abdomen. Hadn't she *always* chosen him? She'd moved to the Green Lands. She'd waited for him to return. She'd married him, chosen him as her lifelong mate. She'd built a life with him. And she chose him every single day.

But the hint of hurt, or perhaps fear, in his eyes reminded her that she *hadn't* always chosen him. Not when it had mattered most. Not when she'd left him to risk her life to go to the human world on a dangerous, unsanctioned mission. Not when his best friend and brother-in-law had been killed. She'd left him in the lurch, all alone.

Tears came to her eyes. They were about to march into the palace, outnumbered, outmanned, and *she* was his fighting partner. *She* would be the one to have his back. And while he'd forgiven her for her betrayal, she realized in that moment that forgiveness didn't equate to trust, and perhaps they had more work to do on the latter.

When you made a vow to share your life with someone, to spend it with them, you no longer belonged to just yourself. That was why they called it 'spending' your life together—you were invested, wholeheartedly.

As they stared into each other's eyes, she held his hands and squeezed. She would *never* abandon him again. Pushing out the word with all the emphasis she could muster, she responded. "Always."

He gave her a tiny nod, then pulled her into his arms.

"Always," she repeated. "I promise."

"Thank you," he whispered.

In the warmth of his arms, nothing more needed to be said. As long as they got through this attack, this battle, they could get through anything.

As they sat in silence, Saff people-watched some more. Ginger and Jon, with their Seeder general counterparts, were the most active, gesturing around the cave, shaking and nodding heads, pointing at maps and blueprints. This hodgepodge little group was far from perfect, but it was the best they would have, and they had to believe it would be enough. Once Soren was deposed, they could stop the battles, stop the war. If they could do this quickly, Soren's people wouldn't have time to flee or move Kaylah elsewhere.

Saff's gaze eventually rested on Rachel and Guillen. She'd never seen Rachel with that kind of smile, that kind of confidence in her expression.

~

Rachel felt Saff's gaze. They locked eyes, having a silent discussion across the room. First, they shared a quick half-hearted smile. Then Saff lifted her eyebrows—questioning, urging. Rachel's face became more stern. She mouthed the word "No."

"What's up?" Guillen asked, having picked up on their exchange.

Rachel took a deep breath. "I'm not staying in this cave."

He bit his lip and looked down.

"I know I haven't been in the parts of the palace that we're expecting to go into. And I don't have as much training as some of the others. But I'm not just staying here to guard the cave. We already have volunteers for that, and that's not why I came. I've trained enough."

He grinned and caressed her cheek. "I can't win this argument, you know. If I tell you not to go … we've seen how that goes. And you'll feel like I'm not supporting you. If I don't fight you, then I'm not being honest with *either* of us about how much I care about you."

She stared into his concerned eyes, a slight smile forming on her lips.

He sighed, gently rubbing her knee. "So, I'll say it once. I don't want you going in."

"You know my answer."

He nodded, lips pressed tightly. "I love you."

Rachel's words caught in her throat. She'd never once hesitated to reciprocate that, not with him. But the way he'd said it, the way it felt—it felt like a goodbye. A 'just in case.'

She swallowed hard. "I love you too. Today. Tomorrow. Always." She forced a smile and gave him a sweet peck on the lips.

*****

Soren had done a significant purge of the guard staff, realizing there were traitors amongst them. The few left still loyal to Kaylah worked to ensure the strike teams and backup would have an easier time reaching the palace, but they had no hope of help on the inside.

Guillen, Rachel, and Heather would be in the smaller group, taking on the unfamiliar entrance, entering first and hoping to get closer to the dungeons where Kaylah was believed to be held.

Saff and Devin were part of the larger group, led by Jon, that would be taking on the more guarded entrance, drawing attention away from the dungeons, and then hoping to take Soren. Based on their last reports, Soren, his wife, and Kaylah were all still on the premises.

Guillen guided his group quietly from the cave under the cover of darkness. They'd be approaching via a different route than he'd previously taken when rescuing Rachel, but he knew the area well enough to get them through swiftly.

The target entrance was an old ground cellar. They cleared debris from the cellar door and shimmed the rusted padlocks open. Guillen slowly undid the squeaky old latches and parted the swollen wooden doors. Clearing cobwebs away, he used a lightkeeper Heather had pocketed to look inside.

Once he confirmed it was safe to enter, they filed in. From what they'd been told, this wing was once used for storage and servants' quarters. It had been abandoned long ago when newer additions were built, grander and closer to the throne room.

Rachel shivered in the cold of the damp corridor. There were only seven Unitas members at this entrance. Guillen headed the group; she was in the middle of the pack. The longer they walked in the dark, the more nervous she became. She pictured the palace layout, envisioning where the remaining Seeder girl was being held, powering the War Vines. Were the three missing girls about to join her? Rachel ached to find them, to free them, to make that as much of a priority as freeing Kaylah, but that wasn't the mission.

This wasn't an extraction.

This was a takeover.

~

Having given Guillen's group ample time to breach the palace stealthily, Saff's team started to make their way out. Jon was coordinating Saff and Devin's team, though he wouldn't be at the front. The Seeders intended to use every tool in their arsenal.

Walking most of the way to the intended entrance, the large group broke up. Four Seeder couples, Saff and Devin included, took flight, soaring to strategic locations, to have an advantage from above. They made sure not to fly too high, or too far out, where the protective barrier caused flight problems. And while traditional human weapons were rarely used by green folk, the palace employed archers—a wise move when your enemy could fly. Completely suppressing your glow while flying was no easy feat, but it was doable, and necessary, to land undetected.

Landing softly on a lower stone balcony, Saff and Devin crouched, carefully making their way to a narrow ledge that led to their target. Not wanting to risk giving away positions earlier than necessary, they had to rely on the others to be in place before they moved next. Two guards were stationed at the door they were aiming for, and two archers on the level directly above. If they could take out those on the ground without noise, they might avoid having to deal with the others.

Devin extended a balled fist, putting his other hand behind his back, helping to conceal the light Saff was pushing to her hand. He quickly flashed his green eyes. Three sets of eyes did the same. He accessed Saff's energy, and flicked his wrist at their target below.

Large darts sliced through the air, biting into a wooden door, and the two guards stationed on the ground. The pounding of the darts against the wood rang through the air, briefly followed by the muffled thud of bodies crumpling to the ground. Unitas Ivies rushed forward to remove the bodies while the Seeders surveyed from above to ensure they hadn't been heard.

The night was still. So far, so good.

~

Guillen's group finally reached the end of the long corridor, stopping at a large wooden door. It was locked, and since they expected guards to be close on the other side, they planned to open it by force, instead of risking the noise of slowly and carefully prying it open. They anticipated six guards in the immediate area. Two by their door, two further down a hallway lined with cells, and two in the stairwell that led up further into the palace. If they could take the six down, especially before those at the stairs alerted anyone, they could accomplish their goal and get Kaylah out, independent of any commotion the other group might cause.

Guillen stood to the side of the door as three Ivies wrapped their vines around the handle, ready to tug. He held two throwing knives ready. He gave Rachel one last pleading look, asking her to stay back. She shook her head, brandishing her own knife. She and Heather hung back, there for emergency healing, as well as fighting if needed. The others would go first.

Guillen directed the group with hand signals and then motioned for those with their vines on the handle to give it all they had.

~

The larger party slipped into the palace. The Seeders up above quietly landed, entering the same door. A pair stayed there to hold the position, while the others barreled down a small hallway to the right. When they turned the corner, they were met by a handful of surprised guards. Several Unitas Ivies advanced, tackling those closest, while the Seeders used their darts for those further away.

It worked.

Miraculously, they'd overpowered the first group of soldiers without them raising the alarm.

And then a bloodcurdling scream rang out from behind Saff. "SOREN!"

Saff whipped around, as did the rest of the strike team.

Raven. Clutching her hands to her stomach, wide-eyed.

What?!

She wasn't hurt.

Everyone jerked their heads about, trying to locate the target or threat she'd called out. A couple of Unitas members shushed her.

It wasn't like 'King' Soren was standing right there, though.

Saff eyed Raven. She should have stayed back in the cave if she was going to lose it and give up their position. She looked absolutely terrified.

Raven took a few steps back, almost stumbling in her retreat.

And then it clicked.

It took only seconds for the team to put the pieces together, but it was seconds too late.

Raven wasn't calling out a danger. She *was* the danger.

The danger *Saff* had begged to bring with them.

Faster than those around her could react, Raven turned to Flora. "Sorry."

Darting down a tiny hallway in the opposite direction, she screamed Soren's name once more. One of the Seeder pairs bolted after her.

Shit. The element of surprise was beyond gone.

Devin pulled Saff back to their mission before she could even gauge Flora's reaction. "Saff, come on."

Traitor or not, Raven didn't matter. Their strike teams had never intended to take on the entire palace staff—nor could they. They needed Soren, his wife, and Kaylah. Once they had them in their custody, this was over.

Saff squared her shoulders and set her jaw.

More guards rushed down the hallway to meet Unitas. Saff and Devin, along with another Seeder pair, Jon, and another Ivy, broke from the group, hoping to climb a nearby stairwell before the guards cut them off. They darted to the base of the stairs as an enemy vine caught Devin's ankle, yanking him to the ground.

Saff had already bounded up a few stairs. She turned and dashed back down, hacking through the vine while a Unitas Ivy covered them, taking on the offending guard. Now free, they climbed the stairs.

They were met by a pair of guards at the landing of the next level, quickly dispatched by the other Seeder couple. Advancing one more level, they anticipated finding the long hallway that would lead to the sleeping quarters of the 'king.'

~

Near the dungeons, the Ivy men tugged at the locked door with all their might. The first pull loosened it, but not enough. They yanked again, and the wood splintered. They retracted their vines as a couple of them moved forward and kicked in the door.

One of the Ivy Unitas men rushed through the doorway, and was swept off his feet by a pair of vines, the closest guard having had some warning from the noise of the door breaking down. Guillen crossed the threshold, planting a throwing knife in the throat of another approaching guard. He pulled out his machete and severed the vines binding his Unitas companion, then took down his assailant.

The rest of the group poured into the new room. The three other Unitas Ivies ran to the stairs, hoping to detain the guards there before they alerted those above. Guillen, the Seeder women, and a Seeder male advanced down the hallway, taking on a pair of guards running toward them.

Guillen stopped, back to the wall, as Rachel extended energy to the male Seeder. He shot darts, taking down one of the guards, but the other continued after another round. Guillen met him as Rachel spotted two more coming from the same direction.

~

As they reached the right level, Jon and the other Unitas Ivy pulled down one of the guards at the edge of the stairwell, then Saff and Devin dispatched them with their blades. Jon indicated he and the other Seeder couple would hold the stairs while Saff, Devin, and the other Ivy rushed down the hallway.

They met the two guards positioned outside of the royal chambers, tussling. More guards sprinted toward them from the opposite end of the hallway. Saff and Devin took one out together, then Devin turned to help the Ivy with the guard he was binding. Saff glanced behind her as a handful of Unitas members emerged from the stairwell as backup against the fast-approaching surge coming her way. The opening was narrow.

But she would never leave Devin.

"Come on, Devin!"

He quickly surveyed the situation, jumping up to join her.

Saff focused energy into her shoulder as she threw her weight against the door, bursting into the queen and king's chambers.

~

Rachel prepared to extend more energy, but a call for backup came from the men in the stairwell. She motioned for Heather to stay and help in the hallway while Rachel went back to assist.

As she turned the corner, three more guards bounded down the stairs. She settled into a defensive stance, Seeder blades and knife at the ready. The closest guard whipped out a vine, and she allowed it to wrap around her extended wrist. Moving energy to her surrounding skin, muscles, and bone, she secured the Ivy leaves in place, embedded in her skin. She yanked the vine and turned, reeling the enemy in, planting her knife in his heart. As his vines released, she struggled to steady her breathing.

She assessed the situation in front of her, counting the guards and her allies at the stairs.

Ripping the offending leaves from her wrist, she shot a glance back down to the end of the hallway to see which group needed her more.

In that split second of indecision, a vine wrapped around her throat. It tugged at her, yanking her off her feet, slamming the back of her head into the unforgiving corner of the stone wall.

With the wind knocked out of her, she screamed only internally at the searing pain, barely hearing Guillen shout *Heather's* name, before all Rachel knew was blackness.

Chapter 41

SAFF BURST INTO THE QUEEN and king's chambers. Had she not used her Seeder energy, her shoulder would've no doubt been dislocated, but she'd strengthened those bones and muscles in anticipation.

With Devin right behind her, she was greeted by a half dozen soldiers.

Devin grabbed her hand. In a fluid, perfectly synced motion, Saff pushed energy to it and he flicked his wrist, dispatching one guard with darts. They separated, extending their Seeder blades, to take on the two closest who had rushed at them, shooting out vines.

After cutting the guard's vines short, Saff made her first solo kill with a blade to his throat.

Luckily, the closest Unitas Ivy from outside came into the room, slamming the door shut. He threw vines at the legs of a nearby settee and dragged it in front of the door. "That'll keep 'em out for a little while."

Now it was an even match. With two Seeders and an Ivy against three Ivies, they could manage this.

With each slice, kick, punch, and dodge, Saff sized up the guards and the room. Soren wasn't even in here.

The stone floors slick with blood, the Unitas members sweaty and nicked from head to toe, they caught their breath. Shouted orders continued to filter in from the hallway; thuds of bodies, grunts and groans.

The three in the queen and king's chambers split up to explore every inch of it—the en suite bathroom, the large closets, under the bed. Soren and his 'queen' were nowhere to be found.

Saff tightened her ponytail. "Of course they wouldn't be here. Not with our forces advancing. Not with Raven sounding the alarm."

The Unitas Ivy wiped his brow. "Is that what that stupid girl's name is?"

"Yeah," Devin answered, squeezing Saff's shoulder.

"So what's next?" Saff asked, choking down any emotion that wouldn't help in the moment.

They could go back out and keep searching, keep fighting. Where would Soren have gone?

Saff folded her arms, trying to recall the palace blueprints they'd studied.

"Why are all the guards outside, though?" Devin asked, right before a loud bang shook the door. The settee moved a few inches.

The Ivy ran to it, pushing it back against the door, holding it in place with his hands, and exerting extra pressure with his vines directly against the door. He dug in his heels with a wide stance, being jostled with each huge pound against the door.

"Need a hand?" Devin started toward the door.

"I've got it. See if you can find some other way out of here!"

"We're sure those aren't our people?" Saff asked.

The Ivy belted out a designated code word. No acknowledgement came from the other side. He shook his head grimly.

Great. And now we're cornered in here. They'd been hoping for stealth and speed. None of that was falling into place.

Devin rubbed the back of his neck. "But why would they be so focused on this room if Soren and his wife weren't in here?"

Why were they? *Six guards in here, too…*

"The White House," Saff said. "Buckingham Palace. The Capitol Building. Probably every castle has them too, right?"

"What are you talking about, Saff?" Devin asked.

"Tunnels."

Both men looked thoroughly confused.

"The tunnel in the cave?" the Ivy asked.

Good gravy. Saff pinched the bridge of her nose. Neither of these men grew up in the human world. Seeders didn't have such large and important structures for lifelong dignitaries. Ivies were secretive about everything.

"No. Humans sometimes build trapdoors or escape tunnels for important people. We need to check under the rugs, look for a fake panel in the wall or something."

"Oh," the Ivy remarked. "Like a pub's smuggling room."

"Uh…" Saff set to work, scouring the walls. "Sure?" She'd never heard of Ivy pubs or smugglers, but why not?

Devin started pulling up the corners of the rugs, pushing dead bodies out of the way.

The banging at the door grew louder, more violent. The Ivy lost his grip and slipped. He quickly jumped up and slammed the settee back in place. "I'm not going to be able to hold this for long by myself."

Saff and Devin feverishly undressed the room. Maybe she was wrong.

The door slammed so hard it nearly buckled, knocking the Ivy a couple of feet away. He scrambled to his feet, thrusting the settee back. Saff rushed to his side, Seeder energy strengthening her as she helped.

At this point, it almost didn't matter if Soren had been in here to escape through a tunnel. They just needed one to get out of here, to be able to search elsewhere. She continued to study the room from her new vantage point.

Devin searched the gaudy wall panels in a far corner of the room. He tilted his head to the side. A sconce was slightly askew.

He went to straighten it, but was met with resistance. He jiggled it, and a loud click followed.

Devin grinned at Saff. "Don't forget I fell in love with you because you're brilliant."

She chuckled. "Not the time. Hurry up." Her muscles ached, and she was expending more energy than she'd like just to hold a door rather than healing or fighting with it.

Devin found a couple of metal ornamental inlays and tugged on the wall panel. It slid to the side. "You're right. Dark tunnel, several yards down from what I can see. Looks like our way out of—"

Devin whipped his arm up, swinging it forward, fist balled.

The moment a handful of darts launched from his fingertips, an arrow slammed into his chest.

"Devin!" Saff screamed.

He didn't answer. But he didn't crumple to the floor, either.

Saff wanted to run to him, but the moment she left her position, that room would be overrun with Soren's extra-strong guards. And she couldn't see into the tunnel; Devin was blocking it as his balance teetered.

"Devin?" she pleaded.

He stood rigid, still facing the tunnel. Her healer training kicked in as she stared at him. Given his skills with Seeder energy, he was capable of surviving that kind of wound, as long as he hadn't been shot through the heart.

"I'll be fine," he forced out with the breath of a single functioning lung. His heart hadn't been pierced. "Go get the bastard," he groaned. "He ran away."

"Okay." Her heart was pounding as hard as the door she was holding in place.

She turned to the Ivy. "Take him inside the tunnel. I'll follow you."

The Ivy shook his head. "You can't hold this on your own."

"Trust me. I'm stronger and faster than you. Please."

He sized her up, then nodded. "On three?"

On three, Saff dug in, her jaw clenched, and the Ivy bolted to Devin, helping him inside the tunnel.

"Is there a way to close it?" she asked, sweating profusely, her skin even glowing.

"Um… It looks like it just clicks into place if we slide it back. There's a handle, but I don't see a lock from this side."

It would have to be good enough. She'd have to be fast enough to make it and close that door before the guards on the other side busted in and saw their hiding space. They might not know about the secret passage. It stood to reason knowledge of its existence would only be entrusted to the highest level of guards, and they likely wouldn't be busting down the door if they assumed Soren had already escaped through a tunnel.

"You're both clear of the entry? Ready to close it?"

"Yes."

Faster than she'd ever sprinted before, Saff dashed across the room, straight for the secret passage. The second before she crossed the threshold, she held out her hands, grasping the sconce with a death grip strengthened with Seeder energy. Her momentum carried her as she ripped off the sconce. Needing speed, she hadn't pumped the brakes. She threw her arms up to shield her face, and slammed into a stone wall, the broken sconce falling to the floor with a *clank*, right as the doorway behind her banged shut and the door of the other room crashed to the floor.

She fought a scream at the pain and exhaustion, listening intently, catching her breath.

All three froze in place.

Hopefully, damaging the passageway's entrance lever had disabled it, and wouldn't draw attention to it…

Guards barked orders from the other side of the panel. "Where did they go?"

That was a good sign.

Saff looked for Devin, barely able to see anything now that the door was closed. She silently joined him, lighting her hand enough to assess his wound. It wasn't bleeding yet. The arrow was still lodged in his chest, sticking out the other side—a nasty broadhead. "How are you holding up?"

"I'm fine," Devin whispered, clearly straining to keep his composure. He was capable of freezing a single lung, of surviving with just one side. For a little while. "Go after him. He's getting away."

Saff opened her mouth to speak. She wasn't going to leave Devin.

Devin's gaze was set on her. "Go. I can manage this for now. Hurry up."

She trusted that he could. He was amazing with his energy. He stood still enough, obviously flooding his chest and lungs with energy, clenching the arrow in place, forcing himself to breathe through his undamaged side.

"You ready?" the Ivy asked.

Making sure not to bump the arrow, Saff leaned in and gave Devin a kiss. Not a passionate kiss—there was no time for that. And this wasn't a goodbye kiss, either.

This was the kind of kiss only a Seeder woman could give. One that transferred a portion of her energy to him. Healing him would be useless with the arrow in there, but this could help him hold out longer.

She was already weak, and might end up too weak to properly heal him before this ordeal was over, but healing did no good if he exhausted his own stores and drowned in his own blood before she returned.

Their lips parted. "I love you." She faced the Ivy. "Okay."

With their way dimly lit by the glow of her hand, Saff and the Ivy raced down the corridor together. They took a sharp left at the end, having no idea where they were going. The tunnels might be woven into a complex labyrinth for all they knew.

Saff tripped over something on the floor, almost face-planting onto the ground.

The bow. Hopefully that was the only one, and Soren had given up on it, preferring a swifter exit without the extra weight.

Eventually, the tunnel did branch out, and they had to pick which route to take in their search. Each short offshoot led to a door just like the one they'd ducked through. They listened for a second at each door, assessing whether it was worth the danger to open it to search the room Soren might have left through.

Finally, they got lucky.

A screech came from the closest offshoot, and they slowed their pace to quiet the thump of their footsteps.

And there he was, just around the corner, tugging on a stuck door with his vines and hands.

Saff and the Ivy rushed him, tackling him to the ground, but he didn't go down easily.

The Unitas Ivy entangled Soren's legs with vines, while Saff fought off Soren's attack. With his legs secured, they needed to disconnect his vines.

"Help me pin him down," she said.

The Ivy did as ordered, and the two of them barely kept Soren down. He was strong. Then again, he hadn't been fighting for his life until now.

Saff aimed her sharpened arm blade at a narrow target on Soren's upper wrist, a move Ben had taught her in high school. A move she'd seen Ben and Devin use on an Ivy general when they'd saved her life. She cut deep, and Soren grunted, but barely bled. His vine from that wrist went limp, disconnected. She quickly repeated the move on the other wrist, then ordered the Ivy to bind Soren.

Soren yelled a colorful string of expletives and threats against the two, until they shoved some of his own vines into his mouth to muffle the sound.

No one came barging through the jammed door for him. It likely led to an empty room, perfect to escape through.

Saff caught her breath, her mind racing as to what to do next.

"We're sure this is him?" the Ivy asked.

She pointed at their captive. "What? That's Soren… Right?" She and Devin would recognize the prince better than almost any other Seeders would; they'd seen pictures when they went to the human world to search for him and Rachel when he'd kidnapped Rachel months earlier, after all. But an Ivy ought to recognize their own prince…

The Ivy shrugged, scrutinizing their captive further. "Yeah. It's probably him. Just wanted to make sure. I, uh, generally steer clear of government officials." He grinned. "More of a fringe kind of guy."

"Okay…" She was a bit on edge. "What's that supposed to mean?"

"Well…" He shrugged again. "Government officials tend to dislike those who illicitly transport items of intrinsic value."

"You're a thief?"

He was visibly offended. "Smuggler. Thief? That's debatable."

Soren continued to fight against the restraining vines and yell through the gag. The Unitas Ivy delivered a swift kick right to Soren's gut. "Shut up!"

Saff was stunned. She could get behind that kind of behavior.

But there was no time for that. The corridors were still quiet, so they might be lucky enough to be able to hide there for a bit to gather their strength and assess the situation, but Saff needed to get back to Devin ASAP.

She hesitated. That meant leaving this Ivy alone with Prince Soren. So much could go wrong. This man had only joined the team with Guillen; he'd never been with them in the Unitas camp. "What's your name again?"

He evaluated the injuries on his arms. "Arlo."

"Saff." She tried not to wonder about the rest of the Unitas team, but she couldn't stop thinking about Flora and Raven. Flora had been recruited by Raven. Raven had apparently been recruited by Soren… "Who brought you into Unitas?"

Arlo massaged his wrists. "Jon—the former guard leading our team. He was like a big brother growing up."

Saff still hadn't gotten to know Jon well at all. But everyone, including Kaylah, had trusted him. It would have to be enough. "I need to go help my husband. Can you watch over this idiot here until I get back?"

"Yeah. I've got him."

"Okay. I'll hurry." She looked down at Soren again. "I'm all for kicking him if you need to, but try not to injure him too bad. We need him alive, and I'm not going to have a lot of healing energy to spare."

Arlo smirked. "I can manage that."

Without hesitation, Saff ran back to where they'd left Devin, though she almost got turned around at one point.

When she rounded the last corner, confident she'd found their starting point, she panicked.

Devin wasn't there.

Did I take a wrong turn? Did they find him?

No… She was sure this was where they'd left him. The hidden doorway was still closed, and a few voices mumbled from behind, but it sounded like they'd given up on searching, and the ransacking had stopped.

A raspy cough came from the hallway behind her. She ran toward it, finding Devin in the closest offshoot. He leaned his shoulder against the stone wall, coughing up blood.

"Crap. Okay. Hold on." His Seeder energy was running out, if it hadn't already.

She desperately wished Arlo could be there to help get the arrow out, but dragging Soren back would have wasted far too much time. "Okay. Hold still." She gazed into Devin's eyes, which were glowing a faint green in his struggle to breathe and keep himself upright. "This is going to hurt." What she wouldn't do for Flora or Ginger right now to numb him at least.

With both hands, she grasped the portion of the arrow sticking out of his chest and, trying to move it as little as possible, exerted precious energy to snap off the end. Devin groaned in obvious agony.

Now she could pull it out without causing further injury. She yanked it out from the other end and immediately jammed her thumbs into the holes in his back and chest, pouring healing energy into them. She winced as he moaned and coughed, struggling to keep it together.

As she sensed the internal tissue healing, she changed hand positions, her fingertips surrounding the holes. As her energy drained, his grimace relaxed.

She couldn't afford to pass out or use up every last drop. "Are you going to be alright if I stop now?"

Devin took a couple of test breaths. "Yes."

Depending on how much blood had leaked into his lung, he might still face further complications, but the important thing was that the bleeding had stopped.

"Okay." She wiped her bloodied hands on her pants, scanning his face. He was still in no shape to run out or get back into the fight. They needed a game plan.

"You stay here. Arlo and I have Soren tied up. We'll bring him back."

Devin nodded. "Thank you."

She smiled weakly, giving him a normal peck on the lips—no Seeder energy this time. "Love you."

"Love you."

Worn out, she did her quickest jog back through the dark corridors, almost tripping over the bow again.

Arlo and Soren remained where she'd left them. Arlo's ear was cupped to the door Soren had been trying to escape through.

"Is someone in there?" she whispered.

"Oh, no. Just making sure," Arlo answered. "Is your husband okay?"

"Yeah, not in any fighting shape, but I think he'll make it." She surveyed Soren. Arlo had added some extra vines around Soren's wrists, which had been wise. It usually took at least an hour for vines severed the way she'd done it to start regrowing.

"What's the plan?" Arlo asked.

Only in that moment did the aches and pains and drain set in. Devin wasn't in fighting shape, and right now, she wasn't either. "How are you doing?"

Arlo's exposed arms, neck, and face had just as many cuts as hers from the fighting. He let out a long exhale. "Gonna be honest. I'm not used to using this much vine at once. If we can take a minute, that'll help."

"Yeah, of course. Let's regroup with Devin. Help me drag this waste of space back?"

"Yes, ma'am." Arlo extended vines toward Soren.

"Hold on." She eyed Soren. "A couple of things first." Fueled by anger, but not backed with precious Seeder energy, she delivered a swift kick to Soren's side. "That's for shooting my husband." He breathed hard, his nostrils flaring, his eyes a bright natural green.

She kicked him again. "That one is for Rachel." And she decided a third might feel nice, but this time she balled her fist and aimed for his face. "And you know what? I like Kaylah, too."

Even if they all died during this battle, at least that had felt good.

***

Saff and Arlo dragged Soren all the way back to where Devin was recuperating. He was still coughing a lot. They'd checked out the crossbow Soren had ditched, but there were no other arrows with it.

Now, the three Unitas members needed to take a breather to allow their energy stores to recover, even if only minimally. And they needed a plan.

They had the usurper, but not his wife or Kaylah. Other Unitas members might have them in their custody, but they had no way of knowing, and they were worn out and injured.

They agreed to take a few more minutes and then assess the situation.

Saff sat next to Devin on the cool stone floor as Arlo paced the area. Devin's breathing was raspy.

She held Devin's hand. "You know, wasn't it you in the cave just a little bit ago that said girls are impossible to please?"

Devin showed a hint of confusion.

"I mean … I kiss you during a battle, but listen to you—one kiss is *never* enough for guys, is it?"

Devin laughed, and then winced and coughed. She grimaced.

"Yeah… I was curious about that," Arlo added. "This is my first time meeting Seeders. Do your lips always … do that?"

Saff furrowed her brow. "Do we kiss with our lips?"

Arlo pointed to his mouth. "The glowing thing."

Saff stifled a laugh, then explained how Seeder women could transfer energy that way, not just by extending it for darts or for healing.

He nodded. "That's hot." His eyes shot to Devin. "Well, I mean, not your wife." He looked at Saff. "Well, I didn't mean…"

Saff grinned, fixing her ponytail, which was now a tangled mess. "No worries."

Arlo swung his arms with nervous energy, continuing to pace their little offshoot. "The last thing an Ivy girl gave me when I kissed her was a slap in the face." He rubbed his cheek.

Shaking her head, Saff fought another smile. Arlo certainly hadn't been a chatterbox back in the cave, but his pumping adrenaline was likely a factor here. While giving off more of a player vibe than her human friend Zach ever had, Arlo kind of reminded her of him. She asked Arlo more about himself as they recuperated. He was an interesting character. Then again, she'd never met a smuggler before.

Feeling marginally better, their energy stores having had a chance to recharge, they had to make a decision. The best choice would be to take Soren back out in the open with a blade to his throat, and demand that all of his people surrender. Even without Soren's wife or Kaylah, it might work. But they could easily be overpowered still. When they took the gag out of Soren's mouth for a brief moment, he refused to surrender, swearing they'd never find his wife, and he would never help.

Not having much choice in the matter, they prepared to step out and demand the guards surrender. They needed to try to preserve the lives of any Unitas members who might still be fighting.

Devin was really in no shape to fight, but he could stand straight, and he refused to leave Saff's side.

The three Unitas members pulled Soren up and dragged him down the secret corridor, searching for a doorway that sounded as though no one would be on the other side.

Finding a suitable door, they filed through it into a closet of some sort. Saff held the tip of the arrow that had pierced Devin to Soren's neck.

Arlo opened the door, and they stepped out into a hallway. They took a left, following the loudest fighting. Only as they reached a staircase did they find guards.

Soren shouted louder and fought harder against his restraints. Saff pushed the arrowhead harder against his skin. "You're going to walk in front of us if you want him to live," she ordered the guards.

After a shared glance, the guards held up their hands.

"Where is your queen?" she asked. "And the *real* one, Kaylah?"

The guards kept looking to Soren for guidance, and Soren kept fighting and yelling, but he was tightly secured and well gagged.

Finally, one of the guards answered. "I don't know where Queen Beata is. The traitor is locked up where she should be."

"Take us to Kaylah," Saff demanded.

The men started to move as ordered, down the stairwell, and they collected a couple more on the way. Saff tried to remember the palace blueprint, but her mind was all jumbled, and she grew wary with each step.

After one more level of stairs, they were met by a surprise. A large one. The stairway led into a grand room, full of guards.

Now to see how this works out... Maybe they shouldn't have worried about the other Unitas members. Maybe they should have stayed in hiding until the outside troops had breached the palace.

This time Arlo barked out a command for them to all stand down, in his most authoritative voice. Devin ordered the guards they'd picked up on the way to join the others.

No one moved.

Saff panicked. They could try to book it and hide again, but they'd have dozens of guards on their heels in no time. Unitas couldn't actually kill Soren—they needed information from him, and if he died, they'd have no bargaining chip.

A guard at the bottom of the stairs shouted an order toward an exit. "Call the archers."

Oh crap. They couldn't handle more arrows.

"I'll kill him," Saff said, flaring an arm blade, resting it against Soren's throat. "Stand down." She lit her eyes, hoping that added some level of intimidation, but it likely didn't mitigate her now shaky voice.

It was a stalemate. Until the archers would arrive.

Devin coughed again. That didn't exactly add to their intimidation factor, either.

"So..." Arlo whispered. "Running away again?"

Retreat might be their best option without backup, cooperation, or Kaylah in the same room. If Saff's party decided to kill Soren, the guards' actions would be unpredictable. Had Soren set up someone to take his place? He didn't have a legal right to the throne in the first place. If Saff killed him, they'd lose valuable information, but he'd no longer be a threat... And it might cause enough confusion?

She couldn't risk it. As a Hail Mary, she tried to think of what Kaylah would do, other than tower over the guards with an authority they might actually recognize. Most of these guards were probably whispers, manipulated most of their lives and forced into their line of work. They wanted freedom, right?

Swallowing hard, her heart thumping in her chest, Saff squared her shoulders. "We know most of you are whisper rifters." She surveyed the room; there were subtle looks of acknowledgement and surprise. "We know you don't always get a choice in what you do, and that you're not allowed to share the truth about who you are and what you're capable of. Kaylah wants to stop that, not keep exploiting you. What has *Soren* ever done for you?"

The guards' eyes focused on Soren, almost in unison. Once they looked back at Saff, their expressions grew darker, more menacing. *That should have worked, right?* Why were they acting like she'd just given them a motivational speech on why they *shouldn't* surrender?

Devin leaned closer. "I think—"

Their time was up. A dozen archers ran into the large room at the base of the stairwell, raising their bows, aiming at the Unitas party.

Saff, Devin, and Arlo stepped back.

"I think it's time to get the hell out of here," Arlo said, only a hint of fear in his voice.

Saff looked over her shoulder, and her hope fell to the floor. Of course they'd sent guards to cut them off. There was nowhere to retreat to now.

"Kaylah cares about you and your loved ones. Soren's not a real king!" Saff shouted, her voice almost pleading. Sweat dripped down her neck and back. "Soren just cares about himself!"

The only movement from the guards was that of the archers as they took aim. Arlo curled his vines in front of himself as a shield, but it wouldn't do much against a dozen archers. Saff stood partially behind Soren, and Devin stepped to cover her more. "Any other ideas?"

Glancing back over her shoulder, she eyed the guards blocking their retreat. There were a half dozen of them, so the three of them stood a better chance attempting to retreat, rather than engaging with the guards and archers at the base of the stairs, but still... *Where's the rest of our strike team?* Were they all dead by now?

Shouts came from the exits of the grand room. Guards barked orders, and half of them ran out of the room.

That was good. Not good enough. *Should we surrender? Would that buy more time?* All of the archers had stayed behind, as well as over a dozen guards.

The yelling and fighting grew louder in the hallway.

No one at the bottom of the stairs gave orders to shoot the Unitas members, but the arrows were still aimed up. The guards on their level didn't rush at them.

Fifty heartbeats pumped in the blink of an eye. Each minute was an hour.

Then the fight poured into the grand room down below. The archers turned their weapons on the intruders—not Unitas members, but Seeder soldiers, the front line of their nation's cumulative force.

Saff's breath hitched with cautious hope, as Seeder soldiers pressed in. She didn't know what the fighting looked like outside, or how many had breached the palace. And Soren's forces had not yet surrendered.

Devin shouted to their troops below that they had Soren.

Saff glanced over her shoulder once more. Three of the six guards decided they didn't like their odds and ran off in the opposite direction. The other three, however, looked like they had made up their minds to take back their king. They charged Saff's group.

Throwing Soren to the floor, Saff blocked the first vine attack with her blades. Devin and Arlo stood their ground, also fighting. Three-on-three wasn't bad odds, especially with a Seeder as powerful as Saff, but that didn't matter with Devin hurt and all of them depleted, especially if these guards were fresh, especially if they had extra strength as whispers.

The rest of the battle was a whirlwind of chaos as Saff's party fought tooth and nail to keep Soren out of reach.

Saff nearly collapsed from exhaustion by the time the remaining palace guards finally announced their surrender, overpowered by Seeder soldiers. She and Devin leaned against each other, both panting. "We should still take him somewhere else until the entire palace is secured," she said.

Devin and Arlo agreed, and they all groaned as they shoved Soren along, back to the nearest room they could find. They shut the door behind them, and Devin slid down a nearby wall, wincing, bloody from head to toe, hacking up more blood.

It killed her, knowing there wasn't much more she could do at that point. Seeder healing repaired damaged tissue, but it didn't miraculously suck excess fluid out of lungs. Still, she moved a hand to his exposed chest where the arrow had pierced, expending additional energy in an attempt to heal it just a *little* more.

Almost instantly, she felt queasy and had to stop.

"I'll be fine." His inhale was more of a gurgle than anything.

She frowned, kneeling next to him, laying her forehead on his chest. She knew what she needed to do next, but before she could force herself to say it, Devin did. "Do you have it in you to go check on the others? See how … well, how everyone else on the team is?"

He didn't even have to say that he mostly meant his sister, Heather. "Yeah, I'll send some soldiers back to help you two. I'll go check it out."

She grunted as she forced herself to stand and balance.

"Don't worry." Arlo nodded to Devin and a thoroughly disheveled Soren. "They'll take good care of me." He grinned.

Saff cracked a tired smile. He was probably just as worn out, energy-wise, as Saff and Devin, but less severely wounded.

She ambled out of the room, closing the door behind her, praying she didn't meet any resistance. Thankfully, the palace was flooded with Seeder soldiers by now. Saff asked a group of soldiers to go up to the room to help guard Soren, and to heal the Unitas members if they could spare the energy.

***

Less than an hour later, Saff and Heather sat on the floor in one of the dungeon cells. The walkthrough of the palace to get there had been devastating. Saff had found Flora, and Rachel, and Kaylah, as well as others.

So many bodies. So many lost.

The stone floor Saff and Heather now sat on was covered in as much blood as they were. Saff was sick to her stomach. From hunger. From physical and energy exhaustion. From the horrors she'd just witnessed. She wiped her bloody hands on her pants, but they didn't come away any cleaner.

"Those are some pretty bad gashes," Heather commented.

Still dazed, Saff examined her forearms. It didn't really matter. Neither of them had energy to heal more right now. Or enough to stand. Or do anything. "I'll survive."

Heather frowned. "Are you okay?"

Saff looked at her hands. "I don't know." Her eyes filled with tears. "I can't believe … she's dead. I should have—"

"Don't," Heather reprimanded. "We did the best we could. We *all* did the best we could."

Saff sniffled, still in shock from the faces of the fallen she'd seen on her way to the dungeon.

And just like her brother, Ben—her friend was gone.

Chapter 42

SHE DIDN'T HEAR ANYTHING SIGNIFICANT when she woke. But she did wake. Rachel opened her eyes, disoriented, not sure where she was. She lay on a soft bed, blinking at the ornate ceiling. She studied the room. This wasn't Seeder style, but it was familiar. This was … exactly like the room in the palace she'd woken up to after she'd been kidnapped.

She started to breathe heavily. A quick visual sweep of the room told her she was all alone. This time, there wasn't a nurse in the room. She had an IV in her foot, but her arms and legs were free, not handcuffed to the bed. She wanted to get up, but her body ached, especially her head.

The door clicked open, and a nurse came in. Spotting Rachel awake and alert, the nurse called through the still-open doorway. "Let him know she's awake! Right away!"

Rachel swallowed hard. She froze, not sure what to ask first. Who was 'him'? Had they been successful? Was she about to go through a fresh batch of hell? Who had made it out?

Her heart soared when Guillen appeared at the door. He was wide-eyed, relief written all over his face, as he rushed to her side.

He crouched and grabbed her hand. "We thought we'd lost you!" he breathed. "How do you feel?"

She blinked. "I… What…" She closed her eyes, trying to focus. "Did it work?"

"Yes. You're okay. Kaylah's okay. Unitas has the palace secured." He kissed her hand.

She bit her lip and started to cry. "Good. Is everyone…?"

He frowned. "We got pretty beat up. But a few of us in the raid made it out alive." He whispered, "We lost Jon."

Rachel's tears flowed freely as she mourned her friend, whose loyalty she'd once questioned. He'd given up so much, too much. Guillen shared the names of the others who had fallen. She wondered how Saff was taking the news of her training partner's passing. Rachel hadn't had much of a chance to get to know her, but Flora had seemed like someone Rachel would have liked.

"And the kidnapped girls?"

Guillen looked down at their hands, rubbing hers with his thumbs. "We got the last one away from the Vines … but … she … um, she's not responding. We don't know about the three who were taken from the safe house. They weren't here, but we'll keep searching."

He looked up with an apologetic frown and wiped at her tears with his thumb. "But how are you feeling? You've been out for almost two weeks. With our combination of medication and your people's healing, we were really worried with how long it was taking."

She closed her eyes again, mentally assessing her aches and pains. The biggest one was her head. She moved a hand up and felt a divot in the back of her skull. "I think I can move everything … and I think … I'm okay…"

"Sorry to interrupt," the nurse said cautiously. "I can remove the IV and leave you two in privacy?"

Rachel nodded. "Thank you."

The nurse completed her task and opened the door to leave. "I'll be elsewhere in this hallway, if I'm needed."

After the door clicked shut, Guillen turned his focus back to Rachel. He searched her face with his stormy blue eyes. "I love you. I've been checking on you constantly." He looked as though he might cry. "I was so worried."

"I love you too."

"Is there anything you need? Something the nurse could do? Or something I could do?"

"Stay with me?" she asked.

Guillen pulled up a chair and held her hands while she regained her strength. He went over their victory. They'd gotten to Kaylah; they'd been right about her location. She was currently awaiting her formal coronation, but had already been declared the rightful queen. Between Unitas campaigning and Kaylah having previously been beloved by her people, the transition wasn't being met with too much resistance.

Soren had been clever, but hadn't paced himself well. He'd stretched his soldiers and assassins too thin, and his grandiose plan—his bargaining chip—as 'leader of the whispers' seemed to have been more of a pipe dream than anything. There hadn't been a whisper uprising.

But there *had* been a stunt uprising.

And as much as the Ivy Kingdom was discontent and bitter, the Mother Vines were the lifeblood of their cities and towns—Soren had been far too confident in his chances of winning his people over.

The Vines didn't just protect the palace or distribute nutrients throughout the kingdom; they were the veins and arteries of the Ivy people's sense of community, so much of their identity, their spirit and pride.

Once, smaller Family Vines had been controlled by a matriarch in each Ivy family. When they'd banded together to form their own kingdom, that power had been pooled, sacrificed, willingly given, by *every* family in the kingdom. In an attempt to unite their people and gain strength, they'd assigned it to one matriarch—the queen.

It would have taken a lot more than what Soren had offered for the Ivy people to truly turn from their queen.

Rachel had known that their win was all but inevitable, or at least had convinced herself there was no other option on the table, but now that it was actually reality, it was all so crazy to imagine, hard to grasp. Kaylah was the person she wanted to see next, out of everyone, though she figured it may take a while—a queen in wartime surely had a busy schedule.

Guillen went on to explain how Unitas was guarding the palace. The Seeder army was still out in force, continually fighting with rogue groups that refused to accept the change in power, the absolute shift away from a centuries-old war. There was still a ton of work to be done, but he assured Rachel they could rest safely. Enough had been done ahead of time, and since the win, that he was confident green folk would be able to move forward with hope in a different future.

The good news was invigorating.

Finally.

Their people could glimpse normalcy.

Finally.

And people like Guillen… They could live a normal life now.

Rachel focused on the hands holding hers. Guillen wore a ring she'd never seen him wear before, carved from green stone.

"Is that … jade?"

He grinned. "Yes. It is."

The victory somehow felt more hollow. "Does that mean…?"

"Yes. It does." He slipped it off, showing her the tiny swirl symbol carved on the inside, then replaced it, the symbol permanently resting against his skin. "Specially commissioned by the queen herself."

She rubbed his hands lovingly. "I'm happy for you. Did you get to be the first Ivy to test it?"

"No. I wanted to wait to share my first time with someone I love." He winked.

"I think you should go." Her voice lacked true conviction.

He raised his eyebrows. "Without you? That's crazy talk. I can wait as long as you need, to be up to full strength. I want to go with you."

She removed her hands from his. "I want you to go." She looked down, unable to keep eye contact. "And I don't mean for a couple of days. Take a break from all of this and explore if it's the right future for you over there. You deserve to find out if a life with humans will make you happy."

"Why would you say that?" His voice conveyed as much confusion as it did hurt.

She pursed her lips. "I love you. But me expecting you to stay is like you asking me not to go into battle. Sometimes we just have to allow those we love to take a chance, to figure out what's best for them."

"I know what's best for me. And that's you. Why are you trying to push me away?"

She fought back tears. Couldn't he see how messed up she'd become?

"Let's," he breathed calmly, "talk about this once you've rested a little more. You just woke up from something pretty rough."

"Yeah… Maybe…"

"I'll stay with you?"

She scooched over, making room for him on the bed, and gestured for him to cuddle up next to her. She loved the warmth of his touch, the scent of fresh mint and juniper berries, but was tortured by it at the same time. They lay in bed for more than an hour. Rachel mulled things over, unable to fall asleep again, her thoughts cycling through everything with each tick of a clock in the corner.

A quiet knock came at the door, and she smiled as Guillen carefully tried to unwrap himself and get out of bed without disturbing her.

Catrina opened the door and cautiously peeked in. Rachel had a good view of her and smiled wider.

Scowling in Guillen's direction, Catrina pointed at Rachel. "She's already awake."

He sighed. "Yeah, well, she needs rest. You should have waited."

Rachel rolled over. "She's fine. I was awake. I'm happy to have another visitor." She started to force herself into a sitting position, and Guillen moved to help her.

Catrina strolled over, sitting in the chair next to the bed. "I'd offer you a hug, but maybe I'll wait until you're feeling a little better."

"Thanks."

"So … you guys have talked?" Catrina asked, her eyes darting between Rachel and Guillen.

"Not about *everything*," Guillen snipped.

Rachel glanced back at him, surprised by his reproach. Then again, she hadn't seen *that* much interaction between the siblings.

Catrina stubbornly pursed her lips, her nostrils flaring back at him. She turned her focus to Rachel, smiling. "Well, I'm glad you're doing better. We all are."

Rachel smirked. "Even your mom?"

Catrina let out a small chuckle. "Well … I'm sorry to say I don't think there will be a lot of invitations for holidays."

Rachel's smirk remained. "Yeah…"

"It's nice to be home. Well … back in our lands," Catrina offered. "For now, we're staying at the palace until things calm down."

Catrina glanced back at Guillen before addressing Rachel again. "Well, I'm going to go. I was just really happy to hear you were up. And thank you, for everything."

"Of course. Let's talk soon."

Rachel watched Catrina leave—she really liked her. She swallowed a lump in her throat as Catrina closed the door, leaving the room to just the two of them now.

Guillen shifted in bed, sitting cross-legged to face her. "She had lots of great things to say about you."

Rachel nodded. "She's a good kid. I'm glad I got to meet her."

"Yeah." He smoothed the comforter. "So…"

"What haven't you told me?" Rachel frowned, waiting for the rest of the bad news.

His eyebrows scrunched in confusion. "I gave you all of the big stuff. It'll take a while for things to calm down, but I promise—everything's fine."

She cocked her head, then straightened. That gesture still caused her head to scream. "Then what is it you two were just talking about?" Her heart sank a little. The tension between Catrina and Guillen must have been about his ring, if there wasn't more bad news. Catrina wished for him to explore the human world, to make a new life for himself.

"I know I'm not alone in thinking you should spend time with humans, give yourself a fair chance to find out if it's right for you." She rubbed the silky bedsheet. "I couldn't forgive myself if you didn't at least give it a try."

Guillen opened his mouth as if to protest.

"Look me in the eye and tell me you didn't join Unitas *knowing* this was one of Kaylah's goals. That not even a small part of you didn't hope for this day to come."

They'd spent *countless* hours on their mission together discussing their cultures. He'd been just as enthralled learning about human culture, as she'd been learning about Ivy culture. Yes, he'd also been intrigued by Seeder society, but a lot more of his questions had centered on humans. It was only natural for a stunt to relate to humans.

Guillen broke eye contact, swallowing. "I promised I'd never lie to you." He shook his head, determination in the set of his jaw. "But

I'm not taking the coward's way out by running away from my problems."

She raised her eyebrows in challenge. "That's really what you think of all those people we met together? Just for taking an opportunity at a better life? You think they're cowards?"

He wilted. "No."

"I didn't think so. You once admitted yourself that it was a dream you had."

"Dreams change. You're not getting rid of me that easily."

She weakly gestured at him with an open hand. "*You* once told me to not worry about our future, to take things one day at a time. But … we're here now. You may think you know what you want, but I don't. I don't know what I'm going to do with my life."

She finally allowed herself to think about life beyond the war. Maybe they'd ask for more help on research with the frequent Seeder rifts, or intrarealm rifting. There was so much they still didn't know about cave rifting and the health risks they faced now that they could rift more than once a year.

Perhaps she needed to spend more time trying to bond with her family back home and helping piece Seeder society back together.

Guillen gnawed on his lip, his face turning pinker. "I wish you'd stop taking things I've said and trying to use them against me."

She rolled her eyes. "Just… We could use some space. You figure out what you want. I figure out what I want."

He ran his fingers through his hair. "Dammit, Rachel! No." His eyes narrowed in frustration. "I mean." He rubbed his face with his hands, exasperated. "I know what I want. Stop trying to talk me out of it! And you might be confused about what you want, but I know what that is, too."

"And what's that?"

Chapter 43

GUILLEN SEARCHED RACHEL'S EYES. "You want to be with someone you can trust, who cares about you. You want to do things that make a difference. We want the same thing."

Magda's death glare flashed through her mind. "There are people out there still fighting against this change. How could we be together right now?"

"I don't care about them." He flopped back on the bed, staring at the ceiling. "And we could start things off right here. We have an offer to stay here, in the palace, as advisors. We could both be happy, continuing to help Kaylah out."

Her eyes widened in surprise. Kaylah had already made more plans for her, for them, than Rachel had imagined for herself at the end of the war. They'd never talked about things that far out.

He sat back up, his eyes piercing her with determination. "I'd throw away this ring, if that's what it took to prove how serious I am. You're trying to break up with me, and all I'm hearing are objections about wildly hypothetical futures and technicalities. But not once have you told me that you want me to leave you alone, because you don't love me anymore."

She couldn't lie. "That's because I *do* love you."

He stared at her. "Great. And I love you. So…"

She studied her hands.

"Or is this about the darts?" His voice was softer. "Because … maybe if you'd had them in the fight… And now you're…"

She was on the verge of tears. "No. That's not it at all!"

"Then why are you doing this?"

She thought about her head injury, but wasn't sure if she could say it.

When she didn't respond, he puffed out a breath. "Maybe I should let you recuperate more."

"I'm perfectly lucid. But maybe that's really the problem." Her biggest concern finally came to the surface. "I have *so* much that I need to work through. And I don't want to use you. I need to learn to be strong on my own." She couldn't look him in the eyes. "You know what a mess I was, and that was before I'd taken lives. I've got a long road to health, and *not* just with my body. I can't ask you to stand by my side. That's not fair."

"No." His voice was confident, firm. "How is it *using* me, if I want to be there? Working through hard stuff, that's what people do together, when they love each other."

She leaned her head back, gently resting it against the headboard. Closing her eyes, she sifted through her thoughts. It was all a jumbled mess. A tornado swirled with pictures of torture, betrayal, death, and all kinds of hurt, fear, and anxiety. The one light that emerged from it all—clear, untainted—was her love for him.

She opened her eyes. "It's not that I *want* you to leave me. Even if we figured out all of my problems, I couldn't forgive myself if you didn't at least step back and consider what you'd give up, okay? What if you realize you want to start an Ivy family of your own someday, but you miss your opportunity because we're trying to make things work out? You need to be open to the idea of things changing."

He reached for her hands. "I *do* want things to change. But I plan to have you there with me. Nothing has changed for me, not about you."

She was out of excuses. Thinking of Catrina, she rolled her eyes. "She might pull a Magda, you know?"

Guillen squinted, clearly confused.

"Your sister. If I stayed here, if we stayed here together. She... I don't think she'd like me so much after that. I know how much she wants you to go to the human world."

His whole face scrunched with further confusion. "What are you talking about?"

"That's what that exchange was about, between you two, right? Your ring. The human world."

His jaw dropped. After a moment, he closed his mouth, his lips forming a smirk. "You know, we're not good at having these moments at the right time."

It was Rachel's turn to show confusion.

Leaning to the side, he reached into his pocket. "She was bugging me to see if we'd had *this* conversation." He pulled out a tiny decorative bag. "I ... had actually hoped to complete your collection. You have the matching necklace and earrings. But I'd hoped ... that if you still loved me ... that you'd consider adding this." He pulled out a ring. It was set with a jade stone intricately carved into a butterfly. "She was urging me to bring up *this* ring."

Rachel gazed at the beautiful craftsmanship, and then her eyes shot back up to his. "What's this supposed to mean?" She could hardly breathe.

"Well, um..." He cleared his throat. "Kaylah said they make them a little different where you grew up, but I thought this fit you better. I... Rachel, life is complicated and messy. Love doesn't change that. It just means you have someone by your side to walk through it with you. Every kind of future I'd want, has you in it. I'm ... asking you to take a leap of faith. Marry me."

She swallowed hard, stunned.

He flashed an embarrassed smile. "Not that her opinion matters much in our decisions, but Catrina wants to add you to the family."

Rachel smiled and stared at the ring, entranced by it, considering the what-ifs. She'd given him options; she'd offered to set him free. It wasn't something she'd wanted—it was something she'd felt she needed to do. She remembered every happy moment together, and even the rough times, all that they'd worked through. She imagined them taking in little ones of his kind.

After a while with no answer, he continued. "I know I've moved fast, and we never even talked about this. I'm not sure if marriage is even important to you. I guess, you know, what you said in the cave really rang true for me. That you loved me. Today, tomorrow, always. That's how I feel about you. If you need more time, I just really… I just…"

She allowed her walls of hesitancy to crumble as she asked herself what mattered most to her. She wanted a place she could call home. That could never be the human world again. It may not ever be South Fortinda. But a person could be a home, and Guillen was hers. Her eyes welled up with tears. "Yes."

They both looked up, locking eyes.

"Yes?" He searched her face.

She pursed her lips. "Yes."

He cautiously smiled. "Okay, you're sure?"

She nodded.

His mouth hung open. "Great. I… I love you. I… um…" He blinked. "Kaylah said guys in the human world kneel, or something?" He started to shift on the bed awkwardly.

She tried to stifle a laugh at his sweet attempts to follow Kaylah's overreaching coaching about human customs. "No. Please. Just come here."

She bit her lip as he scooched closer, slipping the ring on her finger. He gently kissed her on the lips.

Leaning back, he scanned her face with nervous eyes. "You're really sure? I don't expect you to turn your back on your people.

Until I could safely visit, or move over there, and until Kaylah doesn't need my help as much, it could be complicated. But … I'm willing to make it work, however you want."

She answered, more clarity and courage in her heart. "We can accomplish a lot of good, no matter where we are. I don't plan on pulling you away from your people." They had plenty of Seeders back in their lands who could research and rebuild without her. "This kingdom needs us more right now, anyway."

He beamed. "One day at a time. As long as it's together."

Her heart content, she slid back down on the bed, under the covers. She admired the ring on her finger. "There is one problem, though." Her comment was met with concerned blue eyes. "That was a pretty weak kiss for a proposal." She grinned.

He glared at her playfully. "You're still recuperating."

She stuck out her tongue. "I'm stronger than you think. I'll let you know if I'm hurting."

He slid down next to her. Turning onto his side, he gazed lovingly into her eyes. "You *are* strong. Don't forget that." He moved in closer, caressing her lips with a tender kiss, then slowly expressing more, following her cues.

***

It took two full days before Kaylah was able to make a visit, though she'd sent word amidst her onslaught of meetings. In the meanwhile, Rachel happily gained her strength with Guillen at her side, when he didn't have his own meetings to attend. Once Kaylah showed up, Guillen excused himself to allow them some privacy.

Rachel carefully got up from the bed, and Kaylah gave her a tight hug.

"Sorry it took so long!" Kaylah said.

Rachel chuckled. "You should be! I expect a queen to dote on me."

Kaylah smiled warmly.

"You look amazing, by the way," Rachel said as she perched on the edge of the bed. "Gorgeous dress, all the bling. Just saying… I've never been bitter that you look like a supermodel, but I did *not* look this nice after being kidnapped."

Kaylah laughed, flourishing a hand in the air. "That is because I. Am. Amazing." Her smile faded as she sat down in an armchair. "And I didn't take before-and-after pictures from the time of my rescue, to the time Heather and Saff and the nurses were finished healing me. If you know what I mean."

Rachel frowned, positively miserable. She'd just offered the most insensitive compliment possible. "Sorry. Yeah."

Kaylah smoothed out the silky dusty-rose fabric of her dress. "It's okay, you know. We'll always have someone to talk to who understands, right?" Kaylah winked. "Group therapy, on the house."

Rachel grinned. "I love you. I missed you."

"Ditto, of course." Kaylah hummed playfully. "And I understand there's more love in the air, and I *totally* approve."

Rachel raised her eyebrows. "I guess I really need to care about your approval now, don't I? If you're going to be my employer?"

Kaylah grimaced. "Gross. Don't think of it that way."

Kaylah stayed for a while. They caught up on how everything had proceeded and what was to come. Rachel was surprised to hear they hadn't severed the War Vines once they released the last Seeder girl. They instead realized they were a fantastic opportunity. They'd never had something so strong that it could reach all the way across the Green Lands. The Vines were currently inert, but Unitas was going to try to use them—instead of as a way to puncture the Seeder barrier thickets, they'd try to deliver the cure for the poisoned lands. Kaylah expected it to be significantly more efficient than healing the lands by hand, provided they could figure out how to do it.

As for the Mother Vines, the more local ones that had been established for decades, Kaylah would be turning greater control of them over to the communities. She'd formed a council for local representatives to gather and discuss it. As for the stunt communities, she'd formally asked Guillen to step in as a representative. His people hadn't been granted leadership in the past, a voice of their own. They needed the right person to help sort through changes that were to come. Rachel would be appointed to help him and work as a liaison with Seeders born without powers.

It was still in preliminary discussions, but Kaylah and Seeder leaders were already considering redrawing old boundaries. They proposed taking some of the Neutral Woods and designating those places for green folk without powers, Seeder or Ivy, should they want to live there. It wouldn't be compulsory, but it would provide new options for those in the Ivy Kingdom who'd been oppressed, and for the Seeder population that had been forced to live with such drastic limitations.

The last thing Kaylah hesitantly wanted to discuss, before getting back to meetings, was Soren.

"His execution is scheduled. It's set to be public." She pursed her lips pensively. "I ... never thought I'd have to do something like that. But it's what our people need to establish order. It's going to be held next week."

Rachel processed the news in silence. Even now, after all he had put Kaylah through, she gracefully discussed her brother's execution as a necessity for healing, for justice, and not as a hateful, vengeful act.

"This is my suggestion, though you get complete freedom to choose." Kaylah paused. "I think you should be gone. Take Guillen away, try out that ring of his. But before you go, if you want to say your piece, you can. If you never want to see Soren again, I completely understand, and you don't have to."

Rachel nodded. "Thanks for giving me the choice. I'll think about it."

Kaylah gave her another hug. Before leaving, she added one more thing. "We all have demons we need to slay. And while he's hurt both of us, a lot of us, I feel like... What I'm trying to say is ... if you came out of that cell, and he didn't make it to the public execution, I wouldn't fault you. We would make it work."

Chapter 44

GUILLEN HELD RACHEL'S WAIST. "You're sure you want to do this? You don't have to."

"I need to. But thank you." She kissed him. "I won't be long." She drew a deep breath, forcing herself not to fixate on the bloodstained wall down the hall. Her blood. Her near miss.

She'd mentally prepared herself for this meeting. No matter what Soren said, she wasn't going to let him get to her. The guards opened the cell door, and she stepped in, alone. He was chained to a chair, his arms and legs restrained. He looked a little roughed up, but not nearly as much as he deserved.

He grinned at her. "I knew you'd miss me. Conjugal visit?"

She pulled out her knife, coolly. "That would be hard if I castrated you." She smirked as he tensed up.

She continued, "We still haven't found your wife. But we will."

"Screw you," he spat. "She and I will still put an end to Kaylah's idiocy, and get back what's ours."

Rachel nodded thoughtfully. He was truly unhinged, delusional. He'd never really been the author of any brilliant plan. He'd taken advantage of his mentor and co-conspirator's death, carrying the torch. "You go ahead and think that. I'm not exactly concerned. I'd be more worried about your execution, if I were you."

He scowled.

"My apologies, I won't be there. I'll be on my honeymoon."

He narrowed his eyes.

She turned the knife in her hand, admiring the pearlescent handle. "I'd introduce you, but you've met. His sister is going to be one of the witnesses. Catrina is such a sweet girl!"

Soren laughed. "You fell for that compost heap?"

Her eyes flashed green as she gripped her knife, putting it to his throat. "He is ten times the man you could ever be." She'd told herself she wouldn't let anything he said get to her, but hadn't prepared herself enough for that.

His eyes gleamed with defiance. "You're pathetic. You couldn't turn in an Ivy in the human world, and you couldn't hurt me now."

She pushed the knife tighter against his skin. "You wouldn't be the first Ivy life I've taken since then. Or even the second."

His Adam's apple scraped under the knife as his cocky expression melted to fear.

Rachel had already made the decision as to whether she'd take Soren's life herself. She'd thought about what Kaylah had said, about having demons to slay. When it came down to it, Soren *was* a demon, but not Rachel's. The voice that always told her she wasn't enough—that she was a screwup, that she was beyond redemption because of her mistakes—had never been his voice, not really. It hadn't even been her stepdad's voice. The voice that truly hurt was her own, after years of accepting their lies and falling prey to their manipulation.

Her demon was the mess of self-talk in her head. Killing Soren wouldn't slay that.

Though, she'd decided she might not be opposed to torture. They still needed answers, and he deserved more punishment than a simple death would allow.

She removed the blade from his neck, turning it once more in her hand. "I came up with this fantastic idea. You see, I think the punishment should fit the crime. If I said the number sixty, does that mean anything to you?" She didn't wait long for him to respond. "Sixty is an estimation. That's how many cuts I estimate were made in my skin, between restraints, drugging, and War Vine insertions. Each day. So I think it's only right that you understand how that feels. Sixty cuts, for each day I was hooked up. And sixty more, for *every* day each of the other girls was hooked up. Double for the girls that died in your custody."

She furrowed her brow. "It's only fair. And the beauty is, we can keep doing it and just heal you, so we can ensure you'll survive to the end of the punishment. Unlike our girls."

He stared at her, a subtle glare in his expression, but chose to stay silent.

"I'm not going to waste all of *my* time; we've got others that will gladly help. We could even have you looking perfect for the formal execution, isn't that great?"

She raised her knife, touching the tip to his forehead. "Should we start with one here? Symbolically, for the time you stabbed me right there?"

She looked into his cold eyes and realized how similar they were at that moment. She'd been tortured by her mistakes, but it was mostly self-inflicted by a guilt-ridden mind. He'd just epically lost a war, one blunder after another. Unlike Rachel, his pride would cause his judgment to be carried out by others.

Lowering the knife, she instead crouched down. "I might ask them to spare you some pain, if you can answer one question for me." She tapped his knee with the flat of her knife. "Where are our three missing girls that were taken from the safe house?"

His lips curled into a grin; he remained silent.

She sheathed the knife. "Well, just remember, when you're ready for the pain to stop, to just move on to the merciful death part, let us know you're ready to talk." She glared, standing up. "Good luck with the rest of your life." She crossed the cell, grasping the door handle.

"Wait."

She stopped and turned.

Soren searched her face. "My wife is carrying my child. If you find her, could you live with yourself, executing a pregnant woman?"

Rachel's eyes grew wide. Out of all the scenarios she'd planned for in this encounter, this wasn't one she'd thought of. She studied his expression. He wasn't smug or desperate. He'd said it matter-of-factly. She had to remind herself how fantastic a liar he was. Kaylah still wasn't sure if he actually was a whisper rifter, or if he was a charlatan.

It dawned on Rachel how he must feel at that moment. His wife had fled the palace, leaving him to die alone. Rachel almost even felt sorry for him. She considered his question. "Even if I believed you, that's not my call to make."

He pressed his lips together, nodding. "You know what it's like to not grow up with a real dad. What if I'm not lying? Could you deprive a child of a father?"

She swallowed hard, clenching her teeth. She also hadn't prepared for him to open that wound. Or to be so desperate as to make up such a lie. "*No child* would benefit from having you in their life. You're not a father. You're a monster."

She gripped the door handle, ready to move on.

"I'm sorry!" Soren blurted. "I was stupid. I love you. I've always loved you." His voice was full of remorse, his expression conveying regret.

She stood silently as he rattled off excuse after excuse—about how he hadn't known better, about how he deserved another chance, about all sorts of crap that she half tuned out, lost in her own thoughts.

Was I really ever so weak that he genuinely thinks I'd forgive him? That I'd fall for him? Try to save his life right now?

How many chances had she given him when they'd dated, when he'd lost his temper, or had treated her like she was stupid, or had knowingly pushed her past her comfort zone in their relationship?

It hurt to realize that a year ago, she *might* have actually considered trying to fix him, trying to help him, trying to rehabilitate him. But she wasn't that girl anymore. The curtain had been pulled back, and the unstable, selfish puppeteer was now exposed.

And frankly, his death sentence had nothing to do with her. It had to do with millions of other people.

"Please," Soren pleaded, his handsome green eyes glistening. "I can change. I could make you so happy."

"You could never make me happy," she said calmly. "Guillen does. And I…" If she didn't quite believe it yet, she was close. "I deserve to be happy." Yanking the door open, she promptly left the cell, only breathing again once the door slammed closed, once the guards secured the latch.

***

The next day, Guillen was off at official meetings when an unexpected knock at Rachel's guest room door pulled her focus from a journal. She opened the door, and a palace guard bowed.

"Please follow me."

Rachel bit her lip, still wary about being in the palace. "Is something wrong?"

"No, ma'am. The queen requested your presence."

She reluctantly followed him, winding through corridors and climbing stairs. "Where are we going?"

"She's waiting for you in the tower."

Rachel still hadn't taken Kaylah's staff up on the offer of an extensive tour of the giant building, and it wasn't exactly a tour they were on, but they covered a lot of ground. The higher the floor level, the more ornate the décor. As they reached the highest levels, real ivy vines ran along the top of the walls almost like crown molding. Something felt different as she got higher in the palace. It wasn't exactly eerie, but quiet … and not just because there were fewer people there.

They were met by another guard at the base of a short stairwell. The escort had Rachel go up the narrow winding stairs first. Two more guards stood at the top landing, on either side of the only door at the highest level.

Rachel scrutinized the tiny space. Several more ivy vines converged at the landing. She was both oddly calm, and also nervous, to be surrounded by so many muscled guards.

"She's expecting you right inside." A guard opened the door.

Rachel was floored at the sight beyond the open door. Nearly every inch of the walls and ceiling was covered with vines. It was a rather small area, with a massive window at the other end of the room. A border of stained glass surrounded the window; under it sat a padded bench. Facing the window was a throne.

The guard ushered Rachel in as she picked her jaw up from the floor. The moment she passed the threshold and the guard closed the door behind her, a wave of calmness hit Rachel.

"Come sit down." Kaylah's melancholy voice came from the throne.

Rachel strode past the throne and gently perched on the only other place to sit, on the bench under the window. From this angle, she also spotted a large bookshelf inside the room, near the door. Constructed of dark metal, the shelves were closed off with latticework. The latches were busted, looking like they'd been pried open.

She shifted her focus back to Kaylah. "Hey. How are you doing?"

Kaylah sat with her legs tucked up under her, gazing out the window. Her long dress flowed down to the floor. "Not sure."

Something was still off here, and that something included Kaylah. "Pretty cool room," Rachel said. "How long have you been hiding away up here?"

Kaylah continued to look out the window. "Since I got up."

Rachel pursed her lips. It was already early afternoon.

"This is the Queen's Room," Kaylah said, still dazed. "By law, anyone entering without the queen's presence and express invitation, takes upon themselves a death sentence."

Rachel almost smirked at the absurdity of such a law, but Kaylah's face remained completely sober. "You're serious?"

Kaylah's eyes finally met Rachel's. "Yes."

Wow. "Well … thanks for inviting me, then… I'm guessing not a lot of people get the privilege."

Kaylah cracked a smile and shook her head. "My mother only brought me up maybe a handful of times that I can remember, over the years. Though she spent plenty of time here. And it feels completely different now." She sat up straighter. "And I'd bet the kingdom you're the first Seeder to ever be allowed up here."

"I'd say that's a safe bet. Thanks again, for the honor. On the topic of it feeling different … am I going crazy, or does it feel, like … really weird in here?"

Kaylah pointed in Rachel's direction. "This window faces the kingdom. This room is where the Mother Vines end."

Rachel looked around again. She'd never seen a room so overtaken with plant growth—it wasn't like it was a greenhouse. "And how does that work?"

Kaylah drew a deep breath. "What does it feel like to you?"

Rachel bobbed her head back and forth. It felt like a nice place to meditate, honestly. A good place to sort out your thoughts. She could see the appeal—it was quiet, secluded. She shrugged. "It feels nice. Really peaceful. Is that something the Vines do?"

"Yeah. It used to feel that way for me, too."

Used to? "But how does it feel now?"

"I can feel their power. This is where a lot of decisions are made."

Rachel slowly nodded. This … wasn't the Kaylah she knew. It might be that Kaylah was still sorting through her trauma, and feeling the weight of an entire kingdom on her shoulders. But it felt like something more. Rachel was becoming nervous, and it didn't feel right to outright ask 'Why did you send for me?' Instead, she skirted around her growing suspicions. "You've said the Vines answer to the queen. What does that feel like? Do you actually hear voices or something?"

Kaylah let out a short breathy chuckle. "No. It's not like that. But it's feelings, impressions."

"Your Mother Vines… They're a major cause of nutrient depletion in your kingdom, right? You said you were going to turn them back to the people?"

Kaylah's lip quivered, a look of despair covering her face. "I murdered my uncle here. My parents were killed here. The irony's not lost on me that my brother sits in the dungeon and I'm up here, when a few weeks ago it was the other way around."

"He broke your laws," Rachel replied softly. "They all hurt a lot of people. But I know it's still hard."

Kaylah's eyes filled with tears. "What if I'm wrong? I want to do things right. But this is my legacy … and I'm destroying it. I love a human. I won't have kids. I have no family. I'm throwing away tradition."

If the crown princess had only been in this room a handful of times, it wasn't likely Catrina had actually ever been there, but perhaps she knew about it as a downline heir. It had been Catrina who voiced concern about power corrupting when they were back at the Unitas camp.

Rachel wrung her hands, not wanting to say the wrong thing. "You have family. Guillen will always be there for you. And Catrina. Ginger and Nathan. And Eric…" That one was a tricky subject she perhaps ought to have omitted. "And me. You're my sister. I'll never leave you."

Kaylah sniffled, wiping away tears.

Rachel cleared her throat, cautiously curious about a sensitive but related subject. "Guillen told me you have two younger brothers. I still haven't met them."

Kaylah looked down. "Yeah. They're in the care of people I trust right now. This is all pretty confusing for them."

Rachel left it at that. After conversations with Catrina, she'd learned more about their family dynamics. Kaylah's younger brothers were only eight and ten. Kaylah hadn't known them well with all of her time away, and now she was going to be something of a mother figure for them. To add to it, Catrina had confessed she wondered if having the younger kids had been an attempt by the former queen and king to produce a second heir, a replacement heir. Rachel wouldn't touch that with a ten-foot pole. The hurt implied by those assumptions could cut incredibly deep.

"As for traditions." Rachel shrugged. "Not all traditions are created equal. Save the best of them. Make new ones. For your kingdom to come to this point, they chose to lay aside even older traditions—remember that." She side-eyed the jungle of vines surrounding them. "You've made a heck of a lot of good decisions without this room. What would happen if these vines were removed? That's what's going to happen soon, right?"

"It's not that simple. I'll be touring the communities. That'll give me an opportunity to meet the people more, and retrain the Vines at the roots."

Rachel squinted at the half answer, adjusting her seat on the bench. "Will the Vines in this room go back to the communities?"

Kaylah frowned, barely speaking above a whisper. "I'm afraid I'll lose that connection to my people."

Rachel opened her mouth, pausing. "I … couldn't even pretend to understand how your powers work. Or try to tell you what all the right answers are. But I know you'll do the right thing. And I think you need to ask yourself if it's *connection* that you're afraid of losing, or *control?*" Rachel tilted her head, only a slight pain accompanying the movement. "You have a lot of good people in your kingdom; I've met them. They just need a strong leader. And that's you. Not this room."

Kaylah gnawed on her bottom lip.

Rachel touched one of the leaves on a nearby vine. "Are there any other laws I should know about? So I don't accidentally get myself killed?"

Kaylah grinned. "Best friends get immunity. Just try not to murder me?"

Rachel chuckled. "Deal." She stood, running her hand across the leaf-covered wall. The vines clinging to the wall were large, bumpy, and tan, interwoven across a canvas of stone. The leaves rustled, cool and soft against her skin. "Can you tell them apart? If they connect you to the communities, do you know which is which?"

From the throne, Kaylah's eyes followed Rachel's movements. "I can. I couldn't when I was younger, but now I can."

"If Guillen weren't closely related to you, which community would he have been forced to have inked on his arm?"

Kaylah frowned, standing up, surveying the wall. She touched a vine. "This one."

Rachel walked over to meet her. She cautiously grasped the vine, waiting to see if Kaylah would stop her. When she didn't, Rachel slowly tugged it free from the wall. It entered the room through one of several openings near the ceiling. Kaylah didn't stop her, so she proceeded to reach into her pocket, pulling out her knife. "What would happen if I cut it off?"

Kaylah's eyes locked with hers. "It'll regrow, until I retrain them on-site. But I won't be able to feel that connection from here until it regrows over the next few weeks."

Rachel stood on her tiptoes, trying to reach as much of the vine as possible. She held the knife to the vine. "But the people will have less drain on their resources? Sounds like a promising start before your tour to meet the people as their new queen."

Kaylah nodded, mulling it over. "The Vines also help with our rifting barrier, keeping a protective perimeter around the palace." She furrowed her brow in thought. "But just trimming the parts in this room wouldn't weaken that."

Rachel waited for her approval, still holding her knife up to the vine. "Okay. So…?"

"Do it." Her tone landed somewhere between resolve and surrender.

The vine was tough, but with enough force and a little sawing, Rachel cut it loose. These Vines had much smaller tendrils than those she'd seen on her travels thus far. She handed the severed vine to Kaylah. Kaylah ran her fingers over it.

"I wonder what these walls look like under all this," Rachel said.

Kaylah let out a long, slow, measured exhale, gingerly laying the vine over the throne. Then she reached for her own dagger, pulling it from a sheath under the skirt of her dress. "Let's do this."

Rachel smiled as they both picked a new vine.

After a good half hour, the walls were bare, but marred from smaller roots having found cracks to expand. The best friends sat on the bench together, and Rachel wrapped her arm around Kaylah. The energy of the room had dissipated. Now, a *natural* calm was taking its place.

Kaylah laid her head on Rachel's shoulder. "Thanks. I don't think I could have done that alone."

"Any time. I'm honestly surprised you had the wherewithal to tell the guards to bring me. You were pretty out of it."

"I didn't," Kaylah whispered.

"What? The guards came to get me on their own?" That didn't seem consistent with such a strict edict about who was permitted into the Queen's Room.

"I was afraid," Kaylah confessed. "I told them to get you if I was in here too long. I didn't want to become like my mother, at least not the side of her I saw when she'd spent too much time here. And especially not susceptible to anyone else's influence." She picked at her fingernails. "I've never even told Eric."

Rachel rested her head against Kaylah's. Perhaps Seeders and Ivies really did have more in common than they'd previously thought. The most powerful members of their races could also become the most vulnerable, given the right circumstances. And from her own experience, it took great strength to ask for help, to admit that you needed it.

Hadn't Saff asked about this very thing? About the Ivy queen having a weakness?

"You know…" A smile grew on Rachel's face. "I'm not eligible to vote in your kingdom, and you don't even vote for the queen. But you'd have mine."

Kaylah chuckled. "Thanks. I'll take all the votes I can get right now, especially if they're votes of confidence."

Sighing, Rachel examined the marred walls. "Maybe you should commission Saff, or some other artist, to do a mural up here. Something bright that reminds you of your vision for the future, since that's where we're headed anyway." She squinted, looking closer at the junction of the wall and ceiling.

Rachel stood back up, using her knife to push aside bushy stumps of detached vines. "Maybe don't paint the trim. Call me crazy, but I think that's jade."

Kaylah rose, scrutinizing it as well. "Huh … yeah. I guess there's more I could learn about how that works."

Rachel smirked. "Pretty cool. Catrina recited a poem that said all green folk are kin."

Kaylah gave her a hug. "I'm glad you're staying."

Rachel squeezed her tight. "You're family."

"Well, we've got a lot of work to do. Fixing this mess of a realm is going to be one heck of a marathon."

Rachel pulled back, holding Kaylah's shoulders. "Then I guess we better get to it."

Kaylah frowned, nodding.

"Would it cheer you up if I let you call me a lightning bug?"

A grin grew on Kaylah's face. She slung her arm around Rachel's shoulders. "You'll always be my favorite glow-butt bug."

Rachel laughed as they opened the door and exited the Queen's Room. "You only get to call me that in private."

Chapter 45

SAFF AND DEVIN LAY DOWN for the night in the massive palace chambers they'd been assigned, in the softest bed she'd ever slept on, holding each other under satin sheets.

The next thing Saff knew, she plodded down a stone corridor, the crispness of her vision veiled in memories. She'd just left a bound-and-gagged Soren with an injured Devin, and an almost-as-ragged Arlo.

The palace air was cold around her as she made her way through the hallways, as her heartbeat slowed, as sweat stung her eyes and wounds. She feared a guard might slip their restraints, might come out of a hiding place and attack her. She was spent.

Despite the soldiers and captives and chaos all around her, the moment seemed muted, foggy, off. Her legs were twice as heavy as they ought to be. She kept plodding forward, searching, *needing* to know who else in the Unitas strike teams had made it out alive.

There were bodies everywhere, but it was especially heartbreaking when she ran across her first Unitas victim, a Seeder. She backtracked to where they'd initially come in. The last time she'd seen Jon was a few flights up, at the top of a set of stairs.

Shock from the battle gave way to tears as she found his body at the base. She double-checked and confirmed Jon was gone. Green folk weren't invincible, not even whispers. She dreaded returning to tell Arlo.

Saff didn't have to search long before her heart completely shattered. Flora lay on her back, her hair a cascade of burgundy braids. Saff dropped to her knees by Flora's side, feeling for a pulse, but there was none. She sobbed, guilt washing over her. Flora had been so promising, so strong, so talented, so young. But her fighting partner had abandoned her, had betrayed them all.

Saff couldn't move. She just knelt there, holding Flora's still-warm hand, crying. She wasn't capable of moving, of seeing anyone else she cared about dead. She couldn't fathom making her way to the dungeons now to discover what had become of Rachel, Heather, and Kaylah.

"Saff?" Ginger's tired voice made Saff look up.

She sniffled, relieved to see a familiar face, even if it was as mangled as Saff's was.

Ginger gave her a sympathetic frown. "Is Devin…?"

Saff sniffled again. "He's okay for now."

Ginger forced a smile. "Good. Have you heard about the other team?"

Saff's stomach knotted. The team taking on the dungeon was much smaller. That wasn't promising. "No. I was going to head down there to see."

Nodding, Ginger held out a hand. "Let's go together."

Forcing herself to stand and join Ginger, Saff couldn't stop thinking about Flora. She'd never get that image out of her mind. As they walked down a long corridor, away from Flora's body, the palace no longer felt cold.

Saff's face and ears grew warm as she thought about Raven and what she'd cost Unitas. Saff didn't care to count how many she'd killed in this war, but none of those kills had been in revenge. Until this point.

If someone hadn't already gotten to the girl, Saff would. And this time, no one would be holding her back.

She balled her fists, trying in vain to contain her anger and hurt. Needing to take out some of the building aggression, she shifted a wisp of energy to her arm, and slammed it into the wall next to her.

"Saff!" Devin groaned, winded. "Oww!"

Her eyes shot open. Her fists were still balled, but it only took a second to realize what she'd done.

She frowned, devastated, as Devin wheezed. "How bad?" she asked.

He lay on his side, clenching his jaw, holding his ribs with his hands. "Why do you have to be so strong?" he muttered through his teeth. "I'll be fine."

"Come on, let me see." She moved his hands and healed him. While he was doing significantly better with his recovery after two-plus weeks, he still had a ways to go. Getting beat up by her certainly wouldn't help.

"Sorry," she said as she removed her hand.

"You're fine," he said, snuggling up next to her. "I'll be fine."

She sighed, kissing him on the forehead. She'd had vivid nightmares after Ivy assassins had tried to kill her twice in the human world, though never as bad as Rachel had them. Saff was definitely having vivid dreams again now, and while she never woke up screaming, she *had* woken up hitting or kicking Devin more than once now.

Saff had suggested she sleep on the couch in the suite they'd been assigned, but Devin wouldn't have it. As guilty as she felt for hurting him and interrupting his sleep, being together was something they both needed.

"You're right. We'll both be okay," she said, holding him tighter.

Closing her eyes, she tried to fall back asleep, but couldn't. Instead, she savored Devin's body warmth while replaying her nightmare, and how everything that day had gone. She analyzed how they could have done things differently, but it wasn't like it could make a difference now. The fog of the nightmare had lifted, but the scene in her mind was as clear now as the day she'd experienced it.

When she and Ginger arrived at the dungeon, a dozen soldiers had just opened the doors and cleared the area. Saff's feet barely moved as she was permitted entrance; it was like trudging through a marsh, her feet hesitant to walk down the stairs and find the rest of their group.

The first truly familiar face was Kaylah's. "Saff!" Kaylah's face and arms were in rough shape, red with cuts and infection. Two Seeder soldiers helped her walk toward the stairs Saff was descending. Ginger ran down the stairs and helped.

Saff and Kaylah shared exhausted but mutually relieved smiles. "I'm glad you're okay." Saff wanted to give her a hug, but Kaylah didn't look to be in a state where that was a good idea.

"You too. How's camp, and everyone else?"

Saff fought back fresh tears. She couldn't answer that. She couldn't make a list of the dead yet. "I think Devin will be okay."

Kaylah frowned.

Almost tripping over a body at the bottom of the stairs, Saff stepped back to allow space for Ginger and the soldiers to help Kaylah up.

The stillness of the area weighed on Saff's heart and nerves. "What about Rachel and Heather?"

Now Kaylah's eyes filled with tears. Saff's heart stopped beating entirely.

"They're down the hall with Guillen."

Saff forced herself to breathe. *Would she word it that way if they were dead?* As Kaylah was escorted up the dungeon stairs, Saff crossed the landing to the hallway. To her right, all she could see were fallen guards and an open cell door.

To her left was a busted old wooden door; that was the direction Kaylah had been led from. Saff crossed the threshold. A Seeder soldier stood facing an opening several yards down.

Saff willed her legs to move faster, and peeked inside once she got there. Rachel lay unconscious on the floor, her head and neck soaked in blood. A Seeder matriarch cradled the back of Rachel's skull with glowing hands. Guillen knelt next to Rachel, squeezing her hand, his face the picture of desperation and concern.

Heather sat against the wall, hugging her legs, despondently staring at Rachel. Heather didn't look to have any injuries of her own, but she was drenched in almost as much blood as she had been when Saff found her right after Ben had died.

They'd saved Kaylah. They'd caught Soren. But at what cost?

"Can … I help?" Saff offered, not that there was much she could do.

The healer shook her head, continuing her work. Heather finally looked up, meeting Saff's gaze. She frowned and started to cry.

Saff sat next to Heather, and in silence, everyone watched the healer do her work. After several minutes, someone arrived with a stretcher. Saff, Guillen, and Heather stepped into the hallway so the others could carefully lift Rachel onto the stretcher.

Guillen followed Rachel, thanking Heather before leaving down the hallway. Only then did Saff give Heather a tight hug.

"Is he okay?" Heather asked.

"Yeah, Devin will be fine."

"Please tell me it's over," Heather begged in a soft voice.

Was it? Taking the palace back didn't mean the war had officially ended. Saff had to have hope, or at the very least, had to give Heather some. "Yeah. It's over."

Heather sniffled in her arms for a minute. Everyone else had left the dungeon area except for a few guards who were sweeping and clearing each and every room.

The prospect of climbing back up a short staircase felt akin to climbing one of the impossibly tall mountains on the realm's Outer Rim. Not up to it quite yet, Saff instead focused on the open cell door down the hallway. "That's where Kaylah was being kept?"

Heather had her arm around Saff, Saff's arm around her. "Yeah."

Curiosity called Saff closer. They stepped over pools of blood and a few bodies of guards to reach it.

The cell was disgusting, the floors covered in dirt and dried blood. Something glimmered from the corner of the cell—a knife she'd seen Kaylah use before. Saff picked it up and examined it. The tip was bent, the blade covered in nicks.

After looking the room over, the sisters-in-law stared at each other, neither of them speaking. Nothing needed to be said. They weren't lifelong soldiers. Nothing was guaranteed right now. They both desperately needed healing, showers, naps, willow bark, and a gallon of water each. Probably chocolate, too. None of those were options right now. Maybe the water, once they gained the strength to tackle those stairs…

Saff slumped to the floor of the cell, and Heather followed suit. Resting her face in her hands, Saff breathed deeply. "Just a few minutes."

***

Saff turned in bed, blowing out a long breath. By the time she had finally gotten around to hunting down Raven, someone else had already taken her out. Never before had Saff been that livid, but it had likely been a blessing in disguise that she couldn't kill Raven herself. Now that she had a clearer mind, she was grateful fate hadn't afforded her that opportunity, that choice. She wasn't sure what a revenge killing would do to her, and if she could ever be the same person after that.

That scared her.

In the two-plus weeks since they'd been there, Kaylah had ordered the palace searched. Every inch was scoured for information Soren wouldn't give up, like where the kidnapped Seeder girls were located. Nothing was found on their account, but Kaylah had discovered information about whisper rifters, and she'd confirmed rather quickly that Raven had been the whisper who helped in her kidnapping.

As much as Saff hated Raven, new information helped her understand Raven's plight. Like 'Queen' Beata *supposedly* was, Raven had been hiding a pregnancy.

Saff admittedly hadn't always been great at putting herself in other people's shoes. But how would that have felt, to have your powers used against you from a young age, to have an attractive, charismatic, powerful man seek you out, to think he loved you, to think you shared something rare and special, and to have him be the father of your unborn child? What lengths would a mother go to for her child and the man she loved?

Kaylah shared with Saff that Soren had callously admitted since his capture that he'd known Raven was pregnant, and still sent her as a spy, still allowed her to die in battle. When Kaylah had informed him of Raven's demise, he'd remarked, with the warmth of a sociopath, 'That's a shame. I kind of liked that one.'

It felt wrong to pity the traitor. What she'd done was unforgivable, yet somehow, understandable.

Saff rolled onto her back, sighing again.

"Not able to fall back asleep either?" Devin asked.

"Nope."

***

Later that same day, Kaylah escorted Saff, Devin, Rachel, and Guillen out to the burial grounds to pay their respects. Saff's feet were heavy as she walked with Devin's arm around her shoulder. It was too nice of a day to go to a graveyard. The sky should have been dark and stormy, rainy and depressing. It didn't have a right to be filled with warm sunshine and songbirds. Nature hadn't gotten the memo.

Kaylah first showed them the Seeder burial yard. She'd consulted with a Seeder council member about how to respectfully handle their dead. With battles still being fought, and it being several days' walk across the Neutral Woods, they'd settled on a plot of land next to the Ivy royal burial grounds, so they could be buried as heroes.

Devin rubbed Saff's upper arm as they gazed on the soil; yellow flowers emerged from some spots, purple flowers from others. The area had been set up with a picket fence and guards to ensure it was safe and the graves wouldn't be desecrated.

Saff pondered on the site and the names of those she'd gotten to know. She was conflicted. This wasn't one of their traditional burial grounds. It wasn't surrounded by dozens of loved ones from their families and villages. It didn't have the large central tree with soothing energy that she knew from back home. But each of these Seeders had known what they were up against, what they were willing to sacrifice. She hadn't previously thought about where she and Devin would have been buried if they hadn't made it out alive, but it would have been here. It didn't feel as wrong as it should have, to have their fallen comrades so far from their homelands, given family meant so much. It still didn't feel right, though—how could *any* untimely death be?

After a little while, they walked with Kaylah to the Ivy royal burial grounds. A mat of intertwining vines covered the ground. Unsurprisingly, the graveyard was filled with tons of large ornate tombs. The larger the stone, the more important the person. This was the final resting place of Ivy queens and kings, and their families. Passing one, Kaylah shook her head. Rachel and Guillen trailed behind her. Rachel's head lowered as they walked by. Saff's stomach knotted when she read the name on the offending gravestone— Nuren. It was sickening to have his body in a place of honor. She wished she could cover it with a black cloth, or something—a mark of shame. But he had made his mark on history, and *that* mark would bear his shame.

Kaylah hesitated at a much larger set of tombstones—her parents. Rachel and Guillen wrapped their arms around Kaylah. Saff frowned. That had to be hard. Saff had grown up as Mel, a girl with two loving human parents, and then added two loving Seeder parents. Kaylah's family was a mess, and she was rightfully conflicted. Saff and Kaylah had shared some good conversations since Kaylah's liberation, and had *finally* put to rest all of their differences.

Though they weren't technically Ivy royalty, Kaylah had still chosen to bury the Ivy Unitas fallen in a far corner of these grounds. This one was harder for both Saff and Rachel. Saff and Devin strolled over to Flora's grave. Devin held her tighter as the tears came. Flora had been so young, so full of life, and had had so much life still left to live. But she had lived her days with conviction; she was an example Saff would never forget.

"It's not fair, you know?" Saff whispered.

"I know," Devin replied.

Saff had experienced firsthand how impressive Flora was in a fight. But when Flora was forced to take three enemies on by herself, even *she* couldn't win. Saff sighed. If she'd been a Seeder, she might have been able to heal her own wounds ... perhaps could have lived. But not everyone was born with the same abilities and advantages.

Saff still struggled with guilt. She knew she shouldn't. *She* hadn't killed Flora. Saff and Devin had been paired on the strike team— their job had been to move swiftly and seek out Soren as soon as possible. But for every point of logic she held, a counterpoint of grief and guilt contradicted her.

Saff glanced over at Rachel and Guillen, standing by Jon's gravestone. Jon had given off that 'strong but silent' aura. He'd been key in Kaylah's first real move to stop this, when she'd freed Rachel and killed Nuren. Jon had sacrificed a lot to join Unitas.

Arlo had taken the news hard that his childhood buddy hadn't made it out. He'd demanded to bury Jon himself. He'd left for home a few days after the palace takeover, to inform Jon's family of the loss. Saff hoped they'd see Arlo again someday to properly thank him for helping out.

Despite the sadness of Jon's demise, a small smile crept onto Saff's face as Rachel bent over and placed a sunflower on his grave.

Green folk didn't do that—they didn't cut flowers for decorations or gifts or memorials. It was very human, very nostalgic and sweet.

After a few more moments, the group shared hugs and began the walk back to the palace. Saff continued to watch and think about Rachel. Guillen's arm was firmly around her, as Devin's was around Saff. Rachel leaned her head against Guillen's arm. If they made each other happy, then they couldn't be wrong for each other. Happiness was what Rachel deserved.

Saff frowned, her mind momentarily drifting to her sister-in-law, Heather. She hadn't gotten her happily ever after with Ben, but she'd saved Rachel's life that day, down in the dungeons.

Heather was another great example for Saff, on pivoting when life changed your plans. After she'd lost her fiancé, Heather had wanted to throw herself into Unitas and help. Saff and Devin couldn't be more proud. Heather had already returned home to Seeder lands. They still didn't know how their families fared—they had several family members likely still fighting in the war.

"How are you doing?" Devin dared to break the silence with a whisper.

Saff stood straighter. "Ready to go home." They were staying for the coronation, then going back to South Fortinda.

"Me too." He kissed her cheek. "How are you feeling about coming home one short?"

She knew he meant the fact Rachel was staying behind. Like with a lot of things, Saff was conflicted. It wouldn't be a walk in the park for those two, but Rachel had always been on a different path from Saff. She hadn't ever settled in back home with Seeders. But she'd found a home; she'd made one.

Saff and Guillen had shared a couple of good private conversations while Rachel was unconscious. The only thing Saff could find to disapprove of was the fact that being with Guillen would most certainly mean Rachel was truly giving up her Seeder culture. Guillen wouldn't even allow Saff that point; he'd promised to try to urge Rachel to give her family and people a chance, to try to visit often when things calmed down.

"I'm happy for her," Saff finally answered Devin, though it didn't mean her heart didn't hurt. She'd mentored several students, but had only risked her life with one. Had only felt fiercely protective of this one—and she was growing up and walking away. She didn't need Saff anymore. "We all have to learn to let go and move on, right?"

Devin gave Saff another squeeze.

Chapter 46

THE NEXT DAY, KAYLAH LENT Rachel one of her gowns. Rachel chose a simple yet elegant cornflower-blue one from Kaylah's enormous closet.

It had actually been Rachel's idea to have the ceremony so quickly. Guillen hadn't planned on popping the question right away while she was still recovering, but Catrina had all but forced his hand.

Rachel and Guillen knew what they wanted. While they could have waited for things to calm down, or to organize something bigger, they'd decided to start a new chapter before they were thrown into the hectic demands of their new positions. Perhaps someday, they'd have a ceremony that involved more of those they loved.

Rachel sat in front of a beautiful vanity decorated with carved and gilded nature-themed filigree, as one of Kaylah's maids braided her hair. A soft knock rattled the door.

"Come in."

Saff popped her head in. "Just wanted to see how you were doing."

Rachel grinned, sparing a glance at her new ring. "I'm good."

Saff entered, shutting the door behind her. She crossed the room and sat in a nearby chair.

Rachel drew a deep breath, imagining all of Saff's objections. "I appreciate you and Devin attending the wedding."

"It's an honor. We're happy to be here for it."

"But…" Rachel ran her thumb over the soft bristles of a hairbrush she held in her lap. "I'm young. And we haven't dated long. And my family hasn't even met him, and they don't know I'm doing this. And that I'll be living over here for who-knows-how-long."

Saff crossed her legs, straightening a dress she'd also borrowed. "Why are you telling *me* all of that? Are you having second thoughts?"

Rachel bit her lip. She was anxious, but none of it was centered on whether she was meant to be with Guillen. "No. I could never be happier with someone else. I just … know this won't make everyone happy."

Saff shrugged. "Marriage isn't about making *other* people happy. And I'm not one to talk. I married young. Devin was my first boyfriend."

Rachel narrowed her eyes. "And you're still happy with your choice?"

"Every day," Saff answered confidently. "Sometimes, you just know."

Rachel nodded as the maid finished up and excused herself from the room.

Saff gently tugged at creases in the yellow fabric of the dress she wore, smoothing them out. "Family is important. But not all families look the same."

"Thanks. I really appreciate you."

Saff stood, resting her hands on Rachel's shoulders. They looked into the beautiful gilded mirror together. "Ditto," Saff said.

"You guys are going back to Seeder territory soon?"

Saff tucked a piece of baby's breath a little tighter in Rachel's braid. "That's where we belong, but we'll be in touch. We're still working with the council and Kaylah. We're just a rift or two away." She smirked. "I had a queen approach me about a painting."

Rachel met her smile. "Do tell."

Saff pursed her lips. "I'm flattered. But I'm not a pro. And I feel that project would be more appropriate assigned to an Ivy. I told Kaylah I'll work on something a little smaller as a coronation gift, when I can grab some free time."

Rachel thought back to her museum tour with Guillen. Someday, when the dust settled, they could have artists from both sides working together. They could exchange work in exhibits between the nations. Someday.

Saff straightened the chain of the necklace Rachel wore. "Well, things are about to start. I shouldn't be bugging you. Anything I can do for the bride?"

Rachel cocked her head. "I think I'm good. Any advice for a soon-to-be-newlywed?"

Saff looked at the wall, pondering. "Fight for your marriage as much as you did for Unitas."

Rachel beamed. "I will." Her thoughts turned pensive. She and Saff had chatted a bit during her recovery, but there was still so much unknown about their futures. "Going back to mentoring in South Fortinda?"

Saff crossed her arms, wrinkling her nose. "I don't know."

"Hmm." Rachel twisted her lips, nodding. "Yeah, I'd be hesitant too. It's kind of like when humans have their last kid and they call it quits. They know they can't turn out anything superior after that one, so they stop while they're ahead."

Saff chuckled. "You weren't my last Seeder girl to mentor."

Rachel pointed at her. "Last full-time assignment."

"You have a point. But … I've had this conversation with my sisters before. Human parents only stop at the last child because they realize things are going downhill and they can't handle it anymore." She winked, and Rachel stuck out her tongue.

"But in all seriousness, I don't know," Saff confessed. "That scares me. Sometimes I don't like options. Someday, who knows how soon, we won't need all these soldiers, or training in covert ops in the human world. Maybe I'll focus on my paintings, or help with education in other ways." Saff scratched her arm. "I wish I knew."

Rachel stood and gave her a hug. "You'll do great, no matter what you pick." She squeezed a little tighter.

Another knock sounded at the door, and Kaylah peeked her head in. "Hugging without me?"

Rachel and Saff chuckled. Kaylah sauntered over, every bit the queen in a dark plum gown, and gave them each a hug. "Are we ready?"

Rachel gathered another breath, standing tall. "Absolutely."

In a beautiful room at the palace, Kaylah officiated Rachel and Guillen's wedding, with a half dozen witnesses. Saff and Devin held hands, smiling wide. Catrina was just a hair short of giddy. Catrina and Guillen's father, who Rachel finally got to meet, stood next to Catrina, peace in his expression. Ginger and Nathan were happily reunited, ever supportive as they'd been in the human world.

***

After the ceremony, Rachel and Guillen spent their first night as a married couple in the human world. With Kaylah's knowledge and the other girls' discoveries, Kaylah now had the cave near the palace primed to travel there, too. Taking Kaylah's suggestion, Rachel and Guillen planned to be gone for Soren's execution, but would return in plenty of time for Rachel to not be in danger of root rot. The official coronation would take place the day after they planned to return.

As always, the lack of Green Lands energy made it feel colder in the human world, but the crisp autumn air made Rachel feel it even more. Having spared no expense, they honeymooned in an extravagant hotel—at least, the nicest one that wasn't too far from one of their caves.

It was the middle of the night; Rachel sat out on the balcony, lost in her thoughts and wrapped in a blanket. The sliding glass door opened, and Guillen strolled out to join her, also wrapped up. She scooched over on the bench she'd claimed, making room for him.

He kissed her on the forehead. "You okay?"

She smiled warmly, her heart full. "I'm perfect. Just woke up and couldn't fall back asleep. Figured I'd take in the view."

He tugged on his blanket. "It really is colder over here. This is supposed to be the same season as back home? How is it you're not freezing?"

She nodded. "I'm alright. I'm tempted to seek out some hot cocoa, but for now, this blanket and my Seeder warmth have me covered."

Guillen nudged her shoulder. "Just remember, it's okay to ask for help. I would not be at all opposed to helping you keep warm." He gave her a seductive grin.

She giggled. "Offering to warm me up back in bed?"

He bit his lip.

She tried to keep a straight face. "Or were you offering me another blanket?"

He pursed his lips. "You're never going to let me forget that, are you?"

She gave him a toothy smile. "Nope. Never." She leaned over and placed a tender kiss on his lips.

He moaned as she moved to whisper in his ear. "I love you." She shifted and left a trail of kisses down his neck.

"Are you ready to come inside?" he asked, wanting in his voice.

"Just give me a couple more minutes."

He took a deep breath and stood. "Okay. If you're still having trouble sleeping, I don't mind staying up. And if you're *sure* you want to get a matching Unitas tattoo, I *really* don't mind helping you determine where on your body you want to get it." He winked before leaning down for one more smooch.

Her whole body tingled at his touch; she wanted to jump into his arms right then, but remained seated. She couldn't stop grinning as she watched him go back inside. She was elated to be with the man she loved. To have won the war. To have a safe place back home in the Green Lands, a position where she could make a difference.

But everything was still a bit grey. Every day was a struggle, and it would continue to be. Yet, she could confidently smile—things would never be the same. Her sense of safety had been ripped from her in her childhood. But as a woman, she was now surrounded by those who really did love her. And would support her, be there for her, as much as she would be for them.

She thought of Saff. Saff and Devin wanted to have a clutch someday. Rachel couldn't help but think how crazy they must be to want that many kids. But she was also ecstatic for them, that their lands were being healed, and Seeder borders expanded past the tainted soil into the Neutral Woods. Their families would no longer have to be separated.

Rachel was at peace, looking forward to their plans for the next day. She'd finally be able to introduce Guillen to her human mom, Samantha. And … to her human dad, Brad.

It was something of a wedding gift from Guillen and Eric, though they'd never anticipated it that way. Guillen had picked up on how much it gutted Rachel to not know what had happened to the dad who had disappeared from her life when she was a little girl. He'd sent a request to Eric in a letter, to try to find out—the letter she herself had delivered when she brought Guillen's mom and sister there for safekeeping.

Eric had used some Unitas funds to hire a private investigator to find out what had happened with Brad's mysterious disappearance. In typical fashion, Nuren had told a truth, peppered with lies. Brad was alive and well. And he *had* actually freaked out when his wife finally shared their daughter's nonhuman identity, two years into their marriage.

But he hadn't abandoned them willingly. Not sure how to process the news all of those years ago, he'd confided in the wrong man—a co-worker named Rob. Rob—Duke Nuren, Kaylah's uncle—had been serving as a lowly assassin general in the human world at the time. He'd latched on to the opportunity to infiltrate a Seeder family network and learn their secrets, gaining him a position with his brother, the king, in the palace as an advisor. Nuren had threatened Rachel and Samantha's lives, and Brad had left the picture. Brad had looked them up every year, but kept his distance, seeing that 'Rob' was still there, a looming threat.

Apparently, Brad and Samantha had already been reunited. Rachel hoped for her mom's sake that they could pick things back up, and was over the moon that Samantha might have some confidence in love again. Brad had always made her mom happy, and happiness was what she deserved.

All that aside, it would be an awkward conversation the next day. It had taken *one* man in shock, taking a revelation from his wife poorly, to start all of this. To lead to the pain and deaths of so many, his own adopted daughter included in the host of those harmed. Rachel didn't harbor any ill will against him. She couldn't. Had he never done that, the war would still probably be carrying on back in the Green Lands, and here in the human world as well, hidden in the shadows, always locked in a stalemate.

Rachel took one last cleansing breath and spotted a falling star in the night sky. She watched it glide from view, not wishing for a single thing, before returning to bed.

***

After five blissful days in the human world, Rachel and Guillen drove back to the cave. He'd absolutely loved it there, able to walk around so casually with people just like him. The couple agreed to carve out vacations to make sure he'd get to enjoy plenty more experiences, even starting a list of what they wanted to do.

Rachel couldn't contain her excitement at seeing a familiar face at the cave entrance. She jumped out of the car and ran to give Eric a hug.

"Congratulations!" he said.

Guillen walked up and extended a hand. "It's nice to finally meet you. Thank you for all you've done."

Eric gave him a hearty handshake. "My thoughts exactly. Thanks for *your* part in all of this." He pulled Guillen into a brotherly hug. "I mean it. And I'm happy for you and Rach."

She beamed, her eyes glistening with gratitude. But then her joy faded. Eric hadn't been able to attend the wedding. He wasn't able to be with the one he loved. She and Saff hadn't been able to figure that one out.

Eric stayed by their side, and Rachel gave him another hug. He smirked.

"What?" she asked.

"I'm not here to say goodbye. I'm here to escort you two back." He pointed out a ring of his own.

Rachel grabbed his hand. "How did you get it to work?!"

"Nuren would be *livid* to know how much he's done for us. He discovered he could make the War Vines work for him by accessing Seeder blood. But *any* regular Seeder or Ivy blood can be used, with the right symbol, and right words, to make this work. Just like with Guillen's ring, there are a lot of restrictions right now on how the jade is being distributed."

She stared in awe at the ring, shaking her head. Kaylah hadn't divulged how close she was to figuring this one out. "How did she even find the time with all she's doing right now?"

"They said your mentor helped."

Rachel's heart warmed. Saff and Devin were still at the palace, and of course she would have her nose in a book, eager to help and discover more lost secrets of the Green Lands.

"Its use is limited, until they can sort it all out," Eric continued, a grin plastered on his face as he turned the ring. "But I'm kinda lucky, being the fiancé of the queen and all."

Rachel surveyed his face. "We still don't know how you'll be affected. It might not be safe."

Eric shrugged. "The first human to test it made a trip without any harm."

Rachel shook her head. "We still don't really know much about our origins, our evolution process. How our people and powers changed over time. We think humans came over first and *became* green folk. So much could go wrong. Have you really thought this through?"

"Well … your ancestors might have been drinking primordial soup for a century before they went botanical, for all we know. And to me, Kaylah's worth the risk. I'd even drink the soup for her."

Rachel let her worries go. Kaylah needed as much support as she could get in her corner right now. She needed Eric at this pivotal point in her life. They needed each other.

"Take good care of her," Guillen said. "She deserves the best."

Rachel and Guillen walked through her rift first, followed by Eric, in shock and awe. Once they left the cave, he was even more dumbstruck.

"It's so … *green!*"

They laughed at his observation. The Green Lands were called such because of the lush and rich atmosphere, and the botanical beings who lived there. But apparently, to the naked human eye, there was *actually* a tint to it as well—like a slightly green photo filter.

Rachel and Guillen got to be present for the first moments of Kaylah and Eric's reunion. It was beautiful. Kaylah even cried, and probably squeezed Eric half to death.

The next day at Kaylah's coronation, the throne room was filled to overflowing. Afforded special positions at the front were the usual suspects—those closest to her, the honored members of Unitas.

Representatives from across the Ivy Kingdom were in attendance, as well as Seeder leaders.

Kaylah commanded everyone's attention as she entered in a breathtaking gown, which glistened as though beaded with emeralds. As she made her vows of loyalty to her kingdom, she made promises, she gave assurances, she planted hope. She pronounced the end of Unitas as a war movement, and designated it as a new way of life. The official Unitas symbol would also change. It wouldn't just be a flower and an ivy leaf. Behind them both was now a handprint: the sign of the third group, the easily forgotten ally that had stepped up to help end a war in a realm they'd never previously set eyes on—the humans.

Epilogue

SAFF RAN AROUND THEIR FAMILY COTTAGE, tidying things up for the special visit. She threw an extra glance at the corner of the family room where her canvas and painting supplies resided. It was a bit untidy, but she wasn't sure she had the time...

"They're here!" Devin called out.

Squealing, she bolted out the door. She almost bowled George over as she hugged him tight, and then turned to give her love to Pam. "Mom! Dad! We're so excited you could make it again!"

A crowd was gathering around them. "Come inside."

"I'll be in in a few," George said.

"I'll hang back and make sure they don't tackle the old man," Devin razzed.

George gave him a playful stink eye.

Pam and Saff snuck inside while Saff and Devin's kids were busy chasing each other and jumping all over 'Human Grandpa.'

Saff took a relaxing breath as she sat down. "Sorry they're so crazy; usually they're so well behaved. They're just *really* excited to see you guys!"

Pam pointed at Saff. "Never apologize for my grandkids." She sat down and crossed her legs. "How are things going? What's new and exciting?"

Saff thought about where to start. Visits from her human parents were rare, and now that she'd reached full maturity, her rooting had her permanently stuck in the Green Lands—that limitation had never changed, not even with the caves. Though, they *had* discovered matriarchs could actually cave rift intrarealm. The equal energy on both sides of the rift still allowed that.

"Things are good." Saff smiled. "The kids are growing so fast. We love helping with the local education board. Everything's just … really great. And you guys?"

"I'm glad to hear it. We're doing just fine."

A pair of Saff and Devin's kids dashing past the open doorway caught Saff's attention, and her eyes grew wide. "Benjamin!"

A little boy returned to view, scowling.

"Come here!" she ordered with a stern maternal voice.

Pam covered her mouth with a hand, poorly concealing a smile.

"What did I tell you?" Saff asked firmly.

"She started it!" Little Benjamin looked down at his bare feet, wiggling his toes.

Saff's eyebrows lowered as she gently lifted his chin to make him look at her. "I don't care. It's not safe, and it's not fair. If I see you chasing your sister with your blades out again, there will be *serious* consequences."

"Fine." He pouted.

Saff sighed. "Give Grandma a hug and then go out to Dad."

Little Benjamin got a warm snuggle from Pam before leaving.

After he left the room, Saff shook her head. "Seriously, that one. The irony of his defiance!"

Pam smiled warmly. "He looks a lot like his namesake, doesn't he? Especially when he's grumpy."

They both had a good laugh.

"Right?" Saff said. "But he'll be in for a serious awakening the day those girls' powers come in and they're ready for payback!"

Not five minutes later, a little girl came into the room, crying. Her lip quivered as she showed Saff a skinned elbow.

Saff gave her a kiss on the forehead and healed her injury before sending her on her way.

"Really, I swear, it's not always like this." Saff chuckled. "We normally have a ton of family help, everyone's just off doing other things so we could have more time alone with you guys before tonight's picnic." Saff was used to the chaos of large numbers by now, though it might be overwhelming for her aging human parents at a combined family picnic—all of Saff's and Devin's Seeder parents and their kids and grandkids had been invited. It would be a madhouse. The kind of madhouse Saff loved.

She shifted in her seat. "Which, by the way, Heather and her husband—they're hoping they can still have a clutch. They're thinking next spring will be her last chance. Either way, they look like they're doing real well."

"I'm glad to hear it," Pam said. "She deserved to find someone good for her, and live her life. Ben would have wanted her to be happy."

Saff wiped away a tear. Sometimes it still got to her, how much she missed him. Especially with how much she owed him. He hadn't just helped save her life in high school; he'd been the one to give her her extra power, extra energy-wielding ability. At least that was what she and Kaylah had surmised years ago. The timing of his intervention during the assassination attempt on her—during her botched bloom—had been perfect. Theoretically, she should have slipped into a coma, and by the time she'd woken up, her rooting would have likely passed. But instinctively, he'd accessed her energy to fight off their attackers, using just enough to keep the two of them safe, and, apparently, to keep her from losing consciousness, instead allowing her to reap the benefit of additional power for the rest of her life. He'd died never knowing that.

Pam gave her an understanding smile, then slapped her hand to her own forehead. "I almost forgot to tell you about the debacle at the cave on our way here!"

Saff was all ears.

Pam picked a piece of lint off her shirt. "I was *mortified*. Your dad and I went to pass through the cave rift, but it didn't work."

"What?" Saff scrunched her eyebrows.

Pam huffed. "Your dad and I had switched our tokens."

Saff chuckled. "Don't be embarrassed. I'm sure the cave workers see that happen all the time."

That was another awesome discovery Saff had had the pleasure of taking part in with her studies after the war. She still usually called Pam her 'human mom.' But strictly speaking, biologically—Pam *wasn't* human. In a way, they'd always kind of known that. If a Seeder girl didn't go back to the Green Lands by the time of her initial rooting, her powers died out, and she 'reverted' to her 'human form.' But she'd started out a seedling just like her sisters. And like any other green folk, Seeder girls, even those who had forfeited their powers, couldn't have kids with humans.

When they'd expanded their cave rifting trials to try to allow some of these girls to return home to the Green Lands, the kind of charms (or tokens, as a lot of people called them now) that humans like King Eric used, didn't work for them. They finally realized Seeder girls who had given up their powers still had residual Seeder energy in them somewhere. Just like Guillen and others who had been born without powers, they were technically Bomen. 'Bomen' was an agreed-upon title green folk without powers from both nations had taken for themselves—Botanical Humans. Bomen and humans had to use different tokens to rift.

"I'm sure they do have people goof like that often enough," Pam admitted. "I guess I was just too excited about this trip when I pulled them from my pocket."

Saff perked up. "Right! I got your riftmail. You said you were able to learn something exciting?"

"Yes!" Pam leaned forward in her seat, beaming. "We've discovered what village I'm from. My parents are gone, but I have some siblings still in the area. We're going to meet them!"

Saff smiled from ear to ear. Pam had admitted years ago that she'd regretted so casually forfeiting her powers, and the Seeder way of life. "That's so exciting for you! You'll have to tell me all about it. And get me their information—I'd love to meet more family."

"I will! Their village is in the far northwest, so it's not too close to here."

"Will you be taking the caves? Do you need help figuring anything out?"

Pam settled into her chair more comfortably. "No. With your dad retired, we have all the time in the world. And the Seeder council graciously extended our visa long enough for us to take our time making our way there. We're going to enjoy ourselves, taking in the sights." Pam started to choke up. "Finally making my trek home."

***

Rachel gave Guillen a huge hug. After a moment, he released her, gazing into her eyes. "I'm going to miss you."

He moved closer, leaning against her, her back against the wall. Sliding his hands to her waist, he stole a kiss.

"Ugh! *Gross!* Hurry up, Dad, they're here."

Rachel and Guillen chuckled in unison.

"Fine," Guillen called over his shoulder. "Make sure you and your brother have everything you need."

Rachel gave him one more peck on the lips. "That's a good sign, right? When you can still gross out your kids?"

He leaned in for another kiss. "I'm a firm believer in that."

She pulled back after a short smooch. "Alright, handsome. Let's go greet them."

He pouted. "I just got back from the northern council and you're already shipping me off!"

She stroked his chest with a finger, right above the place his Unitas tattoo was inked. "Yeah, well, I think you guys will somehow manage on a boys' weekend at the palace." She poked him in the ribs, and he grabbed her hand.

"Alright. But you and I have a date night when we're back." He walked with her outside. Wrapping his arms around her from behind, they stood and watched as the guards marched down their lane.

To their left was the teenager who had interrupted them; down the lane, their preteen son ran out to meet the approaching entourage.

"Make sure you both behave," Rachel reminded their eldest. "Uncle Eric will let us know if you were any trouble."

He rolled his eyes. "We'll be good, Mom."

Once Kaylah and Catrina were in sight, Rachel broke free from Guillen's arms and ran to hug them. Eventually, the group gathered at Rachel and Guillen's front door, accompanied by several guards. Guillen and their sons also exchanged hugs with his cousin and sister before taking off with a few guards.

"Come on in!" Rachel welcomed in her sister-in-law and the queen.

The three women sat down in the family room.

Rachel grimaced. "I'm sorry I don't really have good places for all of your guards to stay the night… Guillen didn't build this place with this kind of visit in mind."

Kaylah waved her hand while taking a sip of tea. "That's their job. They'll survive camping out there." She took in the room. "I'm glad I finally get to see the place all finished. It's stunning!"

"He always did take pride in his work, didn't he?" Catrina added with a smile.

"Yeah." Rachel grinned, savoring the warmth of the cup in her hands. "Took long enough to finish it, but he wanted something of his own." She set her tea down, making an animated face at Catrina.

"Of course, it would have been done sooner, if our boss didn't work us to death."

Kaylah gasped. "How *dare* you! Off with your head!"

The room erupted with laughter. Rachel stood, offering to give the women a full tour of their house. Guillen had built it from the ground up, but it had taken him several years with all of his duties in Ivy government that he balanced. Rachel's favorite part was the unique zebrawood paneling in the living room.

After their walkthrough, the group of friends settled back down to catch up.

Catrina shook her head. "I still can't believe how tall those boys are getting. Did you guys decide on what Tobias is doing for school next year?"

Rachel sat straighter in her chair. She still couldn't believe it herself. She had a *teenager*. Adopting a five-year-old and an infant when she was so young had *never* been on her list. The circumstances surrounding that decision had been filled with chaos and pain and struggle. Frankly, her and Guillen's first year of marriage could have been described that way as they tried to settle into a 'new normal.' In the end, the timing was right, Rachel and Guillen's little family was perfect, and the day they'd adopted the boys felt like it was just a week ago.

"Yes," she answered Catrina's question. "Tobias is definitely doing a foreign exchange year. I tried to talk him into doing it in Seeder schools, but he was *adamant* that he wanted to do it in the human world." She shrugged. "What can I say? Anything far away from his parents. And of course, the allure of humans is pretty exciting for their kind."

"You're not worried about him being so far away?" Kaylah asked. "It's been a couple of years now since your permanent change, right?"

"Yeah," Rachel said, trying to hide her longing for the world she'd grown up in, the world she'd never be able to step foot in again. "But my parents are hosting him back there, and Guillen can always go check on him. Tobias will be alright." She held up a finger. "Oh yeah, and since he didn't choose a Seeder exchange, we're going to spend some time visiting Seeder family this summer."

Kaylah smiled. "Tell Saff and Devin hi for me. It's been way too long since I've seen them both."

"Will do." Rachel turned her focus to Catrina. "So ... what's this I hear about a suitor?"

Catrina giggled. "Is that what we're calling him?" She took a deep breath and continued more seriously, unable to hide her smile. "He's a good man. And the right kind." She shared a knowing look with Kaylah. "When the time is right, for things to change."

Kaylah cleared her throat. "He *is* good, isn't he? Who was it that made the introduction, again?"

Rachel chuckled. "Always the matchmaker."

Kaylah gestured with her hands innocently. "What can I say? I'm good with people."

A lightkeeper lit up in Rachel's mind as she jumped forward in her seat. "I almost forgot! You'll never believe this. Not to bring up work, but Guillen just got back and discovered the *craziest* thing!"

Catrina cocked her head to the side, and Kaylah bent forward.

"He was doing a regular visit out at the far Bomen colony. He met a couple—a male Boman, from the Seeders, married to a female Boman, from our Ivies." She paused. "They're pregnant..."

Both Kaylah and Catrina's eyes grew large.

"I didn't think that was possible," Kaylah said.

Rachel smirked. "Well ... I guess it is."

Catrina rested her chin on a fist, leaning back in her chair. "I mean ... it would be an Ivy birth. I'm assuming the child would just be an Ivy Boman, right?"

Rachel shrugged. "I don't know. Maybe the latent energy from them both will produce something more ... a mixing of the races, something new? It's something we'll be monitoring closely."

Kaylah arched an eyebrow. "You never know. Every day is a new adventure."

***

"How's your husband's new job?" Kaylah asked the guard stationed directly outside of the Queen's Room.

"Oh, he *loves* it," she replied. "Thank you for the recommendation, Your Majesty."

Kaylah gave her a smile. "Good. It sounded like a perfect fit."

The guard opened the door, and Kaylah stepped inside. It was quiet and calm, one of her favorite places to hide away in the palace. It looked nothing like the room she'd seen as a little girl, or even as a brand-new queen. The ivy-damaged walls had been smoothed out and painted. She adored the bright mural on one of the walls, the style bearing a similarity to works by Monet or Van Gogh.

The throne had been moved a little to accommodate a love seat, and a new bookcase had long ago replaced the one her brother and his wife had damaged as they'd desecrated the sanctuary in their search for information that would help them win the war.

Kaylah strode to the bookshelf, running her hand along the edge of a hammered metalwork shelf. They'd lost so much ancient information in the old war. So many secrets had likely gone to the grave with Soren and their parents.

Some of the books here were ancient, others more modern. *None* of them were in her possession to hide secrets from her own people. She touched the spine of one that she often questioned whether she ought to have kept. It had been found in her parents' old chambers, which Soren had claimed as his own. The book contained names and details of known whisper rifters from back in those days.

It was an odd memento to keep. That information did nothing for her now. Whispers, just like Bomen, had equal rights, the same as everyone else in the kingdom now.

Sighing, Kaylah couldn't resist pulling out the book, making sure a few loose pages in the front didn't fall out. The loose pages had been torn out, kept separately—Soren's targets, or at least some of them. One of the names always left a bitter taste in Kaylah's mouth—Raven.

Of all things, Raven had been training to be a *schoolteacher*. She'd helped teach little kids. That trend popped up a lot in this little black book. Kaylah's parents, or those they'd entrusted who reported back to them, had a system all worked out to identify whispers. Based on observations and data collection, their pool of whispers to target had been narrowed down to two main categories—the assassins, and the spies. Male Ivies who showed more strength, and had already been identified by the Crown as a whisper, were singled out for assassin training, and after their days as assassins, they made it onto a priority list for palace guard duty.

Female Ivies, however, who were identified as whispers, were the true spies. Schoolteachers could report back to officials when little kids, oft missing filters, would blab about things they'd overheard their parents say, things the Crown might find disagreeable. Teachers could also ensure the right agenda and propaganda were taught in those impressionable years.

But the real reason behind having these Ivy whispers in the schools had been to detect the future generation of whispers, to identify them in the first place. Buried in the mythology of whispers was the truth. One of the ridiculous claims that circulated in Ivy society was that whispers were able to 'read your soul, and steal your energy.' That actually wasn't far from the truth.

Under order of the queen, for generations, Ivy children at the tender age of five had been required to rift for their first time. Their teachers trained them on the mental process, how to use their energy with their vines, where they would go to—an established location in the human world—and then return. It was a terrifying prospect for many kids, though they were conditioned to hide that fear, and show excitement. The event was massively hyped up.

What no one had known was that those very teachers were able to read not only a tree's last whisper after it had been used for a rift, but a person's energy—their gift—when they first learned to rift. In interviews following the war, whisper teachers had described to Kaylah how it worked. They had an extrasensory ability at that initial interaction to detect the gifted. They could also read it in the subtle difference in the children's reactions to opening their own portal. These women who had been forced into becoming spies, had also been required to handpick their own future replacements.

Kaylah shelved the book again. Maybe she kept it out of shame, as a reminder of the lengths her progenitors had gone to, or the shame that still lingered for her having made the assumption in the first place that whispers could only be men.

As she straightened the loose pages that stuck out the top, she was reminded of the most likely reason she kept the book. It still held secrets, and she hated secrets she couldn't solve. More pages had been ripped out than they'd found. She could only assume Soren had destroyed them for some reason. His wife, Beata, who to this day had never been found, wasn't listed in the book. Soren himself wasn't listed, but their parents may have chosen to omit him in the first place. Of course, that was assuming he actually *had been* a whisper.

Soren's staunch whisper supporters swore up and down that he'd proven himself to be one of them, but Kaylah wasn't sure they could be trusted. They couldn't really force Soren to demonstrate anything, and he'd needed to die so the realm could move on.

Kaylah frowned. As much as she wanted to believe her brother had only been a charlatan, the truth remained that she would never know for certain.

A soft knock on the door broke her from her train of thought. Eric poked his head in. "Mind if I join you?"

She pointed at him. "You know you never have to ask that."

"I know, but you might want some quiet time to yourself."

Shrugging, she glanced back at the bookshelf. She reached for the second-largest tome and pulled it out.

"Hmm, one of the big ones, huh?" he asked, sliding his arms around her waist. "Planning on staying up here all night?"

"Nah … just perusing."

Still holding her, he pulled her back and sat down on the love seat, situating her on his lap. She smiled. While she loved her larger statement-piece gowns, she usually wore her thinner dresses around the palace and to less formal affairs. They were more convenient, and made it more comfortable to snuggle when she and Eric were able to sneak some time together.

"How was your meeting?" she asked.

"Blech." Eric wrinkled his nose. "Governor Channing can be so long-winded… Especially when it comes to human visitation laws."

Kaylah snuck a kiss. "Well, my dear, I don't think you will ever *not* be a novelty for these people."

"I don't know…" he said skeptically. "I woke up to some growths today… I think I might be going botanical."

She eyed him, knowing full well there was a punch line. There always was. Other than when he'd been devastated to be the first to find a grey hair, he hadn't ever noticed any changes as a human living full-time in the Green Lands.

He raised a hand to his chest. "Cross my heart." He then rubbed his chin. "A *ton* of growths."

She rolled her eyes. "Growing whiskers is something you do *every* day, babe. And if anything, it implies you're transforming into a cat, not a botanical being."

He chuckled. Eric had officially reached the dad joke phase a few years ago, not that they were parents. They'd never wanted kids, and while Kaylah should have technically produced heirs, she and Eric weren't capable of that. Adoption wouldn't have given a daughter the power of the Mother Vines, nor the legal right to succeed Kaylah. And Kaylah flat-out refused the idea of a relationship with anyone could 'sire' an heir for her.

If anything, once things had finally settled in the realm and they'd felt safe sharing their relationship, the Seeders had warmed up to Kaylah even more. They'd always been fond of humans.

Kaylah couldn't live forever, nor would she want to. But she and Eric had a plan for the future of the kingdom.

Would it really be Kaylah, if she didn't have a plan?

Eric held her tight, and she nestled in more comfortably. He rested his chin on her shoulder. "So, more fairy tales?"

She balanced the large book on her lap with one hand, interlacing their fingers with the other hand. "You know me. Always searching for something I may have missed. Especially with that report of the mixed-race Bomen couple getting pregnant."

Eric groaned quietly. "But come on… We all know that's not possible, and what it's going to turn out to be… Right?"

Of course she knew it was statistically impossible… Ivy Bomen women could get pregnant by Ivy men—Boman or otherwise. But they *couldn't* conceive with humans, or Seeders—Boman or otherwise. The woman's claims that she was pregnant with her Seeder Boman husband's child was more than likely a sad attempt to explain infidelity.

Maybe Kaylah would ask Saff on her next visit, which would hopefully be soon. Saff had only missed visiting the palace once in the last dozen years.

"I know what you're thinking. But between you, me, and that mural…" Kaylah shook her head while extending a vine from her wrist, that hand occupied holding Eric's at the moment. With the vine, she flipped open the front cover of the book. "*This* queen will never openly accuse one of our subjects of that. We'll see how it plays out."

"You're right." He nuzzled her neck. "I suppose crazier things have happened."

She grinned, an Ivy queen sitting on her human husband's lap, in a realm filled with unique energy, with so many secrets to their past still hidden, so much of their future to be enjoyed.

Using her vine, she flipped through more pages of poetry, myths, and fairy tales. "Crazier things have happened."

Order Book 4 Now!

Leah never understood why her mom and aunt made them move so much. Or why her family of freaks could extend vines from their wrists. After getting caught shoplifting, again, Leah is forced to start over in a new town and high school. The friends she makes bring her understanding of the world around her crashing down. They're like her. And they aren't … human.

Digging deeper, Leah finds the answers her mom kept from her all these years. Her dad didn't die in a tragic accident. He was a king, murdered by his sister to steal his throne. Fleeing a besieged palace and pregnant with Leah, her mom turned to the human world, where they were forced to live in hiding.

Wanting justice for her parents and the kingdom they once ruled over, and yearning to know how it feels to be amongst people like herself in a realm flooded with energy, Leah forms a plan.

Her ticket to learning how to enter the Green Lands, how to use her powers, and how to get in close proximity to the murderous queen—is one of her new friends. He may be handsome and sweet, but Leah's objective is clear. Date him. Get an invite to his brother's wedding, which the queen will be attending. Take care of business.

The queen has to die.

More by J. Houser

THE SEEDER WARS TRILOGY

THE HEIR'S DUOLOGY

Also available in the

Seeder Wars world!

Magic in the Match is a
series of standalone
Adult Fairy Tale
Sweet Romances.

Magic in the Match
**Fairy Tale
Romances**

A selection of premium book journals. They each accommodate entries
for 250 books and have individual aesthetic touches.

For more information, go to JHouserWrites.com!

Don't forget to leave a review!

On Amazon, Goodreads, StoryGraph and/or anywhere else this book can be found.

This goes a long way to support authors!

Don't forget to sign up for J. Houser's newsletter for publishing news, promotions, and bonus content!

JHouserWrites.com

Also, connect with the author here:

On YouTube, TikTok, Facebook, Instagram, and Twitter under:

JHouserWrites

J. Houser wrote her first novel at the age of thirty-five. Completing eight full manuscripts in just as many months hinted that writing and sharing stories might become an addiction… While her life is not nearly as exciting as that of her characters (and luckily less heartbreaking), she enjoys the journey, the thought process, the romance and relationships.